T0268241

I MET

Death
&
Sex

THROUGH MY FRIEND, TOM MEULEY

Essential Prose Series 219

Canada Council   Conseil des Arts
for the Arts   du Canada

ONTARIO ARTS COUNCIL
CONSEIL DES ARTS DE L'ONTARIO
an Ontario government agency
un organisme du gouvernement de l'Ontario

Canada

Guernica Editions Inc. acknowledges the support of the Canada Council
for the Arts and the Ontario Arts Council. The Ontario Arts Council
is an agency of the Government of Ontario.

We acknowledge the financial support of the Government of Canada.

I MET

Death
&
Sex

THROUGH MY FRIEND,
TOM MEULEY

thom vernon

GUERNICA
EDITIONS
TORONTO · CHICAGO · BUFFALO · LANCASTER (U.K.)
2024

Copyright © 2024, thom vernon and Guernica Editions Inc.
All rights reserved. The use of any part of this publication,
reproduced, transmitted in any form or by any means,
electronic, mechanical, photocopying, recording
or otherwise stored in a retrieval system, without the prior consent
of the publisher is an infringement of the copyright law.

Guernica Founder: Antonio D'Alfonso

Michael Mirolla, general editor
Julie Roorda, editor
Interior and cover design: David Moratto

Guernica Editions Inc.
287 Templemead Drive, Hamilton, ON L8W 2W4
2250 Military Road, Tonawanda, N.Y. 14150-6000 U.S.A.
www.guernicaeditions.com

Distributors:
Independent Publishers Group (IPG)
600 North Pulaski Road, Chicago IL 60624
University of Toronto Press Distribution (UTP)
5201 Dufferin Street, Toronto (ON), Canada M3H 5T8

First edition.
Printed in Canada.

Legal Deposit—First Quarter
Library of Congress Catalog Card Number: 2023949814
Library and Archives Canada Cataloguing in Publication
Title: I met death & sex through my friend, Tom Meuley / Thom Vernon.
Other titles: I met death and sex through my friend, Tom Meuley
Names: Vernon, Thom, 1963- author.
Series: Essential prose series ; 219.
Description: Series statement: Essential prose series ; 219
Identifiers: Canadiana (print) 20230569579 |
Canadiana (ebook) 20230569595 | ISBN 9781771838795 (softcover) |
ISBN 9781771838801 (EPUB)
Classification: LCC PS8643.E75 I2 2024 | DDC C813/.6—dc23

*For Karen, and all the
others lost at sea.*

You may well believe that this seemed to us like the Chaos of old, with fire, air, sea, earth, and all the elements tossed together in one vast and refractory confusion.

—RABELAIS, Book Fourth. Pantagruel: Five Books Of The Lives, Heroic Deeds And Sayings Of Gargantua And His Son Pantagruel

The Day

The Morning of:

Milk

Your neck. Turn it to the right. Now back to straight ahead. Now to the left. The tendons are jacked. That prick had the whole flat of his hand up against the side of your head and pressed, smashed it into the panelling. The wood grain dug zebra stripes into your temple. Nothing gets by him. Nothing is let go. Everything flips him out. You breathe, he spazzes. You walk in the door, his panties twist. You eat, he blows a gasket. Like it's you just being here. You being alive is a major screw-up for him. If you didn't twist your neck loose, he'd've taken you out. The way he looks at you, the way his lips curl—it's like he's peeling you away from life itself. Like there is something in what he sees when he looks at you that is such a disgust, that all he can do is hurl you at the wall, and cast you out.

Ginnie Dare didn't stand a chance when her dad shotgun-blasted her mom in the kitchen, and her sisters in the basement huddled against a wall, and then he searches the whole house—and there she was. Tucked behind the dirty clothes hamper in her bedroom closet. Puts the muzzle under her chin, pulls the trigger. Does himself likewise. Don't trust a dad. It doesn't matter how good you are or how well you can hide in a closet.

Be like the breath streaming from your mouth in popsicles. Shooting out, clouding and then—poof—vanishing. Be like the breath. Disappear. Where that hate can't find you. Instead, hide in plain sight. Smile. Wider. Be the do-gooder. Be visibly invisible. Seen and not heard. Three months to graduation.

You peel back the blankets, untangle the top sheet. Swing your legs over and even before your feet hit the bare wooden floor—there it is. At your throat. In your chest. In the pit of your stomach. A gut instinct. A pistol-whip to the esophagus. You did something wrong. Not wrong like you didn't close the fridge, wrong like *you*. Something about your skin. Your breath. Insane. But you're going to do it anyway. You're going to turn up the thermostat no matter how he rides you. You all have to freeze 'cause he's so cheap. Suck it up, Dad. Jeff.

In the time it takes to travel from the bed to the door, you look back on yesterday. You didn't do jack. Hit school. Did class. Smoked a bowl with Tom Meuley on the Island. You guys hung out. Tom Meuley's got awesome plans about the *magasins* (French, for store) he's going to put up in Paris. That dude.

You're pretty sure you're in love with him. Whatever that is. Nobody really knows if they're in love with anyone. You've never been in love. At least not like how people talk about it. What you feel with Tom is different. More like you want to be eaten by him. You want to be swallowed. Erased. Subsumed. In the deepest core of you, you know you don't matter. You're too much. Be seen and not heard, Jeff says. Think before you act. Your dad appeared at your door last year and said, don't ever think I'm going to have time for you. I don't. So stop looking for it. It's not going to happen. That is the moment your attention turned to Tom. Not as a substitute. But like a, duh, what you are looking for is right here in plain sight. Tom thinks you got it going on. You guys have fun. You mix it up.

Your teeth are chattering. Your dad won't let go of a toonie or two. You got no curtains covering the windows 'cause Mom rags on you saying you need your Vitamin D even in winter. So stupid. Close your eyes. Strategize. Move it. Take the hallway. Don't creak. To the thermostat. Flick the switch. Whack it up. Be here, disappear.

The furnace groans. That plank of moonlight or streetlight hitting you over the head is sick.

Lift your right foot, steal it left. Get that copper door handle in your hand and not breathin' oh tick-tick-tick the thing's crankin' now. Back in your room, you're walking that plank of light, *tst-tst-tst* goes the radiator's rattlesnake *tst-tst-tst* up from the basement.

A dude's at the window. You duck. Peek. Nope. A chick. Maybe. Pressing an eye against the glass. The breath blooms up on the window and then evaporates. Bloom and go. Frost twigs snake out from the face. A woman's. She's watching you. The spill of light falling between the houses ignites her hair. The breeze buoys thin strings of it floating up from a mouth gumming, lips opening, and closing. Her eyes had a green clithridiate glow. Nobody ever accused you of not having a vocabulary. She taps the glass. Like Grandma twiddling her finger at you through the examination window in Oncology.

The pile of G.I. Joes on the dresser is like: Lady, it's two in the morning. A perv, maybe. She's got a thing for seventeen almost-eighteen-year-old meat. She doesn't move. Maybe you're seeing things. Maybe you should whip it out. That'd scare her off. You should go to her, bring her inside—give her heat. A G.I. Joe would.

But the hundred and fifty-three G.I. Joes got their minds elsewhere. *Cobra Commander* hugs 1964 Joe's half-arm to cop a feel. *Real American Hero* has *Marine Navy Seal*'s life-like grip in his mouth. Others are bored and ache; the rest paw at their chins. One hundred and fifty-three Joes. Your little-kid hobby. A push-pinned poster board on the wall next to them catalogues a head count in blue, green, and red ink. What they are and when you got them. Sound off: 1964 *G.I. Joe 27 April 1999.* Sound off: 1976 *Marine Joe 26 June 2000.* Sound off: 1984 *Cobra Commander 22 Nov. 2001*—. Crazy.

Those were the days when Jeff first ditched you, but Joe's had your back. About your mom crawling up the basement stairs, about Tom Meuley, a.k.a. Tad, climbing the chimney at school, about Jeff in the garage. You lay on your back and told one or the other of them about him doing push-ups on the cool cement floor. Dude'd say, *Get me to fifty, Milk. Fifty, okay?* You'd nod, cross-legged as sweat pooled along his spine to trickle lower. How, at the tenth push-up, he grunted like he'd only done one. At twenty, one ankle over another. At thirty, a heave-ho. At forty, the breath swung low. At forty-five, a launch to slap your leg and back to catch himself. At fifty, *Come on, don't be a wuss.* At seventy, he'd stop, wink, and holler at the floor. At ninety, one last slap of his hands and *G.I. Joe's a pussy-shit.*

While Jeff slunk to his La-Z-Boy, G.I. Joe taught you how it takes two to tango, winner takes all. Your mom crawling up the stairs is the story of your life, so Tad climbing a chimney at school didn't get Joe's panties in a knot. He got named 'Tad' 'cause Ms. Beal predicted he'd get himself killed like Abraham Lincoln's son. All because he climbed up a chimney. Take a pill, Lady.

Rappel off Kilimanjaro, then we can talk, Joe said. *Hang by a thread at one-thousand, two hundred and forty-three feet, you got my eye. Outsmart Zartan sneaking MIRC, you're threading the needle.* Joe stroked his chin with real-life hair. *You got real human life and if that ain't what is what, then back to boot camp. Take your friend, Tom Meuley. That's real-life living. Be him.*

But then, in the wee hours of this morning, that woman is staring at you. Wreckage washed to shore, and that aureolin streetlight planking past the Joes to the wallpapered sparrows catching your eye. The shadows of her hair snake past where you stand and beyond to the old skool, foot-long G.I. Joes where it massages their tiny white, blue, and khaki pants. But then—

She's gone. You wait. Breathe. Listen. At the window —peek. She's not in the bushes. Not under the Eiseles' red maple. The house ticks. The furnace kicks on. Like Grandma slipping away.

Now Jeff keeps the thermostat at sixteen. Two weeks ago, you nailed him. You caught him good. You had snuck out of the house after supper. Sat tight at the corner. Archaic Moby in the buds. You kept a bead on the front door. Waited. He came. Off Newcastle Boulevard, Jeff parks in the rear carport of a Longhouse-style apartment building. A cul-de-sac gives you cover. The ice wind lifts your hair snapping into telephone wires. You hunker down. He ducks inside.

You get right up next to the building. Listen. Frozen dog-doo bricks at your feet. Two floors. Six apartments. Scrunch down. A door. Windows on either side. Stay low. You make it. Locked. Crap. A side door. Zip to the far end. A window. See him, maybe. From out here. From the first floor. Blood drains from your knees. Through the window, a kid picks his nose watching TV. A lady stepping around to a fridge. Not hot. A car pulled into the carport. A tall drink of bearded water got out of his car. You blocked his path.

The Dude: *How's it going?*

You: *'S all right.*

(You bat your eyelashes. He held the door with one arm.)

Dude: *You live here?*

Don't blow a gasket. You: *I do, I do. We're new. Um, Albert. I'm Albert. Um.*

He said his name, you were stuck on his lips.

Dude: *Hi.* He let the door go. *See you. Albert.*

You dawdled, quote-unquote, digging for keys. When you couldn't hear his boots anymore, you listened outside of each door; the freaking creaking floor cracked loud as dried sticks. Someone creeping close to a door. You freeze. They stepped off. Three doors, then four. Listen. Boom. Got him. Jeff's yapping slipped through the crack.

Got me. Got you. Yes, honey. Got me. I'm just saying. I am just saying. I am only human, hon'.

Aren't you all. You snuck back to your car and let the plot unfold. In the wee hours this morning, with that woman in the window gone and the furnace cranking, you turned to face your Joes. You had a plan. Your squadron, your posse, your sacrificial lambs. You Spartan lovers would take down the Athens of Jeff together. Get a giant Glad bag and the Joes inside. Get the Coleman tin of gas. A bomb blast would explode Jeff's new Saturn. Sick.

Sessy

Imprisoned by the walls of their bedroom, she needs sugar. Her world comes together in the crunch of a cookie crumb. But, no. Don't. Do not, Sessy. You are fat. You are a cow. God knows she's heard it since the day she was born. You are—

Her boy's foot on the cold floorboards creaks.

She digs her forehead into the night table. Oh, Milk's going to venture out to the sea of the hallway and jig the thermostat higher. Brave, beautiful lad. Her, too. She could do something. She could help. She gropes for shortbread in the drawer, gets the plastic package in her teeth. Tears. Adults always throw their kids into the sea. To the bastard Jeffs and the Ern Trues.

Jeff's breathing guts her. Like the rips of her cartilage when he kicks her down the basement stairs. Like that chair hitting the wall when she threw it at his head. She is no one, if not his. She promised. From the high branch of a low tree just before he popped the question back then, a handshake deal.

She nibbles. Okay. The sugar pumps through her veins. The carbohydrates do their dirty work. She tears open another package. And then another. She does it all without making a sound. She gets a leg free of the comforter. She'd never shake free of the snake that grips her around the neck; that is Jeff. Her boy, though, could flee free.

Milk creeps into the hallway. A soldier. A patrolling guard against the freeze of the night. But he would not have to do this alone. Not this time. No. Tonight, she would help him. Tonight, she would not cast him out on the waves. No matter how hard she paddled, no matter the lengths she went to, slit, gutted, and quartered mind, body, and soul it had never been enough. Jeff had *her*. She had one leg free and, letting the shortbread wrappers fall to the carpet, she pushed herself off the mattress.

'Ssh.' Jeff sunk the fat of his hand between her thighs. He yanked it to her back door. Pulled her other leg and flipped her onto her belly. 'I got to peel your orange, darlin'.'

She clamped her legs just like she'd done to that branch back then. Men spear any living thing. Oh, it had been so different. *She knew he would ask her to marry him. He went all hang-dog tightening his belt and pulling his pants up. She hoisted herself up into that red maple disappearing into its leaves. Her skin ached to a tune tangled in the leaves. A sweet touch even when she didn't deserve it. A cup of tea when her belly ached. No way.* Tonight, she had no tree to climb but snagged another packet of shortbread.

In the hallway, Milk stopped.

Jeff squeezed and squished.

Oh, wait for her, son. Wait. She would free herself from the monster. She would strike him down, take your hand, and the two of you would flip the switch.

Against his wishes, against his will. You, you, Milk. Yours is a life worth living.

Tonight went all wrong. Goddamn Jeff. He never pulled his shirt up to press his belly to hers anymore. *She had climbed down from the red maple for him. He snookered her and disappeared into a squeeze of curl lotion and anger over what he'd lost.* These days, slamming his fist into the table. Sending the silverware and two of their yellow glasses to shatter on the linoleum. And then Milk. Kids should feel they exist. They matter. But there he'd been, staring his dad down teeth gritted white-knuckling. His fragile body getting slammed into the dresser, all his G.I. Joes flying off. The way he, oh, he twisted his neck to grab hold of Jeff's arm, clawing at his throat for air. And, at long last, reaching to her begging for help.

In the moonlight, Jeff snatched her hand, pulling her back down to clutch his cajones. 'I got one. Come on.' He had a stiffie.

'Oooo, ooo, yeah,' she cooed with one eye peeled at the crack under the door for Milk. 'Good for you, Jeff. I got to pee.' She'd slip out and the two of them, she and Milk, would turn the heat up. She'd take the blame.

'Let me go boom-boom.'

She listened. Milk had to be in the hallway by now. If he turned the thermostat by himself, there's no telling what his father might do. Jeff's 'boom-boom' lit dynamite.

She kicked.

'Oh, yeah, baby. Oh, yeah.' Dear God let his turtle duck inside.

He pinned her down and poked his cock in. *Back then, that head meant care and attention. She knew he would ask her to marry him and so slipped up the trunk of the tree her mom and dad planted in their front yard that first year they took flight from Nebraska. They ripped her from her best friend Ellie's arms. She couldn't bear it. Her mother had pried them apart to stuff Sessy in a car, slamming the door, and telling her father, Uncle Louise, to gun it, Lou. Gun it. The shocked, freckled, and sunburnt six-year-old Ellie stumbled backwards up the stairs reaching out to balance herself.* This picture had burnt into Sessy's mind.

She can hear him. Milk's pulling himself along the wall by the sticks of streetlight coming through the elm. The scruff of his socks a symphony. Oh, if only she could reach him. The kid is getting himself in thick. 'Wear one.'

'Let me in first.' Jeff spread her cheeks.

'I'm not clean.'

He dug into his drawer with a free hand. 'Don't got none.'

'They're there.' She'd grabbed a handful of condoms from Milk's school.

He got one in his teeth. 'You do it. You got fangs.'

'I got to pee.' God lingers in one more piece of short-bread. Just one little crunch. *Back then, if she climbed down, he would pop the question. An aperture narrowed. This is the moment. She brought her knees in to grip the sides of that thick maple branch, to hold this knowing deep within her. Do not forget. No matter what happens, Sessy. He wants you. You count. A line of ants marched the length of the knobbled wood she straddled. She is the queen Jeff means to serve. In the yard below, her mom, Adele, dad, and Jeff passed back and forth calling Sessy, Sessy.* She'd fling herself to the hallway, the shore of her boy.

Jeff pressed into her.

The furnace rumbled down in the basement. *For two days and two nights, she had stayed in her tree. Should she say yes, should she say no? But, suspicious, as all writers are, of when their characters go to sleep (even Shakespeare understood that) the story can't progress with its heroine asleep, she opened her eyes to a sparrow beading its eye at her, and then to Jeff still weeping at the base of the tree, holding himself with both arms repeating* stupid stupid stupid. I'm here, *she had said. His blue eyes turned skyward to her, the spirals of his permed mullet catching the breeze, he reached out his hand as he came to standing.* Not for long, *he said.* The seed sown, the battle won. The animal climbed down. Being dumb and gullible pumped through her matriarchal blood. She couldn't shake it. Love comes first. Love trumps all. To be owned is life. What a racket. She had swung free from the low branch of a tall tree. After playing house for a couple of years, Milk came, she dropped out four credits shy of her honours English degree and Jeff, watching mother and son cuddle, took on a wound seething with jealousy and bitterness. And so began a full-on assault against the very idea of her existence. As long as he had his job, as long as the empire reigned he kept a lid on. But then, with his being laid-off, something long buried unearthed itself, shook itself free of its shackles and lifted its face into view: now snarling, now framed with curl-crème. It must have been sometime after, maybe around the time he got his D.U.I., that *she* came sniffing around. Sessy had pulled at her own hair and plastered old photos in scrapbooks all to delude herself into thinking someday soon, if she could just figure it out, he could care again.

'Do not blow your gravy in me.' She caught her breath. Don't be scared, *he had said back then in the breeze, wiping the tears from his eyes and taking her claw in his own.* Jump. *And she did. He held her. She belonged to him. She mattered. No matter what friends she had to ditch, what fingering other men did; no matter how fat Adele, her mother, told her she was, she mattered. She was somebody.*

Her boy's eye must be up close to the thermostat dial.

'Nah.' Jeff plunged in. And out. And in. And out.

She got Jeff's thing in her fingers. Fucker. No condom. She punched him. 'Don't give me AIDS.' She knew all about Tom Meuley. It could happen to anybody. She knew what she knew. She found that phone.

'I'm not.'

'Put one on.' Oh, God. If she got AIDS and died, who would look after Milk? What would become of him? So close to making it. Almost eighteen. Almost ready to take on the world. If she died—.

Milk closed his door. Just over the threshold, he stepped on the heating grate. She could hear it.

'But you're cattin' on me, Jeff. Doesn't that—.'

'Nobody's 'catting'. On Nobody.'

She gripped the mattress. 'AIDS—. Happens. Tom. Meuley. Has it.' Oh, God. She might never reach that shore.

Milk had moved to his window now. She just knew. Her boy, a poet sentry guarding the landscape of sullen front yards, desolate living rooms, and vacant, snow-ridden sidewalks. Jeff straightened his elbows working to some grand push. 'Oomph.'

'They left his file. On the counter. I saw. Jeff. When. When they got. Drunk, I had to. Go up there. To sign. Papers. I saw.'

'Nah.' Jeff plunged in. And out. And in. And out. As if he were staking her to a tree.

'I. Saw.'

The sausage went flat. Jeff rolled off pulling at his grey wolf bush. 'Yes. Come on.' He straddled her head. 'Open up.'

Milk had gone quiet.

'Can't go in both ways, Jeff.'

'Suck it, suck it, suck it.' His thing flopped on her chin.

She clamped her lips. 'It's not clean.' She'd get him. She'd get him and *her* and wrap her sweet boy in her arms. Her son would never believe that he didn't matter. She'd make sure of it.

'Stop that.' He worked his finger into her mouth to pry it open.

She chomped at it with her teeth like a pack of cookies and got the flat of her foot at his ribs shoving him with everything she had. He fell off.

'Hoo.'

She had the fight of her life on her hands. A plan to spook Jeff good. To put the fear of God into him. To get him to straighten up and fly right. She could hide out in his parking lot at work. Out by those antelopes, wildebeests, and giraffes in the parking lot of the Humane Society of Canada (HSCAN). Jeff hoodwinked his bosses to buy titanium big game shells and casings that became sculptures of murdered animals. Today, a herd of big game statuary galloped across the grand savannah of their East York parking lot. Come winter, snow collected in the dip of the moose's shoulder or the crook of the grizzly's paw. The whole thing glittered with the melting water and the rush of that creek a little farther out.

She'd wear her clodhoppers and strap on some gee-gaw—maybe Milk's bicycle helmet. Park her Tercel on the street and hike out on foot. A storm, maybe, would gather force with every step. Hail'd pelt her. Driven by the wind and rain, she'd claw her way across blacktop, through snow drifts and speed bumps. Her back against the driveway wall, one eye peeled in front, the other behind. The rhino would hide her completely. From the rhino to the wildebeest to the Cape Buffalo, the lion to the grizzly, to the caribou, to the moose. That Saturn would be mincemeat. 'What time are you going in to work?'

'It's stiff again,' Jeff said, marvelling at his carrot. 'Come get it.'

The light leaking from under Milk's door went dark.

'You parking by the rhino or the wildebeest these days?'

Ton'

His shift over, Ton' took his sweet time getting to the 54 Division locker room. His soles stuck to the linoleum, sticking and squeaking worse than that St. Andrew's cross he tied that kid to doing Detective Constable fieldwork. Jesus. The City of Toronto cleaners wouldn't know the scrub side of a sponge if their life depended on it.

He undid his buckle. He loosened the leather. He ain't an ass man for no reason. Take the American Sutton Horst, straight ahead, reaching for his Puma and bending over. Goddamn. That is true patriot love in all thy sons command. Ton' leaned against the locker to take in the view. 'Hey, States.'

Horst's little bum clenched. 'Phff.'

The squats he does to mould those mounds.

The kid got his panties in a twist. 'Don't call me "States," man. Wow.'

Ton' slipped his belt off. Smooth, like the rolling sweet moors of sugar cargo down at the Redpath docks. He coiled and cracked the strap. Then, the buckle.

The dude ought to just give it up. No reason to fight so hard.

Paperwork filed, Ton' logged out. A better kind of fucker would call his wife. But 'Schelle'd be sleeping. He flew out the automatic steel door and smack into the biting crack of 54's downtown back parking lot with that storm stewing. Grey-bellied clouds elbowed up from the lake. Come his afternoon shift, it'd be cold-cocking snow by the barrel.

Shoot. He ought to get some. He could. Man. But with that crap coming down, he'd have to shovel Albert's and Ale's driveway; there'd be CUPE'd calling a strike action; there'd be J. getting him and Shafiqq to shovel. But, shoot. He ought to.

He shouldn't. By the time he got onto the Gardiner Expressway, the Datsun skated. No traffic. A straight shot, blasts the heat, sunroof cracked. He drove his Z432 Fairlady, his blood orange baby since high school shop class. Gets him to YYZ in seventeen, downtown in under twelve, and the Village in maybe ten. No Taurus flies that fast.

He shouldn't. If he went straight home to 'Schelle, he'd be out cold as soon as he hit the sack. Man, it's only one-thirty a.m. He could. Nah. That would be bad. He took Spadina Rd. The city lit all grey fire. He spit a jet-stream catching the expressway lamps and lighting up the night sky. Hell yeah. What the hell's Life worth living for if you can't get some "bad"? If he closed his eyes he wouldn't even be in the city. He'd be flying. To College. Past streetcars. He would do it. Why not, nobody he knows goes there; why shouldn't he, 'Schelle had no right—a wife, a spouse, a partner—to tell him what's what. She's not the boss of him. What she don't know won't kill her. Julio and the High-Kick Dancers. Silver sugar hot pants. He scored parking on Maitland. If somebody saw him, he'd tell them he's there doing his job. A detective returning to the scene of a crime. If he didn't go into places like this, he'd never find out the truth. Like who's trafficking the Mac-10 pistols? It's the little ones; the ones like snub-noses. He bet Pat-Pat's got his finger in that pie. But Ton's after the big fish. He cracks Mac-10s, and he makes Detective Constable. He could cover for Pat-Pat. The old guy would owe him. Pat-Pat owing Ton' just as that Detective crown goes on his head means he owns the whole division. He decides what investigations go forward. He calls the shots regarding promotions. No one'll touch him then. Man, if Ma could see him now.

He jumped the dog crap snowbank and jammed up right into a flock of diamond-back queens snaking to the front door of CELL BLOCK. Jesus. Focus. He dug his hands under his armpits. Two dudes in blue tank tops and white shorts. The other a judge, some lawyer, some stockbroker.

Inside the doorway, he held up the doorjamb holding his breath against a cloud of Aquanet. The stained ceiling leaned over the tables. The line delivered him to a Little Miss Moffat curtsying past the threshold saying 'Guttenknock' licking her lips, twirling a sandwich board that read 'TONIGHT!! Every dime to HIV/AIDS/HEP C. COUGH IT UP!'

Ton' leaned back hard and casual. His bicep bent to bulge and impress. He stroked his jaw. Look at them. A fag in a plaid fedora. A brown boy in a pink shirt. The stage empty save for a baseball circle of light.

'*Well you can tell by the way I use my walk, I'm a woman's man/No time to talk—.*'

A car crash in a red wig got his chin. 'Easy, Tiger. Debbie Demonic, baby.' She chewed the fat of her hand. '$20, smart-boy.' She's a sausage stuffed in a silver tube top. 'Take it all in, Cowboy. Give it up.' She licked her forefinger and straightened the DROP IT HERE sign taped to her tits.

Ton' could take it. 'You don't know how smart I am.'

'Nine big ones. Fat. Officer.'

'You don't know I'm an officer.'

'I think I do. You can call me Debbie.' Her huge bosom bent her sign. The bells dangling from her chest ding-a-linged. She pursed her black lips. A waft of his mother-in-law's perfume floated across his nose.

'What's that you got on?'

She rang her bells. 'You just grab one if you want.' One split orange nipple—pierced through with a ball and chain—tipped out. A real bag of rocks. A steel worker, probably.

'You want some milk? Look at that mouth. Come here.'

He held his breath, leaned in a little closer and Debbie gave him a peck. He let her. He could do that for AIDS. He tucked a twenty in her smackers. 'Stay warm.'

'You keep me warm. Enjoy.' Debbie took first one twenty and then another from the dudes behind him. Then, she vaulted the table, spun around, and shook her bells. 'Dings for your dongs, Gents! Ladies! Three minutes!'

Ton' worked his way to the bar and got himself the good stuff, Kettle One. Why not? He tucked himself behind a pole. Julio didn't need to see him right away.

Noisemakers blew as two dudes rubbed their noses together. A guy poured a beer for another one before sitting down. Fairies. A suit stroked the bare arm of a bodybuilding Sumo Wrestler-type. Fags got it so easy.

The crowd started stomping their feet. 'De-mon-ic. De-mon-ic. De-mon-ic!'

In one leap, Debbie took the stage. 'All right. All right! Quiet!' He, she—whatever—horned off like the foghorn at the Spit. She did a spin, a curtsey, and then froze.

The lights fell. A knot twisted around Ton's esophagus, tightening. Like when Ma went.

The room fell dark. The baseball-sized spotlight widened to ignite a red velvet curtain. The glitter ball spattered spinning dots of light as a leg shot out in a silver go-go boot. The tendons, the thigh—in a perfect line with the stage. Julio.

A drumroll kicked in, the curtain parted, and there they were can-can high-kicking. Two in purple-pink frizz wigs, maybe Diana Ross, maybe Bozo, held-braced Julio, in chalk-white hair, as he flipped to high-kick on his hands. Moving upstage, the two curtsied underneath the disco ball and backed away. Still on his hands, Julio lowered himself to lay his gold titty tassels flat on the stage. He did one, two, three—five push-ups, and extended one boot to a point before bending his other leg to make a '4'. Fucker. Straightening his legs to the ceiling, he spins his boot toe in a teeny circle, and then lets his legs fall into splits, still the whole time up on his hands, and brings his legs together to scissor-kick, before he does a complete 360, flips himself over and back onto his feet right-side up, spinning into a pirouette en pointe. The crowd went nuts. Ton' couldn't wait to get a handful of this fucker. But then he flipped upside down again into a handstand.

'Ladies and gents, this boy is working, okay? Let's get some dollars up here.' Debbie twirled the microphone and shook her bells.

Loonies landed onstage. Then, fives and twenties. A hundred. Faggots just throw it down for each other. Maybe a thousand dollars, fuck fuck fuck. Debbie kicked back in.

Julio did upside-down push-ups. Sweat glistened on his torso. A smile plastered to his face. His veins bulging.

'Now, our boy here, his arms are getting tired.'

Julio caught his eye. Ton', he mouthed.

Damn. Sweet. Man. Yeah. This little fucker is going to get more than a beer. The kid lowered his legs down and then hopped back upright.

After the show, Julio landed next to his table, hands neatly folded.

Ton' could put on a show too. He tilted back in his chair. Take a good look.

'Papi.'

That twist to his gut hit again. He landed the chair back down. He dug at the sticky and gouged table. 'Don't they have the table wipers here?' He pulled the other chair out for Julio.

Julio didn't move.

Maybe Ton' should stand. He stood.

Julio sat down. *'Gracias, senor.'*

Ton' got Julio's chair straightened around. That Asian twink leaned in and goosed Julio. *'Ay, papi!'*

'Quiete.' Julio pulled his chair closer and folded his hands under his chin. *'Hola.'*

'Yeah. What're you having?'

'Nada.'

'*Nada* nothing no way. You got to have something.
I'm treating. After a performance like that? Come on.
Dites moi.'

'*Que bueno, papi.*'

Ton' winced. 'Damn. That's cool. When you talk
like that.'

'*Si. Papi.*'

When their beers arrived, Ton' poured Julio's for him.
He had to do that. It's common decency. He shouldn't
look Julio in the eyes. The kid might get the wrong idea.
It's plain decency. And fucking. He studied his scratched
wedding ring. The fibreglass ceiling tiles were stained
with brown water damage. The light system seemed
even older than the equipment they had at the Buffalo
Correctional facility rec room.

The music kicked up.

He pumped his calves to the beat and then leaned
into Julio.

Julio put his finger to his lips and sipped his beer.

A woman carved into the wall panelling by the bar
with a penknife.

Ton' shouted over the music. 'They probably last
redid this place like, I don't know, in the 1970s.' He
inched his chair closer. Julio had his ear to the ground.
Maybe he had a little news on the Mac-10s. 'You know
a guy named Pat-Pat?'

Julio didn't hear and drained his beer. Ton' got up to
the bar, bought a fresh one and poured it into a glass for
him. 'Have another. I got to ask you—.'

Julio laid his arm on the table.

Ton' ran his finger along the vein there. 'You've got
some real muscle there, man.' He took his finger back.

And tucked in real close to Julio's neck. The dude smelled like cloves.

Julio didn't budge his arm. 'Go on, *papi*.'

The oiled part of Julio's hair caught the light. His eyelids half-fluttered. 'Nah. Thanks.' Julio set his beer down. He reached under the table, found Ton's hand and lifted it back onto his forearm. *'Eso es.'*

Ton watched his finger nudge into Julio's skin. Soft. Like 'Schelle's.

He pulled his chair closer to Julio. He got an arm around him. He tucked his chest in close. His nipple dug into Julio's upper arm. It hardened to the rhythm of Julio's breath. *'Chica*. You know, *"Chica," Chica*?' Julio's arm seemed to stiffen and then melt some under his hand. 'I got a thing to ask you.' The back of his neck heated up just then. In times of worry, Ma put hot wet towels there. Not 'Schelle. She never did that. 'What do you know about—?'

Julio looked up at him, same as he did at the greenhouse. He leaned in a little and tilted his head.

Man. The way the dude looks at him. Ton' had to have that mouth. He got that whole fricking rosebud into his. After a minute, maybe thirty seconds, an eternity, he let his tongue creep in. Salt and Bud. Ton' drew Julio's chin up to see his eyes. 'You're a good dude, dude.'

'Gracias, por favor.'

Ton' kneaded the muscles roping Julio's spine.

At the foot of the stage, at a table, a blonde woman leaned in and rubbed noses with a dude at her table. She pulled his face close to kiss. Maybe that wasn't even a girl.

'Schelle looked at him like that. Her aquamarine eyes. Vast landscapes opened to him there. Yesterday, on her back with her feet in the stirrups as they did the IVF, they gripped each other's hands through the entire insertion procedure. He told her to squeeze but she didn't answer with words. Maybe the stuff would stick this time and he'd be somebody's dad. She held his gaze. Her jaw tightened (like her dad's). And landed him in those turquoise pools. For two hours, he read to her from a book about a black woman in Nazi Germany. God made her eyes. And God put a hunger in him to consume. He couldn't help himself. The way they all looked at him. Julio—Jesus. He couldn't give that up. What boiled into Ton' ripped the space between him and 'Schelle sometimes. When he and 'Schelle made up their kiss looked like that blonde lady-man rubbing noses. 'Schelle is no idiot. The error of his way is not forgotten. He had the scars to prove it. She had the tears.

She and her mother collected their tears in used jelly jars. Family heirlooms.

'It's called legacy, Mom.'

'It's old-timey stupid,' her mother Ale said sitting on the edge of the bed. *'Ton's right.''Mom. It's not stupid,'* said 'Schelle.

'It's dumb,' said Ale. *'Us women over-sentimentalize.'*

'Grandma Hickman got all her tears in there.'

'Not all of them. Grandpa had Mrs. Strawberry Preserves on one end of the property and Grandma Hickman on the other.'

'I'd give anything to meet them.'

'No, you wouldn't. Trust me. T-R-O-U-B-L-E.'

'And all their tears are still in there.' 'Schelle held the jar up to the light to see the floating debris. It seemed

like pale apple cider vinegar with the mother still in. *'Still.'* When her mom, Ale, went up to pee, 'Schelle unscrewed the lid. She dipped her finger in and tasted it. Borax. She sipped. It tasted the same as those root cellars in Arkansas. *'Mom,'* she told Ale when she got back, *'they're real.'*

'Don't count on it.'

'You're not throwing it away, Mom.'

In their family, when a mother dies, she passes the jar to her oldest daughter. That daughter, and her sisters, if she's got 'em, mix their tears with their mother's. 'Schelle asked what happens if her daughters have daughters.

'Don't worry about that,' Ale wiped her wet hands on her slacks. *'Just watch the bats in the garage.'*

Albert, 'Schelle's dad, caught bats circling in their backyard from time to time with a butterfly net. He nailed their carcasses over the garage door. The wooden siding there was pocked with black splotches like a windshield on the highway. Kind of nasty, in Ton's opinion. Why he did this wasn't discussed. It's Albert's thing. Maybe a stress reliever.

That jar of tears had become like a female crucifix. But, boy, when Ton' and 'Schelle got into it, he could get her goat.

"Schelle, if you went up to pee, I could pour out your tears and rinse out the jar—.'

'Right, Ton'.'

'I didn't. But how would that feel, 'Schelle? You treat me the way you do.'

'The way I treat you?'

He had goofed up. Only once. Okay, maybe slightly more. *'God, you are such a baby sometimes.'*

For a coordinator at a wreckage haul company, 'Schelle wasn't stupid. *Chlamydia. And you don't know how I got it?*'

He couldn't be sure.

'Bat's, Ton',' she said. *'I got it from bats.'*

Ton' had no idea what that meant. The only bats he knew were her dad's. *'It had to be before we met, 'Schelle. I swear. It lies dormant.'*

'Dormant?'

'That's what they said in training. It wakes up and boom you got it.'

'Yes, Ton.' Boom. I got it.' Her eyes welled up and spilled over.

"*Schelle. Don't think what you're thinking.*'

➤ A few feet from the stage, Ton' got his hands back to himself and then sat on them. No Mac-10 news tonight.

With a tassel in his teeth, Julio wrapped himself with his arms. Ton' polished off his vodka. He bopped some to the music. Sweat trickled from his pecs. Julio gripped his chair.

This place is an armpit. 'Hey, Julio.'

'Si—.'

'Don't *papi* me, okay.'

'Si—.'

The air got thick. You can't breathe in a place like that. 'Is there, like, another show?'

Julio eyed him. 'No. *No mas.*'

'Ah. Ah-huh.' His palms got wet.

'Si,' Julio leaned back and folded his legs.

Ton' wanted to say something like don't make fun of me, I'm married, ha-ha. But, he didn't. He stood up, drying his hands on his pants. Fucking Steam Works in here.

'Officer.' Julio stepped up to him and traced Ton's moustache with his finger. *'Mijo.'*

'And don't "Mijo" me, okay? I got to blow.' He air-walked his fingers as if Julio couldn't understand the words.

Julio nodded. And smirked.

'Okay. Good show.' He bolted.

On the way out of the club, Debbie Demonic got him by the collar with one hand and pulled at her pump with the other. 'You are not going to leave Esteban there by himself.'

Those tits like barbells blocked the door. 'Night.' He squeezed through.

'Esteban.' Fucking faggot liars. Can't even come clean with their name. Jesus.

At home, he snaked into bed next to 'Schelle, the light of his life. The moon laid rectangles of glare onto those porcelain dolls bleaching their rosy cheeks and blinkering their gold-painted earrings. Albert, her dad, handed them over to 'Schelle to care for since Ale, 'Schelle's mom, only whacked with the feather duster these days.

Next to the dolls, that jar of tears leered at him. From the 1800s or something. One of 'Schelle's great-grandmothers had run off from the Trail of Tears to Arkansas or somewhere, they just kept holding that jar up to their cheeks. Rivulets of tears inched down the glass like his forehead pressing into Ma; like a Mac-10 poking the small of his back.

Sessy

Later that morning, but before Milk woke up, she wrapped the camera in a towel. Holding the downstairs railing across from the front door, she craned her neck to listen. From upstairs, Jeff's hotsy-totsy *Paco Rabanne* beat his fish stink to her olfactory whatchamacallits. With his peeling oranges last night, she'd missed it when Milk got back in bed. Once the kid got under good, it seemed like he didn't wake up for nothing. But, according to Milk, going to sleep is like being lowered on a rope and then yanked back up. Lowered a little and yanked. She knew exactly where he got that from. Secrets do that. They'll string you out, rope your neck, and then yank you back into place.

All those days with Owser. All those afternoons where, in one sliver of a moment, she could have been lifted. She could have been transported up through the slats of that roof. But she wasn't that girl. She lay there and took it.

Her boy, too, had some secret life. Like that taking up last year, that wearing their clothes inside out that he and Tom Meuley had started on. Shirts inside out, pants seams showing. Boys, boys, boys. Mounting two steps at a time, she ripped a lily-white hair from her cheek.

She nudged the door open. Quiet, quiet, quiet. Tread lightly. Don't peep, don't breathe. She got the lens in. Jesus. Musk funk. Holy Criminy. Perfume of the Gods. Pong. Teenage ass and sugar dew breath. She pushed in.

His mouth cocked open, his eyelids fluttering. The shortest eyelashes she ever saw except when her brother, Adam, burned his off. Milk had the bugeye blephora that the actor Michael Caine did. His eyes surged upon you, sun-beamed through lash stumps, spilled from the sockets and took a person in. Those were the arms that held her from harm's way. His gorgeous globes tipped further to green these days, in December, but would take on a yellow tinge come summer.

He had his T-shirt on right. His shoulder blades and neck were still rounded with baby fat. The chubby he sucked in when awake folded along his hip. She aimed her camera with one hand and lifted his T-shirt to see the small of his back. Oh, she could kiss that sweet spot. One touch there soothed him as a baby. If she had a dollar for every coo she got blowing air there. The lens purred to capture that honey cream skin. He unloads into his dirty socks. Adorable. She got a couple of shots off with her free hand and would get them into her albums. They'd all be grateful someday. Jeff wanted him out. O.U.T. She could make it better, maybe. Their story isn't over. Jeff would see the lengths that she'd go to win him back. She hit the St. Lawrence Market with his sweet-loving stink-smelling dress shirt. She needed to confirm the additional evidence she had gathered. And get lemons.

She took the shirt to Mr. Full-Lips and his brother, Mr. Long-and-Lanky, selling spices and dry goods in the St. Lawrence Market basement. Those Italian boys have a lot more than raw almonds and dried dates to handle. The goods are on display with those two. A couple of O.G. biscotti. If she were twenty years younger, she'd brown bag those two. No chocolate dip needed. Popcorn, the chick who really ran the show down there, piped up. 'That's cardamom.'

The brothers, clearly refugees from an Italian sausage festival, passed the shirt back and forth over the dried pineapple.

Sessy made up a story that, ha ha ha, the shirt is her dead father's. She got her accent just right. 'It's for-ah special-ah. My ma-ah, it's her 90th-ah.'

The guys rubbed their chins. Maybe they didn't speak Italian.

'We wanna to make-ah, you know-ah, a special meal-ah. Just like-ah she did for my papa-ah.'

Popcorn didn't see the fuss. 'You gotta know cardamom.'

Mr. Full-Lips tipped his head one way, and then the other. God, he knew how to wear a tiny waist. Those big shoulders veered down into something more than an oversized toothpaste tube but smaller than a pickled salami. He brought the shirt to his nose again. 'Me, I say cumin.'

Mr. Long-And-Lanky, his brother, took the shirt. This one had triceps that bulged erect just resting. 'Nah. You don't listen.'

'That's like, you know. Turkish, Middle Eastern.'

'Persian,' said Popcorn. Long-and-Lanky handed the shirt back to Sessy. 'Cardamom.'

'Bastard.'

'Excuse me?' Popcorn stepped back.

Daddy's been lyin'.'

At that veggie stand cash, her cards were declined. First the Visa, then the Amex, and then the mother-effing Mastercard. She knew why.

'Doesn't work.' A Miss Thing Cashier handed Sessy's last card to her. And then twisted snags out of her hair band.

Sessy pushed the card back. 'Sorry. Try it again. It works.' She had to bet back home. After last night, she had to see Milk before he goes to school. Maybe he had bruises.

The woman heaved her shoulders and tugged at the hair on her neck.

Descended from mammoths, probably.

She got a thumb good into her hip, swiped the card again and folded her arms. Her lips thinned. 'Nope.'

'You must be doing it wrong.'

'That's not possible.' Sessy couldn't do anything right. Never not no way.

When she first married Jeff, his mother, Joanne, dropped that it wasn't her first time at the rodeo and if Sessy didn't want Jeff wandering all over titty heaven, she better have a good mincemeat.

Mincemeat?

Girl. Girl. There are a lot of titties in this world, but there is only one mincemeat. I know. I'm going to teach you. You get one present from me. Mincemeat. You make mincemeat the way he likes and trust me he will stride right by any other Tenderflake pie crust. Don't muck it up. Don't go getting to be a big fatty-fat-fat like some chickees do.

Sessy didn't know mincemeat from a hole in the head. Before her lesson with her mother-in-law, she asked Petra, a typist whose lazy eye Sess' held open so she could get her drops in, said try Aisle 6 at Metro. It looked to Sessy like somebody took a dump in that jar.

Oh, I'm telling you, Joanne chewed at her nail polish. *You better make it yourself. You better make it the way I say. I have been to the rodeo, Missy. I rode the bull. You.* Joanne took a long draw off her Kool 120 extra-slim cigarette. *You might look like a young little thing, but you got the spine of an old crow. Sessy. Who gave you that name? I always ask Jeff, what kind of name is 'Sessy'? Is that a birth certificate like Lithuanian, name? Want a Kool?*

Sessy wouldn't know a Lithuanian if they squeezed into her sandwich bread. She tucked her lip under.

It's not hard. I told you. Don't buy that mincemeat crap they got at the store. They put cleanser in for filler. It's got ammonia. Formaldehyde, they got that in there. Hexamine, naphthalene—god-knows-what-all. You make it. Don't be scaredy-scared of a little fat, okay? You still got room in the waistband. Suet's good for you.

Suet, like sooey?

Suet like suet, Sessy. She ppffed. *No suet, no pie.*

So, Sessy had gone to butcher in the Market and got the suet gunked up like clogged arteries. She got the venison suet because Jeff would never go for the elk.

You're so fancy. Elk—not me. Bovine is fine is what I say. Joanne flicked her smoke into the sink. *You just cook up that meat on the stovetop, cover it with your water. Don't overcook it, okay. Get it tender, set it aside. Don't rush it. Let the meat pitch off. Leave it there. In the fridge, overnight. Don't discard the water. Don't rush it.*

Got it.

Now in the morning—depends on what time women like you roll out of bed—you scrape off the fat. If you sleep all day, the fat'll be rock-hard. Don't dig, scrape. You don't want all your meat soaked in fatty fat, okay. I use a spatula flipper. You use your fancy fingernails or whatever you got. Cut your meat up into little squares. Cubes. That into the pot. You got a pot, don't you? Get your raisins, your apples, your vinegar, your suet. You got your molasses, your cloves. Do not forget your cloves. Get everything in, cook it down. Two hours. Don't burn it. Don't rush it. Okay. Suet is time intensive.

Sessy stewed the raisins, cut up the apples, cubed the venison. She got it all into Canadian Tire jars. For pie, for Wonder Bread, for full-fat ice cream.

Jeff wanted to know how come there wasn't any cloves in it.

Go brush your taste buds.

I don't see 'em.

I am not your mother. I grind my cloves.

—— Today, the check-out girl at the register got her weight over to her good hip, adjusted her knock-off hair band and spit the last bit of something on the floor. Christ. Pumpkin seed.

'That doesn't seem altogether sanitary,' Sessy offered.

'It's not.' The girl leaned over her gum-pocked counter to whisper. 'But neither is you folks coming in tracking god knows what in here—urine, feces, spit— you all track all that in all this food every day. I get rid of one seed and you make some crack.'

Sessy peeled her loafers up. 'Well, you ought to mop this place now and again.' She handed the girl her Interac. 'You do have luxurious hair, though.'

A lady leaned in around Sessy but dropped an orange. 'Excuse me, pardon me.'

The universe pushes, you got to push back. Sessy kicked the orange out of the woman's way.

'Asshole.' The woman crawled after her orange.

'Accident.'

'Credit, debit?' The chick tightened her hair band. She licked her finger and wiped at the yellow caking on her shirt. She took Sessy's card. 'Debit. Please.'

'PIN.'

Spinach, cabbage, and red Swiss chard piled around the cash. Dammit. If she kept her eyes alive to what he puts inside of himself, Milk won't be clutching his gut like his grandma in some tube-hung, Pine-Sol'd cancer ward.

Don't think she didn't know all of the crap her boy fills himself with when she's not around. Don't think she didn't know how he gets himself up with ibuprofen and acetaminophen every chance he can; don't think she didn't know he probably smokes cigarettes even. The kid pickles himself in anti-biotic'd, growth-hormoned beef, Cheez-Its and nitric acid pepperoni and sausage pizza. She could tell. Armpits do not lie.

'Doesn't work.' Miss Thing pulled snags from her mop. She must grease that thing with WD-40.

'Try again.' Her neck seized up. Her C1 vertebrae. 'It works.' Air flooded her knees. He did it. Oh. She snatched her card back. Think. Think. Jeff cut off her Interac.

'Use cash.'

There's more than one way to skin a cat. Lie. 'That must be my daughter-in-law's card.' She held it very close to her eyes as if she couldn't see. 'Oh, yes yes yes. "Sessy"? Ha! Phff. That is not my card. My name is Abigail. My son will take care of this.'

'You want the lemons?'

Life cuts a lady off, strands her and leaves her as dust in the wind. The woman calling her "asshole" snorted behind her clutching her orange.

Do not tell Sessy about peeling oranges.

She bolted from the market. Get out. Air. Breath. Inhale. Oxygen. Sessy took the railing, mounted the sweating stairs, and before she pushed through the moose-hatted oh-honey-look tourists licking the red sauce from meatball sandwiches and cleaning their mouths with the backs of their forearms. A ghost hurtled at her. Her reflection in the glass-panelled double doors. It was she herself. Her! Sessy stopped in her tracks. Her coiled back reflected, took on an aged and gnarled twist. Her soupy locks of hair lifted into the wind, scratching at the sky. Her! Herself, a hooded and floating ghost. Jesus. She smashed through the crash bar, landing in a square of the morning sun.

Out on the west deck, she could see to the docks where the freighter smokestacks loomed over the Gardiner Expressway. Black, orange, and simmering.

Jeff went too far this time. It'd cost him. She got herself out to Front Street. If she couldn't get lemons, she'd find something else. But, wait. One door slams shut, another opens. A panhandler strummed a guitar, nodding and smiling to folks lugging booze from the liquor store.

A no-talent nincompoop who wouldn't know a musical note if it walked the length of his nose stabbed the senses with some Barbie-doll guitar version of "Stairway to Heaven." Hell, her dead mama could hit the notes of that song better than that. Not this guy. *'When she gets there she knows, if the stores are all closed, with a word she can get what she came for.'*

She came for lemons. But stood empty-handed. She planted herself on the corner, right where everyone would see her: from the Market, from the LCBO, from Spring Rolls, from Starbucks, from Rainbow Cinemas and the Metro—right across the street. Goddamned. She cupped her hands so the people could drop their coins in. She dropped her purse between her legs, planted herself in front of the guy—and belted. *'And she's buying the stairway to heaven.'* She hit the notes. Every single one.

'Excuse me,' he said, raising his voice. *'There's a sign on the wall, but she wants to be sure—.'*

Sessy wasn't waiting for no tone-deaf caterwauler—*''Cause you know sometimes words have two meanings.'*

'Lady—'

'Listen, pal, you want to sing a classic, you got to at least try.' He wasn't stopping her. *'In a tree by the brook, there's a songbird who sings—.'*

'You got to be kidding me.' The guy got pissy. Men never give women their due. 'What would you say if Robert Effing Plant walked by right now? You would shrink in shame. Wouldn't you? If you wouldn't, then you should think twice about getting out of bed in the morning.' Just let him try to start something. She crooned. *'Sometimes all of our thoughts are misgiven.'*

A woman in a long, fur coat eyed her up and down.

Sessy could do this. 'Miss? You have a dollar, don't you?'

The woman squinted at Sessy and moved on.

A man pushed a stroller through the handicap door of the LCBO. She clocked him. He slowed down to pull a blanket over a jug of Stoli while balancing two six-packs and a bottle of white wine on the stroller lid with his free hand.

She had never let booze that close to Milk. 'Excuse me—.'

He waved his hand at her.

'There's a feeling I get when I look to the west!' She followed him a few steps: *'And my spirit is crying for leaving!'*

The off-key panhandler blocked her. 'What do you think you're pulling? I work here. This is my slot. 'Kay? Don't get all up in my stuff just 'cause you had a bad day in your little housey.'

'I don't have a house-y. My husband has a house-y. And he's thrown me and my boy to the curb.'

A delivery van pulled up. A man in a blue uniform landed on the sidewalk and pulled up his zipper. He hurried up to the Spring Rolls sign fondling keys on a chain from his belt. He leaned over, got his glasses to his nose and squinted.

'Excuse me—.'

'Sorry, I just can't—.' He scrunched his mouth up to see better.

She'd get him. 'Your pants are—.'

He grabbed his zipper. 'No, no. They're not.' He hurried into the building, patting his crotch to double-check.

Time to up her game. Her hair had been casually, but delightfully, arranged on her head. She dismantled that and got it knotty with her fingers. She ground her yellow scarf in the wet dirt of a city planter and then wrapped it around her shoulders. She flicked the dirt as if she were a high-class something or other, and tucked a linden leaf next to her brow. A small twig protruded near her occipital bone. Perfect. She chewed the crux of her hand. If she ripped her skin open, maybe that would be enough.

Two women approached. One with a whipped cream frappé and clutching her oversized leather satchel, the other a mummy in a fur wrap. Before Sessy even got close, Satchel Lady lifted her arms to her, 'My arms are full!' The other yanked the woman back. 'Mom, this is a vulnerable person. Treat them like people. You've got whip crème on your chin.' The woman froze, while the Yanker wiped her chin. 'It's her circumstances, Mom.' She handed Sessy a fiver.

Shazam.

The mother sniffed and her daughter hurried her on.

Look the part. Sessy hung her head slack and pouted.

A crisp-creased banker tore up the pavement. His cell phone rang.

'Excuse me, sir—?'

He twipped a twenty from his breast pocket, handed it off and answered his phone.

Excellent. She flipped her hair over to keep it messed good. And then she saw them: lemons.

Across the street, Metro had a display of shiny lemons blinding in the sun. She leapt off the curb.

Cars honked. A little girl pointed and her mom pulled her away. Watch out!

Sessy stepped back up. They got to let people walk. At a break in traffic, she flew to the lemons.

A kid, Milk's age, rushed up to her. 'Oh, Mrs.—?'

'What?!' She clutched her chest for effect. 'You scared the living daylights out of me.' Her cover was blown.

'Sorry, I didn't—.' The boy, too polite for his own good, bowed but then stared at her.

'Well, you did. What? What do you want, young man?'

'Mrs.—?'

'Peg. Peggy. My name is Peg. Golly.' Goddamn it. She hung her head. Never be herself. Never. Never.

The kid hoisted his monogrammed backpack higher onto his shoulders.

She stuck her hand out. 'Got a five?'

'Are you sure you aren't who I think you are?' He let his backpack drop.

'No. Yeah. Yes. No. I mean. I don't know you.'

'Oh. Sorry.' He looked up at her, self-conscious. He stretched his mouth one way and then the other. He handed her a loonie. 'Sorry.'

Jesus, she's a monster. 'Take it back.' She couldn't take a dollar from a little boy. If she could, she would work for him.

'No. No, Mrs.—.'

'Golly. Peggy Golly.'

The boy stepped back. 'I'm not a little boy anymore, ma'am. I make my own money, I clean contagion labs.'

'Holy cow. You're just a child.'

'Take it. I get paid on Friday.' He lifted his shoulders. 'I know where I am going to sleep tonight.'

She snatched the dollar back. 'You are so right. I just wonder where I am going to lay my head.'

'You do?'

'Yes. What do you think this is? Make believe?'

'Aren't you, though—?'

'No. Yes. No. Yes. Fine. It's true. I am Milk's mother.' She pulled her scarf tighter and wheedled that twig from behind her ear.

'Those lemons really throw off bright.' He shielded his eyes. 'I'm Scott.'

'Scott. Well. Do me a favour, if you want to help the homeless and those down on their luck. Don't let anyone know you saw me here today?'

Scott shook his head and backed away. 'Okay.'

But she could see it in the way his shoulders sagged. He wasn't going to.

'See you. Milk's mother.'

Watch and learn, Scott. Don't ever double-cross a lady.

Milk

The shit's hitting the fan. You hauled yourself out of bed. Whoa. Right. Check that. The dresser is vacated. Dust halos circle where the Joes were. Wicked. The Joes are packed. A Glad bag in the backseat. The thermostat won't be the only heat rising. Kaboom. That woman had stared in the window. You got your eye against the glass to see any footprints in the snow below. Nada.

In honour of Tom's coming along on your mission of *Destructo* tonight, you got on one of the *Paris, Je t'aimes* T-shirts he brings you. With one hand on the doorknob before turning, listen. Your fingers smell of gas and ass, but the hallway is scented with lemon. The coast is clear.

Downstairs in the kitchen, your mom's slicing lemons. Steel knife in one hand, she reaches, gets the cupboard open. Snatches a cup, sets it down, takes the coffee pot, fills the cup. All one hand. She can't look at you. Pushes the cup to you. If I toss that percolator, she says, he'll have to spring for a new one. Your grandma got that for us four hundred years ago.

You skit to a stool.

A mozzarella stick disappeared down her gullet with barely a blink. I'll never get used to such a teeny belly.

She had bariatric surgery two years ago and went from the size of a military troop tent to a Barbie beach van in like three months. They re-jigged her intestines to by-pass her stomach.

The coffee bit good.

I just get so full, so fast. She spun the blade. I eat too much and POW. Pow, pow. Yech.

Your mom is the epitome of swallowing *it*. She has to.

She kicked a drawer shut with a free foot and cut into a new lemon. Then, got lost in thought. I'm too dreamy.

Way before she got super fat, she'd lollygag out in the backyard, nibbling chips, oiled up and roasting—bikini straps undone. A greased cobra curling in the grass. Her fingers and her feet paddling to Neil Diamond.

You and the guys from the 'hood peeked from around the garage.

You whispered in a hiss. *Mom. Your top.*

My top what, Milk?

It's—.

Don't be so sensitive.

You'd watch her through the trash cans paddling her feet and working her glutes. *A gracillis has one place to be and it is not the ankles, Son.*

She snagged another lemon. Like your dad says, make better use of your time. I, for one, he says, am nickel and diming us to death.

She looked good today. You could tell she had an idea. Purpose. Mom, you're kicking it up a notch this morning.

I got my boxing gloves on.

Use 'em on him, would you?

We're a team, kid.

━━ Last night, you crack the front door open. Your dad's sitting at the other end of the room in his La-Z-Boy waiting to pounce. You missile in. He launches to block your way. A finger twists a coil of his greased-up hair.

A thick snake of hamburger smoke circled the room. *Stop.*

The scrapes and clinks from the kitchen meant your mom leaned on the sink.

You're fucked.

You seen all these I.T. jobs? He points at the paper newspaper draped over the arm of his chair. *Paper?*

In 1986 or something, Jeff mined a mineral combo that let them sink microchips onto the deep sea floor. The deeper the dive, the better the circuits. The weight of the water pressed increasing the potentialities of electrons and so the kinetic energy possible had become infinite —until the circuits broke. But Jeff's circuits triggered crashes. The old days didn't have surge control. He got downsized in the downturn and paid bills doing contract system maintenance for HSCAN and their affiliate animal shelters. Jeff got the Acting Regional Director of HSCAN Tech position because in the old days he was the new guy.

I didn't get where I am by pussy-footing.

His frenemy Kenny from his old job tipped him off that his old company is bidding on new circuitry. Big man Jeff thinks he's gonna knock 'em dead with some fresh idea. Watch out, dude. Things surge in the modern age. *The Circuitry Network—K-Tek Pop* (Japan), *Blaue*

Linie (German), 빨간 선 *"Red Wire"* (South Korea), *Caustique* (France)—and a whole bunch of other conglomerates were yanking their business if they didn't come up with a circuit breaker to end all circuit breakers. Jeff had two weeks, Kenny said.

And don't come in there dressed in that suit. Jesus.

It's on me, Sess. On me. It's do or die. This is my shot.

Truth is, those days are gone. He's better off saving boa constrictors running loose in Leslieville or coyotes roaming over from the Rouge River woods. He won't admit it. Which means you and your mom get shit.

Jeff slunk to the kitchen and pulled the three chairs out. *You two can't bring yourself to sit down?*

Your mom ran the faucet. Opened the oven door, slammed it shut. She set a long glass pan of tomato-hamburger-squash lasagna on the table.

Jeff massaged his split ends.

I ate.

Jeff stabbed a tomato from the salad and wolfed it whole. *Why bother? Why go to the trouble? He doesn't care.*

Duck, dodge, weave.

You ate, Hon'?

You nod.

Doesn't care.

Hanging yourself wouldn't be enough for this dude. *Sit down.*

Fine. You're sitting.

So—work is work. Hours are the hours. Nothing lasts forever, eh Milk? He sized you up. *You get it from her,* he tapped his knife at your mom. *Where do you think your name came from? Evan. Even. Even you. Even you have got to amount to something. Right?*

Sure.

So—so, so. So, so, so, so. Right, Milk? He clawed a piece of cheese from the lasagna. He rubbed the back of his neck. *Goddammit, Sessy, sit down so we can eat. Jesus.*

Your mom stretched her waistband and sat down.

Cut her some slack. *Jeff, what is with you?*

Don't call me 'Jeff.'

Your mom passed you the salad.

HSCAN doesn't know what they got in me, they—.

You heard it twenty-thousand times.

Trust me. You can't count on nobody. Right, Milk? Jeff felt the bowl for heat. *You get to a certain point. You're not prepared. Boom. Life comes at you.*

He took the salad, tipped the bowl onto his plate. *You get in on the ground floor—.* He shook a last tomato out.

Don't take every last tomato, please. Jeff.

I'm hungry.

Well—.

You don't like salad, Sess.

She didn't. Your turn next.

You get your veggies from Pringles, right? Jeff poked you in the shoulder. Hard.

She wants salad, Jeff. Give her some. You scraped some of yours onto your mom's plate.

Jeff stabbed a tomato from her plate. It disappeared into his gaping maw. *There. Now we've both had vegetables. Are we going to make supper that exciting?* He jabbed at the lasagna. *The one thing you can count on is the evolution of technology. Believe you me. I know, trust me.* He hoisted a dripping brick onto his plate. *Goddamned soupy.* Steam floated up and dissipated.

Now seemed like a good time. *I'm going to go—.*

You're going to sit—.

Let him go, Jeff.

I don't see him all day, we, I come home from the workhouse—.

You backed your chair out.

Jeff yanked it back.

Jeff. Your mom tore a piece of bread.

You could play this. *What? Jeff.*

Let him go.

You bolted. Tripped. Got the wall. Took the stairs two, three, at a time.

He leapt from his chair.

Fuck fuck fuck.

The world's not all G.I. Joe, Milk.

He's got the stairs right behind you.

You got to have insurance. He clawed at your heels, but missed and slid down.

It's insurance, Milk. I-N-S-U-R-A-N—. He called up the stairs, one, two at a time.

You barreled down the yellow hall into your room. Shut the door.

He shoved in before you answered. *I just think about your future.*

You studied the chip in the corner of a floorboard.

You know in I.T., our whole deal is hope, son.

Don't call me that. There is no future, Jeff.

It will. It does. His face went dark red. *Do not Dad me. Do not Jeff me.*

Your mom creaked up the stairs now.

Man, you piss me off, son. He swung from the doorjamb, got a hold of your T-shirt, and spit. *I could throw you out that window right now.*

Sun Tzu says the hawk breaks the spine of prey with timing. You went loosie-goosie rag doll.

He growled and shoved you into the bulletin board.

Do it, Dad. Jeff.

His Brut shave stuff coated in your nostrils.

With one hand, he scratched at the sparrows flocking in the wallpaper.

Dad. Jeff.

Your grandmother and your mother lied to you. You are nothing special.

Your mom knocked on the hallway walls. *Boys?*

You're going to get the hell out of here the minute you graduate. The veins in his neck throbbed, and his glasses had slid down some. *You are nothing. Will amount to nothing. I see it. The writing's on the wall.* He brought you in closer again. *Eff. You.* His breath hissed in a soak of burnt cheese and browned hamburger. He loosened his grip. *Eff you, Milk. Evan. Even.*

Your mom hovered in the doorway now.

The minute school's done, he's out. He stuck a finger long into your face. *Start looking before. It's an owners' market.* He thumped from the room.

Your mom held her cheek. And fugged at the Funyun on her finger. She looked away then, too.

━━ Then, this morning, you had hurtled back downstairs. Something bit your ankle. A burr. From tromping in the middle of nowhere with Tom. The Spit.

Your mom threw a scarf. You said something about his curl-relaxer, didn't you?

Whatevs. In the car, you scraped at your yellow teeth in the rearview mirror with your fingernail and tucked the Glad bag of G.I. Joes into the backseat boot wells. Digging in your backpack for a pen for calc, you found a peanut shell instead. Tom Meuley's. Hell yeah, you rolled into class. You turned your button-hole inside out and dropped into your chair with Smith going off on William Lyon Mackenzie. There's another dude not afraid to blow things up.

Sessy

Time to teach the old man a lesson. She got the lemons sliced and her boots on. Oh, God. This is her time.

A vast canyon opened in the nether lands of her gut. Upon that scarred and bitten landscape, she, Milk, and even Jeff hung from some cooked-up cliff. Chunks of rock tumbled over the edge. The abyss pulls. Don't look down. Her days now were swinging one leg out to Milk. Grab it, Son. She could not yet let Jeff fall. Gripping with everything she had, she swung an arm to him. But, at that great height, Milk looked to Tom Meuley crouching on the ledge above. Jeff called her stupid for even trying.

She swiped the lemons into a big Glad bag and—. Shoot, shit. Juice dripped from the cutting board to the linoleum. She got her microfibre sponge. She pawed, scuffed and splattered. Shoot. Shit. Christ. It took everything she had to lift that bag onto her back. Jesus. Tote her weary load, why don't she? She could take it. But, she needed nourishment. She put the bag down. Shoot. *Shit*.

She opened the fridge and made a clean sweep. If she could just fill herself up. If she could make it so that there was no more room. If she could pack it so that even she, herself, could no longer find a chair. Milk, mustard, olives, ketchup. Fat-free cheddar. Christ goddamned. Butter, bread, jam. Eff. But she had to eat something. Multi-grain raisin. Whole grain, fruit. Two slices and a slab of P.B. & J. She licked strawberry off her thumb. Maybe Jeff or Milk beat her to that can of candied prunes. A week of smooth moves and no weeping. The only sensible, existential response to war is food.

But, by God, she needed liquid. Her mouth cracked into the earth of sweet Jesus Christ lost in the desert. Very dry. God, she could gag. She got a handful of chocolate O-Yos. Take a slug of no-fat soymilk. And another. Christ goddamned. One more. Now, now she could breathe. She pulled her waistband down. Fat-free don't count. She pulled her tee up, and then down, to fan herself. Her coat fell to the floor. Jesus, they'll bake a lady alive in here. She deserved a reward. After all that she'd done. All those lemons. Maybe that shortbread lay waiting up there in the back cupboard. She hoisted herself up on the counter, braced one foot on the edge of the stovetop and the other on the sink and, Jesus, making sure she didn't fall, she got the door open with her free hand, and reached back, way way way back, she couldn't get around to see in there but she could feel doing a Helen Keller—*et voilà*. She swiped at the dark corners, tearing at the cobwebs slathering her face. If she could only reach that same corner deep inside of herself. She fingered the box out as best she could and dropped it on the linoleum then, easy as pie, she landed on all fours getting all the pieces because her life depends upon it. Christ goddamned. Eff. She squatted on the palm-frond linoleum. She would never gain her fill.

Eating again, Dummy? is what her mom used to say to her. And so every single time a morsel of food passed her lips—every cracker, every spoon of cereal, every sip of water even—she hurtles into the oblivion of not mattering, of being no good, of what the demons knew long before she ever saw—she had no right to be here. Eating isn't the problem. It's being. It's living. It's breathing.

Her doctor laid it all out after her procedure, she could eat whatever she wanted. Eating is life. Chewing is sex. It is the pterygoids anchoring the muscles churning, the mandibular grinding, the un-masticated chunks writhing and squirming this way and that with acid-laced saliva pushing into the opening of the esophagus. That one act connected her to what it meant to be alive. She couldn't get her breath; her knees were skinned now.

Focus. She'd take those lemons out to where Jeff parked—. Her mother had a one-track mind. *Eating again, fatty?* Oh, if Sessy could just keep one thing in mind at a time. She'd park out on the street, and slide out to Jeff's car, she'd lie down—. He might see her. Really see her. But people need protein. Back up on the counter, a hard-boiled egg lay huddled and lonely in a bowl. Gone before she noticed. People need fruit. An apple winked at her. Time to go. She snatched Milk's bike helmet off the hook and fell through the back door.

Out in the driveway, in the car, her stomach seized. She gripped the steering wheel. She dug her feet in. She hugged Milk's helmet hard into her tummy. Sweat bubbled along her hairline. She cracked the window. Cold air digests. Her stomach wrenched. *Do it, Sessy. Do it.*

She lurched forward. A ricochet shot from her sternum to the underbelly of her ribcage. Oh, God, how could she not, after all of this time, be like everybody else? She heaved, lurching the door open just in time before retching an orange spray into the ice-drenched wood chips lining the hedge. The condiments (ketchup, mustard, jam) came first, straight past the trunk of the silver maple. And then the solids (olives, cheese, and multigrain raisin bread) smeared a brilliant ribbon of chunks into the perennials. Finally, the hard-boiled eggs, peanut butter and chocolate O-Yos cleared the Eisele's bushes. That is how you spell relief. Her stomach thrust out and then back in. Out and in. Out and In. In, further. People don't know the cost of svelte—. She jammed her finger down her throat to get every last bit up-chucked. She got a handful of snow. Wiped her face and dug into her bag for what was left of the lipstick. She spit, putting the blueberry helmet on the seat next to her and checking the rear-view mirror. Her gums ached from the stomach acid sting but the teeth were clean. She wiped the limp strands of hair from across her brow like when her mom made her lug that effing Hoover for exercise. Her thumb stung from the lemon, her mouth sour from retching. A little pee let loose. God. She couldn't keep all that food down and the piss inside her, too. No. No. Now. She got out. She'd scrub the seat to-night. But first her lipstick. She skimmed it one way across her lips, and then the other.

She scooped snow with both hands covering the vomit good. She got a rag and *detacheur* stain remover from the trunk. Once the fungus-brown seat got scrubbed, she got back behind the wheel. She opened her legs to let air into the moist. She checked for gawking Mrs. Eisele and dug the *detacheur* into her pants.

She clenched her teeth. Dug her nails. Shut her eyes. Her brain on static. She fought for an ideological branch, a philosophical root, a metaphysical saying—anything to hang onto but everything tore from her hold. Her mind collapsed into a mud-soaked riverbank. Little did she know that spinning, scrambling, snatching at straws which used to take her weight wasn't nothing to hold onto. She—daughter, wife, mother—had no roots to hold now. Now, the ground turned sinkhole. Now, a gaffe— her very existence—opened to swallow the whole earth, the driveway, and her. Right here in North York, the earth trembled. She turned on the ignition and gave the Tercel some gas.

She cracked open the trunk. Oh, for a Pizza Pocket. Oh, for a carton of milk and something sweet at 7-Eleven. Not Oreos, Nutter Butters. P-R-O-T-E-I-N. The taste in her throat made it too soon to ingest. She threw the rag and stain remover in the trunk, climbed behind the wheel, shifted into reverse and checked her face in the rearview. Her jowls had gotten bigger. She reached into the back seat to feel for the extra food she'd brought with her. She pulled her cheeks down, and then back. She didn't look so bad. Maybe. Sort of. Oh, if only she weren't herself.

Peeing her pants. No wonder Jeff didn't want her. She'd never amount to anything. Fat, ugly and stupid. Smelly. Old. She checked the car seat. A plank of sun burned in through the windshield and right onto the spot of stain remover. The elongated stain had evaporated in the shape of Alaska crab legs. Fat, stupid, ugly. Stinky. Jesus, what an effing catastrophe her life rose to. Ugly, fat, stupid. Putrid. No wonder Jeff went catting.

Tiny wisps of steam lifted from the spot, gathering and dissipating.

Forget food. No more. Okay. Maybe grapefruit, Diet Coke and water. She could take it. Eff her mom. Apples. Celery. Carrots. Who wouldn't stuff their gut? Bran. Power bars. Skim milk. Eff food and Uncle Louise, too. She had to pee, now. God, what she'd do for a wig. But this helmet would do it. She clenched her thighs. How come she couldn't just blend in and be like everybody else? Fat chance.

Most kids don't have to explain their dad's titties. Most kids don't have to explain their mom writing her name in the snow when she pees standing up. Oh, she had a long history of people shape-shifting. Take Uncle Louise, her 'Dad' with a yoo-hoo fuzzier than a bear claw. Take her mama and her friends with their low-hanging balls. Her mom said she ought to write a superhero book someday and Louise'd do the pictures. A book of lady Superfriends. Forget the men, just think about those ladies. Think about the girl monks, the housewife soldiers, and the nineteenth-century cross-dressing female politicians. Think about the criminals, the misfits and the masters of the aeronautics sphere. Think about the bearded ladies, the Sapphic killers, and the lady *pyrates* of the Caribbean. Any girl could be a lady James Gray, a soldier of the Royal Marines, capped with her triangle and good to go. She could be a private in the Civil War 95th Illinois Infantry Regiment chopping her pigtails and bringing down Vicksburg. But Sessy wasn't that kind of girl. Not like her mother, not like her dad. Not a revolutionary, not peeing in the flower bed. She clenched tighter.

As she backed out of the driveway, the sun splintered through the windshield. A flaking had fallen overnight crunching crisp snow under the tires. No sliding, no fishtailing. Peeling down the road, the ice held her.

Out there in the parking lot at HSCAN, no one would I.D. her. He never took her to any work events. Nobody there knew she existed. If they were gazing over the lot from a window, the blacktop would stretch from where they stood all the way out to the tree line where that Mud Creek trickled still. All they'd see would be an alien creature, not like the others, skating along in Milk's bicycle blueberry helmet. At a stop sign, she waited.

The lemons had scented the car covering up the puke smell. A sour taste coated her throat. She dug in her purse. Fisherman's Friend. Vicks. Something. She found a peanut shell. And piddled some.

The Afternoon of:

Ton'

Under the covers, Ton' listened. He sniffed. Bacon. He poked his head out. Smoke from the kitchen lassoed a beam of sunlight cutting through the drapes. 'Schelle's gone to work, probably. She should've got some of the sausages he's slinging. *Not-everyone-thinks-about-getting-off-like-you-Ton'* tone: *we might find out we're parents.* Listen.

Everyone like him sleeps late to hit the four-to-midnight shift. Those pussies at 54 Division all want daylight hours. Not him. Not his partner, Shafiqq.

He wouldn't make it to 'Schelle's in-vitro deposit today. His stuff could swim upstream no problem. Their trouble came from her insides. It can't be pushing his junk back out. His dudes can't stick to the walls getting squeezed out.

The silverware drawer slammed shut in the kitchen. She's still here.

'Ton'!' Give the props to 'Schelle, man. Bitch make a sandwich, is what he's saying. Bacon grease dribbled on iceberg: fried egg, mayo, black pepper. Sriracha, baby.

Damned. 'Yeah.' Come do business, baby. 'Yeah?' His five fingers could not fit around the Leaning Tower of

Pisa he held in his hands. If he had a boy, his little man'd be just like him. Equipped.

'Ton!'

Bam. She slams the silverware drawer again. The racket she makes.

In the fat of his hand is a gift from God. Community property. Dudes don't keep a piece like that tucked in their pants. Sharing is caring, man. He pulls a dude or lady over, up to like sixty even. Age is a state of mind. He performs. Ten or fifteen minutes. It don't take long. The time it takes Shafiqq to feed his kids lunch. Ton' works alone. Gets a customer (he can read their burning eyes) to the side of the road. Licence, registration, insurance. Clockwork. A cock of the eyebrow, a sideways glance for the coast is clear. A pull at his stuff and bam. A ticket to paradise. He fills them up and makes them whole. Let them eat cake.

At the marblesque en suite bathroom sink, he softens his stubble with warm water. Spreads the shaving cream. 'Yeah.' He got some more directly onto the meat of the shaft. Minty-fresh tingle. Pump the goods, cement the day. Man, the flesh on that motherfucker. Artisanal, man. Bespoke. Religious. Take it.

'Ton',' Mom spoke out loud.

Now, she's banging around in the closet.

'You and me, we're going to visit.'

The cream goes on smooth, ear to ear, throat to mouth. Base, shaft, head. He draws the razor over that sweet throat. He'd teach his son, someday. Not one jowl. Flex the delt, torque the arm, trip the 'cep. Not an ounce of—.

'Ton', I'm leavin' the mayonnaise off okay? You got chub at your belt.'

He pinched his waist.

'Get fat in ten years, Hon'.'

Dang. He digs a finger in the crevasse at his hip flexor. Eat that, 'Schelle. Feel that. Dig in, mo-fos. Pump for God's good creatures. Pump. Pump. Pump it. Pump, pump, pump. Not one finger takes it all. Yeah. Pump. Pump. Pow. His stuff comes up good. Thick. Oh, man. Pump. Yeah. Rocket. More. Spray. Shit. Oh, man. Yeah, man. Fuck. Shit is dew drops. He wiped spill from the sink, mirror, and tip.

'Ton',' 'Schelle busted into the bedroom spinning a rag and pitching it all '92 Jimmy Keys. It nails the door-jamb and slides to the baseboard. 'Do those, too. Before you go. In the cracks, too. And your gook.'

Aw, man. He'd show her cracks.

'Don't even, Ton'.'

'Hon', I got to be at 54—.'

'Before. You. Go.' She ducked back to the kitchen. 'The food grade H_2O_2 hydrogen peroxide on the counter. A'ight? Use that. Don't burn yourself.' By the back door, she crunched paper grocery bags. 'I'll be back, flat, legs up. As long as they tell me to.'

Sweet. Toothpaste caked the mirror. He swivelled around to catch a glance of his behind dusted with black, animal fur. Once he got his pants on, he got down on his knees. He worked the rag digging at the dust-crap-gunk from where the moulding meets the wall. Mama used a vacuum but Ale, 'Schelle's mom, his mother-in-law, didn't think that got the germs off so they used a wet rag coated in the stuff that takes skin off: food-grade hydrogen peroxide.

She stuck her head back in. 'Don't burn your hands. It's super strong.' And then disappeared.

He'd show her 'super strong.' Take that lady he saw at the Petro Canada. That chick dug at her gummed-up wiper blades with a yellowed fingernail.

'Be good out there tonight, Ton'. Be safe.' The front door shut. 'Schelle pulled her key, clicked the bolt, and knocked twice.

'Schelle never took one minute to listen to his heart these days. If she did, he'd tell her that old lady at the gas station scared the bejesus out of him. It's what happens when you get old. He'd tell her: *Right, so, old lady gets out of the car. Old. Ancient old. She's on a cane. Pulls down her hat for the wind. Gets out. But there's overhead speakers, right? Above the pumps. And she's bopping to the music. She's digging and mouthing* why must you be such an angry young man? The future looks quite bright to me. *She busts it, no sound. Wailing. Her car is like a 90s. A Taurus. Like your dad's, 'Schelle. We are never getting a Ford Frigging Taurus. Like your dad's. No way. This lady's got a station wagon one. A 90s one. Packed to the gills. Every fucking thing the woman owned. She probably has to eat dog food. In the States, old people have to eat dog food. It's getting like that up here. The lady's stretching like up over the windshield. Like holding on to that glass for dear life. When you're old you want to be on your own, not to get taken care of. People do anything to stay free; eat dog food. Freedom and hanging on—it's their air. She hauls herself up to get over the windshield farther, but goes wobbling, drops her cane and tips back. Fucking falls back.*

*Jesus. To the cement. I run to her, Ma'am, ma'am, ma'am
—you all right? She's lying there on her back blinking gaw
gaw. Like right now, 'Schelle, I went to my knees to help her.
Dog crud frozen in the ice. Okay? I took her pulse. Readied
her neck for CPR. She wallops me. Whoa, slow down, I say.
She could've been your mom, 'Schelle. I got her elbow, got
her up. She jerked to the rubber rainwater lip around the
windows and pulled herself to the hatch. I backed off. A bag
lady. Somebody's mother.* Just 'cause she got chlamydia,
'Schelle's got no time to listen. If they get a kid, though.
She might listen then.

By 4:15 him, Shafiqq, Horst, and the rest of the
squads were huddled at the tables in the arena-shaped
briefing room. Radios, man. Beeping, squawking. Buzzing.

Lieutenant Jamarandu banged his steel book on the
chipped table. And tapped the blackboard with his
knuckles.

'You all deaf? Turn it down.' Some jerk-off blinked
the lights.

Horst twirled his wire-rimmed glasses on one finger.
'Wow.'

The room reeked. Like rotten egg-soaked pine cleaner.
Shafiqq studied the dots in the floor tile.

'Don't get in my stuff, Officer Horst.' Jamarandu had
bigger fish to fry. A tiny plastic bag of what looked like
coarse rock salt. Meth probably. 'Who is not checking their
back seat? Again.' He wagged the bag in front of them.

Ton' covered his nose. The department's cleaning
stuff. 'Schelle says it's the chemical neurotoxins in manu-
factured janitorial products.

'I want to know. Who pulls out their back seat, sticks their fingers in the crack, and removes the unit after a pickup?'

Ton', for one, stuck his fingers in cracks. Just sayin.

'They found this in a certain back seat. Okay? Dig your fingers in. Pull the seat out.'

That plastic baggie had to be Pat-Pat's. Definitely. Like they're gonna bust him. He's got rank. Ton', though, had someone else to take down. One of these dudes deals Mac-10 semi-automatic rifles. He'd nail them; he'd get Detective Constable. Hop right over Constable Shafiqq Sinha.

'Remember what we found back there.'

They found a Mac-10 stuck in the rear seat cushions two months in a row.

'We can't have weapons packing in the back seat.'

Something's cooking. Macs pop up for good reason. They pump. A .9mm does 1250 rounds a minute. Macs traffic. That one the Lieutenant held up now—that's a sale that didn't go through. Ton' knows from experience. With Pat-Pat.

━━ At Sherbourne, the Don Valley river carves out the ravines from which nineteenth-century Castle Frank mansions spring. Far below those glittering living rooms, the stink of homeless crappers and Toronto cast-offs had stewed since the 1930s. Gay boys throw themselves to their demons off the viaduct bridging the Don Valley Parkway (the D.V.P.)—the expressway sewing the northern suburbs all the way south to the lake.

In Ton's second month at TPS (Toronto Police Service), on the bush side of Sherbourne past the Bloor

Viaduct, he and Pat-Pat, his trainer, pulled to the curb. Just a pit stop. It being winter, Pat-Pat told him to sit tight by the car. *'You mind your business, Anthony. I'll mind mine.'* He patted Ton's thigh.

Anthony. Only his dad called him that.

Those stairs. He knew the trees at the railing since they were saplings. What Pat-Pat maybe didn't know is that those stairs descended into more than a ravine. Ton's dad built those stairs on a city contract he won just after he, Ma, and Grandma clawed their way to Canada. When he and Ma would drive past, she'd stick her chin out some.

Pat-Pat got a thermos bag out of the trunk. *'You just chillax. Okay?'* At the top of the stairs, Pat-Pat, stomped his boots free of gunk. He clomped down each stair until his head dropped out of sight.

Ton' hopped out and leaned against the car.

A jet came in low over the lake passing to Pearson airport. Traffic crunched by with the grumble of Ma's throat gunk.

Ton' crept to the steps. And peeked over.

Pat-Pat gripped the railing below.

'Pat-Pat.'

Pat-Pat waved him off. He nudged one foot a fragile step down.

What a girl. *'I got you.'*

'Back off. I got it.'

Ton' jumped down. Took his arm.

'Get off me.'

'Off you. You'll break your neck.' Ton' took a step, testing the ice. *'It's just a little steep.'* Ton' could break his neck out here. *'Like you got a heights thing?'*

'I did the CN Tower walk, okay?'

Ton' jumped a couple of steps back up and then down. *'Pat-Pat.'*

A white glob in a freezer bag lay in the leaves and a dust of snow beyond the stairs.

'Dammit.'

An older guy came prancing up the stairs. Show-off. He nodded at Pat-Pat.

At Ton', though, he stopped. He took a breath. His mouth screwed up. The lips jerked back baring stained teeth and darkened gums.

Do not even. Fag. His whole life. Only that guard in Buffalo never wanted anything from him. Fags get up to business in The Ravines. The man ducked up the stairs.

'Pat-Pat—.'

'I don't have to tell you nothing, Anthony.'

'Think fast.' Ton' jumped and landed two steps down. The whole rack of stairs shook.

Pat-Pat freaked. *'Ton'!'*

No one had ever called him that before. It fit. "Ton'"

He eased another step. *'Pat-Pat, Jamarandu's got us at Lawrence and Yonge. Not here.'*

'I order you.' But Pat-Pat's legs shot out to the side. *'Ton'!'*

Ton' snatched hold of Pat-Pat's collar. He pulled him up.

Pat-Pat locked eyes with Ton's pleading. *'Rock for Mac-10s for cash. Ton'.'* Pat-Pat had a sideline selling seized meth for Mac-10s. *'Everybody does it.'* Pat-Pat got his arm free. *'The buyers are down there.'* The dealer buys the meth from Pat-Pat, pays the guy for the weapon, takes the gun, and resells it on the black market. *'One shot is seven K for me. He gets upwards of ten K.'*

'Who?'

'What do you mean "who"?'

Leaves rattled in the beech and aspen above.

'Who? Who runs it? Who gets the "upwards of ten K"?'

Pat-Pat shook his head. 'Somebody that doesn't want to be known.'

Ton' didn't see nothing down on the path. 'Buyer's're not going to just stand around 'til you get a toehold.'

'I slipped Anthony.'

Ton' reached out a hand to lift the guy up. 'Call me, Ton'.'

Pat-Pat backed into the railing. 'Anthony.'

'Ton'.'

Pat-Pat cocked his head and snatched the brick hanging on for dear life. 'Whatever. Back to the car.' The bag held more than a glob. Smaller snack baggies had been folded in.

Ton' got his hand in Pat-Pat's face. The tiny nose hairs there were caked with dried beads of snot. "Give me that stuff. I got it.'

Pat-Pat chewed his cheek. And dragged an arm across his nose.

'I trick this like that.' Ton' snapped his fingers. 'Boom. Like that.'

Pat-Pat pulled out the pack. 'Seven.'

'You don't sell nothing for seven. Twelve. If he's telling you ten K, it's twenty. At least.' Ton' bolted the stairs two at a time with Pat-Pat lighting the way with the cone beam of his flashlight. At the fourth step from the bottom, he leapt to the path. Pat-Pat killed his light.

The shadows blossomed amongst the trees. They rose to meet him. A cascade of dried leaves tittered.

Looking back up behind him, he could almost see his dad. Loading planks. Building stairs.

The trees began peeling themselves one from the other. Not trees at all, some of them. Dudes and chicks. Afterglows, almost, shadows shuffling from the grey light, slipping bills into his right hand while the left handed a pack off, one for the other, the shiny silver strip of duct tape catching the lamplight. His role same as it ever was. To feed the hunger. The deals got done. The packets got bought, and the spooks thinned into trees. Wind ripped through their tippy tops. Traffic slogged over from the D.V.P.

⬛ Back at roll-call, Jamarandu barked. 'You don't have time to remove the seat unit, you stick your fingers in there and—.'

'No Mac-10s back in my seat. Wow.' Horst massaged his thighs.

That dude's trainer is paying off.

'Just make sure you check, 'kay?' Jarmarandu slapped his Call Book closed.

Ton'd stick his fingers in, man. He ran his fingertips under his nose. Julio.

Sessy

She parked across the street from the HSCAN parking lot. She ate her bag lunch and watched the thin line of shadow cast by the Tercel antennae move across the hood with the sun. Just when the light lost that mid-afternoon burn, she balanced Milk's bike helmet on her head for protection and disguise. Her hair greased right, rank and rancid; her breath rumbling, her eyes set. She'd straighten Jeff's curls, all right. He'd come home.

A Cape buffalo, a wildebeest, a moose, and a giraffe. A rhino. Jeff's HSCAN fundraising idea. Donors buy spent-shell casings stamped with their initials which, in turn, are soldered onto steel animal skeletons. Big game tearing across the parking lot savannah. Their pelts reflecting shots of glare in the sun poking through. How they must wish to fly. How they must wish to drop their burdens in a trample of hooves. She'd take the rhino first, and then the Cape buffalo. One of the herd, she would disappear beneath their sagging bellies and smooth, thick legs. Past the moose, she'd risk a run out into the open, pop the trunk, and lay the lemons down.

A cormorant tittered on that rhino's horn.

She hoisted the bag of lemons to her back, sinking low and shooting out her left leg, and then her right. She spun lifting her leg good, her toe *en pointe*. She held the skate up long enough to catch a glint on her knife blade. He wouldn't ever skate like this with her back when she lugged the lard of a moo-cow. If anybody were remembering her, they'd piece her together, bit by bit, limb by limb, ice cut by ice cut. The memory of her would fade, she could only hope.

Her blades cut the ice same as Grandma Jean Sloan skinning rabbits. Sess' pressed on, provoked and inspired as any day-old Miss Chatelaine. She passed the rhino, the Cape Buffalo and the cormorant now hopping her way. She launched herself forward, hand-waving and her boot rubber slipping smoothly 'til she landed right behind the trunk digging her toes in to stop. The wind clipped through her air holes. The stinging air kissed her cheeks, a freedom surged from her belly scar—the horizon unspooled past the creek at the far end and all the way over the far hills towards Mississauga. And there it was. Jeff's Saturn. An overblown cherry ready to pop.

Isolated. Removed. Parked between the lines and hogging two parking spaces. Entitled. Insufferable. Oh, but Jeff had to know the lemons would come from her. No one owes him loyalty. No one else's life depended on the sunlight rays of his attention. He would know it was her. No one else loves him like her. That car ought to be out there alone. Sacred. Separated from the others. This is their love. If only they could unplug what had gotten so confused. If only *she* would go away. Jeff knew as well as Sessy that lemons mean loyalty. That St. John the Baptist brought them to the baby Christ way back when he still pooped his pants. Jeff could read the signs. He would return to her loving arms. Or else.

She started on the far side of that late-model pomegranate tin cup. Got the helmet up onto her forehead. And then, ha ha ha her heart started thump-thump-thumping and her finger cuts stung from the juice oh god oh god this felt so good so alive so what she ought to be doing and then every one she laid especially when she got that first one little slice down oh and there it landed. There it lived. Just like she saw it in her mind and then the next one and every single one, there they were; and even with the little rivulets letting go and loosening themselves in tiny rivers off the roof over the glass down along the window seal overflowing and leaving a mark, a scar, a difference before it dropped off down below. She drew another out and laid it next to the one before. No stopping now, she kept on to lay a sixth, a seventh, a next one and after she got all the way around the front bumper there must have been forty, more, fifty maybe she didn't even know how many lemons she laid, but she kept going and going, and then coming around in full view to where she could've been seen, dancing along, laying them faster and faster so now she made like a pro and got clean past the back door on the driver's side then to the trunk again where she started sort of; but she couldn't remember where she started—but before she knew it, oh, she forgot to breathe, she got right around that back bumper and Holy Toledo there comes the first one back in sight, she gained on it and, boom, there she was. She did it. The last one down.

And then—an old woman appeared. Standing there. Not two feet away. Watching her. Sessy slammed her helmet back down. But the woman's eyes left Sessy to land at some fixed point beyond. The ground trembled a little. The wind, probably. Sessy ducked low, dug her heel into the ice and pecked at the car window as if she'd forgotten something inside.

The woman marched by. One careful step. At a time. Cigarette in hand. Purse clutched. The robin's egg hood half down. The strap slacking, her coat flapping. She stood still, inhaled deeply, let the air go, and stepped. After three steps, she stopped again. Her eyes tearing, the wind biting. Her gaze unflinching. She felt around for her strap but, caught in the wind, she could not get it.

Sessy hurried to the tiny thing, but then slipped only to right herself. Now, she dug her toes into the glacial asphalt. Her helmet cocked off. And, when she got to the woman, she cupped her face, pulled her hat down and held her face on account of she looked so so so—what's the word—disparaged. Resigned. Lost. Unattached and untethered. She belonged everywhere and nowhere. Disturbed. Homeless. Or both. She blocked the woman's way and tied her straps snug as if she were Milk a hundred years ago.

The woman pressed forward.

For crying out loud. She had to know the wildness of the woods back there.

The ground rumbled. Canadian Air Force jets taking off from the Islands probably or heavy trucks passing by.

Unthinking, she soothed the woman's back with her hand. Maybe she could guide her back. Maybe she'd gotten loose from a long-term care facility. Maybe she was like Sessy's mother clawing at the glass window, doing her best to bust out. Jeff could come any minute. Dang.

A bell rang inside HSACAN.

The woman puffed her stub smoke and stepped forward. Two more feet and the butt fell from her hand. One foot in front of the other. Her eyes pinned to where Mud Creek used to be back there. It cut through a wood that got paved over. Lady, come back. Maybe the lady had a screw loose wandering out here in the wilderness behind an industrial park.

When they first came from Nebraska, all this grew as grazing land. Back before Adam was born the woods stopped near the Don, cutting all the way out of Old Toronto, and fed still by that poor old creek. Before that, Indian land. Uncle Louise and Adele had dragged them all out here, long before there was any such thing as an HSCAN or great bullet-sheathed beasts gunning toward Etobicoke. They stood looking at the hills and fields of their new land, sniffing the air and twiddling their thumbs wondering what they'd gotten themselves into. The glaciers carved a trench out there and the water rushed rough. Back when trees still held the water table. Like they do, men buried the creek to park cars and handed nature to water management computer programs. That creek, like this woman, had kept on. Zombie-like.

The ground shivered. Horses were galloping towards them, maybe.

Maybe the old dog slipped out through an unlatched storm door. Maybe lost. Maybe dementia. Sessy had lived five years worried sick thinking of her mom ripping out those tubes and, doped up, wandering away. Her mama getting hurt on her watch would cut far deeper and sharper than any blade. Adele had a lot to answer for, but no way in hell Sessy would let her wander into the bush unattended. There are wolves out there.

The woman padded out across the parking lot to a rough line dividing the asphalt from the dirt. Sessy could see cragged edges of the rock cut through, kind of like mini-versions of the escarpment up by Muskoka and the Kawarthas. She hurried after the lady, holding her helmet in place with both hands.

She thought about those Japanese exchange students taking the wild for granted. They're always backing themselves to flip over the railing at Niagara Falls and getting broken on the rocks and tangled in the branches below. Nature is not a picture, kid. They just don't know. And just how would kids know things aren't photographs? They are jagged and sharp-edged. Fall into them and you'll die. You'll drown and be swept over and you won't come back. They find the bodies, far down below, limbs hooked and flailing around some trunk, the legs swirling like seaweed in a whirlpool downriver. There's that story too of Alice Munro's, all about her relatives clearing the land and—maybe her cousin, Thomas Laidlaw—that had a big tree fall straight on top of his head killing him instantly and how they had to leave his body in the shed all winter because the ground froze too hard to dig but not wanting the animals to get him before the thaw. That happened way outside of the city. Out in the middle, out there by Elmira or somewhere west and wilder than this parking lot.

Where the asphalt ended, an embankment fell off. The woman held her hands up as if she were about to step on a tight rope and squatted down carefully to her knees, then onto her bottom. And began scooting down the embankment.

That rumbling closed in on them, but from above. Top of the upslope across the stream.

For the life of her, Sessy couldn't figure out what the crazy goose had in her noodle. Out of clear view of the windows now, she pushed her helmet from her face. 'It's cold down there, Ma'am. It's wet. It's winter. There's a storm coming. Ma'am, there's a storm coming tonight and it's supposed to be really bad and if you get wet and stuck down here who's going to get you out? You won't get out of there maybe.' Her concern went unheeded. Not a person in this world listened to her. Not one.

The woman kept going. And then stopped. She extended her arms and brought them towards her body as if she were smoothing the surface of the water or welcoming some loved one home. She looked at the upslope on the opposite bank, and then upstream. And then very slowly taking in every bush and plant her gaze drifted in an arc to around behind her and down the creek. And then she straddled the creek. She stepped forward and got one foot on either bank. She scooped water and seemed to be offering it up creek, up the slope and then down creek. The woman drew water from the stream running between her crouching thighs. She seemed to draw it from her innards. And then, slurped it down. And scooped up another bit. She turned and offered it to Sessy. "No, thank you." Oh, to be that brave. To be that full of beans. To offer the pure liquid gold of one's stream to sip.

Something up top the hill opposite—a flash of white at the top of that slope—caught Sessy's eye. The

woman looked, too. Her mother. No. No. Grandma Jean
Sloan. What? Her mother's mother. She blinked. No way.
No one. Nothing there. Just dried, spindly reeds left
over from Nature's attempt to take her land back. The
lady's going to get knockered.

Sessy ought to do something. She'd only get wet;
soaked, for sure. Catch a cold. Just so this old squirrel
could sow her oats slopping in the ditch. The woman
sucked some juice from her hand. That pearl flash came
again. What?

First, though, there were snips of what looked like
her mother's wispy hair teasing up from her balding
head over the crest. It was her mother. Mom. What? The
very body and face of her mother pinning her with her
gaze. Sessy looked behind her. And then to the right and
then the left. She hollered. Mom. The old woman never
looked up as Adele began her descent towards her, IV
tubes hanging from her arms clear as snakes dangling—
as if she'd just snuck off from Toronto General. But her
mother had got dead and was buried—what is this? Not
her. Can't be. It's a reality show. A hidden camera. A circus. A game show. She must be on the verge of winning
something. Maybe it's a space-age, high-tech parking lot
fair with 3D Princess Leia's coming to town. Holy
Criminy. Behind her—. No. Grandma Jean Sloan came
on now, in that dark dress dotted with tiny flowers and
her fake pearl necklace, shuffling on account of her bad
hip. She too had got long gone. She wasn't no more no
way. That couldn't be her. Her dead mother and grandmother were the tip of the iceberg.

Before Grandma Sloan got far and, following her
mother, Edith Nordheimer mounted the crest, it had to

be her, wearing pelts not yet cured and their blood draining into the fine lace netting over her silk dress, then on the far side of Edith came Phyllis Dietrichson from *Double Indemnity* motioning to her actress Barbara Stanwyck to hurry up and, Sessy hadn't even seen it, but just ahead of those two trotted Victoria Barkley of her all-time favourite TV show *The Big Valley*, all the way from Stockton, California with her six-gun and leather skirt. Before she could look fast enough a whole line of folks swarmed up behind her mother and Grandma Sloan, Edith, Phyllis, Barbara, and Victoria: Edith's husband, Samuel, Tommy Thompson, Steve Douglas with Uncle Charlie, Walter Neff pushing and shoving his actor Fred MacMurray, that must be the way it is for poor performers, the people they play shove them around expecting them to climb hills faster and make like they know what they're doing, all these folks pounded forth —then here came Billy Wilder, the director of *Double Indemnity*, and her brother, Adam—is he dead, too? Here came Arthur Ashe, Rock Hudson, Liberace and, holy smokes, Rudolf Nureyev leading a determined, but weakened Jack Layton trailing his bike. Behind them came, sure enough Sir Sanford Fleming and then then then the ground shook even more, not from who stomped over it but from what gushed up from it, volcanic eruptions of heads and then bodies of the dead and buried descending toward Sessy and the old woman, tens of them sprouting up, first the head, then the shoulders, then the torso, all the way to the legs and gnarled feet; hundreds to the right, the left and straight down the centre, they now dotted the entire slope as far as the eye could see, all of those ghosts making room for the new ones, she couldn't believe it, some lifted the earth as they came rearing their heads while others tore through it with a rage that must've accounted for some of the grumbling but that wasn't the end, no, just like that amongst the hundreds, now thousands of indentured Chinese materialized, followed by First Nations men holding their babies, slathered in war paint, women suckling others, children with ropes around their necks pulling even younger ones, the wounded and starved, some in old timey dress like she'd seen in the movies others like they just came off the rez two days ago and the thing about it, the thing that caused all of that rumbling; all of that earth shaking came from their footsteps, yes, but something else entirely, too. All of them mumbled: 'Kkkchrtrnchll, kkkchrtrnchll.' As they got to the stream, some holding onto the shoulders of others—it being awfully slippery—but fighting to say the word they were saying, that old lady got back into action.

She cupped her hands in the water. Lifting them, she offered it up again to Sessy, first and then all those folks swarming in.

Horrified at the rot and stink, Sessy had shrunk to her knees, covering her mouth. She must be hallucinating. Up through the bones of her knees came the ground, and the guilt she carried just for being herself, shaking. It thundered in the roots of her neck, and her shoulders, and seared into the tendons sealing it there. She had been doing so well. She had stayed so focused. Now it came again, this burning hate, this fire, from every direction. As if a nuclear bomb blew from the ground zero of her insides and everything she had been and done. This bomb would never dispel and never let her go. It would never vaporize. It would leave her writhing on the blacktop of the HSCAN parking lot. All she did was plot one lemon lay with a little helmet on her head. One ring of lemons around the teeny car of a catastrophic catter. Nothing's never okay. She pushed herself back to standing. Jesus.

Imported CNR workers from Head Tax days, cracked lips, racing eyes, beat down gumming as they scooped imaginary food into their mouths with their blackened fingers. They pushed and shoved and elbowed each other for a chance to lap from her cupped hands. The woman offered it up creek, up slope. Down creek. Up creek, up slope, down creek. Up creek. Up slope, down creek. Each time, tens of hundreds sipped from the palms of her hands. She extended her hands, straightened her elbows, and offered drink.

Sessy made herself move. One foot in front of the other. She had to go get to her. The lady could drown. Look at the crook of her beak, the tilt of her chin. She'd seen that somewhere. That beady-eyed sparrow on the branch of the red maple where she'd hidden from Jeff. The school secretary eyeing her from her desk after that nutcase gorilla Ern True shot up Milk's school. She clapped her hands together. Maybe those kids, that cute little Suong and the one that got it in the forehead would appear—maybe somehow her endurance could undo the carnage her living wrought. Turn the world right today. Turn it. Adjust the dial. Do good. She checked the hill.

A blood-spattered lace skirt shrunk to a sliver and vanished behind a red maple. Up there, leaves scrunched. A chipmunk went in chattering. But, as night does when it overtakes the dusk, of a moment, all those people fled back up the hill, some vanishing into it as easily as they burst forth. The upslope returned to a snowfield. The embankment blanketed in the last snowfall trickled a stream down to the old girl. No footprints, no children, no movie stars, no aboriginals, no labourers. Not her mother nor Grandma Sloan. But that old bulldog had her hands raised to the sky moaning for all that had fallen away.

"Kktchrrtrchll," she wailed, now into a piercing call.

The dolphin scream pitch stabbed into Sessy's ears. She shook her head hard to shake the squeal loose; she covered her ears. Oh, she knew who this lady was.

The Toronto Historical Society newsletters did not go unheeded by Sessy. Don't think that the story of Edith Nordheimer flinging herself onto her beloved Samuel's closed casket (the end had been explosive) got lost on her. It took every ounce of strength to pull her off. "Animal, or bestial" is how her sister, Adeline, described it in a letter. "But that is the nature of God's good grief." The gathered mourners gasped, lurching up and towards her from their elegant, carved pews. One good slap from Adeline did the trick. The blood in her cheek filling the imprint of her sister's hand.

Edith dabbed her tears and smoothed her skirt. She steadied herself on the podium and forced herself to speak. *"You."* She eyed every man in sight. She lifted her arm and pointed her long finger at one, two, three and then, in a sweep, at the whole room. *"You meet Samuel Nordheimer,"* she gulped. *"He sleeps right there!"* And raised her other hand to meet the first with a fist. *"You have met a man when you meet Samuel Nordheimer."* She told the story of how she had whizzed from the dining room to the living room of the grand castle Samuel had built for her on the banks of the Vale of Avoca and discovered a tiny gold box on the floor in front of her. It is only chance that she didn't step on it. Just as she pulled at its even tinier maroon ribbon, she shook it instead. It seemed empty. She lifted it to her ear and shook again. Empty. She knew her Samuel. Always, he himself. A flutter erupted in her tummy. That prankster. But, two can play this game. She replaced the box on the floor exactly as she found it. Stepped back out of the room and reached for the bell. She must remind Cook that this household prefers zucchini to be sliced razor thin, dribbled with a titch of apple cider vinegar, and spiced with two twists of black pepper from the mill. When she lifted the bell, a note dropped out directing her to the stables. Oh, her whole body was filled with goosebumps. She could only imagine what her man had in store for her. She tip-toed to the stables. She could take the upper hand in this game. Getting a good grip on the heavy leather strap, she pulled the barn door open. Jacob's Ladders streamed through the majestic pine slats of the walls aflame in flecks of hay dust and fleeing mites. *Oh, Stable Boy*, she called. *Hello.* Up in the lofts, sparrows tweeted. Other than her breath, and the increasing beat of her heart, no human sound emerged. The boy must be fishing for trout at the new Rosehill Reservoir. With the scrunch of boots on straw and the Empire under siege from every side, Samuel stepped from behind a stack of alfalfa bales, holding an overflowing picnic basket and softly singing "Men of Harlech." The one-legged Ukrainian boy, who shills for coin at the St. Lawrence

Market, hovered past the hay pulling his bow across a violin. And now, according to the papers, Edith returned the favour. Just steps from her husband's coffin, she sang to him the words that wooed her that day: *"Rocky steeps and passes narrow, flash with spear and flight of arrow, who would think of death or sorrow? Death is glory now!"* According to those in attendance that day, she sang to lift her spirits and, with any luck to raise his.

Outside, under their weeping willow, they sip wine on the blanket Samuel spread and, after sending the boy away, would mount at least one Jacob's Ladder as Samuel feeds her teeny pieces of Cornish game hen sprinkled with rosemary, spoonfuls of iced sorbet and nibbles of the sweetest longhorn strawberries any woman could ever desire. From atop the huge boulders long ago planted by the glaciers to plant in their lawn, the lovebirds take in the view all the way to the lakeshore. Down in the ravine, they plop onto the bare rocks, their hot, bare feet dangling into the cool, rushing stream. All a man had to do, Edith thinks, is cool her feet in summer and giggle some. Life is that simple.

That old piano player, Samuel Nordheimer, had to be a good roll in the hay, conjured Sessy.

By the transitive property, ghosts have a way of slipping in amongst the living. They soak through pores. They pump blood with longing.

➤ She led the woman up the bank, carefully. God, she wanted to get rid of that helmet. She'd lose the lady down the bank. Up top, the woman looked up creek, down creek, and up slope. And turned to Sessy and said, 'Cut your trench well, cut your trench well.'

The loon had lost her crackers, no question.

In the Tercel, she got her helmet off and blasted the heat. The woman warmed her hands over the vents.

For once something worked out. 'Where can I take you?'

The woman pointed.

At the first turn, Sessy asked, 'So, where to now?' The woman pointed right. She turned right. At the second turn: 'And?'

She pointed left. Sess' hung left.

Next, at a traffic light.

The girl jerked her thumb right. Sess' copped a right. The goat gave no mercy. Right, left. Right, left. Sessy slammed on the brakes. 'You got I.D.?'

The lady pulled the hood drawstrings over her eyes and clamped her teeth.

Life's too short to chase old ladies out of creek beds. Sessy pulled up to 54 Division. In the gold-flecked lobby, she sat her in the green, plastic chairs. The duty desk officer would help her. The woman would be processed, photographed, and remembered in some small way before being planted with others like her under the Gardiner Expressway. She'd be on the seas again tomorrow. The same journey all over again.

Holding the lobby door open she waved to the old girl. And then licked her finger. Goddamned that lemon still stung. So went her first visit to 54 Division that day.

Milk

Oh, man. Fourth grade, maybe fifth, your teacher, Mrs. Vertie Dison, hoisted a stained canvas bag of letters onto her desk. She emptied its contents. White envelopes flit onto the desktop, followed by blue ones cascading onto the floor; one folded, orange half-sheet shot over the others before landing on the floor. Dison's butterfly nails plucked at the letters. Thirty-five snot-nosed, butch cut, spit-soaked, and pony-tailed nine-year-olds leaned over their knees, waiting. Dison's swollen feet squeezed out of pink sandals crowned with cracked and yellow nails. Barf.

These letters, people.

Scott Heintz pipes up scoring points. *You're gonna ask us how'd they get here?*

That—. Dison tapped the map and then the pile of letters, *is the question, Scott.* She came around front, leaned on the desk and pushed her heels off. Her gaze landed on the maple leaf collage at the back of the room. *How does anything get anywhere?* One thick toe aimed at the class while her ankle coiled around the desk leg. *Let me tell you. I have a nephew in oil. Big oil.* She tapped the desk. *Was in Oil, now in combat in Afghanistan. The*

Canadian Armed Forces. C-A-F. Our army. Obviously. Now, and he met all of these kids and he knows that I know you. Obviously. Can you imagine people so far away thinking about you? Imagining who you are? Well, he asked if they would want to write to you. And you to them.

Scott Heintz blows a gasket. *Can we write two?*

Start with one, Scott. Now, their English—the words might be hard to read at first but I want you, five at a time, to come up, choose any letter, read it and then we will write our own back to them. Okay. Look. Carefully. Her eye caught the orange letter on the floor. *One of these is written to you.* She smiled at Suong, sitting on her hands. *Yes, to you. Afghanistan. Okay. War. Death. Okay? Dismemberment. Agony. Blood. Okay? Okay. Orphans. Abandoned. Rejected. Okay. Alone. Bereft. But—hope. After all that even. Hope. Kids just like you. There.* She air-drew, *Y-O-U.* She slowly unfurled the wall map. It snapped back. She eased it back down. It fwapped up. She caught it and held it.

Evan. Get up here and hold this.

You crawled out from your desk.

Don't block the map. Hold it from your knees.

She knows you'll make the least mess of things.

Good. There. She tapped a pinkish-orange pancake-shaped country. *The snow plains of Khakon. Okay. Right.* She pointed to a place in the northeast. *Now, it's way way out. Not a lot of mail. Not a lot of love. You give them mail, you give them love. Right? Okay?*

She tapped you on the head with her ruler. Even in sixth grade, you wanted to be all: bitch, don't even. But, you smiled.

The map snapped back.

Jesus. She spun to you. *Okay.*

You and Tom got different classes that year. In his class, he climbed the chimney.

Who'd like—?

You shot up your hand. So did Scott.

Oh. All right. Evan, Milk. Milk. Evan, rather.

Everyone groaned.

And Amy. Dante. Vahid. And Brittany.

Mrs. Dison—. Scott stomped his feet. *Asshole.*

Scott. We take turns in this class. There are plenty of letters. Keep your pants on.

He took a blue envelope so you nailed the orange. You ripped it open. It read: *My name is Asaan Farhad. Seven years I go. I English words. Me love.*

You showed '*Me love*' to Mrs. Dison.

In their language, the object comes before the verb.

You don't know what a direct object is? Scott Heintz sticking his prick in.

You had two words for him: *Le subjonctif.*

He thrust his crotch at you.

Mr. Heintz.

What do you think he means? Mrs. Dison scratched the back of her calf with that thick toe.

━━ In Lab, you checked your email. At the desk next to you, Vahid, a creative, hammered out a drum solo he'd work out with his band, The PoorMeHaveNots, after school. Your belly is full, the lights are on. Nobody's shelling the school. But your shoes stuck to the tiles. Orange, apple, grape. Juice, gum, goo. Sweet.

Lund roamed the rows chewing his 'stache.

Mr. Lund?

Evan.

Lund.

Evan.

It's so so clean in here, dude. Like not.

Evan, my blackboard hasn't been scrubbed since 1982. The front leg of my desk is tacked with masking tape, it smells like you-know-what from that diabetic ferret they rescued. They traded union janitors for right-to-work so the floors stick. But count ourselves lucky. American schools don't have TP.

What's our excuse?

Aspiration, Evan. Toronto's is an aspirational culture. He pointed at your screen. You've got mail. And five minutes. Finish up.

> From: Tom Meuley
> To: *milktoast@HSCAN.net*
> *Subject: Strange Attractor*
> *13 December, 2012 6:28:05 AM EDT*
> *Attachment: CGI Julia 3*

Life, dude. All organized.

> From: Mom
> To: milktoast@HSCAN.net
> Subject: Photo(s)
> 13 December, 2012 8:46:02 AM EDT
> Attachment 1: Little Milk Couch
> Attachment 2: Clogged Arteries (graphic)

If I don't tell you, who will?
Mr. Lund blinked the lights for his two-minute warning. Vahid drummed his thighs.

From: asaantakah@stc.com.af
To: milktoast@HSCAN.net
Subject: hi
12 December, 2012 2:34:08 AM EDT

Tooth man Sakar buy. Me on base not live. Family gun. English good not write. G.I. Joe PC. One day to more you.

Time is up. Go. Tonight, Tom Meuley would know what to do. Clock Jeff, then hop a plane to Kabul. You reply.

From: milktoast@HSCAN.net
TO: asaantakah@stc.com.af
Subject: Re: hi

You on your own, Asaan? You at the American base still? I'll come. I can come.

You could do it. No one's telling you not to. There is nothing separating you from this desk, to Pearson airport, to Kabul International. Pick him up; he boards the plane back here. You're eighteen in five months, you adopt him. Fuck optics. Your mom could adopt him. She'd save a kid's life. That shiny white teeth fucker *bought* his brother, Sakar. 'Family gun die.' Shit.

It goes down on a normal night. Quiet. Still. Birds squawk. Faucets drip. People asleep. Dreaming. Breeze kisses their skin. The moon low. Squint to see. Asaan wakes up. His father and mother hurry past his bedroom door first one way and then back the other. His sister, Kasi, swollen with child, rockets past his thatched door. The yellow of her *parahan* flashes. His toe lands on the cold, dirt floor. He closes his eyes to see better.

Kasi—.

She careens to the front. Pads to the back. Stillness. Not a peep. Not a bird.

A pounding at the door. The mud walls loosen, chips fall. The thumping reverberates against bamboo poles and the packed dirt floors. His mother shrieks, the door crashes open. Soldiers shove in. They drag his sister by the hair past the crack at his door, the soles of her muddied feet trailing. She snarls kicking and slapping. His father shouts to *wait*—*who is it*. The steel scrapes the floor as Papa lumbers from the back lifting the AK-47. He cocks it.

Gunfire. Spray. His father falls. The brass shell casings tinkle.

A nightjar bird clucks its *apel-apel*.

Asaan holds his breath.

His mother hurtles at the door. Screaming. Another spray of gunfire.

Now, a snow finch chirps *tsing-tsing*.

Kasi scrambles back inside calling, *Asaan, Asaan*—. But then throws herself at the soldiers, growling. Gunfire. Spent shells clink on the garden stone.

Asaan: stock still.

Weapons drawn, slamming doors. The soldiers hiss in English: *Hostile.*

Asaan must be caged in one of those metal storage dorms they have; the wind rattle at the sheet metal, pebbles pelting the sides.

Maybe better if you enlist. On one condition: the C.A.F. sends you to him or nowhere. Go. You have no life here. Nothing you do or say matters. Go. Mean something. Right. You're back where you started. Stuck with you.

➤ After Lab this afternoon, you and Tom Meuley kicked it on the hood of your Cutlass across from Burnout Island. The smokers huddled under that twig standing in for a tree, blowing on their fingers, and shaking their lighters for fumes. Cradling their bowls.

Above them, cormorants uncoiled into black ribbons over the lake.

'S sick.

Yeah. Smooth.

Yeah, no, sick. Asaan's brother got sold, dude.

Two burnouts tore off bee-lining over a curb.

Tad pulled at the tiny burnt gold hairs on his upper lip.

The birds moved into an arrow formation.

Dude. It's so not solvable.

They're screwed.

Who?

All of 'em. Asaan. My mom. Afghanistan.

One cormorant at the tail end of the arrow split from the others. Heading to the Spit.

They don't choose, dude.

Who?

Those birds.

No. Like my dad, my mom, Afghanistan, man. Me. Everything's a prison.

B.T.W., can't hang tonight. Got windows. The BTO bank booth.

'S cool. After.

Nope. Sleep.

He had some something going on. Like with his body.
School.

Tad. Screw me, man. School's like so easy. It's this—
you pull at the seams exposed on your jeans. We're not
good, man. Tom, we do not have it going on. You pressed
your hands flat into the roof of the car. If you were to roll
right now, maybe you could fall into order. Cohesion.
Coherence. We don't matter. Your dad's gone. Like all the
time. Like always. My dad's a fucking prick. My mom
lives to barf. We don't count. They're stealing and selling
kids. That seals it. Nothing fucking matters. I sure don't.

Tom nodded at the birds. They matter. Flying. Shitting.
A whole section of the Spit is paved over with guano.
They have to live, man.

Tad got your knees in both hands, spread them apart,
leapt off the hood and buried his face in your thighs.
That makes your heart pound.

Fractious. All right. Tonight.

Webster said Tom had a condition. What if he's like
really sick? You drew a constellation in the dust on the
hood: Tom, you, your mom, Jeff, an indeterminant variable. It's solvable. People just got to want to. I'll go. I'm
getting him and his brother out, maybe. I should.

The cormorants thinned the farther they flew.

If we don't, no one will. You jumped off the hood.

What's up? Tad squatted.

The birds were gone.

His Adam's apple pulsed.

Life, man. Terminal, right?

Maybe he's got bird flu.

Your mom spells it out. Store-bought *chicken is not meat, Milk. It's Tupperware for viruses. Really. Someone sneezes, you don't know what you're getting. Each particle tab of virus is smeared with thousands of keys, all pronged up, ready to plug into the pores of your gullet; they're primed, polished and ready to socket in, to unlock their nucleus, Milk. And man o' man, watch that death party unravel. Lay out the welcome mat and replicate it 'til the cows come home. An assembly line of squiggly pooper things but all protected in their little cocoon, going down down, burrowing in. In your sniffer. That's Mother Nature. And then, boom. Pow! Explodes with funk DNA. Flying monkeys, son. Viruses are flying monkeys. Bird flu is like that. And you better care, Milk. I'm telling you. You got a chicken, it's hatched from a mother hen that's never even been outside or breathed fresh air. That changes the lungs, Milk. Birds—chickens have lungs, just like us, and so then the chick gets a little older, gets into a brawl or two and it gets pecked, but the wound can't heal because where they live is so cramped, it's dank and damp, no oxygen, it festers, okay, pus, all right, then, they are packed with anti-biotics so that their immune systems don't work, and when that chick dies from infection, from not breathing, from no care by anyone, not even its mother, it's just like us, that chick, now chicken, keels over, and the body is taken out of the cage, if and only if, this is what I'm saying if the other chickens don't eat it. That's right. They are driven bananas in there, they become cannibals. Just like us. They're desperate. What's left of the bird is thrown on a conveyer belt, dipped into pools of electrified water to make sure they're dead, yanked back up, fed through the de-feather thing, their necks stretched, heads whacked off, and then shipped to Chinatown or somewhere; same with the feet, off to Chinatown for all those soups they make; and then the corpse, full of virus and crap and antibiotics, packaged in down at Metro—if I ever, ever catch that freaking test tube wrapped in gristle going past your lips, I will be done. Absolutely done, Milk.*

You clip the curb. He sneezes. Bird flu's coming at you right now, maybe. That's probably what Tad talked about with what that poet aunt told him. Replication.

You put the Cutlass in park. Eased the seat back. You could take a toke.

He nicked the spliff.

Is it dead?

No sparks.

If you could melt into the skin of his Adam's apple, you might count for something. You got your feet up on the dash too.

You look at me like you're in me, Milk.

Ton'

Before Jamarandu saddled him with Shafiqq, Ton' cruised stealth east on Carlton. Jarvis to Sherbourne to Parliament. July, August. Hot. Late night. Lone wolf. Prowling. The headlights caught those glittering shorty shorts. Fancy silver. Bent over digging in his thigh-high patent leather lemon boots. Showing off his money-maker. Maybe a hooker. If Ton' played his part, the kid might spill dope on Mac-10s—among other things. Dudes like him have their ears to the ground. He lowered the window. '*Y'all right, buddy?*'

Julio shot over jackrabbit, leaned into the cruiser and puckered his burnt orange lips. '*Ay.*' His eyes locked on Ton's, traced his chest, and tracked his nipples pressing through 'Schelle's press creases. '*Thank you, Officer.*'

Ton's hand went to his thigh. '*Just checking.*'

'*Gracias.*'

'*Okay. Well.*'

'*Yes.*'

'*Have a good night.*' Ton' zapped the window back up. Julio stepped back.

He pulled away. But then stopped. Brought the window back down. Julio hurried to it.

'*What's with the get-up, Chica?*'

'*Yo soy High Kick.*'

'*Nice.*' Ton' had a 'high kick' for him. '*What's the scent?*' Ton' tapped the kid's fucking cherry nose.

'*Pachuli para la prosperidad.*'

'*Que bueno.*'

'*Si, gracias, Mijo—Officer. Tu tambien. Me gusta.*'

'*¿Tu gustas?*'

'*Me lo gusta mucho, Officer.*'

He popped the locks. '*Vienes.*'

Julio wriggled into the front seat. Sat on his hands. '*¿A qué vienes?*'

'*Jugar, Baby. Jugar.*'

'*Que bueno.*'

By High Park, he had to pull Julio off by the hair. '*Wait, dude.*' Oh, man.

The kid pawed at him, wanting back on.

Ton' had seen that hunger. In the eyes of more than a few of those he pulls over and in those of the kids lined up to see Raymond Baumgartner. Raymond didn't treat Ton' like the others. He wouldn't. *Not you*, he said. *Too sensitive. You'd fall in love, haha. I see you.* Maybe. Maybe not. Raymond Baumgartner had split him open, though. And he ain't never going back.

⟋ God knows the kids lost to the boot heel and pogo-stick of Raymond Baumgartner. Ma babysat Raymond after Ton's brother drowned. Raymond oversaw the lunch table at Ma's house. He'd slurp the better part of the baked mac and cheese down his gullet. Ton' and other tykes cower under the lip of the table. Being a gimp kid, Ray'd squirm onto the tabletop. He spun a fork with the toes of his right foot and a knife with the left. He ate with his feet. Bits of yellowed cheese product flicked from his gummed-up braces onto his corn cob thalidomide leg.

Raymond may have had pimples for arms and legs lost to purpose but he could run a playground. On one gump leg, he wore a platform shoe with a sole six inches thicker than a hockey puck but built of the same stuff: rubber-bullet material. It landed thick, heavy, and hard. God's little deformity tore after the little fuckers in his sights. A bullet-smelling fear. No one outran Raymond Baumgartner. If caught, forget it. He kicked, punted, and pow-pow-powed taking skin from shins, back, and head. The best Ton' could do was to curl into a ball, cover his head, and wait 'til it was over. A real superstar. A heart-breaker. God threw a bone to Raymond. Ladies smelled out what the good Lord gave him. Chicks lined up to buy a ticket to his thrill ride. He packed a pistol closer to an overgrown summer zucchini than a pop bottle. But God likes a plot twist.

But boys got a thing for baseball and home runs too. He paid Ton' five dollars a day to herd the older boys behind the garage with his snow shovel. For a fiver, the boys could squeeze around the hole yanking their mon-keys. Ton' collected their money and reminded them not to make a mess on the outside of the garage. The young get messed up easily so Raymond split his audience ac-cording to age for moral reasons. Boys sixteen and under in one group, seventeen and up in the other. Only boys. Keep it clean. Four to six at a time, they'd huddle to watch the girls take a thrill ride. Ton' kept a lookout.

The lines of guys to gawk grew longer than ladies coming for the main event. Word got out to local high schools, wrestling clubs, and the Sons of the Empire. Adults, coming home from work or walking to Schmidts bakery, had to push their way through the lines. Raymond's joy stick jockeyed the mayor's coke problem for best-kept secret. Ton' gave his notice to quit.

Raymond insisted that he stay. Ton' didn't want to tell Mama where he got the money to pay her electric bill. Raymond upped Ton's pay from $7 a shift to $8. This helped but didn't take away the tightness in his tummy. Turns out, the boys weren't all there to watch. Some of them wanted a little more. Like Ton'.

Raymond accommodated his increasing market base. He systematized his operation. After the ladies cleared out, say on a Wednesday or Thursday, he invited the younger boys; the eleven, twelve or thirteen-year-olds, flush with cash after collecting for their paper routes, to come a bit closer to his high-speed drill.

'Go and get down and have a good look,' he'd tell them. 'Go ahead. Touch it. Fifty cents. You can. It don't bite.' Five bucks, if they wanted to lick it. Ten, if they wanted to put in their mouths. Fifteen, if they boarded the gravy train. But not Ton'.

Ton' ducked outside. He listened to the night swallows burrowing into the neighbour's elm and ash. Raymond reminded Ton' he could take advantage of his "employee benefits." Ton' got up close but none of that did it for him. He had fallen for the spider in Raymond's eyes. If Ton' partook, he'd lose the spider forever. Even at eleven, he knew this. Years later, the spider in Ton's eye caught its flies.

Ton' wasn't the only one. An older boy lost his heart to the skin in Raymond's game. He sobbed, beat his breast, and tore his hair. Swore he'd die without more and more and more. Raymond, though, didn't go for dating. The kid had ridden the popsicle since he was twelve. He begged for a happy ending. Love is harder on the young. Raymond rolled his eyes, but love wants what love wants. The kid took it badly. With tears flooding his cheeks, he spilled the beans to the cops squirming on a green plastic chair in exchange for them looking away from his side-action pill deal. *'He's doing it right now with the kids. I can show you where and when.'* Raymond did time in the pokey. Being a juvenile, his court records never went public. At eighteen, justice worked its magic and Raymond worked his. First as a community organizer for the Progressive Conservatives, and then as a candidate to capture the youth vote, Ray ran a campaign ad featuring himself and a catcher for the Blue Jays stroking a signed baseball bat mobbed by a bunch of kids. Looking close, the hunger in their eyes is real. The clench of their jaws. Life is never as long as it is cruel. On election night, Raymond promptly plowed his specially outfitted pickup into the backend of a semi-truck. Ton' learned from Raymond. The scent and spit of appetite.

As they walked across the lot, Ton' killed the volume on his uniform mic. He led Julio to the Grenadier greenhouse by the neck. No one went in there. The bolted door rarely locked. That close to Christmas, Ton' couldn't barely breathe for all poinsettias. Nobody breathes anyway. This wouldn't take long.

Julio blocked the greenhouse door with his back. '*I tell you something.*'

Tell me, baby. '*Tell me who's moving Mac-10s?*'

'*Papi—.*'

He'd asked too soon. Ton'd deal with the matter in hand. '*You're clean, right?*' He stroked his package.

'*Si, papi.*' Julio dug his heel into an ice patch and poked a finger into Ton's chest. '*What's your name?*'

'*Officer Friendly.*'

'*Que bueno. Well, Officer Friendly, I tell you before we go into a little story.*'

He got the fucker in his arms and cupped one silvered ass cheek. '*Dime.*'

A nip of poinsettia zipped through the doorjamb.

'*I tell you that when I first come here and learn English good. You, you know?*'

'*I know.*' Ton' got his fingers in under the elastic foil openings.

'*Well, they tell me about what los Bathhouse Raids, you know?*'

'*Before my time.*' He got the tip of his index finger farther in.

'*Yes. This story, I think. Los muchachos. I know. Them officers. And I promise myself. I would be my who know muchas polices.*' He flit his arms like wings and then held his throat.

'*Cool.*'

Julio's pucker weakened to Ton's fingertip.

'*How about that? You like that?*'

'*Si, papi.*'

'*Good.*'

'¿Pero, papi?'

'Si—.'

'*You cut me off,*' he coughed to demonstrate, '*mio su puta, papi? Entonces—.*'

No problem. Ton' understood the deal. He plugs his cord into the kid's outlet, he gets a bead on the Mac-10 traffic. Life's a trade-off, man. Even a greenhouse visit. He kicked the glass door open and lifted Julio onto a table. Near the end, Ton' cut him off—and exploded. Julio clung to his thighs. He would not let go. He gulped. He gulped. His epiglottis stayed open. Like the last pulsing notes of a trick mix. Ton' pulled away.

Julio stroked his sternum. '*It makes me feel like a man.*' He flexed his arms.

Ton' zipped up. '*I'll take you back.*'

They'd hit the greenhouse four times since then. The last time Julio asked if they could hit a Wendy's. Aw, man. They'd have to "talk" talk. The last thing he needs is a Kitty Macqueen High-Kick Girl boyfriend.

Man, they'd be dead before Jamarandu tucked that Mac back in his panties. Let 'em hit the street already. The downpour's gonna bury the cruisers. It'd be thin ice tonight.

'Just we don't need any Mac-10s back there. This—.' Jamarandu wagged the bag again and laid it on his desk running his finger along the seal.

'Mac-10s are the ticket, Lieutenant. We need 'em all right.'

'We don't need this.' Jamarandu had to piss and moan. 'We don't need Downtown raining on us now.'

The department had just got investigated because of some fake, fabricated charge of police brutality from twenty years ago. Don't even get him started on that mess.

'Okay, I got some incentive for you.' Jamarandu tapped the tabletop with his pen.

Here it came.

'We got a low D.U.I. number, okay. One word: quota.'

Chairs pushed away from the tables, radios cracked low and pens tapped.

'I'm just saying, you know we got to. So, I am going to help you out. On two counts. First, assignments. Ton', Shafiqq: the Spit, Queen from Yonge to Leslie. Pat-Pat, you do the field coordination on a sobriety checkpoint on the D.V.P.' More chair scuffing. 'Horst, you got Front Desk.'

'Wow.'

Pat-Pat lifted his chair some and set it down hard. 'Checkpoints are like traps.'

'Whatever gets you through the night, P-P.'

Pat-Pat waved him off. 'Dude——.' He gave up.

Horst sulked. Maybe, Ton' got it wrong. Maybe that Mac got tapped in his unit.

And just like that—the sun speared past a bank of clouds igniting the corner of Ton's desk. A good sign, maybe. He pressed the pad of his finger into its heat.

At Maitland, they hadn't even barely got started when the Eden radio went dinging saying to call Albert.

'It's 'Schelle's dad.' If Albert's calling, Ale's suffering. 'Shoot out over and back out Eastern.'

'Are you going to want me to come in?' All of a sudden Shafiqq's all nervous.

'Man, Shafiqq. Stop pissing, it's my mother-in-law. My father-in-law.'

'I'm just saying.'

'I'm just saying. If you do go in, don't say nothing about 'Schelle's IVF today.'

'I don't gossip.'

'Whatever.'

At the house, the front walk lay thick with ice pack. Ton' tromped up the porch steps.

'Don't kill yourself. It's slippery. Sorry.' Albert held the screen door open. 'They say it's hitting hard tonight.'

'That rain'll be more ice. 'Schelle'll salt it.'

Albert pulled the door closed as it blossomed with steam. 'Your friend, he's not coming in?'

'Nah.'

Albert shut the door and rubbed his hands together. 'Cold, cold. Thanks for speeding over.'

'A brother's got to do …'

'So.'

Albert had moved the hospital bed into the dining room. 'Oh.' Ton' lowered his voice. 'So, you got it set up.'

Ashen strands of Ale's hair snaked out from under the sheets.

'We did. Students are good for something.'

Ton' rubbed his hands together. A block of shit-stink hit him. He smiled.

Albert smiled back. He tapped the thermostat. 'Cold, eh?' He whacked it harder. 'Sticks sometimes.' A baby of his would need heat staying here.

They might wake Ale.

'She doesn't hear anything. Drugs.'

Ton' rubbed his hands together again. 'Right. What can I—'

'I know you're—.' Albert rubbed the back of his head. 'I'm sorry.' He twisted a hand towel he took from his pocket. He handed it to Albert.

'Okay.' Ton' patted Albert on the shoulder. 'Cool'. He pulled him in close and held him. He whispered in his ear. 'We got this.'

The refrigerator kicked in, humming.

Albert nodded.

Ton' removed his belt and slipped his hands into thin plastic gloves. He hummed a low "Life is a Fantasy" like his *abuelita* would have wanted. He unfastened one side of Ale's diaper and then the other. Like he'd done it a million times, he slipped the palm of his hand under her lower back and lifted it while pulling the messed diaper out with the other.

Albert handed him the large, moistened wipes and with a few more wipes, Ton' had the job done.

Albert kissed his wife on the forehead.

Ton' washed his hands.

'I got to get more gloves.' Albert smoothed Ale's hair. "Schelle'll come tomorrow.'

They stepped back out of the dining room.

'She can't see her mom like that.'

'She can take it.' He peeked out the window. Shafiqq sat there.

'Next time bring him in.'

'He's a yard dog that guy.' He got in close to Albert's ear. 'He stinks.' Ton' stepped for the door but tripped on the torn carpet.

Sessy

Sessy pulled away from 54. She had to see the look on Jeff's face with her own eyes. He'd get spooked and she'd rope him back. Maybe he doesn't know what true love is. Even after all of these years. He doesn't know the lengths she'd go to to keep their bond. She didn't drop from a tree a hundred years ago to leave it all in the dust tonight. Every single knot tied tonight roped her to shore. Or not. She had plenty of time to watch him freak, say her peace, and lay the law down. She headed back to HSCAN. But Milk. Oh, my god. She had to go home, first. He might need supper.

At the front door, she called for her boy. Her voice reverberated against the ceiling at the top of the stairs and into the empty. She'd wait for him. No, better. She'd order pizza. She wouldn't cook at all. She laid the lemons down. Her blood pumped. She was free. Free. In one leap, a Nadia Comaneci. She leapt to the doorway moulding. And hung. Living room to the right; kitchen, to the left. Front door, behind; upstairs, ahead. Lemon scented the air. Her fingers stung. All the times she watched Milk tear through this gate, shooting through to whatever pitched next for him. Beautiful Milk. She could imagine him poking into some young yoo-hoo and lifting her to Kingdom Come. One front flyaway to take the stairs two at a time. Oh, to be a girl again!

Sessy came up as that red-haired girl wiser than her years. The one that everyone goes to with their problems. The one that got others in touch with the truth of the matter. She earned that. She had to love herself. And so was fucked. Who was this 'she' she was going to, someday, love? Where is 'she'? 'She' never was where Sessy stood. 'She' skittered out of sight the instant Sessy glanced her way. She had plenty to say about others but couldn't see into her own skin.

Milk's scent reached her before she passed the thermostat. Something metallic clung to the air. He and Tom Meuley must be filing down those squeegees he uses for his windows. Tom is an industrious kid. He studied the professional window washers in Paris, and then in New York, of all things. But, not just any window washers. The one's for the skyscrapers. Then, the ones wiping windows at intersections, too. The desperate ones. Those guys know how to clean well and clean fast.

Plus, Milk's mom (that's what he called her), *they taught me that if you line the blade with at least a pound of lead with a rubber strip, you got to use the heavy thick rubber, then you can use it to pop windows open to bust free a TV or jewellery or whatever from a house, bam, this squeegee does that. You cut the glass. Doesn't even shatter the whole plate. You got to pound it to bring that down.*

Seems like it could hurt somebody, she suggested.

Definitely. Milk knows. I wrote a paper about those window washers for Mr. P. Got an A. Their squeegees literally busting open skulls of dudes they want to bring down.

In the latter part of the summer, after it got too hot for Tom to be in New York or Paris, he'd come back to Toronto and the boys had spent way too much time, to her mind, rejigging the squeegees with lead. Once the weather turned, they used the blow torch to melt the lead out back but filed and smoothed the things in Milk's room. In the hallway, the lead hung in the air. She put her nose close to the moulding of Milk's room and then her own. The lead and spite and sweat of their years soaked into the wood there.

Upstairs, that den of sick (she and Jeff's bedroom) lay at the end of the long hallway painted the exact colour of her Granny Smith green. The architecture in this house cracked her open: the walls gripped her elbows, the ceiling crunched her neck, the carpet swallowed her. The creamed Brussels sprout bedspread curdled. In that sewer of dreams (their bedroom) she got her fingers deep in the faux marble sofa cushions looking for change. His rot got to her. His nasty rubbed all over the couch. She dug good. A quarter. An effing dime. The mould green walls cast a pall on Jeff's *Venus de Milo*. She hiked a loogie and hit that bitch in the clavicle. Her fingers stung. Lemons. Loyalty.

In the bathroom, her fingers cool under running water. She sucked the sting.

That is how germs get in, Sessy, her mama told her. *Don't just put any old thing in your mouth.*

Sessy wiped her finger on her jeans.

What are you, a pig?

Sessy scrubbed.

Cracked hands equal hard work.

She pressed her forehead into the mirror.

Oh, get up. Life's a bitch, live like one. You're not the first, you won't be the last.

When she tapped her mother on the shoulder to tell her about Owser, Adele cut her off. *Forget about it. Put it out of your mind. The rest of us do. You'll learn.*

But Sessy didn't want to learn. Her stomach hurt "down there." Maybe Adele would talk to Mr. Owser. *Think something else.* And, by God, she did.

The more she distracted herself, the less she could feel. Her mother was right. For the longest time, she didn't hurt. She didn't feel at all. She knew exactly what she would feel if she felt. She could tell you what she should feel. She could listen with concern to her friends fighting with their parents or getting dinged for the first time or breaking up with boyfriends or girlfriends; she could tell them how they feel or might be feeling—but she, herself, could not feel.

She spent long hours on the cold basement floor, a steak knife at her wrist, carving thin arrows there. If those winged scratches were to lift from the skin, they might fly, the way they do in cartoons, and pierce her throat, her budding breasts, her heart—maybe she could feel them then. The timing of the cuts had to be just right. She made sure to cut on days when she had enough long sleeve shirts but on the other days, she had food. And comrades.

She and her friends used to see who could eat more and then who could barf more. The winner got to take on a Mama's Pizza sausage pie—solo. They would sit around over at Tammy B's house. Her parents were always at ANAVETS. Up in her room, they rinsed their hair with glitter water. Oreos, Nutter Butters, Pringles, and Doritos packages scattered across the comforter. The first inning brought plates of tamales and cans of Pepsi Light force-fed on top of pepperoni pizza, Hostess Fruit Pies, Twinkies, Ho Hos, and Little Debbies (her favourite). After, they'd huddle around the bowl singing *She-bop, he-bop, a-we bop, hey, they say I better get a chaperone, I can't stop messin' with the danger zone, a She-bop, he-bop, a-we bop* and they'd keep going and going and going until one couldn't take it and they get themselves so *hey batter-batter* up, boom, and one of them would spit, bend, and retch into the toilet, hurling loud deep and hitting it out of the park, and then that one'd gag the other one, and then another one, and another one, 'til one after the other and sometimes more than one at the same time let chunks fly. A sextette of vomiting princesses. They'd be laughing and wiping their mouths with their forearms and then pretty soon, they'd start in on the second round and shoot their puke zipping 'round the bases, so to speak, with their hands at their faces like the *Home Alone* kid and get going all in again until they had pulled their 'jammies and night dresses up to their mouths wiping the sweat and saliva from their brows, coating their hems 'til pretty much all the fabric got soaked through and somebody had to open the window and Tammy B'd bring in her fan to air it out or they never would have stopped getting sick and then finally, even the last one that had nothing, absolutely nothing left inside made it to home plate, and even when two or three stuck their fingers down another's throat that is the person that won the free Mama's pizza for next time. Just then Sessy would Thelma Houston her friends ("Don't Leave Me

This Way") as they backed out of the bathroom getting cleaned up and pelting each other with Jean Nate. Spent, they piled on the floor, and then the bed, their legs entwined into each other, their hands and arms holding each other's backs, hips, and hair. Puke don't lie. But it sure smells like home. Like family. Like friends.

A lifetime spent to "think something else." Feeling was a country whose borders remained closed to her. Until Jeff slammed Milk into the wall. He'd done it a million times but last night changed things. His whole hand gripped Milk's throat pressing him into the wall. Milk, choking, beet red with purplish white blotches reached out his hand to her and she could do nothing. She froze. She let him down. The grace of God made Jeff let her boy go. But she, herself, had done nothing. She couldn't feel. Owser stared her in the face still.

   Yesterday, when he finally came back home, Jeff unloaded in the loo. She knew something fishy was going on. But she had to find proof. In between his grunts in the john, she dug through his wallet, his shoe box receipts, and through the numbers on his phone. She didn't recognize the last number dialled. She hit 'redial'. That woman's voice: 'Patricia.'

'*Yes.*'

Foreign. Fancy.

'*Yes.*'

'*Yes, hello.*' Sessy whispered so Jeff wouldn't hear her. '*Jeff?*'

Oh, boy. She had him. That effer. She hung up. She planted herself in front of the loo. She folded her arms. Come on out. Come to Mama, Brother.

When the toilet flushed, he bolted out like a beetle on fire.

Sessy slung the cell phone at him. He ducked. It smashed into the wall, shattering.

'647-383-9090.'

Jeff stayed down. He covered his head.

'647-383-9090.'

'What "647—"?'

'Oh, you know what "647-la-dee-da".'

'Sessy, I do not—.'

'You do.'

'I do not.'

'Oh, have the balls to stand up for your little cutesy-wutsie.'

'I do not have any 647- cutesy-wutsie.'

'Oh, right. Act like you don't have that number imprinted on your medulla oblongata.'

He hurried to the nightstand.

'Looking for these?' She dangled his wallet and credit cards. *'Spit it out.'*

He stood straight. All huffy and puffy.

'Come on.'

He pursed his lips.

'Then, what's that cardamom shirt smell?'

He smelled his shirt. *'Your Dollar-Store soap.'*

'Oh. My Dollar-Store soap. I don't have wootcha-wootcha carda-mama soap.'

'Whatever. Give me that.'

'Come and get it. Effer.'

He lunged, growling.

'Ha! Ha.' She jumped on the bed. *'Come and get it, Carda-mom Boy.'*

He vaulted, but she did a Spider-Man and landed by the door. *'Catch me.'*

Jeff surrendered. On his belly on the bed, his face swollen and sweating. His eyes were wild. He had no fight. He ground his face into the duvet.

Chicken. *'Now where's your piss and vinegar? Ha.'* She flung his wallet at him. *'Don't think I don't got your number.'*

━━ She made her way back to Milk's bedroom. That damned floorboard in the hallway groaned. She pulled her foot back.

'Honey?' She put it down again. Pushed his door open. 'You home?'

He wasn't. His blankets twisted and spun like some kind of crazy serpent. She flipped them over, looking for dried stuff. God knows what he did with the comforter. *It makes me sweat*, he says.

The room had fallen into grey the way it does this early in winter. The windows were freezing up. The rivulets streaming down from the day's thaw thickened with the cold.

She buried her face in his pillows. Oh, the smell of that boy. Safeguard and his lavender oil. Like her mother.

It's like Grandma before, he says. Sessy's mother did her first dance of cancer when Milk hit third grade. Lavender oil masked the chemo smell.

If you want to smell like an old lady. Give her a taste. She got as full of him as her lungs could take and held his pillows to her chest, and then licked the 750 thread count case, letting every fibre soak into a taste bud. To absorb her boy. Into her cells, under her skin. She flipped onto her back. But.

Something is different. She swung her legs off the bed. No. She looked behind the door, then under the bed. The dust, unbroken. She did a 180. The dresser. Empty. No G.I. Joes. No *Actual Hair Desert Storm Arab Interpreter*—. A mother knows. She can smell her boy.

At their old abode, she had a real stink sanctuary. The basement. A hole to flee to. A respite from the storm of her days. Buried just past the pile of dirty laundry, the washer: a throne in the cocoon of her catastrophe. She listened to the boys above: Jeff thudding to the fridge, Milk tiptoeing in from TomTad. Jeff freezing, Milk holding. Jeff padded back to his chair, Milk doing a fly-away up the stairs, crash-landing halfway and then pounding to his bedroom. The sweet ticks of their castle.

All three of them dumped their laundry onto the concrete floor. Stink T-shirts and sour underwear tethered her to the shore of her family. Reeking to high heaven, their spit, their ejaculations, their tears wove the ties that bind.

When he was still a little guy, Milk tip-toed down the stairs scaring the bejesus out of her.

Do not do that. She put her long, blonde hair behind her ear. *How long have you been standing there?* What a duck.

He ran to her and held her legs. *Mom.*

He'd be lucky to make twenty years. No skin for this world. *What, honey?* She tickled his ear with her fingertip.

He yanked his head away. *Mom. I can't grow up.*
How come, Honey?
There's no room for me.

Oh, you're going to set the world on fire or something. Just duck the flying Staples signs is all. If it could happen to that weather reporter (decapitated in a strong wind), it could happen to her boy. *Think something else.*

He eyed her. A kid that age chewing over *the future?* What future? Nuclear blasts. Toxic poisons. Rivers running dry. His body a food bank for cancer cells. BPAs weren't going anywhere. *Your job is to play. Play. Have fun. Play. Go to school.* She got up close and put her forearms on his shoulders, giving him her weight.

He didn't flinch.

She got some of Jeff's underwear and held them out to him.

He wrinkled his nose.

Go on.

He flicked them into the washer. And then rubbed his hands clean on his pants.

A little funk never killed anybody.

He scrunched his nose again.

Some people do a lot of speed racing in their shorts. She goosed him.

He bit his lips together and folded his arms.

You're old enough. Wipe better.

Tom Meuley is going to study math.

Math? For crying out loud. *No way that kid is. Doing math?*

He's got ambition.

Who taught you that word? Jesus. Get me those T-shirts.

Milk pitched them into the washer.

His dad said he has stick-to-it-tive-ness.

Don't hold that against him. Tom Meuley's a good influence.

Mom.

Milk.

When will I know?

At twelve.

How come?

It'll flash before your eyes. Like that. She snapped her fingers.

He held her legs. *Then, what?*

Then, you go live your life. You do what the Good Lord-That-Is-Nothing-But-Tall-Tale tells you to.

The fluorescent began clicking and blinking. Off. On. Off. On. And off. In the dark, her fingers traced the clammy walls reading the hieroglyphs carved there.

What if I don't know?

You will, Milk. He wouldn't let go of her legs. *Come on.* She pulled at him. He clung tighter. *You will. Everybody's got a place in this world. We just sniff it out.*

He loosened a little. *Where?*

She poked him in the belly. *Right there. Gut Instinct. Go get the big knife. I'll cut it out to show you.*

The Evening of:

Albert

Ton's cruiser crunched off in the night numbed with the snow stretching to Steeles. A car alarm dinged. The streetlights blinked on. Afternoon fell into evening.

Albert let go and the curtain fell into place. There, on his doormat, he teetered in a current unspooling into Lake Ontario. In open, so to speak, Albert dug his heel into the torn carpet and nudged his toe into the ripped linoleum. No more repairs. On the edge of the bed, he rubbed Ale's silky skull. You just lay there all buttoned up. Pretending.

Maybe I can't won't tomorrow. That boy wiping my bum. She clicked her teeth the way she does making a funny. It's—. It hurt to move her neck.

He's young. He can take it.

Cops are pussies. I had a dream—

Woot, woot. He twirled his finger and then burrowed his forehead into her purple housecoat. Lots of boys wipe a lot of asses.

He wiped her mouth. America.

Don't call me names. In the dream I was, I think it was me—

You. The grey of her pupil paler than this morning. But how flush with blood the pink meat of her fore-arm. Canada.

Oh God, to make her neck move. That hurts. Oh—. We flew off the curb, I think. Fighting for focus, she dug her fingertips into her forehead. Don't call me Canada.

Don't call me America.

My last breath. You're calling me names. Oh, Canada. I had a railroad spike—

My country 'tis of thee. You started it. Back before 'Schelle came, they could really fling it at each other. Don't call me Czechoslovakia.

Don't call me Lichtenstein.

Don't call me Gary, Indiana.

Her lips clung to the sippy cup. A piece of paper, maybe. Hammering it—

Your lips are dry.

She pursed tight. The orange juice under the heavy lamp had warmed on that Sanka-stained collection of Carol Shields. Bring me my tears.

They're at 'Schelle's.

I got more. Under the cookie jar. Oh—. Yes. She tapped her temple. It was—. I squatted—was that me? Over—maybe.

You don't have that stash of tears.

'Bet you I do. But not that. Not—water, maybe. In the wide open. Under a hill, kind of. Cool through my fingers—. She laid back on the pillow.

The fridge rattled up as he wrestled a fork tine free in the top drawer. Sure enough. A Kerr jar on the second shelf under the cookie tin, behind the staple gun for bat tacking. Bat tacking. His "dirty rotten faggot" bat-tacking is what Ton' called it. If he only knew.

Ton' in blue. A badge. A gun. The personification of juridical-legal procedures. The law itself, he decides living and dying. He is the 'he' that wipes the beloved's ass. Tonight, Albert stood the staple gun on end. If he were to pull the trigger, a steel staple would shoot into the glass container there shattering them. Fracture or stability. Life or death. He pulled himself to standing. Tonight, he is no different than these glass jars. He and Ale are falling now into a vast field of indistinction. Suspended: only hours remaining for him; days or weeks, for her. As long as there is life, there is hope. Whoever said that never walked the precipice. Hope, indeed, springs eternal. Or it ought to. But 'hope' requires potential. He has waited a lifetime for the law of public decency, vagrancy, stigma, or shame to throw the book at him. To put a knee on his neck. To ring the alarm. Tonight, he would leap free of the laws which had long ago been struck from jurisprudence. A ring of crusted and yellowed sediment-scarred Ale glass jar. Dried up. Empty.

What-ifs aren't good for nothing. The rip in the bedroom carpet stretched from her cedar chest to beyond the box spring. Yarns squirrelled out from the edges. A syntax weaving now, next, and then. All of their years, a perverse prayer. A twisted incantation. A call to run from one desperate second to the next just to get here. Progress, like law and potential, was long gone.

The years folded back onto themselves. Back into whoever he was before signing the mortgage documents all of those years ago; his vow to have and to hold, for richer for poorer, for better for worse—to do the right thing. To do his parents proud. He should have known better. There's no stuffing desire. There's no packing it away. The bare life must be lived; nothing more, nothing less. No strictures, no boundaries. In flight. The bats he's stapled to the garage speak. They call to fly. Their dried-up carcasses scribble a hieroglyph of scripture meant just for him. What-ifs are long gone. He pencilled a note for Ale: *Out for cash. Bat-removals. BRB.* From bare life, one must always seek.

What if, dropping to the wet leaves of the ravine, his look would be returned? What if the man approaches, what if he consents? What if he gives himself to a stranger to whom he owes everything and nothing? With every stranger taken in, a screw tightened. A window narrowed. An antenna stuck to static. As if the random universe shook him loose. To move into that no man's land of black ice where the law of the-way-things-are strips the look from your daughter's suspecting eyes. Seals the deal with she to whom the life is given. Each time he returned home, and pulled back into the driveway, he turned the ignition, reached into the fruit-syrup-coated bait jar, and with tongs, extracted one squealing and leathered batling, opened the car door, and dashed its terrified body onto the concrete driveway. Once or twice did the job. He'd staple their limp, slivered wings onto the siding. And there, by his decree, they waited for him to take flight. It was time. He had lived his 'random.'

➤ Ern True, once a perfectly likeable kid shot the school up. He gave As to that piece of shit, writing about Viktor Frankl, the camps, and social behaviourism. Ern brings his Luger and a rifle to school for an up-close show and tell. Albert came out of a door above as Ern came into the stairwell above. One glimpse of Ern tromping up the stairs—the rifle snout and camouflage rising into view through the railings, his bullets and his gear clanging—and Albert stepped back through the double doors, looked right and then left. He hissed at Susan Billings, the new English hire, to get back fast into her classroom before he ducked and disappeared into a doorway just as Ern whipped open the glass doors behind him. Albert closed his eyes waiting to feel the metal barrel under his jaw. The kid stomped past. Albert dodged to the other side of the doorway, out of sight. He swore he heard poor William Thibidault then. Maybe he didn't. He didn't dare peek around the corner. Whatever he heard was silenced by Ern's bashing into Davis' classroom door. And then silence. A single crack of a bullet. And the schuff of a body hitting the floor. Glass broke and he knew he ought to go help whoever just got shot but he backed farther into the corner of the stairwell. He turned his head into the corner. Screams and shots fired. And fired.

Sirens rang. More boots pounded up the stairwells. Radios and mics squawked. Maybe Miss Billings got away. He waited. Footsteps clomped to him, a hand grabbed him by the collar from behind, and dragged him from his hiding place, and back through the double doors. "Go," an officer said. Albert made his way down the stairs one at a time as his joints filled with air and he wondered what was wrong with him. Albert, seeking only solace in a brutal and violent world, had forfeited his place amongst the rest. Tonight, then. The void.

Albert had one more 'random' left in him. To find Tom Meuley. The kid had no idea his greatness would be the swing of a squeegee.

The Robaxin pain-relief thinned in his bloodstream. He knelt at the rip in the carpet and prayed to God and Ale to forgive him for what he was about to do to himself. To 'Schelle. To Ton'. Her breath soothed his skin. For he and Ale, each on their own roads out, forever would come soon enough. He nudged her jar to be in reach. After gathering himself, he felt around in the dark closet for that woven Bay Street shirt 'Schelle got him for his birthday. The tie with purple triangles. Her breath routs the quiet. On his knees now. Take us in your grace. You got to. God. In your grace. He inhaled the stale berry stink of 'Schelle's old talc blue baby blanket. Maybe someday she'd wrap her child in it. If Ton' were to think back, he would recognize Albert. He would remember that night on the stairs. Albert had been stopped in his tracks by the young man's beauty. The skin so smooth, the dark lashes. To look like that is to hold secrets. Albert had his number.

Tom Meuley is strong enough to do the deed. He could take it. He could recover. He let slip in his paper which nights he cleans the bank windows. Which one where and when. Tom Meuley being there is the only luck Albert still needed. A person's got some things in them, but not others. Nothing that can't be faced. The refrigerator, the tears in the carpet, that rip of the linoleum; her sleeping there, that thin breath, that fresh-wiped bum.

You want to know the future of a country, ask a teacher. They'll tell you. You want to know your future, check out a tenth-grade homeroom. Every 8:35 AM

Monday to Friday, your future sits there picking its nose, charging its phone and texting its mom that it's staying late to do homework, smoking out and cruising in its limo. That's the future. Anybody that thinks otherwise hasn't been paying attention. Your future's swimming in wet dreams and dodging desks with boners. A teacher'll tell you what's to come and who's going to do what. Take one good look at homeroom and unfurl the days ahead. Kids know the cost of being seen. Every morning in homeroom. The faces pinch back raw nerves in exchange for getting along. Parents' terror on their kids' faces. Pupils tighter than tight. Facebook has them pawing at their cheeks, Instagram sucking in their tummies, Foursquare taking on the floor, Snap folding their bone arms around their tweeted waists. Old folks don't blink, but it's expected from them. It's in that black and white of Duchamp playing Cage in a game of chess in Brick Magazine. They study the board, their fingers poking and pulling their cheeks and jowls.

A Tom Meuley, though, stares right back. Tonight, he'd find Meuley on The Danforth. The kid had one ATM client out there. Dad is in Paris, and Mom god knows where. That boy might make it. No iPhone: no follow, no tweet, no friend—ing. Social media is a sticky hieroglyphic web meant to curtain oneself from the living, he says. In his midterm, Meuley laid out how he got the idea to patent his leaded squeegee by committing Facebook suicide.

He'd seen teams of kids in New York hired to squeegee at intersections. With soldered lead strips lining the rubber, their blades zipped glide on glass. His leaded squeegee leans into the glass leaving no tracks. No grit, grime, blood or bullshit. As if it wasn't there at all. No streaks. Meuley'd laid it all out in an essay. Two pounds of lead. Albert would strike the first blow and hand the squeegee to the kid.

In the moment between finishing the essay and giving it a grade, Albert saw how Meuley, but not Milk, could weave his demise. People would ask, rightly, how he could do this to a kid. Perhaps by divine right, perhaps by evil, perhaps by neither and something else altogether, his role was to execute the sentence that Albert, once indicted, commanded. Those that can take what Life owes them on the chin. This is God's great equalizer. It's how a person becomes themselves. Tom Meuley will understand. Nietzsche said God is dead. But teachers, too. Nobody knows anything. Everything is a disguise. As metal bites into his skull, Life blinkers forth. In that instant, he becomes the bat stapled to the garage. He takes flight.

Milk

Tonight the plan was: get Tom, find Jeff's Saturn, and explode the G.I. Joes. Where Tad's gig was, a banking machine booth tucked between hills of plowed snow overlooking Pape Ave. Overhead, gorged, grey clouds dragged themselves blinking through a bush of silver maples. Wicked.

A canyon carved into your stomach. Something about Jeff pinning you to the wall makes it no different than Asaan's brother getting sold off. Like your insides are the rock formations cutting along Afghan back country roads. You could tear down those treads, like maybe Asaan is doing right now, hunting for his brother. Stealing Sakar free mattered; his brother mattered. You matter. Probably. Maybe.

That day in the bleachers, Mr. P. sat riveted studying the huddle and break of the varsity football team. You fingered a hole in the bench, watching him. Ask.

A car alarm blew in the parking lot. A flock of Canadian geese grubbed for worms. Air Show weekend. Schmidt's bakery smell wafted over varsity football practice.

You hung onto the bleacher's steel railing. Down a few rows, Mr. P.'s eyes'd bead out under the deep furrows in his forehead tracking Tanker Holloway or Dante Breton, his hands flat on his thighs. As the scrimmage played out, he'd pull them up to his hips and then back to his knees. His skin grey like Grandma's that afternoon in the stairwell holding onto her railing. Ask him.

The car alarm stops.

A bat hangs from your ribcage but Mr. P. anchors you.

The guys hit. Crack. Crunch. Their breath dissipates. Silence. Fighter jets swoop in low. The girders shake. The alarm squeals again. The guys bolt. The geese scatter. The jets' roar thins.

Mr. P. folds his fingers under his chin.

The birds freeze. The jets fire back. The players hold. The engines scream. The geese explode into the air. Confused. Darting. And then float back to the ground, scratching and pecking. The alarm stops.

Mr. P. smooths his comb-over.

The guys on the field break their huddle (*Ho-ah*!) into a scrimmage line. Calves turned out, asses to the sky. (*Break!*) First down. Ho-ah.

Mr. P.'s hair'd whip up, he'd pat it down.

You landed next to him. *What's up, Mr. P.?*

He nodded.

Don't let me get in your way.

I'm just watching. His hair whipped up, he smoothed it. *All that blood down there. It comes up in their cheeks, just like one day they're—blossoming.*

The guys roared and then hustled back to the scrimmage line.

Tell him you know. Those bats got to be about one thing. He's like you. Like how Dante and Tanker could've been to him like Tom is to you in another time another place. Like how you lost the thread.

What's up?
You trapped air under your top lip. *Nothing. Hanging.*
The guys beat down the field again.
All that hitting. I never did sports.
Ask him.
My wife's out there digging today in her flowerbeds. You think she can smell Schmidt's from here?
Do it.
You caught me out. Don't tell her. I better take her a fresh loaf back. When you're in love, Milk, treat 'em right.

Maybe instead ask him if it was his wife's insides eating her like the thing with your grandma. Those weeks ago, even then, you could feel the bricks in your insides loosening, the grout cracking.

You and Tom had seen his wife, Mrs. P., floating down the hall clutching an envelope to her chest. After Ern went nuts. Her steps tiny, her face static, her hair thinned —like grandma's. Like your mom's. Cancer-chemo'd green skirt, teeny pearl chain, sweater buttoned up.

As she got close, Tom shoved you into the lockers. Then, he got all up in you with his tongue. The back of your neck sweat. Cool your jets, dude.

She drifted by, a dream ghost lady, down the hall. Tiny beads of sweat surfaced along her hairline.

Somebody blew their nut on a pencil sharpener.

Nobody stopped Mrs. P. Her arms were folded over her envelope as she tucked a Kleenex into her sleeve.

Through the windows of the Main Office, you could see them leaning over the desk. Mr. P. flapping the envelope, pushing his glasses up, her pressing her forehead into his. He ripped the envelope open and read the paper. He put it on his desk and took her hand. You waved Tom over, but she bolted out smelling all lavender. Tucking her tissue still. Somebody's dying.

Mrs. P. tucking her Kleenex into her sleeve is like Grandma gritting her teeth against the chew of her insides. Instead, she'd go after your mom saying how fat she was and didn't she know how hard it is to be a woman.

She's out there digging to put bulbs in for spring.

Oh, before it freezes.

Mr. P.—I got to ask you—.

Another car alarm sounded. The birds pecked. The guys broke.

Your wife brought an envelope to the office.

Who said that's my wife?

Google.

The alarm died. The birds pecked. The guys huddled. Mr. P. chewed his cheek.

It's none of my business, Mr. P. You dug your pencil into gum stuck to the seat ahead.

I'm not who I thought I was.

Oh.

Nope. Nobody is, Milk. Nobody.

The guys had come over to the bottom of the steel bleachers. In one fell swoop, Dante lifted the huge, full water jug over his head and, lowering it, spurt water into his mouth, guzzling and then moving it in small circles drenching his face, head, and torso. Tanker had his shirt off already. Dante lowered the jug, shaking water on him. Dante passed the jug and stretched out on the bench. Veins rose out of his cleats roping their way up his calves to under his thigh pads and must've been connected to those that bound his forearms and massive hands cradling his helmet on his tummy.

Ask more.

I'm mum. He bit his lip.

Tanker lay on the bench, head to head with Dante, doing leg lifts and smacking his belly.

Your tummy fizzed. *I'm going to be a Sociologist.*

There's no money in it.

'Cause of you.

Tanker had his shirt back on. He, Dante, and the guys regrouped in a huddle. The Canadian geese stole away. The Civic drove off. You stood up. *It's winter, about.*

Milk. His mouth looked carved like a pumpkin. For reals.

Yeah?

Nothing. He turned his gaze back out to the guys.

At twelve years old, Sakar is baked Bacha Bazi. The dancing boys. He will learn the moves. He has to. Hop right, tinkle-tink, hop forth, snap-snap, hop back, tinkle-tink, drop to the rump; the breeze billows the silk and the earrings glitter.

If you were a bacha bazi, a Sakar or an Asaan, you would pack your sack and take a hike. Your brothers and sisters would bawl. Crates'd strew the floor. Dinged and singed pots and pans would line the walls; pillows and mats'd stay put and shadows'd triangulate at the door. As the buyer pulled through the doorway and towards his truck, your parents would peel your fingers from the doorjamb, the grain of wood chewing your thumb. But letting go is easy once his guttural push mirrors your mother's breath acting. Sometimes boys like you would escape. They get their men drunk, they fall asleep; they snatch their patched purses and vanish into the snow plains of Khakon.

If you could get over there, you'd get Asaan and Sakar under the protection of the Canadian Armed Forces. Not the Americans. You'd get one at a time to an airbase. He'd dance for you and you'd explain he doesn't have to do that. He'd insist. He needs to perform. His memory's faded. What he was before seems long gone.

You pulled at the thread unspooling from your jeans.

Mr. P.'s finger found the threads at the rip by your knee. He tore them loose. And then patted it there. *Maybe.*

Maybe that was the thread hooking Khakon to Tom's ATM booth up there on that hill. It threads you into the night.

Ton'

Once they got onto Steeles Ave. from Albert and Ale's place, Shafiqq got all slack-jaw staring straight ahead. 'You are a frog in a well, Ton'.'

Harsh. 'I don't know what that means, Man-no. You know who's pushing Mac-10s.'

'Dude. See, like that. Like you hop in a well, dude. Your eyes doot-doot, man.' Shafiqq's hands left the steering wheel as he shook them. 'You miss the writing on the wall. Don't see the forest for the trees. If you're a frog on a lily pad, you don't just look over the edge to the water. The answer to the Mac-10s is probably staring you in the face.'

The dude is messed up. For one, Ton' wipes his mother-in-law's ass. Frogs in wells don't do that. 'Right. "Doot doot," dude. To be a detective, you got to be a collector.'

'Just don't be disappointed by how far you don't get.'

'Do not be disappointed. Yo, you "do not be disappointed." I am a Speed Racer to you, man. You don't even know Speed Racer. Go, Speed Racer, go. That's like from my dad.' Man.

Drunks squatted on the pylons outside of the 24/7 mini-mart.

Cops got to open their eyes. 'You got to look for traces of the crime. They tell the story. One to the next, to the next, to the next.' Ton' rat-a-tat-tatted on the door panel. 'Don't frog me, man.' He whipped down the visor mirror and clocked his hairline. 'I wipe ass.'

'My grandmother used to collect *Ek Onkar*.'

Same with Ton's grandmother. His *abuelita* brought her *tarascas, carambas y marimbas* from El Salvador. She played in a band down there. They came up in the 1980s, crawling all of *El Norte*, sniffing through sewer tunnels, peeling leeches off their necks, and skinning rats for food. They picked oranges straight up from *El Refugio* through San Diego coming through the Central Valley, hugging the Sierra Madres taking up as many tomatoes as their grubby mitts could grab, splitting off from skinhead baseball bats gunning for their lives all the way, even taking the Mississippi in the dead of night to Chicago. His dad did house construction in all of those new suburbs coming up from the cornfields out there, but couldn't get legal even with Reagan's amnesty. Canada took them in.

Along the way, they snagged turtles, cockroaches— Mama said you never have *nada* 'til you have had scorpions fried on a rock in honey, mescal, butter, and grandpa's spit. *When you don't have, you do.* She put the shells and claws of crawling things into dried squash for instruments. She kept them all the way to Canada. *'Los Gringos.'* She'd shake her tummy at Ton', screw up her face and while he clung to her dried skin ankles. At St. Catharines, in a sea of semis, screaming mini-vans and trucks loaded with pigs going to meet their maker, she threw them in a dumpster. Illegal imports.

'Your grandma put two and two together.'

'Illegal vegetables, illegal people.'

'It's called choosing her battles.'

After, his *abuelita* made new instruments with cardboard paper towel centres. A few squash seeds or eggshells, add some rice or popcorn and coochie-coochie to Aldo Nova. *Life is just a fantasy / Can you live this fantasy life?*

'See how your mind wanders, Ton'.'

His mind wanders to connect the dots. Man. No way. Take 'Schelle, for instance. Take her great-grandma and that jar of tears. That chick jumped about as far from white as him. And she threw it down. A slave, man. But a slave of Indians. That lady cut out from soldiers, ducked up into the mountains and slept in a cave for two years eating roots. You got to respect that. 'Schelle didn't even know about her great-great-great grandma, and Ale probably didn't either. Albert told him. If that woman showed up in their living room, 'Schelle'd never see herself in her face. People ought to think about that. They ought to think about how memory changes your face, your skin, your muscles—today. Memory lives in the skin, man.

'Pay attention. People want to kill us out here, okay, Ton'. Think Mac-10s.'

Ghosts will not be denied. 'You can't say I'm a frog.'

'Study, Ton'. Take the test, be a detective.'

'We could be Study Buddies, Shafiqq.'

Shafiqq made some little croak sound.

'Now who's the frog? I am a study guy who knows the ins and outs of this culture.' Shafiqq wouldn't know about like Sir Sanford Fleming. Not William Lyon Mackenzie.

'I been Constable rank for one and a half years, Ton'.
I came to Canada at seventeen. I think I got the culture.
I use hand sanitizer, don't I?' He got his teeny bottle out
and squeezed some into his hand. And then Ton's.

'It's a dead giveaway, Shafiqq. You say no to everything. We say "yes" over here.'

'Canadians don't say "yes". They say "sorry".'

'We are a shy and retiring people. Walk down the
street in Toronto, what happens?'

'People welcome you with folded arms.'

Dude looks every gift-horse in the mouth. 'Actual
care hurts, Shafiqq. People disappear into it.'

The dark seeped in under the Gardiner. 'Dude, can't
we get out into the light some?'

Shafiqq fiddled with the radio and stopped it: *I got
a Nikon camera, I love to take a photograph*—.

They rode in silence. Up by past St. Lawrence
Market and slowed down by St. James park.

'I am going to tell you. You can just shut your ears.'

'Can I Ton'? Can I just shut my ears?'

'You might learn something.'

Shafiqq punched the radio off. 'I'm listening.'

'So my idea is that I will collect evidence. This is when
I am a detective, right? I will collect evidence but you
won't see me putting a case together—. That's a trap.'

Shafiqq rolled down the window, stuck his head out
and closed his eyes.

'What I'll do is different. I'll collect evidence, right,
just like always but what I bring is one crucial piece. I
am not going to string the story "together." No. I am
going to let others string the story together. I will get the
credit but they will do the story-telling. See? Detective

work is all story-telling. You lead the horse to water. You lay it out. All I do is present. I am not going to tell anyone what X, Y and Z means. I present, they story. What it means surfaces. Like a toad from underwater.'

'See?'

'What?'

'You can't help yourself.'

'What?'

Shafiqq stuck his head back out.

'The problem people run into is when they make it all personal.'

Shafiqq chewed hard on the inside of his cheek.

'Nothing means anything until you get in those nooks and crannies in between the pieces of evidence. You know the blood spatter X, the knocked over lamp Y, the busted teeth Z. It's math.'

'I bet Jamarandu eats this up.'

'Jamarandu doesn't have nothing to do with anything. Mac-10s are bigger than him.'

'Frog.'

'You got to make something of yourself, Shafiqq.'

'What do you say we head up Church Street.'

'So you can gawk.'

'Somebody up there you don't want to see.'

Dude played him. 'I'll go. I'll see anybody.' He better not run into Julio. He smelled his fingers. Flower something. Old lady smell.

Milk

The Danforth goes quiet on a winter night. The Eastern kids racing cars, the Greeks shuffling to Chester, the hipsters huddled under the Palace. Evening pulls its shadows from Kingston. Tom's ATM booth glows up there, but he's nowhere in sight. Emptying his bucket, maybe. The mission is underway. Tonight's gonna amount to something. Jeff will feel the sting of burning ABS plastic in his throat. The storm tears at your forehead, cheeks, neck and chin. Get Joes into Tom's limo.

The snow unfolds onto the Cutlass's roof, coats its windows, and blankets the street. The snap of the passenger door latch echoes against the darkened church across the street. Not one car down toward Pape or east to Coxwell.

Drag the bag of Joes from the Cutlass' backseat into the street, then load them into the limo's backseat. Three steps. The black generic garbage bag splits. Fucking cheap Jeff. Shit. The Joes skit into the street, slide amongst and under the cars huddling at the curb. *Desert Storm Joe, Cobra Commander* and *Action-Pilot Astronaut* pile in the slush and offal. *Storm Shadow* with *Astronaut's* helmet hooked to his arm, *Snake Eyes'* neck caught in *Captain*

Claymore's armpit, and all of them caught by *Crimson Horseman's* backpack. They mangle into maple leaves, Lick's burger wraps, flattened Du Mauriers and 40s of Labatt's. Like *Quick Kick's* Humvee detonated by *Viper*, gasoline fumes fuel the mission. Poof, boom. Fireball. You scoop them back into the bag and drag them.

The temperature dropped. If you could only be *G.I. Joe Quick Kick* riddling *Zartan* posing as *Ripcord*. Tonight, *Quick Kick, Snake Eyes* and *Desert Storm Commander* would climb to where you could not: the volcano on Cobra Island. Staggering to the top, giving it everything they've got, against all odds sapping their energy banks knowing that nothing's guaranteed; the charred and scarred rock scorch soles and the suffocating shrivel punches their lungs to rip open their flak jackets and leap. Soldiers do that.

You heave the bag up. No way you'd be here tonight to deliver these Joes to their final flame if *Quick Kick* had not executed his daring escape as *Viper* gunned down their convoy. If he couldn't save the lives of *Duke, Falcon* and *Cross Country Commando*, he'd never be interned in Arlington National Cemetery. The Joes' beady eyes catch you. *Quick Kick*, and you.

You are neutrinos. Electrons crack your snaps, buttons and zippers; expose dough bellies and dive faster than the speed of light. You tear ahead ducking rocks, winding through crevasses, surfing the jagged maw of an Afghaned, snow-field universe, to the upper known limits of speed and beyond—just as velocity ricochets Time backwards. Neutrinos slip out of Time, speeding past the Twin Towers, Che Guevera gunned down in the jungle; tearing past the boot-rot and blood-crack of trenches in the Somme and the nineteenth-century Trail of Tears to the eighteenth-century cave-in of Parisian streets mirroring the twentieth's contamination of the Donlands. It is in an oscillation so twisted that one shrinks—no, erases—to get a clearer view. You zip past You as you were tonight, and then oh oh oh falling away into some quantum drainpipe. You could imagine *Quick Kick*'s ABTC six-pack disintegrating alchemical tonight, all weakness and susceptibility. Vulnerability girds you. Neutrino. Tonight is untethering a boatload of weakness.

Marine Joe falls back out. You dropped the bag again.

Shot out by the sun, a neutrino passes through any material undetected. Its only trace is the fact that it is no longer there. Presence by absence. Being seen but not heard. Visibly invisible. It's tracked by super-sensitive, Grade A equipment at CERN or the super-magnet in the cornfields outside of Chicago. It heaves itself through stone and bitumen buried under volcanos like *Zartan* and *Billy*. No weight, no colour, no mass, no smell. You are a neutrino. Ice ruts snatch the bag as does the smell of Jeff's ass on the couch in their *Venus de Milo* room where your mom has her pictures of you and she and him and Grandma and Uncle Louise spread out and, even though it's winter, sweat pools with underarm cream leaking down the sagging fat of her arm; and you see yourself at three in a striped shirt and cock-eyed hat; at eight, treading water at Charlevoix, that lake water mossing in your nostrils. Every one of these Yous disappear leaving what didn't get lost to the waves: you. Your squinty pig eyes, the spare tire at your waist, and the lopsided earlobe. All of those Milks are this one.

If those Milks hadn't oscillated into you now, no one would know that they had existed. You would have passed right through pulled by antimatter. Who's to say it's not Circe's spell feasting on the sorrows of sailors and netting a whale; now clutching the bow, now spouting for breath? The limo is Telemachus' ship paddling to find his father, Odysseus. Say it isn't so. The two of you, too, you and Tom, unmoor from this night riding to the ocean's deep. The limo can slip through drifts and pools tight and sweet. Black and shining in gunk salt slush, freezing and melting. Salt and slush, freezing and melting. It's a ship casting from kith to kin to hunt for Jeff. No. Better. Consider another: *I am game for his crooked jaw, and for the jaws of Death too, Captain Ahab.* He is who claws at the rock on that failing dune: *He is not the whale for we know where he lurks.* He is not the Father for we know what is in his heart. The monster awaits his turn.

Lift the bag up. Two steps. Drop. The streetlight reflections stretch along the limo's extended side panels as ancient clippers oaring home. Up, two, three. Drop. *Bow to stern, son,* Uncle Louise would say. *Bow to stern.* Up, two, three. Drop. December. The weather blows free the sails unfurling for Odysseus and his witch, for Ahab and his whale, for Tom and his You. Pop open the limo's rear side door.

Up, two, three. Heave. *In a limo you are present,* Tom says. *That's me, man.* Bury your treasures deep past the stalagmites, across the Aegean seas of scraping the seats and roiling seat belts, clamping the snapping jaws of built-in ashtrays and slipping amongst the long-dry crystal decanters. You wedge the bag of Joes' behind the limo's front seat.

I got things to do. The limo, says Tom, is all about hiding in plain sight. *Nobody drives a Saturn to stay on Earth.* Jeff does.

The current pulls.

It yawns into that little inlet with Uncle Louise. Your legs dangling, the bass gulping.

He laid his paddle, its green paint chipped and flaking, over his thighs. *Some folks—take your mom—have a harder time when reeling in their line.*

Ah.

Them bass want to get hooked as much as you want to hook them. Bass aren't different from Ahab's whale. Sailors weaken at the sirens' call. They got to matter, Evan.

━━ Tonight, about now your mom would be at home plugged into her iPod pining over Jeff and his fancy perm: *Love on the rocks, ain't no big surprise / Just pour me a drink and I got a goodbye.* Fingering herself over *My Three Sons.* Mooning to Fred MacMurray (a.k.a. Walter Neff) as Steven Douglas chasing Robbie, Chip, Ernie and Uncle Charlie (a.k.a. Fred Mertz, the first) long after Barbara Stanwyck (a.k.a. Phyllis Dietrichson, a.k.a. Victoria Barkley) showed him the business end of a gun barrel. One finger in her pants, one pasting her pictures. Scan, print, and paste. Scan, print, and paste. Scan, print, and paste. Four by sixes, five by sevens, eight by nines. Albums with black stick-on triangles for the corners.

You got to do it like that, Milk, it looks more old-timey. People think they're real. She treads water in a pool of Pringles, Doritos, Little Debbies and wallops of Diet Pepsi. *To whet the whistle. I'm not going to eat all this. I'm not a cow.*

Not anymore. Not since she got gutted. Not since her days as an orangutan. Not since she couldn't breathe. *Oh, I love you so so so much. One Little Debbie. One. They're not good for you. Hydrogenated oils.*

You're eating them.

I may look like a svelte screen siren now but I'll always be a Two-Ton Tina in my mind. I am a rusted hull. One of those old ships cut up and beached we saw at the ROM.

Burtynsky.

What you see before you is the result of a knife and a tying-off, so I cannot—. Your father cut the rope—come here. Look at these pictures.

You pack into the Greco-Roman loveseat next to her.

I eat to keep this mop on my noodle. She pawed at the limpish strings hanging in blondish strands. *One little thing and boom upchuck. I can't help it, Evan. I eat, I boot.* She picks at the corner of the picture where she's a housecoat mascaraed China Doll Queen throwing an egg at the camera. *We all did our eyes that way then.* She rubbed the photo album page with a finger. A shot of her on her yellow towel in the backyard with her straps undone. *Those boys were all perverts. Gawking, gawking. 'Cept Tom Meuley. Oh, TadTom.*

A shot of your Great-Grandma Jean in her coffin.

Old Jean-er-roo got out the door shipshape, didn't she?

You cover your face. Don't stare at the dead.

Don't she look just like Mama? Look how sunk her cheeks are. The wax hands folded. The family cowering around the body. *If that is not a ship of fools.* She yanked a hair from her ear. *Always has a Kleenex in her hand. Spit can in her pocket. Ladies don't keep those anymore. For spit juice. Blech.*

Mom wasn't done.

Mean? Shoot, she used to call Uncle Louise at work saying your grandma's done with not being normal and don't think it's a done deal—.

What's not a 'done deal'?

That your grandma gets her head on straight and steers towards the shore of normality. Nor-mal-ity. Like the town in Nebraska.

She offered the bag of chips.

Have five chips. Serving size is ten, so half is probably safe for human consumption. These're not good for you, Evan.

She flipped to a picture of your hand poking out of the water.

Like that holding yourself underwater. Sick. Sick, Milk. Sick. That's my mother's fault.

The bends are your thing, not Grandma's. At nine, you saw on Google how you could hold a rock that weighs as much as you do and then walk into the lake and let it pull you under. The body makes all the right oxygen-nitrogen exchanges. Hold your breath. Hold it. Then, squat, drop the rock and shoot yourself up. Surfacing, you have the bends. Stoned. Dizzy. Nice. You waited on your knees by the dock for the bubbles to come up on your skin but Grandma Adele called you in. Tonight, the bends would unfold. Surfacing. Crazy. Tight. All the right exchanges spinning.

You ain't none other than Odysseus too, said Grandma Adele. He's knocked off his raft and pressed down: his knees buckled, bulging arms hung limp, his body swollen. The surf throws him to a beach, cut by coral, and left to puke. Getting all the right oxygen-nitrogen exchanges, it is this exchange paving the highway unfurling before him. Now you are that grit girl Nausicaa coming upon him, as an accelerating atomic particle tractions itself, passes what it once was, and plunks into one of the quantum pipes shooting onto the sand. You are like Odysseus, his massive heaving brine-encrusted torso as some other him. Maybe where Grandma found herself after the breathing machines stopped.

Death is to have just spun through. Grandma probably poked around to see what's what. She probably dug her foot in to get a toehold in the sand. She wondered, naturally probably, what the eff. She lifts her hand, it's not there. She feels the skin, it, too, is no more.

Come the moment you spin through, pinging down and out, you'd be thinking, oh, don't forget way back when Mom, Tad. Tad. Effing Dad. You would breathe deep to smell fresh cut green grass one last time, to rope you in. You would lasso deep on the banks of that river there, your lungs filling with the past piss brass coat buttons in the closet where one of your great-great grandpas hung his ghosts for larvae, like you, to feed on clutching up for air. No matter the blooming alveoli, to be smothered, to gulp for nothingness. Pining for a toehold would be one regret, the Eaton Centre another. You think of how you never touched those fibreglass geese flying way up close to the ceiling there. You wouldn't miss the stores. Not The Gap. But those geese, those Canadian geese that crap phat all over the football field and down by the lake but then just when you least expect it lift off like they're spirits or ghosts or some container of something greater and fly dolorous and ragged dragging their umbered carcasses skyward. And, The Spit.

⟶ In the limo's driver seat now, you finger the steering wheel. The wiper blades stick. Wipe the fog, scrape the frost. Curlicues map the glass-like riverbed birds swooping down to the snow plains of Khakon. Like where Asaan is. Look both ways.

Afghan boys like Asaan and Sakar get sold so that their families can eat. They get protection. But you think of after the boys are taken away; how their mothers press their faces into mud walls clawing at the clay. Fifty bucks goes a long way. Getting all the right exchanges between moms and dads, sellers and buyers. Betting on collapse, defeat, and the opening of new markets. Capitalism.

Tom Meuley (a.k.a. Tad), is way more of a capitalist than you. He is *une capitaliste*. His plan: first, a U of T math degree. Then, retail. Not just retail retail. Money-earning retail, river deep mountain high. Take his dad. Lit major. French lit: Baudelaire, Balzac, Proust. *Mais, une capitaliste l'étrange, il m'a dit. Le plus exemplaire.* Lives in Paris. He is so far a capitalist, he's a socialist. Commercialism is the contemporary, practical manifestation of *recherché à long temps*.

What Tom says: *it's wickeder than that.* He sticks his finger in your ear.

After graduating, he intended to open retail a outlet called *Magasin de Desir*. Desire to the nth degree. *It is all algorithms,* he says. *My algorithms get it so that not only everything can be predetermined as a commodity but also every freaking exchange is gotten just right inside the confines of the magasin. You look at someone, it costs you. You are attracted, ka-ching. That is from Walter freaking Benjamin. Write that name down. You just have like a key card on your person, in your purse, in your pocket. You venture down an aisle, desire triggers sensors, vectors track you and you pay. You breathe, you pay; you breathe, you pay; you breathe, you pay.*

Impressive. You pulled at the loose threads on your jeans.

No one wants to just look at their computer screen forever. People are going to go to stores, into the stores my dad and I are going to build, the Arcades Nouveaux Niveaux—that is a good name: "New Levels." A play on words and a play on the wallet. And customers are going to go just so they can buy authentic exchanges between them and other people. It's all about sincerity. The more people get stuck behind their computers and with their buds in, they are, right, still human, so they are going to need, not just want, they are going to need that sincere exchange with other human beings, and they will drag their sorry rich asses aux Arcades and pay for it. Babies die if they are not touched. You watch. Every everything can be sold. My algorithms will calculate, and predict, exactly what it—a glance, a brush of the hand, an inquiring look—could be priced at. Watch, look and learn. Be like me, Milk. Make plans. Calcu-lus. In-sid-i-ous. Okay. Inside out.

Tom thinks out-of-the-box. That would not be the last time that phrase came into play today. Ever the entrepreneur, he made his own job cleaning windows. He called up five stores—a DVD store, a mobile phone store, a raw sushi store and the bank. Whatever it costs to get their front windows cleaned, he'd do them for 20% less. If it cost them ten bucks an hour, he'd clean for eight. To boot, they had the privilege of putting an unemployed youth to work. He was up there, right now, pulling his final strokes. Wiping down his two-pound leaded squeegee and dumping his bucket.

Flakes float to the ground like mattresses.

The brake light blinks. Blinks. Flitches. Blinks. Your teeth chatter. The heater whack-a-whacks. Where is he? You couldn't see him through the rear window.

Shadows goad from the skimpy trees past the curb.

When he finishes this ATM booth, you guys hit the road. The plan is: cruise around in his limo. Isotropic. Bonfire. You get out of your Cutlass. The air bites straight off. At the front bumper, you slip, hop up onto the snowbank, and balance on that metal strip. And then, there he comes. A hawk winging his grey army coat; a shadow blinking in periodic headlights. He hops onto the back bumper. And, then again. Then in one squeal collars you to the car. The glass stings the fat at your belt. His 'fro in your face, he goes in fool for your neck, chewing such a spoon of you you could have boned and died right there. You shove him off. He yanks your shirt up and pushes you back off. Don't go all fag on me.

And he gets another mouthful before gravity slides him to the sidewalk.

Sick. Ha.

You land next to him, then moved to the hood. Your mouth won't move. Inside, a spoonful of your Mom's lasagna is in your throat. You are not going to boot. You are not.

Inside, he claps his hands and slaps your thigh the way he does. Rips your shirt up to chew your tummy the way he does. Goes down to tug the hairs there with his teeth; you get his mop in your hands and for a split second you have him. The slick soft, the cotton of his threads. You push him off.

Sup? He rat-a-tat-tatted on the dashboard shooting. Sup, sup.

If you had to point your finger to a moment when you fell into one drain and then another and then another, where you were bulleted onto that beach heaving for air, it is exactly here. To be him. To chew his tummy, to taste those hairs.

He shores you up pulling so close. Then, presses back into the window. Don't look at me like that. I got to just see you, he says. He gets himself back up against and into the corner where the seat belt coils. He sprinkles weed into a paper.

And it is here first that that same momentous pull of light, molecule, atomic and rock hurtles you ahead. That you as neutrino, as *Quick Kick*, as metaphor, launch. Ready, set, go.

You got your coat inside out. You peel off your boots, Tom unzips his coat. His smell—rust leaves. You undo your jeans, he cracks his fly. His smell—burnt cinnamon. You worm yours, his drop fast. You, one leg back, he pulls two. Your undies fall fast, his undone. His smell—smoke ash. Your *Je t'aime* T-shirt up, he pulls and wrenches. You, the coat sleeve sticks; him, a no-snag clamp. The two of you had gotten good at buckling your belts from the inside. A thing you two do since Tom turned his guts inside-out in the principal's office. Like, literally, up-chucked his guts under her beady eyes on the dog pillow. Follow the one thread soaking in puke juice.

That day Smith showed the quote-unquote "Coolies" movie on the Canadian National Railroad, Tad downed a fifth of Jack at lunch. He couldn't drive, so you drove his dad's car back to school. That day, your heart jumped out of your chest driving. Hit the curb twice. At Statler, the steering wheel flew. By the skin of your teeth, no-body died. Tad stumbled, fumbled and dragged himself to fifth hour. You ducked into Smith's as the bell rang.

Ten minutes later, Vice Principal Webster leaned against your classroom doorjamb tapping her nails.

Busted.

She wagged one of those fingers with the cabbage jewel rings. An orangutan totem pole folding its arms. A Medusa gorilla with a stick up her kazoo. Like her hair snaking off her noggin. Animal. Her face didn't move thanks to the Botox her husband got her for Christmas. She pointed at you to follow. She tore off down the hall-way trailing rank perfume, you hurrying to keep up. *Do you not know how dangerous this is? For Mr. Meuley? You know he keeps saying your name? I mean, why am I pulling you from class? Do not tell me you don't know, right?*

Under her office window, Tom Meuley twisted into a dog pillow on the floor.

Whips is at the vet today. She tucked her nose into her elbow. *Tom Meuley's lucky. He's got a soft place to lay his head.*

A string from one of Tom's jeans seams sucked up barf juice in an ink-spill-sized puddle next to him.

Webster extended her toe out to the tip of a small rug near Tom and kicked it out of the way. *Ick. Gag me.* Oh.

Don't oh on all of this. You know, Evan.

You didn't.

Tom Meuley's vulnerable. She dug her cuticle and then licked the finger. *Very. Treat him that way.*

Tad stunk. Drastic. *What's 'very'?*

Very, very. Mr. Meuley lives with the consequences for

his choices. I'm opened-minded but boys like you pay your money and you take your chances.

The wood-panelled office reeked: 'boys like you'?

Ugh. If this gets into the wood in here. She pulled her hair behind her head and lifted Tom's coat. The inside dripped puke. *Blech. My wig doesn't flip over boys like Tom Meuley vomiting. See, Milk? He's going to have to wear his coat inside out to get home.*

Should I like take him home now?

No. You're not getting out of class. You boys. Just 'cause your yoo-hoos work, you get yourselves into all sorts of trouble. Come back when the bell rings and help him home.

Outside in the hallway, you pressed your tummy.

The lights glared, and pans clanged in the school kitchen around the corner.

The coast clear, you punched a locker.

On the way back to class, you turned your flannel shirt inside out. When you ease back into your seat, the darkened room blinked with the flickering movie projector. Silent newsreel movies. Chinese men, long tracks, sledgehammers, pick-axes. Sneaking peeks at the camera. *The Blood of Our Century of Progress! Iron!* Came up on the screen. If those iron tracks are the blood, then those men laid the veins.

Iron, Mr. Smith said, *is a living montaged thing. Particles, just like you Suong, just like you Julie.*

The P.A. buzzed loud static and every head in the room cocked up in that direction, waiting. The speaker fitzed out.

━━ Tad gets his feet back on the dash. Lights his spliff, flicks ash with his fingertips. Now you planted your feet on the dash too. He inhales one, two, three times to take it in deep and holds your face to his lips. A ribbon of smoke curls out into your nose. You breathe, taking him in. Something of him rises in you. He reaches over the dashboard to wipe the fog from the windshield. His sleeve smears gunk in the crack opened up there last summer when you two stole bread loaves.

Dude, ick.

He wipes it clear with the other sleeve.

━━ That day, you had parked on the road out past the Leacock Museum and the Orillia Millennium Trail, slunk into the field shoving each other shushing to not get caught. He pulled your pant leg tackling you into the wet grass, pinning you down getting your teeny belly button hairs in his teeth—for the first time—'til you were squirming; he rubs his own tummy pulling you, with one arm up off the ground, along that path to a door wide open to an empty bakery kitchen, just a timer ticking is all, and like you had to do it, they were right there for the taking, you got five or six loaves braided, buttered, and burnt; huffing so hard 'til you fell slam on your butt; 'til Tom hiked you up spitting crumbs and mouthfuls, back out the door, and you two gritting your lips sshh, sshhh, ssshhhh, you tripped and fell hurtling yourselves through the bush to the car and effin' missiled that bread like a football into the back seat and died there on the road, laughing so hard you couldn't breathe but hung on to the rubber seals where rain and snow water leaks in tiny streams, and no one ever came, they never busted you, never read your plates even when you peeled out on the gravel that stone hit the windshield nicking it to crack a twig fissure squizzing up to those rubber seals.

━━ With each of you holding that fine thread, you pulled away from the curb earlier tonight. The snow crunched under the tires. You switched on the wiper blades to scrape the glass. You squinted, getting lower than the steering wheel to see. A strangle of cars flooded the Danforth. You pulled into the traffic swept along by snowflakes the size of Frisbees spinning into the night.

Sessy

She pulled her car around behind the wildebeest and killed the ignition. She'd wait. God knows, she'd spent her entire life waiting. But Life taught her: don't count a chicken 'til it shakes its shell. She and Jeff met way back when. He got her hook, line, and sinker.

Jeff strutted into the psych lab to be a paid participant on a project researching the role that history plays in the emotional processing of visual imagery. As an English major, Sessy'd been hired to write up session reports. They stuck EKG and EEG sensors to his rock-hard abs, at the arteries near his groin, and next to the tufts of his armpit. If tighty-whiteys make the man, Jeff was full grown.

Later, when they were out for coffee, it was the way his finger stroked the lip of the cup, first, and then the tail of his mullet that got her. He listened. He heard her. He did the psych test for the $80 honorarium but also to study the sensors since he used the same technology to map the microbial impacts of soil-based resource extraction. *I don't want anything from you*, he said. *Just to be with you*. For two years, he kept up that song and dance. She promised herself that no way in hell would she say *I love you*, unless she absolutely had to. But some people got to learn the hard way: love's got its own momentum. It log-jammed into her, pummeling her insides to the point that her hands'd get sweaty and she couldn't breathe around him. She just knew he was going to ask her. And so bolted into a tree.

Tonight, the engine ticked. She cracked the window to keep the glass from fogging with her breath. She wanted to see it. Every second. A few squares of office lights glowed like teeth at the rear of the HSCAN building. Their glare cast a black curtain on the woods past the asphalt. Maybe that old woman would be all right. Maybe they'd find her a bed in a shelter. You don't never know. What they do to old folks around here is anything but pretty. But, look, some of it is their own fault. Look at her folks. Look at her mother, Adele. Her dad cut his own breast off.

Don't tell Sessy about nutty old people. For all she knew, that bird had slipped out of the loo at 54 Division. Right now, she could be back in the creek cuttin' her trench well. Just out of sight. Don't kid an old kidder. Old goats like that can hustle. She could be out there at this instant, past that asphalt, teeth chattering and hood-string twisting in the wind, lifting drink to those ghosts: *cutchrtrnchell*. Take care, Sister. Taddle Creek takes no prisoners.

The temperature had dropped another ten degrees. Sessy got her wig right and sunk low to just under the dashboard lip. And waited. And then, there he came.

Jeff stopped at the necklace of sliced lemons roping his cherry-red Saturn.

Hah.

He squinted. He looked at the other cars in the lot.

Oh, yeah.

He nudged a lemon with his toe. He took three steps back.

Got you.

He ran up one side and down the other.

Got you good.

He darted over to the nearest car and then back. He kicked at a lemon. And then knelt to smell it.

Yep. That's real fruit. Peel that, baby.

He got in his Batmobile and, not seeing her, looked right in her eye: his own worst enemy. He glanced to the right and then the left. The lemons gummed up his traction and he ground his tires shooting lemon pulp onto the rhino, the giraffe extending its neck, and the sheet metal hyena awaiting sponsorship. Once he got loose, he spun right—but not towards home. Sessy followed.

He tore up Newcastle straight past Meijer's—where he took a left onto a side street, slipped along two blocks, and cut a right into a *cul de sac*. Sessy pulled to the curb and killed her lights. Got ya. The backs of her knees dripped with sweat. Out here, the air reeks like Chinatown-Dundas come stink-piss hot August. He spun his tires up into the driveway of one of those mid-century clapboard apartment buildings. The Saturn slipped into a carport. Whoever this bitch is, her rent is $600 a month for two bedrooms and a 24-hour asbestos buffet.

He balanced his way across the blacktop ice disappearing through a door.

Two can play this game. She left the Tercel to zip up the dog-poop-pocked driveway. Some crack-ass popped open the door Jeff had gone into.

She dropped to her haunches.

The man jumped back in. Fraidy Cat.

She stood up.

Keeping a tight hold on the door, he poked his head out. 'Uh. Ma'am?'

'Yes.' She smoothed her hair-do, now a rat's nest.

'Can I help you?'

She fingered her delicate flaxen mane. 'Yes.' She made the door in two steps.

'We can't just let just anyone in.' He closed the door to a slit. 'People get high out here.'

'Do I look high?'

'Um.' The guy twittered.

'You think that I am high, as you say?'

'No. No. I'm not saying you are. I'm just saying.'

'I am looking for——.' She cocked her chin at him 'Number 14.'

A cat landed on the dumpster with a thud, kicking up snow. The guy gasped, bringing his hand to his chest.

Pussy. 'Patricia, please.'

Nervous, the guy shook it off and opened the door wider. 'Is that Number 14's name?' Now he leaned out to Sessy like he wanted something. 'You know. Maybe you can help me. I asked her out when she just first moved in. But I could not remember her name.'

'Patricia.'

'Too embarrassed——.'

'Between you and me, I'd say ask her again.' Why not go all the way?

'You think so?'

'I do.'

She skated past him trailing a finger across his chest and into a vestibule no bigger than a closet 'You're going to thank me later.'

'That way.' He pointed down a long hallway lit by fluorescents the size of cookie sheets. She twittered her fingers at him. He twittered back. She blew him a little kiss, he brought his hands together in prayer. Jesus. What is happening to men? He left the building.

The apartment units lined the hallway but only on the right. She stepped closer to a door and pressed her ear to the plywood grain. Jeff's squawk could cut particle board. Nothing. She hit the next one. Pressed her ear. Nada. All along that hallway, she listened at each door. Luck be a lady tonight. The rotten floorboards holding up the stained barf-yellow office pile creaked louder than those outside Milk's room.

'No. I'm telling you.'

Him. There he is. Number 14. The backs of her knees and her thighs gushed. God does work miracles. Death does come knocking.

'Jeff. Jeff. It can't be just you. I mean, lemons?'

Sessy pressed her ear into the door to get every word.

'It was, Patricia. It is.'

Patricia. Insect. Beetle. Centipede.

'Don't be paranoid, Jeff. It's some kind of team-building morale exercise.'

'But—why? It's like sick. Demented.'

Sessy covered her eyes from the hallway glare. She sucked on her fingers.

'Like sinister. Dark. In the parking lot.'

She licked her lips.

'In the lot. At HSCAN?'

'Well, don't ask me.'

'I know what lemons mean. Loyalty. Betrayal. Capital B. Could've been Kenny.'

The light under the door flickered, the floorboard wheezed and the door flung open.

Sess' ducked, pressing herself into the wallpaper.

Jeff hurried out holding a garbage bag.

She hid behind her hands.

'Jesus!' His mouth fell open, he dropped the bag— and bolted back inside.

But, she had him. 'Don't you—.' She got him at the collar and yanked him to her.

He wrenched his neck back, his face and neck swelled with blood and exertion.

He never once beat her at arm wrestling. 'I'll choke you. You—.'

The door pressed hard against her foot now caught. He shoved. She rammed the door with her left hip. She dug her shoulder in. 'Don't you—.'

Jeff screamed an animal shriek—and then weakened. The door flew open and then slapped back. They both jumped out of the way and right back into position.

She slammed the thing into the drywall behind.

A living room. She looked around. A plant. A lamp. A child. A little boy clung to a wall. A love child. A love palace. She took it all in. Oversize windows to bleed beams of morning sunlight. A real ceramic pot with a blooming Judas Tree. Her hands came to her face.

'Sess'?'

The walls, a cascade of pussy pink.

'Is that you?'

A holster, a handgun. A certificate from Toronto Police Services scrawled "Patricia" in fancy letters.

He took one step.

Her mouth would not move. She dug her nails into her palms.

He came to her, across the threshold. His heart returned, his fingers soothed her hairline. He eased her platinum wig straight. 'Sess.'

Air slammed into her knees. She stepped onto the beach of his gaze. Confusion crystallized into clarity. Now she lived. On this desolate shore her hope, his touch, a beacon. If only her mouth would move she would utter, *take me back*. She swung at the waves pounding at her, the shards of fracture crowding in. The two of them could leave this place, speed down this rinky-dink hallway to that café on Charles St., that one with fireplaces, brick walls and those wooden stairs that lift you from the brutality of sidewalks. Jeff laid his hand on her shoulder. With one eye still on those Judas blooms, she let him lead her back into the hallway. She took off her wig and let it drop. Her breath caught at her throat.

She, animal, stepped forward. 'She.' *Her*. It. One arm stretched high along the door jam, the other folded along her goddamned sexy hip cocked and ready.

Sessy's sunglasses followed the wig to the floor but before she could retrieve them, Jeff had them back in her hands. She folded into his chest. The fur there warmed her. And reeked of cardamom.

That woman cocked an eyebrow at the love birds—deep down that is who they are—and cleared her throat. 'Who let her in here is what I want to know.'

Sessy held onto Jeff with one hand and balanced herself against the wall with the other.

'Don't faint,' he said.

The woman screwed up her face.

'Let me call *54*.'

'Patricia—.'

'—Can't you see?'

This lady, this *Patricia*, must be blind. Love could be seen. Love could be felt. Love could be heard. She couldn't know passion. Sessy dared to rest her hands on the small of Jeff's back. He stiffened, and she dug to find each vertebra.

'I'm calling—.' Miss Free and Easy started to close the door. Jeff wedged his foot in. Sessy pressed harder. Into the bone. That settled him. 'Jeff, she's manipulating you.'

He braided around to talk to that hussy. 'Honey—.'

Sessy dropped to her knees. She laid her palms on the top of his shoes. Facing up. 'Come home.' If she willed it harder and enough, if she shoved herself back into his heart, if he would gather her in his arms, if she could rid this moment of herself and make it like she wasn't there, then everything that drove him away would disappear. If she could remove herself and make it like she wasn't there. If she had a knife she would cut this thing, this her—her own self, out of her own gut, her own breast, her own arm. If she only knew right where it, her, had buried itself. She would cut. She would hack, slice, and dice just to free the girl. She could find that her—like a purple kidney—and cut it out. She had no map, no compass, no schematic but she could feel it. Under her belly button. A polyp. A tight, metallic knob. She could smell its rank, rot, and grief. The smell rose inside to her sinus to just this side of a taste. Acidic, acrid, and sour. A wet sponge left too long in the sink. Who she is. A cloth cut like no other. Her. Her despair pooled in the gaze of that that that woman, that vampire, taking her in like some kind of sick beast. Roadkill. She herself. She. Sessy. Her. Her being her. Her existence made everything wrong.

Jeff got her elbows and lifted. She fought back. 'Home, come on, Jeff. Home.' She wobbled towards the surface. The dizziness. The oxygen. She'd lost the heart to kill him. People only kill the ones they love. And them only. She didn't love Jeff. Love is action, not latching like a mussel.

The woman flapped her wings at the door.

Sessy stepped back from Jeff.

That lady moved back, too, chewing on her long brown hair, 'How'd you get in here?'

'For eff's sake, Sessy.'

'Jeff.'

'This is my wife.'

Patricia talked through the hair in her teeth. 'Well. Is she crazy?'

Sessy hadn't thought this part through. 'Jeff. I am begging you. Please come home.' She dropped to her knees.

'Get up.'

She could remove herself.

'Jesus.'

'She's crazy.' Patricia peeked over Jeff's shoulder. 'Look at her.'

Sessy leapt off the floor, snarling. How come she crouched on the floor? How come she grovelled? What had she ever done but be the most her? 'Yes. Yes, you cruel heartless piss-ant bitch of a lady. I am crazy. Very crazy.' She growled, and spread her wings; now condor, cormorant, criminal. Her game to maul and skin alive.

The woman jumped back into her apartment and swung the door.

But Sessy's foot blocked it. 'Now, what? You Patricia.'

'Don't call me that. You can't call me that.'

'You.'

'Go home, Sess'.'

Sessy had one arm on the doorjamb but with her right, she got Jeff's collar in her grip. She brought his face close. 'I will. With you.'

Jeff dropped his arms. 'I can't.'

'Give me a reason.'

'There's nothing there there.'

Sessy let the door go and in one fell swoop ripped her coat zipper open and busted the buttons on her blouse. She yanked her bra straps down, baring her breasts. 'I am a container, Jeff.' She shook her whole self at him. 'My body is yours. It is a container of everything I have ever ever felt for you. Do you think I just fill myself up with nothing? There is here there. Take it. Jeff. Please. I belong to you. I am your Tupperware. You are my virus. You fill me, Jeff. I am as Milk's G.I. Joes are. Skin, not plastic.' She rubbed her hair on his cheek. 'It's better than real life-like. Take me.'

'Well, I am sorry, Jeff. I have to call the police. She's cuckoo.'

That chicken-feather chihuahua woman still clung to her door. It had to be pushing seven-fifteen, seven-thirty by now. In the time that they'd been in the hallway, she caught a glance out of Patricia's windows. Outside, the evening had fallen off. Those Judas Trees blooms were just outlines against the black Etiobokean sky now. Jeff's face fell into shadow. His gaze was a greyish-brown blob.

Out in the parking lot, a car engine gunned. And then revved harder.

Sessy leapt wild onto her man. 'HOME,' she screamed.

Milk

Toronto's lateral artery, Bloor-Danforth, stitches a wound of commercial buildings onto the city. Now, the Danforth landed you two on Bloor by Jarvis at a juncture stented by blight and funeral homes. Tad poked at your bag of G.I. Joes in the backseat.

Cripes. It's heavy. There's a whole bag. How many you got in there? They aren't in dress uniform.

The two of you used to cut suits and underwear out of magazines to Scotch tape dress the Joes.

One hundred and fifty-three.

One hundred and fifty-three G.I. Joes.

Jeff's got a hard-on to get rid of them. I'm taking him up on his offer to grow up. Kaboom.

Tom folded the legs of *Desert Storm Actual Hair Arab Interpreter.* You recycling them?

Jeff is dogging my mom, dude.

She started smelling spice—.

Perfume?

Nothing gets by my mom. *What is that smell?*

Cool. He flipped the radio.

1010 Newstalk says tonight the worst storm ever would slam the Midwest, accumulate steam over the Great Lakes, and take out the eastern seaboard.

Dude. Tom.

Winds 50 to 70 KM/H. We ought to bag it.

No way, man. Like dandelions don't even bend over at that speed.

The CN Tower backflips.

At the AGO, an art piece mapped out which neighbourhoods would be zapped when the tower collapses.

My limo can take it. You gunned west. Past the ROM, past High Park even. Out into newcomer flats enforced by multi-culti gangs. Tonight is the bends on steroids. Dude.

Chill.

At Keele, you hung a right and sped up to Highway 400. Dude. We going to Vaughan?

Black Creek Ossuary, man.

Milk—.

Hang on. You jogged over to Jane, hung a left, up to Newcastle and hung another left off Eglington. You got into that cul de sac across the street from Jeff's love nest. You killed the engine and ducked under the dashboard.

Dude.

Get down.

Dude, it's dead out here. It's like Walmart land.

You reached into the backseat, keeping an eye on that building. See that Saturn? A red two-door Saturn coupe stewed at the far end of a carport. Recognize it?

Your dad's.

A stand of trees trembled between you and the carport. You'd have to cross the street.

You and the folks were in the pine mountains, high up in California. The cliffs lurching up on either side. Your uncle, Adam, lived alone in a cabin up there. Every time your dad went to turn across on-coming traffic, a pair of headlights blasted at you, and he'd slam on the breaks. A left-hand death turn. The first time. Like a bottle of ants shaken up in a jelly jar, you'd all grab the ceiling, the window glass, the armrest. *Jeff! Don't!* Your mom'd scream. *Jesus, Sessy! I'm not! I'm not.* The second, third and fourth she'd shut her eyes and bare her fangs. *Jeff!* He'd creep out into the creamy fog and boom. Headlights speeding at you. Shit. Jeff gunned the gas, tore out into the lane and holy effing mother of god shit a pair of headlights roared right at you. This is it. This is biting it. Horns blasted ahead and behind. You sailed through. Cast onto the shoulder, the three of you heaved for air.

➤ A recon pays off. You knew exactly where to find Jeff—and his Saturn. Cross your fingers you don't run into that tall drink of bearded water you batted your eyelashes at. You unloaded the Joes. You pointed to the slopes of the hills, the stands of trees across the road. Propping all those hills and trees up are the bones of indigenous people. Those are the people propping up the land on which you stand.

Dude, they're like cement piles. Tom couldn't get his zipper up easy. Inside out-ness can suck.

Taking a stand against the weather, a row of saplings shook along a low potato-shaped hill.

It's the start of the Black Creek drumlin out here.

All bones, man. All ossuary.

Don't slip.

Tom got a corner of the bag and the two of you balanced yourselves on the ice, across the street and around back to the building's carport.

People move out here to die. Senilicide. Invalidicide. Eglinton West.

You are going to bury your G.I. Joes.

You pulled the can of lighter fluid from the bag. But am I?

Wind whipped rattled the fibreglass roof of the carport. Jeff's Saturn tucked into a parking spot at the far end.

Tom snatched the can. No way.

You handed him a *Gung-ho Joe, Stalker Joe,* and *Duke* from the *Rise of Cobra.* Do your worst.

African-American Adventurer fit perfectly into the exhaust pipe. Tad artfully arranged *Gung Ho* and his team into a cone-shaped Tower of Babel.

I'll keep a lookout.

When he finished, you soaked them in lighter fluid. Their plasticine skin shone, their uniforms darkened.

Milk, he whispered. Dude, this whole place might go.

That end of the carport—definitely. The whole thing maybe. The building, no way. The flame radius for poured liquid gas is tight. Maybe a window cracked. If Grandma Adele were here, she'd say don't get your panties twisted up. Here goes.

You skittered off towards the apartments shushing Tom. You hunkered under windows, scrunching along to the second of four windows and pulled yourself up to peek through blue curtains.

A boy, maybe six, balanced on a chair reaching for a low pipe on stained pink cotton candy walls.

You dropped and stepped on to the next one, adding to the story in a whisper. Whole freaking Ontario, Canada man, it's all a burial ground. What we're doing is perfect.

Not me. Tom leaned against the building and then hunched down into the snow. I'll wait in the car. He covered his face with his arm.

Dude.

It's not me.

I just wanted to—.

No way, man.

Home. A woman screamed. Home.

Your mom. Tom stood up, listening. His fingers gripped the sill, the blood squeezing his knuckles white.

You peeked too. Big plants on a dining room table shielded him. A woman's arm propped open a front door. The side of Jeff's head and his blue checked collar were in the hallway.

Sess' ... The rest garbled.

BAM! BAM! BAM! A pounding shook the windows and walls. You dropped down. Sess ...

Somebody thumped and pounded walls snarling and growling, doors slammed.

You pulled yourself back up to get a look inside. The little boy stood in a corner, his back to the wall.

Home, Jeff, home. That's your mom.

Tad shot off, first. Then, you.

Out front, a city plow groaned lifting its shovel. It pulled away rumbling over packed snow.

You caught up to him. Dude.

Man. This is all—.

You pushed him back towards the carport. If I can take it, you can take it.

No, no, no.

What am I, man, if I can't even stand up for myself? For my mom. You dug out your lighter.

This isn't right. His face had twisted and lost focus. Nobody stands up for my mom.

Bodies were stampeding downstairs towards the back door twenty feet away.

You got the lighter next to *Talking Adventure Team Commander*'s pocket. And clicked. And clicked. Again. Again. Shit.

A ticking growled in from an electrical box attached to the carport. It sped to a hum.

Tad snatched the lighter from you, shook it, and clicked. It took. A thin flame gently gnawed first in yellow, then with a blue-green core. The Commander's pocket and then his life-like beard ignited. He lit *African-American Adventurers'* pants in the exhaust pipe. The flame devoured the little cotton pants. Run.

Tad shot back to the car slipping and sliding. You caught up, ducked into the car. A mound of flames engulfed in black smoke snaked up to the Saturn's trunk.

Tom had *Marine Joe* in his teeth. Not *Marine*. He threw it into the backseat.

Jeff'll guess it's me.

Go, go, go.

You stole, headlights out, into the night.

'S not about your mom, Milk.

He cuts into her, Tad. You drew a finger up and down your gullet. He hollows her. It's like the land out here, cut and hollowed out from First Nations to plant their bones and pave over for Wal-fucking-fart.—

He flipped the radio back on.

The scales got to get re-set, Tad. My life is a burial ground. I am the Black Creek Drumlin. I am an ossuary. I'm surfacing.

Tad tightened his lips. That doesn't make it right.

Sessy

Sessy shut her eyes to the fluorescent hallway lights. That bitch had a good chunk of her locks in her grubby mitts. Pain tore at her scalp. Cap that cow. Breathe. But, him. Him. Jeff caught her by the elbows, and lifted her by the forearms, his mouth ever so jagged and askew. He could read the text of her eyes: the years, the doing without, the mop-hole in the centre of her face. He must love her still. He has to.

He twiddled her blonde wig to his thigh and dug at the office-style plush carpet with his heel.

A brackish stain bloomed into the threads, mushrooming and buckling the rug at the wall. Near the door, the weave had split into bruised worms of fray.

No unknowns are woven there, Jeff. No hidden wisdom under your heel. She longed, oddly, for that heel to squish her throat. She longed for the full weight of him to force the truth of her into the open air. She, as split and frayed as that carpet, longed to gather the pieces of her life. If she did, she might speak. But her mouth didn't work.

He let go of her arms and flipped the wig to her.

Sessy's knees ballooned with air. She put one foot forward. And, then the other. And, then the other. An exit door loomed at the end of the hallway. She hobbled towards it, pulling herself by the gloss white walls. The walls were acres of snow field—now blinkering with a muted orange flicker.

That buffalo felched. 'She's faking, Jeff.'

'I don't think she is, Patricia.'

Oh, she was not faking it. Didn't he see that he was taking the wreckage of what was left of her and throwing it to the hounds of a flitting desire? Didn't he see that despite peeling her orange and shoving Milk against the wall that she she she would in a heartbeat take him back? Didn't he know that actual true grit and spit love heals all? If there's one thing she had learned, it is that letting go cuts a girl from what *is,* from everything she knows but that a little demonstration of tenderness, of vulnerability, opens a gully through which love can flow. Sessy collapsed against the wall and then to the floor. The thin blinks of that flickering light reached for her. Some galaxy ricocheted at her from far far away.

'What an actress.' That she-goat leapt past Jeff to stand over her, jabbing her finger at Sessy panting on the floor. 'What a car crash.'

She fluttered her eyes to focus. That blinkering orange cosmos beckoned her.

She had been a girl when it happened. Out walking the dogs. A cinder landed at her feet. A vertical rectangle flickered on the side of the neighbour's house. Her parent's room on the second floor flicked orange-yellow flashes onto the Dennison's house. She raced inside yelling *FIRE, MOM! FIRE!* And her mother raced upstairs before herding Sess' and Uncle Louise back from the flames. *Go, go outside. To the curb, git Sessy git*—she tripped and fell down the stairs and Adam, coming out of nowhere, pushed her at first and then dragged her by the arm out the door to the other side of the street and when she looked back her mom wasn't anywhere and before she could even think about it she started in screaming *Mom* and soon enough the sirens could be heard from far off and then louder and as they were getting closer, everyone mumbled *here they come here they come here they come.* A blanket came around her. She pulled the blanket closer and shook her head. She pretended to shiver. She forced tears into her eyes. She covered her face. She moaned some.

'Faker.' Patricia poked her with her foot.

Sessy slapped at that sow's leg and pulled herself up. 'Fire.' She flung herself down the stairs, shoving open the door and beheld the Saturn in glorious flames. She moaned, for sure. But now she clasped her hands and wailed. She shook her head and threw herself side to side. She giggled. Holy cow. The flames chewed into the car's hood. Heat burnished her cheeks. She spread her arms to the joy in her belly. Burn soaked into the skin there. A grin plastered on her face. Her boy to the rescue.

Jeff came around the corner and through the doorway, he stopped in his tracks. Entranced, he inched forward. His mouth fell open.

She guffawed now, slapping her thighs and clapping her hands.

Jeff threw the wig at her. 'It's not funny!!'

He shoved past hurtling himself towards the flames, shrieking, 'Oh, cripe cripe cripe.'

Oh, Milk'd done it. He had really done it. That's her boy.

He wheeled around to her. 'Your son! *His* G.I. Joes. Your. Son. These are effing G.I. Joes! They're on fire—.' He snatched at the tree drooping low over the carport.

Obviously. She howled.

'HE'S BURNING MY CAR.'

That did it. Sessy threw herself at him, tearing at his belt. 'You don't know that—.' She growled and hissed, cornered and feral. 'You don't know.' She knew. 'You don't know that that's him. You don't know what you know.' But she did. 'You always blame Milk.'

'It's the "Desert Storm" one!' Jeff darted towards the fire but hopped back from the heat. 'They're melting. Look at them. The arms are shrivelling, they're stumps. That head, the real-life hair is on fire. My car is on fire. He wants to blow me up!'

Oh, to be blown up. To be reassembled. To be riddled with fracture, to be held together by a strong thread. Frankenstein never had it so good. To be sewn with care, love, and kindness.

Jeff straddled the carport's support pillars pulling himself up and muttering incomprehensibly. The flames caught the tree trunk now, blackening it.

'Honey, get away!'

He spun around the pole not two feet from the fire.

'Get away from there!' Jeff would hurt himself to spite her and Milk.

He leapt up to reach the branches and leaves. 'It's fuel. Got to get rid of the fuel.'

'Come down, Jeff. Don't die.' She is the fuel. He is the fuel. Milk is her gasoline.

He-who-brought-her-from-a-tree dropped to the asphalt, pulled a folded canvas tarp from somewhere and began pounding the flames chewing at the hood.

That slop cardamom gorilla squatted next to her, chewing the side of her hand. 'What kind of kid wants to blow up his dad? He ought to be put away.' She stood up. 'What kind of monster—?' She pushed Sessy. 'What did you do to him?' She got a hold of Sessy's neck and yanked her head back. 'Your kid's trying to kill people. You people are insane. Nuts.'

Damned straight. Sessy snarled. Her cheeks warmed. Go ahead. Snap the neck.

The burn bloomed up now licking at the carport roof.

A fuse box exploded. Jeff hopped back.

Then that man from the front door returned, tearing out of the building with a fire extinguisher shooting foam. The Joes hissed and sizzled in their writhing.

A bitter chemical stung into Sessy's nostrils.

Landing on the flames, the foam evaporated until even more piled on, and then so much more that the flames suffocated.

Mr. Fire Extinguisher yelled at Jeff, 'Get a shovel. Get something. Get that plastic away from the car.'

Jeff found a snow shovel against the far wall and scooped the hill of sizzling G.I. Joes out of the way.

The blackened car smoldered. The engine wouldn't blow.

Jeff wept.

Sessy fled to her car. 'Don't think you don't deserve that.'

Jeff folded his arm over his face, crying. On the porch, he gripped the doorjamb for dear life staring at her.

Patricia had crawled back into her cave.

Sessy dug her crispy nacho chips from the glove box and ripped the bag open with her teeth.

Jeff ought to go back inside. He didn't have to stand out there on the porch all totem. He don't have nothing to prove. He'll freeze to death. She gouged for dried gum under the seat lip. Stop standing there, Jeff. Save yourself. Go to the Patricia whom you love so well. Leave me on the rocks exposed to wind, sand, and weather. Go.

She shifted the Tercel out of neutral and gunned it. And then revved it some more. A cloud of exhaust ballooned out of her back end. Breathe that, suckers. She had tipped the iceberg of loneliness to expose her devotion.

If Jeff wanted to gawk, she'd give him something to gawk at. He'd come back now. He'd be too shocked to resist.

The Night of:

Ton'

Crawling up Church St., iced leaves crunched under the cruiser's wheels. Ton' held his breath. And held it. Like being underwater. Like being locked in a stink-funk squad car just to get delivered to a blackmailing man-fuck suck-bottom queen. He clawed at the gummed-up window button. The glass crawled down, wheezing. Freaking cold. 'You reek, man. That curry.'

'Curry is my toothpaste, Ton'.'

'Man. That is—.'

'It's my deodorant.'

'Nah, nah, nah—.'

'Stop with the ethnical harassment, Anthony.' He adjusted his cornmeal-coloured Dastār.

'Do not call me that. Do not name-ically harass me. I'm dying in here.'

'It's curry, Anthony. It gets in clothes. The dead pigs-dead cows in you I have to smell.'

'Whatevs.'

'The flesh you eat rots in your gut.'

'Man. You don't stop.'

'Put a piece of meat on the sidewalk in August, Ton'. That's your insides.'

Jesus.

'Eat yogurt, Ton'. Kefir. That dead meat rotting in you. That's why you're getting fat.'

'I'll tell you what's fat.' Ton' grabbed his crotch. Christ Candy-ass-falafel-chick-pea-eating-lentil-curry-spit-prick.

Bloated clouds lumbered up Church St. looking for trouble.

What bible says Ton' has to wipe ass, stew curry piss-stink, and get called fat?

A gaggle of smokers huddled under the heat lamps at Hair of the Dog. At The Vibe next door, guys lined up waving sparklers for a Q-Weiner Fest. And there he rocked it. Julio. Stalker. Silver shorty shorts. Sparkler in hand. Pirouetting on a parking meter. Sees the squad car, and jumps up like a schoolgirl. Fucker. Man. He looked good. Very good. Damn. Streetlight refracted off Julio's aluminum neon crotch. Shit. Groin meets thigh—muscled, taut, edible. Fucker-fuck-fuck. Julio shot that leg over the parking meter and lowered it perfectly perpendicular to the sidewalk. Stalker.

Ton' swiped at the dash. 'They don't clean the units right, Officer Sinha.'

'Julio cleans up, though.' Shafiqq slapped Ton's thigh. 'Who?'

The flock of fags fluttered. Julio landed his leg at the curb.

Shafiqq tooted the horn. 'He's got it going on. Eh?'

The traffic stopped. Ton' sunk. 'What. Evs.'

Julio clicked on the glass. Shafiqq rolled down the window.

'Oh, Papis, it's so cold out here. My shorts.'

'You drinking, son?'

'*Si*.' Julio flashed the Canadian national flag painted on his fingernail. '*Solomente uno*.'

The Ontario provincial shield was plastered on his thumbnail.

Ton' hit the window button. Shafiqq's window rolled back up.

'Papis!' He fluttered his fingers. Every single remaining fingernail a different provincial flag.

Shafiqq hit his window button. The glass rolled down. 'Julio's cool. Aren't you cool, Julio? Nice nails.'

Ton' punched at the horn. Twice.

The limo ahead of them blinked its brake lights.

'Papi. You used to like me.' Julio poked his face.

That fuck talked right to him. Jesus.

Julio shot his whole arm in the window, reaching across Shafiqq's chin and wiggling the Maritimes: New Brunswick, Newfoundland, PEI and Nova Scotia in Ton's face.

'Back off.' Ton' slapped Julio's hand. 'Don't Atlantic me.'

Shafiqq tapped Julio's forearm reaching across his chest. 'Sorry. Officer Gonzalez is undercover.'

'*Si. El sabe. Yo sabes muchas*, Officer.' He gave a thumb's up with a fleur-de-lis. Quebec.

Fuckin' Shafiqq probably googled his phone number.

Julio leaned in further. 'Don't make me want to.'

Fucker fuck fuck.

'Want to what, Julio?'

Ton' fingered the veins in the door panel. He had to pee.

'There appears to be some unspoken something between you two.'

Julio passed his tongue over his teeth. And stood up. Time to break up the party. 'No. There's not.'

Julio twiddled on the door rubber. Shafiqq pressed into the steering wheel.

'Dude, let's go. I got to pee.' Ton' squeezed his thighs.

'Hey,' Shafiqq called to Julio, 'Excuse—.'

'Don't.'

'Can my partner use the loo in there?'

God damn it.

'*Yo lo espero.*'

'I'll bet he does.' That's all he needed. To get cornered in the loo with that kid and those shorts. Man.

'*Papi, tienes muchas problemas.*' He rattled off Manitoba, Saskatchewan, Alberta and the red inuksuk of Nunavut on his left hand.

'*"Muchas"*, eh?'

Faggot probably videoed them at the Grenadier Greenhouse. He'd YouTube it. Ton' ought to pack those shorty shorts with a little bag of something-something. The fucker dug his thumbs into his silver panties.

'*Ay, Papi. Y yo espero que tu no tienes muchas muchas problemas.*' He traced the squiggly line-cutting tree from the tundra in the shield of the Northwest Territories.

'What. Evs.'

His fucking peach pecs spilled into the window.

Ton' lunged at him from his side. The fucker tripped and bit the concrete.

Shafiqq held Ton' back. 'Chill out. Assault, okay?'

Ton' sat on his hands.

'Go inside before you piss your pants.'

Shafiqq unlocked his door.

Ton' popped his door, got a good footing on the ice, kicked that big ass limo ship ahead of them and planted himself next to Shafiqq on the sidewalk.

'I will come with you if Officer—.' Julio didn't know Shafiqq's last name.

'Sinha.'

'If Officer Sinha comes.'

Great. A piss party.

Ton' got the third urinal. Shafiqq took the first. Julio, the middle.

Man, bro'. 'You like it right in between, don't you, kid?'

Julio pulled the front of his shorts down. Nothing to sneeze at. Shafiqq hid. Chicken.

Julio let loose a good, strong stream.

Ton' cut loose.

Julio blew a firehose.

Shafiqq finished up, didn't even shake his thing, washed his hands and leaned against the wall.

'Nice show, eh?'

Julio blasted. Ton' trickled.

'*Papi, no quiero nada.*'

'You.' Ton' shook himself at Julio. 'Don't talk to me.'

'Ton'.'

Julio's stream still pounded.

Ton' didn't take harassment lying down. 'How come you got PEI and New Brunswick on one finger, huh? Where's your accent? You were all *eso es* at the Greenhouse. *¿Tu me recuerdas?*' Ton' zipped up.

Julio's water cannon showed no signs of stopping.

'Those are not actual insignia. Nova fucking Scotia and Labrador-Newfoundland can't get one fingernail.' Ton' stepped back to the urinal. He squeezed.

Julio's fine, thick stream pressed on.

'Jesus.'

'Esta nada.' He flicked a pinky nail. *'Este lo Yukon, mijo.'*

Ton' 's got a couple of drops out. 'Man.'

Julio shook, stepped back, and pulled up his silver panties.

Shafiqq snapped his fingers 'Guurl, you two have an unspoken conflict.'

'Don't, Shafiqq.'

Julio got a dab of hand sanitizer, rinsed and propped the door open with his boot.

'A'ight.' Shafiqq stepped over Julio's boot. The door squeaked close.

Julio adjusted his shorts and puckered his lips in the mirror.

Goddamn, Ton'd take a slice of that pie. He got right up behind the fucker. 'You got me all self-conscious out there.'

'Be nice, Papi.'

Ton' got a cheek in either hand.

'You remember, Papi. The first night in High Park. You remember what I told *a ti?'*

'Hot.'

'No, Papi. I mean I did it.' Julio Ontario'd his Adam's apple in the mirror with his bird finger. *'Tu ne me recuerdas.'*

'I do, too. I remember.'

'I am in you now, Papi.' Julio fingered his belly button. 'Got me a beer. Your hand on mine. Touched my forehead. I am in you.'

Heat flooded the back of his neck. The restroom probably didn't have a lock.

Ton' pulled Julio's shorts down. 'You looking for trouble?'

Julio caught his hand.

But God gave Ton' two hands. One slipped in between Julio's thighs.

Julio softened. '*Tu y mio*, we trust each other.'

Ton' dug in some more. 'No videos, okay?'

He pulled up his shorts. 'Your wife, Papi.'

Aw, man. Not 'Schelle.

'*Si. Ella.*' Julio turned Ton's chin. He had to see himself in the mirror.

The scar on his arm shined in the skin light.

'Schelle lunged again and got his face with her nails. She spit at him. He ran for the couch but she leapt with all fours—a cracked-out baboon. Squealing, snarling and gouging. She tore into his scalp, her tears spattered his forearm. She got a good chunk of meat from the muscle there, blood-smearing his T-shirt. She swung her arms like they do in Mama's church. People hollered in tongues and swayed back and forth.

'*Stop, 'Schelle.*' Don't move.

She dropped to the floor hammering the carpet. '*You can't, you can't, you can't.*' She spun into their bedroom. '*The IVF might've stuck, Ton'!*'

The bedroom door stood ajar. Her footsteps thumped. Back by the bed, he bet. He listened. One step, two step. He bit his shirt collar. The floors didn't creak. He didn't do nothing bad. Like he'd hurt his unborn baby.

Shit. He put his service revolver in the lockbox. With live rounds. Man. Think, Ton'. She could get the piece, tip-toe to the door. Bam. Shit. Sweat flooded his neck and clavicle. He got his back against the wall out of the line of fire. He made a very, very—very—light tap. He's not perfect. One misstep. One teeny human error.

Like, there's no genetic test for chlamydia. She didn't know. Not really. People get it on toilet seats. It's hers, probably. Like he even ever got one STI. Okay. One. *One*. That once in high school. Okay, so what. Twice. But just gonorrhea. Everybody gets that. It doesn't count. Two times. Right? Right. Okay, maybe sort of. He couldn't remember. Like how does anybody remember 'how many times'? Life is getting dirt under the finger-nails. Okay. Like, he had to live.

There's every good chance it's her fault. She probably caught it in a panty store. Trying on G-strings, thongs, and the V-Kinis. A lady's yoo-hoo leaves skid-mark heebie-jeebies. Fuckers. Threatening their unborn chil-dren. Now she's going to blow his head off for an infec-tion she brought home.

He rapped harder on the door. *"Schelle.'* He turned the doorknob. Slowly. Here it comes. Call 54 Division. Get the SWAT team. Turn the handle. Do it.

He slammed it open. Bam. The drywall cracked and crumbled, pieces tumbling inside. He dropped to the carpet. Stay low. Duck. Ladies be batshit crazy. One last moment on earth. A short hallway separated the door of the bedroom from the larger area where the bed, dresser, and the window stood. He peeked into the room.

The corner of the window curtain wiggled in a tiny breeze.

After, neighbours might say how they had heard the boom of the gun—they'd probably think it's a door slam. *They didn't seem like those kinds of people,* they'd say after.

Blood spots from his arm dripped onto the cream carpet. Red blooms. He stayed low.

'Schelle sat on the bed. Her arms pressed into her forehead.

Bedspread clean. Floor and dresser—all clear. Maybe it's behind her.

He could leap, knock her out flat, and snatch the gun before she did.

He got himself around on all fours. Ready to jump.

She held that old crud tear jar to her cheek. A dribble of tear collected at the lip falling inside. She put it between her knees and pressed her arms to her chest. She gulped. A sort of chirp-squeak erupted. Another tear came. She let it flow to dangle from her chin. She wiped it with the back of her forearm. *'We're one more in a long line, Ton'. I thought we were different.'*

Ton' crawled to her. *"Schelle."*

'Don't "'Schelle" me, Ton'.' She squinched and turned away. *'Don't.'*

'I just—.'

She wouldn't look at him. *'I told Mom I don't need this jar. I'm an asshole. Stupid.'*

'Not stupid. 'Schelle.'

Before he could blink, she back-handed Ton' into the wall. Man. The bone in his good cheek throbbed.

She smiled some. *'I got your number, Ton'.'*

In the washroom light, the scar from that chunk of meat shone slick. Julio wrapped his arms around Ton's waist.

Outside, Julio bowed to Ton' and Shafiqq. He winked at Ton'. 'Bang, bang, papi.'

Fags. 'Aren't they something, Shafiqq?' Ton' fun-sucker-punched Shafiqq, getting back around the limo and into the front seat. He slapped Shafiqq's thigh. 'You got to show 'em what's what.'

The traffic wasn't even moving at all. That boat limousine, bigger than a Town Car, blocked them in.

He got in front of Shafiqq and hit the horn three times. 'What is it with this freaking ship?'

Sessy

She could give Jeff a ride. No. Let him walk. Milk comes first. He'd know right where to find her. At home with her photos.

Hurtling down Eglinton, her chip-stained finger tracked the long, spongy scar running up her gullet. Starting at the slice above her yoo-hoo up to her too-da-loos. These days, they sew folds on the inside feeding a garden hose down the esophagus. She sucked her finger dry, still feeling the press of the blade through the anesthetic. Nothing more than a poke that left her gutted wide open flopping around like one of those big bass Uncle Louise stomped on in the bottom of the row boat.

After the surgery, things went smooth sailing for the first few years. She had the drill down to a science. She'd eat to the point of needing a poo, but instead, she'd upchuck. Washroom upchuck never fails. No need to be a party pooper. Eat what you want and boo-da-loo down the loo. That damned Princess Di gave upchuck a bad name. If God makes you a fat pig, then eat like a sow and puke like one. Mothers pass the goods to their daughters. Thank you, Adele.

Her mom got hold of Sessy's hair and pushed her to her knees in front of the toilet bowl *Lean your noodle in there*. She got her fingers down Sessy's throat. *Like that. Like your tummy's upset.*

Sessy lowered her head just past the brim. *Mom—.*

Get low. Don't mess the rug. Adele leaned against the sink and poked two fingers into the back of her own throat. *Do that.*

In turn, Sessy taught her friends how to stay thin. Most of them already knew. But the proof is in the putting. Take Milk's friends. On her towel in the backyard, she'd get up on her elbows just enough to show off the nipples her Maker marked her with. They could barely contain their little pee-pees. She would, very slowly, draw lipstick across her lips looking in her compact. They would peek. She leaned up a little higher on her right elbow. They'd giggle. She'd keep lifting. A hush fell over them. Nobody likes a fatty.

One day she lifted up and goll-darn-it her waistband pinched. She let the belt out a notch. And then another. And another. And another. She bought a new swimsuit. Black is more slimming. No amount of puking seemed to work. At home, she took to wearing sweats. She wasn't no show pony. The gold chain he got her got stuck in the skin of her neck. She killed it. And nearly killed herself.

That scar carving up her belly got its start with Jeff reading the paper and thinking maybe she ought to try this new surgery they had. Bariater-something.

No, it is cool, Sess'! He shook the paper. *They just bypass your stomach.*

Wouldn't a person, uh, die?

Uh, no. You still get all the nutrients you need, they make you a little pouch or something. You take vitamins.

Men are always finding new ways to cut up women.

Sess'.

Tell me, Jeff. How come they don't ever think up ways of cut men up—?

This is for every—.

Yeah, yeah, yeah. You know three men got it just to hoodwink one-hundred and forty-six thousand women.

Not everything is a grand plot.

Don't be too sure. You're not a writer.

Don't look a gift horse in the mouth.

She sucked in her stomach as far as she could and went to re-tie her sneakers. She put her foot up in the chair, instead. Fine. Jeff had a point. *Okay. You paying?*

I will. He laid the paper in his lap. *But Sessy, my love. It could kill you. They say there's a risk. 2%, at least. Maybe higher.*

You're late to the party, Jeff. I watch Oprah. I have done my research. She hadn't read a word. *Don't think I don't think long and hard about it.* She had never thought of it before in her life. *Maybe it is time.* Maybe she'd be in the 2%. Jeff neatly folded the paper and squinted.

Fine.

He stood up. *Sess', I love you whatever—.*

Oh, sit down. Don't get your panties all tied up.

She took the Roux-en-Y; the one as common as macaroni & cheese, according to her doctor. Like skinning a rabbit, her guy got his scalpel and cut good. The blade lifted the skin, the gristle peeled loose. There glistened layers upon layers of melt-in-your-mouth pot roast. Pure marbled fat. A stem to stern gutting. They divided her bowel and stapled the stomach to the size of Barbie's cocktail clutch. The two ends would recognize each other and lock in a leak-proof seal. A little less chomping and a little longer in the sun and the lard would disappear. And it did. Fast. She fit a size two by Thanksgiving.

But, goddamned that fridge loomed. She bought truckloads of food. Starvation drove her to Metro over and over. Now, she couldn't tear herself away. Suzanne Somers, Weight Watchers, and not to mention Oprah were in complete agreement about how to shop to keep the chunk off. She would start in Meats reviewing her list widening her stance just enough to feel the cooling draft blowing from the meat bins tickling the inside of her thighs and up the back of her neck. Hit the fruit and vegetables, side-step the film crews to snatch an eggplant, she'd put her bum to the vacuum-packed ham and Selection pork cutlets. Something fishy went on back there with all that movie-making at the Metro. She didn't care. Next up came pizza pockets, pudding pops, frozen blueberries, Ore-Ida hash browns and 3-for-1 9" pie crusts. Frozen pizza, tortillas, corn dogs, pasta poppers, oysters au gratin, oriental chicken souffle; and breaded mozzarella sticks packed with protein. Get the yogurt cakes with lemon poppy seed for fibre. An apple spice cake; a Carrot and Apple, too; Chocolate, White, and Gooey Glazed Love Cake with caramel hazelnut filling cinched the deal. Stuff and boot, baby. What she'd give for one of those right now.

Getting gutted is no cakewalk. A few months after the procedure, she safety-pinned one of Jeff's socks to the other in the basement, but her gut wrenched throwing her into the washing machine. A dry heave and a slam down. Oh, no no no. Not now. She could not die now. She'd gotten so thin. Sixty pounds left in the dust bin of history. The concrete floor cooled her cheek. A tear opened in her pinkish scar.

A centipede tip-toed around her face. It studied her. Her efforts were all for naught.

The floor seemed to coagulate into a mattress; swirling, perma-chill memory foam.

The insect's antennae tapped at her nose.

Air stop-gapped at the back of her throat. The back of her neck seared fire. She pulled herself along the floor, flat except by the drain, to the bottom of the stairs and then, one stair at a time, she heaved herself up to the kitchen landing. Maybe she could get a grip on the linoleum, maybe she could snatch at the phone above. Her hands and shirt were soaked. Reach, tighten, drop. Two effing stairs separated her from the kitchen phone. Clenching her teeth, she got a hold of the top stair and hauled herself up. Damn. She landed—and screamed. Her slit gaped open, her chompers open wider than ever. A flood of eggs, toast, yogurt, blueberries and the two waffles she ate for breakfast flew from her throat splattering the cupboards under the sink. Seven undigested blueberries dropped to the floor in tiny rivers of fat-free vanilla chunk chowder.

Milk thumped fast into the kitchen. She gripped his foot for strength. He inched close to study her. The stink of Safeguard and lavender whirled up her nose. She grunted. He stood up. Not moving his foot, he spun around and punched out 9-1-1. Milk held the phone while they asked her to say her name, which day of the week it was, and what was the Prime Minister's last name.

That ding cost her two days of her life tubed up and spread-eagled in the hospital.

It was the anastomotic leakage that got her. Her bowel dripped at the seam feeding abscesses on the walls of her abdomen. Gastrojuice seeped into the stomach cavity. They gutted her again but this time left her open to heal inside out.

Back at home after the carport explosion, which may or may not have been caused by Milk, she took the stairs one at a time. With the sting of burning G.I. Joes in her nostrils, the storm of history stopped. Photos. In them, she found her bearings. She got one of those albums from way back in Nebraska. From way back when. She got the one with her grandparents in it. Grandma Jean had shelves of them.

She peeked out the front curtain. Tom Meuley's limo or a taxi bringing Jeff could come at any moment. The computer dinged the first notes of *Nothing Compares 2 U* and she snagged the honey wafers and chips from under the bed. She'd sit tight and thumb through memories. Jeff'd come crawling home soon, maybe. Milk'd have to lie low in his bedroom with his efforts to blow them all to Kingdom Come.

The desktop appeared with its snapshot of her, Jeff, and baby Milk. Taken in Milk's first year, Jeff dangles his son by the collar of his onesie with one arm while the other hooks Sessy around the neck. She pushes Jeff away with one arm but reaches to Milk. Sessy stopped chewing. It's right there. Hiding in plain sight. The years of her marriage were no more than a Grab & Go market aisle of danger and hate. She should have known better. She should have protected her boy. A pressure burrowed into her throat. She withdrew her hand from the chips and studied that baby's eyes. The same ones she looked into this morning slicing lemons. That kid sees things with those pig eyes born of a million fathers before his own. She didn't deserve a child like that. She snagged a handful of chips and fed them into her chopper. If only the people in the photos could help her. The worst thing about modern life is people got to figure everything out for themselves. Back in the day, you could ask a Grandma Jean, an Uncle Doo or a Pistol for advice. Now, she had the photos.

The dead posed there cobbling themselves together around the dining table spitting tobacco chew and playing *Aggravation*. They pulled lawn chairs into the shade, their burgers smoking on the grill. The men poked their heads out from under car hoods, the women cut up tomatoes for canning. She knew well and good that her dead, ever so skillful, could help her set Jeff right and keep Milk from his claws. The dead have seen it all before and long to be called forth to tell their tales. She tucked into the loveseat with Grandma Jean's albums.

Sessy came from a long line of lovers and blunderers. The well from which she was drawn is bloody and the apple did not fall far from the tree. Seems back then in Nebraska, they only ever took photos in front of that old pigsty-fence or on the porch. In her family, lovers get left behind. Madeleine, Grandma Jean's mama and Sess' great-grandmother, in her frumpy, black dress with white pansies, her arms folded just under her tits hanging so low they practically raked the leaves. She still had her teeth. That means the early thirties. Still, every single one went down fighting. Everyone looking for trouble. The stories are in the pics.

Madeleine hanging on a fence, biding her time. She followed more than one man down around the bend in the road. The first time she divorced her husband Pistol, she broke his heart, took their daughter (Grandma Jean) and married another man (with five kids). Pistol threatened to walk to Omaha and throw himself off the bridge there. It took three years, but she relented, ditched the good dad, and remarried Pistol her one true love. But what's good for the goose is good for the gander. Pistol took a turn at the rodeo and fell in love with a hotsy-totsy. On his wedding night, their daughter (Grandma Jean) found her mother hanging from a roof beam by two hands; a noose around her neck. Being nearly eleven, Jean cut the rope and Madeleine dropped into her arms. By midnight, Madeleine had downed a couple of shots of family good stuff, collared Pistol in the parking lot of his honeymoon motel, and beat the bejesus out of him. She patched him up, kissed him on the forehead, and sent him back to his new wife, Hotsy Tots.

To spite Pistol, Madeleine married a third man. She ditched him right as Hotsy Tots left Uncle Pistol. Pistol and Madeleine married again. But wandering hens don't stay long on the farm. Madeleine got a job far away at Pontiac Motors in Detroit. She left Uncle Pistol and headed east to better times and better days. In Michigan, she met a Dutchman, fell in love with him, divorced Uncle Pistol, and spent the next few years working the assembly line and taking Dutch's fist to the gut and the side of her head. Sessy traced the picture of her great-grandmother Madeleine on a motorcycle in those Michigan years. Her smile bares her fangs giving the cameraman a run for his money. A hard worker, she soon bought a house. She sent for her daughter, Jean, to join her. She divorced the Dutchman.

By then, Uncle Pistol's third wife, a preacher-lady, found God for real and begged Pistol for a divorce. By the 1960s, towards the end of their lives, Madeleine and Pistol stumbled back into each other's arms and remarried just before Alzheimer's kicked her noodle for good. They did their best, from all accounts, to make life hell for each other for what time they had left. In her family, Life has a way of bringing all the loose threads back together. It'd be the same for her and Jeff. And Milk. She had to believe that. She turned the page, dug for another wafer and that's the last thing she remembered.

Milk

The night deepened. You made your way back towards the downtown Core. Bursts of streetlight ignited Tom's forehead. He chewed the inside of his cheek. And yammered. To Tom, the whole night seemed like slipping through a Parisian arcade. Like Victoria below Adelaide to King. He says in Paris, you see the name *Passage Brady* or *Passage Vivienne* brass-embossed in the tile, embedded in the sidewalk. And, what you see is what your attention is drawn to: iron and glass-wrought tunnels of stores; stamp shops next to knick-knacks; next to Indian places next to Gaultier next to D2 in a 19th century railroad car; moss crawling up—there'll be an angel with her arm outstretched; dripping walls, snaking cracks; wood shutters up where the sex workers hang their wares. And you know what they're reaching out for?

Clientele?

Where do you think I got my *Magasins des Desir* idea? Pimps rope customers once they enter, once you're in, you can't get out—. Tom pressed his feet into the mud rugs. *Les passages* started legit. As rain shelters for opera-goers, but desire likes the dark. Dens of sex workers, their pimps, ne'er do wells of the *demi-monde*. But guess what their parents and maybe even grandparents grew up listening to—.

Moans and groans.

Les Bateaux des Mortes. Which went on for decades. Where do you think the catacombs came from?

Underground? He did not want to talk about exploding carports.

Thirteen centuries from when the city started to the Revolution they dug limestone from under the city to build palaces and stuff. But, they never replaced the stone. Thirteen hundred years go by, guess what happens? Boom. The street opens. Literally. Whole streets, whole blocks even fall into the earth. Buildings drop. It's over. Carriages ka-boom; wagons, people walking their dogs—the ground opens, one massive yawn; boom. In they go. Starts at Denfert, into hell right? To Montparnasse, up to the 15th. And, they don't tell you this in the display, it's at the same time that pamphlets and posters are getting plastered all over with Marie Antoinette getting it from Shetland ponies and Russian Wolfhounds and the Germans, of course, and the Treasury is getting emptied —know why?

The Americans.

Exactly. What Americans forget today is that the French, Louis XVI and Marie Antoinette, at the urging of Benjamin Franklin and their very own Lafayette, emptied the French treasury to support the American revolution.

If things are collapsing, it's usually the Americans.

They're shovelling cash to the Americans with one hand, and digging out the earth under their feet with the other. Pay for one revolution, cause another. The ground fell out beneath them. The King orders a study—.

But.

There's thirteen centuries of people dying in Paris. Cemeteries, and I am not yanking your chain, literally start exploding. Bodies pouring, putrefying, oozing, flocculating goo-gunk slime, decaying heads and skin and all kinds of crap, bone plus don't forget you got all the horses and cats and dogs and anything that just like here in Toronto were just loaded into a big pit and it just stays there decaying, smelling. Summer comes in flies and maggots. Winter comes, and it freezes. I mean. You know. Think like your mom's mincemeat out on the side-walk in August. Thirteen centuries of cemeteries pour into the streets and come out of people's basement walls. Total ooze-fest. The smell, you know, smell that. Out here all you can smell is gas but think what those people were smelling. And breathing. People massively sick. Typhus, all kinds of crap. So the Prefect of Paris orders that no more burials in Paris. But people are still dying, right? People don't stop dying because of an order. So, official history don't tell you this either. They burnt bodies in dese-cration. They had to. None of them got proper burials. *Homo sacer,* man.

I don't know—.

The ones burned without prayer are cast-offs. Excluded. Unworthy right? They can be killed but they sure can't be sacrificed. They're exempted from the nor-mal rituals. The Prefect gets the idea to move the bodies of some buried nuns popping from their graves to where they'd mined out the streets. In that limestone. They reinforce them, in the bones go. It's a massive project. Takes a decade. The nuns are just the beginning. Wooden wagons start rolling through the streets of Paris carrying the dead, all hours of the night, ghost ships to the quar-ries. *Les Bateaux des Mortes.*

Les bateaux des mortes/sont pleurées
le chanson des vivre, le cri des mortes/
ils ont sonnais, la trompette a announcer
leur passage, ils m'ont passer
ce soir, ils me porterons demain——.

Is that a real song?

Does it matter? *The boats of the dead are crying, the song of life, the scream of the dead, they're heard, the trumpet announces their passing, they're passing me tonight, they'll carry me tomorrow——.*

Wicked.

The sound, Parisians at the time all remember long after it ended; wagons creaking and rumbling over the cobblestones, getting pulled out of mud pits——. Years and years this goes on. Decades. Thirteen centuries of bones and bodies under the city. Think how those wagon wheels echoed into *les passages,* all of that iron and glass, they—

The 427 got closer. He grit his teeth and cracked his window.

Take this to the D.V.P.

The D.V.P.'ll be crawling like ants.

Get off at Bloor.

You two weren't any different than those ants and beetles you used to catch and burn under a magnifying glass. Your pincers burnish first, purple then orange, and ignite. Your insides roil from your mouth and asshole until it is just your brain, singed from its edges, lifting the wire for your mind to flee. Your insides evaporate in a teeny puff of vapour where once throbbed moist scutellum. You ducked into the right lane towards the 427.

Crossing the path of a cement truck that would kill you as soon as look at you, a bough of streetlights passed overhead. You've been on the lam your whole life. Tonight's no different.

⬤ Once when you were stacking in his book closet, Mr. P. rapped on the doorjamb and caught you sneaking his Max Weber, the father of Sociology. He said he'd be in the Teachers' Lounge. Your heart caught. Barf.

Don't have a knip-shit, Milk. You think I put you back here just to stack books. Don't be so sure.

You had *The Protestant Work Ethic* tight in one hand. The fluorescents blinkered revealing the outlines of hundreds of dead flies.

He took the *Ethic* and thumbed through it. *I ever tell you about my friend from Cambodia? You want to know about no-objective-scientific-analysis-of-culture check out my friend from Cambodia.*

How come he shook you like that? How come he could see the hoax of who you are? How come you wished to run for your life?

Take a breath, Milk. He chewed his thumb. *The worst thing that can happen to any of us is that we die. And that can't be so bad. Everybody does it.* He messed your hair with the fat of his hand.

Black hairs poked from his cheeks. His Old Spice reached your nose.

Some of us come into the world, Milk—. We come in thinking we're interlopers. We've snuck under the barbed wire and got to get to the other side before getting caught. But we keep running. And running. Read Hume. People like you and me mistook resemblance for shame. Mimesis for guilt. Care for crime. Read Heidegger. He eased the Weber onto the shelf. *Don't let me get all heavy on you. Let me tell you so the story doesn't get lost. True story. A student from Cambodia. Two thousand years ago, in the mid-90s, I took extra hours teaching. Harris's reign of hell era. Advanced English. And this student, Asian. Maybe Cambodian, maybe Vietnamese. As kids, we saw these people on TV with the Americans causing trouble over there, we got to know what they look like. You know, Pol Pot? The Khmer Rouge?*

No idea.

Hitler'd run from these guys. Pol Pot's enemies were people he considered insects, bugs, rats to be exterminated. He systematically set out to kill every last enemy: six-year-olds, a mom fleeing with her toddler, some dad pawing at a rice paddy. They were a virus infecting, polluting the sanctity, the pureness of his people. That ought to sound familiar from Smith's class. It's all Jim Jones. Slaughter as liberation.

That you knew. Guyana.

This student named Rose. Nice guy. Rose's family, one night, they're sleeping. It's late. The moonlight coming in. His mother curled on her mat snoring. Khmer troops tromp in. The village knew that stomp. His mother bolts, drags Rose out of bed, he screams, he pleads, he kicks. She wallops him and puts her hand over his mouth and her own. Drags him out back, throws him far as she can into the jungle. She heaves a squash after him. He finds it and holds it waiting for her and his dad and his brother and sister. He sits where he landed and listens to all of the screams and shouts coming from in front of his parents' house and he said that before he even knew it he'd backed up so far that he almost fell into a ravine back there. Echoing things to come.

He sat there on the edge. Not a peep from the village. Whispering. Little heads bobbing in the bush. No words, they creep, stay low, go farther and farther back into the jungle. Never been that far. A hole once where they used to throw birds and lizards into is back there. They'd chase wild boars to fall down into this hole. A deep pit. A root cellar, like. Count ten trees into the bush and make a hard left and there it'd be.

The class bell rang. Students circling the door would drain into the room, thundering with *get-off-mes* and *whassups*.

Ignore that bell. The kids drop into that hole. To wait. And, they wait. It's in the earth, right, they can't hear anything. A cocoon womb. They pulled a bamboo camouflage roof over it. A Tupperware container lid, you know? Sometimes, they didn't come back for those animals. Just left them to rot. Methane, hydrogen sulfide, carbon dioxide, nitrogen. Loose lid. A ladder thing dug into the walls but rungs had come loose in the rains. A few are stuck in good. They huddled in the deep. And, it's not a big hole. There's like 20 or more crammed into it down there. They are all crammed in there, tangled, arms, legs, hands in the other's faces, necks. And so the kids are in the hole, quiet enough to hear their breathing, they're in the earth, right? And then, Rose said, it got even quieter. Kids covered their noses and mouths, not because of the smell, which you'd think, but to hear better. Not one of them made a peep.

Out in Mr. P.'s classroom, kids began charging in. Desks scootched, windows squeaked open.

Mr. P. leaned back into the classroom. *The A.C.'s on, Baxter.* Mr. P. fake yawned. *Never. Gives. Up.* He signalled for the students to hang on.

The next morning, they wake up. A little light got through. They're lucky that gas didn't kill them.

Mr. P. stepped forward and lowered his voice. *He dreamt of Major Anthony Nelson. He remembered that. You—oh, forget it.* He turned away and then turned back, hopeful. *You don't know* I Dream of Jeannie, *do you? Jeannie? Blink-blink?*

He had folded his arms, one on top of the other out in front of him. *Blink-blink?*

He mock threw up his hands and lowered his voice. *They got out of that hole. Imagine. Walking through the trees; a jungle. He said it wasn't the skin and legs hanging. It was they'd recognize someone's bracelet, a neighbour's head or a hand cut off—you know you imprint and recognize these things even strange parts of people's bodies that separated, identify. The smell, too. Not like the hole. Different. Pleasant. Out in the open, the insects hadn't gotten to the bodies. So it couldn't've ended too long before. He said it was like walking into a butcher's shop. A melon and metal smell. Maybe 'cause they were so hungry. They all get together now out in Vancouver or somewhere for reunions. But the smell is what they don't ever talk about. Nobody does. How good the fresh meat of their moms, dads and neighbours and aunties smelled. How—appetizing. 'Appetizing,' he said.*

The bell rang again.

He leaned into the classroom. *Right with you. Read 95, the first two sections. Pop quiz in 20 minutes.*

Groans. Someone lifted their desk and let it slam back down.

Mr. P. turned back to them. *Baxter, that isn't serving your cause.*

He ducked back to you. *Those kids lived in that jungle for two or three years. They weren't the only ones. Hundreds, probably thousands of kids stayed alive out in the jungle. They all lived together out there. What do you think Max Weber would have to say about that? They get together, these kids, they find each other. They get themselves food and shelter. They make rules, build shelters. They did all of this because even though a force wanted to exterminate them—they knew that they were not insects, bugs, or rats.*

What happened?

Found. Refugee camp. A good number made it out. To Thailand. Germany, the U.S., Canada. I remember Rose 'cause of that story. That 'smell' story. He had the thickest German accent coming out of this Cambodian face.

You hadn't eaten.

That's isolation, eh? Sometimes you don't know what you're here to do until you meet someone astonishing. It wakes you up.

He gave you a hug and wrote you a late slip.

The 427 landed you on the Gardiner East, off at Jarvis. Jog over to Church and head north. Cruise through the Village. There might be something happening with the gays.

Sessy

She blinked. At the bottom of the stairs, her forearm wore the wafer box. If she had the strength, she would push herself up. She nudged her knee. Stiff. Half twisted onto the foyer tile and the living room carpet. How long had she been here? The last thing she remembered, she had boxed up the pictures and photo albums. She had dug for a cookie. But then—poof. She listened. The fridge hummed. A car crunched past. No creak of Milk's floorboards. No tin hammering of Jeff's REO Speedwagon.

She didn't think she was dead. To prove it, she smooshed her face deep into the living room carpet. The odours of the living. Jeff's peppermint foot rub. Milk's lavender oil. Orange juice from way back when. The wreckage of history, their lives in smell. The echo of lived life, of love, of crushed hopes and anguished dreams. There had to be a science to smell, there had to be some math behind it. Smell is just another word for Tupperware and nothing left to lose. It captures the broad fields stretching between molecules of odour where imagination dances.

But wait. All of those times on the road, perfumed by piss and pizza, back and forth, being with her mom and

Uncle Louise here in Toronto, and going to visit bat-loose crazy Grandma Jean Sloan in Lansing, Michigan. In her unconsciousness, she had just been there. She closed her eyes. Maybe she would just stay here on the carpet.

━━ They had been passing Vaughan and then again after crossing the border and heading south. Old Grandma Jean Sloan held her bladder—a real bank vault. Sessy could not. No matter how she complained, Grandma forbade pee stops. *Girl, don't you even think about it. Into my house and onto my sheets after oozing around on some infected public toilet.* She handed Sessy a Folgers can from under the seat. Sessy steadied the can between her legs and braced herself on the door. And let it rip.

Soon enough, the Ambassador Bridge reared its blood-orange horns over the Detroit River.

Don't it look like pliers turned upside down?

The bat winged pillars of the bridge flew against a bruised sky. *Sure does.*

The closer they got to the border, the more Grandma's breathing tightened. *Just what he asks. No nice-nice. Facts. They're American. They twist anything into story.* Leaving the United States terrified Grandma Jean. *I just feel safer on American soil.*

Sessy knew enough to keep her mouth shut but oh to be kept out of the United States. To be so lucky. *We like living in Toronto—don't we?*

Oh, wouldn't that be the end of the world. Me, in that place?

There's nothing so bad about Toronto.

Everybody's face is stuck. They don't feel nothing, Grandma complained. *Where's the piss? Where's the vinegar?*

Grandma had a point. Adele, Uncle Louise, and Sessy had a semi-detached next to nice High Park. *That's about what I'd call those two*, Jean called it like she saw it. *You don't get to put a dress on and know what it is to be a woman. You don't just buzz your head and put on a flannel shirt to be a man. 'Semi-detached' is right. They aren't never getting free of who they are.*

Grandma fiddled with the radio dial. Static buzzed.

That Canada wouldn't do for me. The government pays for everything. I work for what I get.

Static scraped the insides of the speakers.

To have everything handed to you on a silver platter. Free this, free that. That ain't human. Going to the doctor every day just 'cause you can is a waste of money. That's why they moved over there. You grow up, you promise me to do right by me and make yourself American.

At the border booth, Grandma rolled down her window. She held her driver's licence out with two fingers.

The man in the booth looked at Grandma, and the car and then spotted Sessy. *That your daughter?*

My daughter!?

Your granddaughter?

My granddaughter?!

Ma'am—.

Just funnin' you. This is Melissa. We call her Sess'. Don't judge her by the pee on her shirt. Canadians never learned her to hold it.

Purpose for your going to Canada?

My daughter lives over there.

Where does your daughter live? Is that your granddaughter?

Toronto. Yes, yes and yes.

Nice city.

Some say so.

Is your daughter American?

Excuse me?

You heard me.

He—ha ha! Grandma loved to get bullied by her countrymen. *She. Sure is.*

Why doesn't she live in the United States here?

How much time do you got?

Sessy would watch her grandma chew her lip, glance at her, and settle what to say.

Let's just say it doesn't suit her.

It is a free country.

It is, Officer. For the time being. Some of us are proud of that.

Good day, Ma'am.

Some of us, she might say taking her licence back, *are willing to die for it. Right, Sess'?*

But Sessy didn't answer. She and a black crow on an orange pylon were in a staring contest.

Grandma'd hand the licences to Sess' to put back in her purse. Off they'd drive, straight into the bowels of that demon. They did have Sir Pizza over there. Grandma had gone east from Nebraska a hundred years before to work at Oldsmobile in Lansing, Michigan. While Grandma worked, Sessy couldn't go outside because the blacks might get her. Malcom X had grown up there and his daddy died there under mysterious circumstances just down from the Capitol.

Sessy did, though, have her own room with pink pin cushions. And, after Grandma went to work, she'd call up Sir Pizza and then lie flat on her back downing one slice of pineapple pepperoni pizza after another. As long as she didn't move much, she could leave her pizza boxes yawning wide on the quilt cover, roll to her side groaning when it got too painful, and then, keeping her stomach tight, force herself to chomp every single slice and crumb before Grandma got home. Then in an whirlpool flush with vomit, she could collapse in the clutch of retching and cling to the toilet's porcelain. Her face grinding into the pink fur bathroom rug, reeking with the stink of Grandma's pee splash and her own puke, she got as close to being an American patriot as she had ever been or ever would be. But the raw physical torture of being in the U.S. had a history: one that Sessy did not quite register as it unfolded.

She vaguely remembered sitting on the front porch back in Lincoln, Nebraska with Adele, her mom. Adele had just sat down after peeing in Grandma Sloan's flower patch. Sessy watched the pee sprinkle the wildflowers chosen some for colour, but mostly for their names: *Bouncing Bet, False Boneset, Buffalo Bur, Beardtongue, Snakeroot*. Her mom had Sessy's hand in her free one. *Pee left to right. You soak the roots that way.* Come midsummer, she peed in the flowers to balance the soil. *With the pollution, you got to keep the pH right.* A couple of wolf whistles didn't deter one drop.

Sessy's mother, Adele, and her father, Uncle Louise (née Louise), were outlaws or as they liked to say, 'gender refugees.' Facts suffice: Uncle Louise (née Louise) birthed Sessy. Adele (née Adam) gave the sperm. She'd also given the sperm years before for Sessy's older half-brother, Adam. He was the product of an unfortunate encounter in the Fontenelle Forest but one she would never deny. Adam fell in love with a poet that may or may not have gotten lost in the Vietnam War. He followed suit and may or may not be kaput. Uncle Louise, then, was Sessy's bio-mom, but her dad-dad. Adele was her bio-dad, but her mom-mom. Way back in Nebraska, her parents spun tales of female Revolutionary War soldiers crossing the Potomac with George Washington, lady Civil War soldiers suiting up with yoo-hoos plain as her own and Amazons with breastplates broader and golder than Cleopatra's birthday hat. Amazons were lady warriors all right but they were, above all, Radical Ladies who didn't fit into the common mould. Cutting your titty off for a better draw of the bow isn't for sissies. *Wonder Woman had it going on,* explained Uncle Louise, rubbing snake oil into where one of his breasts used to be. *But that is not, trust me, what kept Captain Steve Trevor in her game. You just wait 'til I tell you about the Radical Ladies.*

Adele folded her arms and stomped her feet some. *Tru-u-st me. Everything, even pee, washes away.* Her mom hitched her housedress and settled on the porch next to her. A parallelogram splintered through the ice tea to the spindle sidewalk slit. Adele stretched her long legs down to the third step. Sessy got her shorter ones just past the first. They would lean back on their elbows, cross their ankles and soak up the sun.

Sometimes people don't know what to do with other people, Sess'.

Couldn't we move to a place where it's for sure?

It's as sure as sure gets. The best bet you get is the best bet. Where you want to go? Florida or California or China? Getting there's the easy part. Close your eyes.

Sessy did.

Imagine we drive into town, okay? In the Impala. All your car sick has it smelling all gut goulash. Her mom'd goose her. *Let's say it's someplace we could afford down there, like the panhandle of Florida.*

What's the panhandle?

It's a piece of Florida down there. Jacksonville. We roll into town. We look for a house. Now you know, I walk into a room. My voice being what it is. I am just who I am, okay? Uncle Louise, his voice is what it is. We just are who we are, okay?

I can see someone, a lady, showing us a house.

And is there a gaggle of people behind her? 'Cause I can guarantee there will be a gaggle of people.

I don't see a gaggle.

Do they come up to us?

I don't——.

Do they say hi or give us their names?

Okay. One does. One man comes up and says hi and he's glad to have us.

He's glad to have us. That's nice.

Can I open my eyes?

Just wait. So where are we going to live?

I don't know, Mom. I don't see.

She did, though, see Mr. Owser ogling her while her mom and Uncle Louise got settled in Toronto. Sessy had to stay with bat-nut Grandma Sloan in Lansing and Owser lived next door. His name became 'Owser' 'cause that's the sound Sessy made over and over when he first fiddled with her. Sick to her stomach, she hung on for dear life. He scraped her into the carpet, burning her cheek and knuckles. She kicked at him with everything she had, but he'd clamp his hand over her mouth and hold her down. In these trying times, she imagined pretty Queen Elizabeth, her good and gracious Queen.

Owser'd come on her face, wipe her cheeks and fore-head; get the gook from her hair and let her gorge: Hostess pies, big thick slabs of chocolate cake, caramels in crunchy paper. The forcing down wasn't so bad if she could stuff herself. He'd get his arm around her and hold her too close, asking *didn't all that taste good*. That's about as good a difference between the U.S. and Canada as you could get: one had *Yoo-Hoos* that just kept com-ing, the other Queen Elizabeth with a smile that never cracked. Sometime around then, Adele taught her to upchuck. *You got worms,* Grandma Jean said.

Tonight, Sessy squished her cheek into the carpet —and had a flash. Her gut guided her compass. Its radar pinged from one craggy rock to another, distin-guishing one isthmus from the last. Not the molecules but the feeling. Not by science but by force of will. Now, at the bottom of the stairs, she ground her knees in and burrowed further in the green shag. She pressed the side of her face as flat as she could. The bits there dug into her skin. Eggshells, dirt particles, and cookie chunks; punches, slaps and hits. Boulders of bread crusts, the pointed tip of pins, and the hair strands of care; the groping, the poking, the holding down; the strong arm of a woman and the remains of an aspirin. Come sum-mer, a trail of ants. She pushed into the emerald weave and hauled herself to her feet. Jeff. Get him.

She thought of Milk's pillow away, upstairs, in some foreign land. She thought of that Scott, the kid who nailed her at Metro, wandering aimless, crisscrossing traffic and dodging street bums. An avalanche rumbled like at the HSCAN parking lot. All bets are off. All at sea. Nourishment. Jeff, oh, Jeff. She did not know the road that had brought her to a shag carpet clogged with the shipwreck of their lives.

Wobbling to the kitchen, she took a slug of soymilk. So good. A spoon of peanut butter could do. Protein works. She took another slug. And popped a couple of olives. She squirted a little ketchup on them first. You got ketchup, you need cheddar cheese. Cheddar cheese with a slap of peanut butter washed down with soymilk and a couple more olives with two squirts of ketchup. Those feelings of emptiness withdrew. Her stomach hung low now squirming with ballast. She got on the horn to Magic Oven for pizza.

Her thoughts unfurled. Her whole family soaked in the misguided shenanigans of lovers gone wrong and their wandering hearts. Oh, the pain they have caused. The sufferings they've wreaked.

Just drawing her fingers across the fogged photographed images of those lost souls could bring *family is family* to mind. Fiddling is fiddling. Family is a Mommy-Daddy-Me; a thing in the world; a mattering. It's right there in the pictures: Toronto: her arm lifted to throw an egg at the camera. Another one, same time: Milk toddling in the backyard. Another: Jeff squirting her and Milk with the garden hose. Family. The love, the hate, the spit. Family has scent. No cardamom-shilling Patricia smells like them. Jeff's bounce with a honey doesn't change blood and fact. Milk can get with Tom Meuley all he wants and she can lay all of the lemons she needs. No diddling's got a blade sharp enough to cleave them from her breast. It's physics. Hound-dogging don't mean a thing.

The doorbell rang. Pizza.

Milk

Outside of the city, the Green Belt got twenty centimetres.
Not on Church St.

Gawker.

Yeah. One dude lassoed another with a rope of red
hair—and tied him to a bike post. A whole gaggle of them
worked him free. A loner waving a sparkler tugged at his
junk in silver panties. He blew smoke rings from a long
cigarette holder into the mouth of another spread-eagled
on the hood of a car. The whole line of them went into
a can-can of high-kicks and sparklers. The silver panties
one lifts his leg straight up, clears the parking meter at a
full perpendicular to the sidewalk and suspends it mid-
air. Damn. With the ice and snow caving in.

That's called L2ET, says Tom.

L2—?

Living Life in Enemy Territory. Agility. He rubbed
his finger and thumb together, thinking. We should get
more G.I. Joes, dress them up and then pass them out to
these guys. They probably don't even know a Joe. He
pointed at some Edelweiss Heidi walrus packed into a
tube top fourteen sizes too small. Bitchin'.

They know G.I. Joe. His abs, man. You would have given anything to join that can-can line. They'd never want someone like you.

The dude with the silver shorts teetered over to a cop car twittering his fingernails. He leaned in the window. Dang.

Cops don't seem to mind.

Depends on the cops.

Those shorts chewed the dude's *cajones*.

The traffic snarled. Two toots behind and that cop car flashed its lights. Tom lit a stick.

Don't pull away yet. They'll bust you.

They're going to bust me.

You let the car roll forward.

The cops whoop-whooped their siren. And poked their noses out.

You steered to the curb.

The cop car wound in front, lights flashing—and passed by. The officer tipped a finger to you.

Couldn't be looking for you two. Nobody saw the limo parked by Jeff's.

Let them get ahead. Out of sight.

Dude, we're so not on their radar. After a few cars passed, you pulled into the traffic. It bottled again at Wellesley.

He flicked the rest of the spliff. Hang a right. Take Parliament up to Bloor. To the cemetery.

The sanctuary of concrete angels, St. James Cemetery, came up on the right. At the curb, Tad bolted from the car. Leave the limo, he called over his shoulder. He did a sideways kick at the padlock. It hardly budged.

You hopped over the curb and did your own best throw kick at the padlock. Nothing.

He shook it. No prob, man. He mounted the iron gate grate in a leap and swung his leg over the top. And dropped to the other side.

You clomped into a pool of cigarette butts, hoisted yourself, and dropped into the graveyard. The cold jiggied up your leg. Why we here, man?

Tad had disappeared into the ash tombstones brushed with lichen. Hurry up, he barked from somewhere in that grey-brack soup. It's cold.

You stepped into his tracks, getting your balance on mouldy tombstones.

Tad had climbed up hung from a stone angel's face. He licked her cheek before snatching a Canadian flag from another grave and wedging it into her mouth. There.

Lighting the lighter, you read the angel's podium: *Passed into the arms of our Lord, December 11, 1879.* Practically today. A streetlight glared through him into shadow.

He caught you watching, dropped to the ground and blew on your hands.

You're cold. He bared his teeth. Like that?

You tucked your fingers into your pocket.

We're like those guys in the 1920s—. He focused on another spliff, lighting it, taking the smoke in; one, two and passed it to you. No time to lay off.

You toked. The ember glowed. Grandma Adele loved to watch mosquitos fill with blood from her forearm. One, two back at you.

Tom took the joint. Leopold and Loeb, he said. They kidnapped and killed a boy just to see if they could. Saw it on TVO. We're like those girls taking bricks to their mothers.

We only blew up G.I. Joes. You both had to be thinking Ern True. What if you killed somebody at Jeff's carport? We're more Sal Mineo *Rebel Without a Cause*.

Right. Plato. The internet's got a million gifs of Sal on the museum steps getting killed. One had a purple thunderstorm crossing through it; another one, gurgling lava; another's with planets spinning; one with *Giant* James Dean in dripping oil staring at himself in *Rebel* staring at Sal Mineo on the steps. In one, Natalie Wood is sitting in a rowboat holding James Dean in her lap but she slips out and disappears in dark water. Another's got this re-enactment: Sal Mineo goes down on this guy in his garage but the guy stabs him yelling *faggot*. Your boot got caught by a fast-food bag.

Milk. Tom blew into his hands.

He ought to get to the point. It's cold in the tombstones. Dude, it's—.

I killed Mr. P.

A bus groaned to a stop out on Parliament. Its doors wheezed open.

He's in the trunk.

The bus doors exhaled. And closed. The bus coughed into action.

You heard the words he said but their meanings scattered. There's no connection from Mr. P. to Leopold and Loeb to James Dean to Plato to Natalie Wood to the waves to like here in the cemetery scenting with spliff.

Take a toke. I been holding this in all night. He passed the smoke back. He made me. Where you were waiting for me out on the Danforth. At the ATM booth. I don't even know what would've gone down if you showed up at the door.

Your fingers wouldn't come together.

He begged me. Milk, it's like all a fog; like a gushing from here—

Tom made these motions like shoving ocean waves away. He lifted my squeegee—I used, oh—Milk. Tom pressed his head into your chest. And then popped back away. I used one of the ones we soldered with two pounds. Why me, man? I made those to do a good job.

What 'good job'? What 'those'? Mr. P. put squeegees in the trunk, maybe. But 'He's in'—.

He just takes it and slams it into his own head. Over and over. Like so fast. No stopping. But then he's like stumbling and falling and reaching for me; clawing at the wall.

Mr. P. hit himself with Tad's squeegee?

I was just doing the windows thinking you know that it wasn't leaving any streaks, that we had something, that —oh Jesus Christ fuck me—that we could market them and—Milk, I couldn't stop him. No way I could stop him. Tad shook his own head in short, tight jerks. Bam. He—wrenches it out again. He's begging me. He's got my pant leg. Please. Please, he's saying. I couldn't. No way. But, then, I don't know—. I could. I had to. I took the squeegee. And I just did it. Tom's hands were up now as if in a bank robbery.

A pink plastic straw forked through the grit and snow.

Your mind took off; a flying saucer boomeranging out and back.

Another bus roared up on Parliament. Jesus. A cacophony. The ground shook. The trees rattled. Its hydraulic doors breathed open and then closed. It gunned the gas and pulled away.

Milk. Dude. Nod. Do something. That is not me.
You stepped back to get into light.

Not me. Not me. Milk. Do not be scared of me,
okay? Jesus Christ, not you. You—. He spun away and
plunged off into deeper snow. He stood aways off now
waving his arms at you. Go. Run. Get away from me. Do
not stay here. Go. Take the Bloor way out. Run.

Long before you made any decision to stay or go, the
earth had opened and you were grasping for a hold, sliding into a crevice; a crack; a crossing over to some strange
land; unknown and terrible. You leaned on one of the
stones. The mould moist to the touch. Plastic lilies, their
dingey yellow petals ashened in the grey light, sprouted
at the base.

A smell hit you. Mould to pesticide. Pond-muck to
Vanish. The same smell as Mr. P.'s house when you and
Tom helped him set up his wife's hospital bed.

Since you saw her in the hall before, Mr. P.'s wife, Ale,
had not done so well. Tad and you went to their house
to help him put together a medical bed for Mrs. P. in the
living room. She couldn't climb the stairs to the bathroom anymore and Mr. P. thought Tom could figure out
anything. *We'll log your time as your volunteer hours.*

To graduate in Ontario, you got to earn at least forty
hours as a volunteer.

But I'll pay you, too. On the down low.

Mr. P's house smelled sour rotten and nitric. He led
you through the dining room, where the smell got
stronger like it'd soaked into the clay-coloured linoleum,
and past a tall glass china cabinet in which you—there
she sat. Asleep in a chair. Her mouth hung open. Spittle
cake at the lips. Hair in limp strings like Grandma's.

Her skin the colour of your mom's green Halloween eye-shadow. Her legs veined, blotched in purple; thin and leathery. You folded your hands. Mr. P. must be her primary caregiver.

Mr. P. grit his grunge teeth just past the doorway to the kitchen. *I'm old. She's old.* He rubbed his hands together. *Sorry for the smell. The windows can't stay open as much with the weather.*

You two shrugged.

Tom nudged you to keep moving. You covered your noses past a stack of magazines and newspapers spilling off a dusty pipe organ.

Mr. P., What's your wife's name?

Ale. He reached out to muss your hair. *Thanks for asking.* He clapped his hands together. *Let's do this.*

Ale snorted a little in her sleep.

So. Whoops, shoot, uh—let's see—right. He half-turned and looked for a moment back into the dining room but then past the kitchen. *Right. This way. Through to the garage out back.*

Through the kitchen and out into the backyard. A large rectangular box leaned against the wall of the garage.

Above, like fractured ink spots, black-brown blotches arched up the sides of the garage door, across the middle, and down the other side. Berries.

Bats. Dried up. A phase. Mr. P. nodded up towards the square garage door.

You studied the blotches.

Dead. Long dead. Get close. They can't bite you.

Holy Toledo. Out of the blotches, spindly, dried legs, tiny claws and miniscule snouts emulsed from the wooden planks. Microscopic nail heads glinted from chicken wing thighs. Stretched out and away from their bodies, dark net-like wings stretched in futility. Your jaw hung open.

With one finger, Tad lifted your chin to shut your claptrap.

A phase.

And, said Tad.

Tell.

A thing. Call it religious. Call it an epiphany. You two of all kids know what an epiphany is.

You did.

We had all these bats. They'd be out here chirping carrying on, wild, darting around. Nighttime, going after mosquitos. Moths. Summer. So my daughter, 'Schelle, get it in her head that the bats're going to attack her, the dog, Ale. She—her mother has this jar. It is a jar of tears.

Tears?

Like tears *tears?*

Tears. Tears. Like you cry. Tears.

You could just see the bats flying and the girl crying.

She wouldn't stop crying about these guys, swoop-swooping up and down. Dusk time, especially in summer. So, Ale's got this jar of tears and 'Schelle would get so upset that she'd——. I get the bright idea if I catch a bat——. I got a bat house, you seen them? I nabbed the bats in there when they were sleeping and I tacked them to the garage, the ones I could catch. She could see those darned dead bats after they stop squealing and feel better. Only dead bats. All dead. All dried out. But bats are like tears and fears, they just keep coming. These are just some of the ones I nabbed during her whole growing up. Cats and raccoons like to nibble on them. They don't stink.

How'd you kill them?

Kindness. Mr. P. clucked, *No, I wrung their little necks.* He dug an instruction manual for the hospital bed from a plastic pouch tacked to the mattress. *Read?*

Do the tears stink?

Both you and Mr. P. looked at Tom.

Yes.

They say they're easy to assemble, with springs in there—The tears?

Mr. P. cupped Tom's chin in his hand. *The rails.* He let go and ran his fingers along the length of the crate-like box. *There's the whole nine yards—not the mattress, that's tomorrow. So ...* He went over to the far end of the thing and pulled it from its lean on the wall. *It's heavy. 165 pounds. More.* He tilted it back so that it leant back again. *So ... one of you get one end and I'll get the other. We'll drag it.*

Once all the rivets and pull tubes were hooked up and the casters on, you couldn't smell his wife or the house anymore. Like the bats. Weird.

At the cemetery fence, you both held the bars. You climb up there with him, you're in. You go with him that means you're complicit. An accessory after the fact. At the least, doing something with a body you're not supposed to. You'd figure it out. There's no way you're leaving Tom to handle this on his own. No way he did it on purpose. No way.

You pulled yourselves up to the top and balanced there. No dropping out. No going back.

Ton'

The storm barreled in from the Maritimes slamming head first into the pounding from Michigan. Atlantic wind is brutal. P.E.I., you don't muck with. Moncton ain't fooling. Don't even talk about St. John's. In a crueler world, a storm'd make folks stay home. But come bad weather, Toronto spills its guts: stabbings, shootings, assaults, suicides. He and Shafiqq better take another leak before all hell broke loose.

They peed over a crag of rocks spilling off the Spit. Shafiqq's dribble glistened in thin strings on the granite chunks. Seagulls blinked, shivering amongst steel cables.

Ton's piss obliterated the snow caught between the boulders. Volcanic, man. Fuck Julio. Out here, the stars can be seen. Out here, breath.

Geese burrow into the abandoned, homeless lean-tos. Shafiqq's man-funk stunk from the water's edge. Yuck.

Ton' had a talk with Lieutenant Jamarandu about getting another partner. How come he has to put up with that stink? Like what if he has a newborn baby?

'He's a pant pisser.'
'Shafiqq's a good cop.'

'*Every fucking night.*'

'*Easy.*' Jamarandu doodled on his legal pad. '*You racist?*'

'*We pee-draw our names in the snow.*'

'*You both got short names.*'

'*His is long.*' Ton' pressed his forehead into the wall.

'*Maybe you're the one that needs a break.*'

'*It's not a health and safety violation?*'

Ton' attempted to broach the subject with Shafiqq by taking a historical approach calling on the Great Dekanawida. Think of the First Nations, right?

Shafiqq had other ideas. '*Do not cherry-pick First Nations, dude. You think it's right to crunch somebody's throat with your knee. Making their head explode, or whatever you say.*'

Every cop thinks about that. '*I say "pop".*'

'*Ton'. Let me tell you something about the difference between you and me.*' Shafiqq nudged him towards the lake.

Ton' held his breath. The dude reeked.

The waves crashed into the shore. A goose hollered.

'*See those clouds, those clouds are stacked up like mattresses up there.*'

'*Same as my mama's fat rolls.*'

If only he could've disappeared into her. He dug into her torso with fingers, hands, and feet.

Mama rubbed his back. '*All and sundry.*' The mattress caved with her weight.

'*Smell the wild.*' She'd heave herself up and lean him out the window with her tree-trunk arms. '*Maybe it smells now just like it did back then. Back with those that began. Dekaniwanda.*'

The breeze squeezed in between their building and the one right across. She'd take the air in. Fill her lungs. Let it loose. *'Papi took me to sit in the tall grass. You and me'll smell the wild rye too before we're through.'* she said.

Ton' held his breath.

'You see those rocks out there, Ton'?' Shafiqq shook himself dry.

Here comes Lesson #236.

'You see those rocks caked in ice? Those blocks are lives, Ton'. Stories.'

Steel, industrial cables caught the blink of harbour lights in their coils.

'Those are what remains of desires snaking to the sky. That's human.'

'It's junk.'

'Man, dude.' Shafiqq knew better. Hell, even his dad did. Shafiqq's dad taught him that "The Spit," constructed out of discarded building materials from building Old Toronto, had transformed wire and cable and brick and concrete into dirt and plant, muskrat and rabbit, and wild birds chittering into and out of the rectangular houses enthusiasts like himself laboured to build and maintain over the decades so that what his son saw before him today would be a protected wildlife conservation and recreation area. Migratory birds, mammals and reptiles nestled amongst the construction dump trucks and Lake Ontario's pounding.

'Ton'. The ground we're walking on came from somewhere. Bricks, clay, stone, cable—Life. Kitchens, bathrooms, bedrooms like where your mom rubs your back; offices,

factories. People get us to now. The throats you want to jackboot hold our story. The Spit is a book, an encyclopedia —a text, Ton'. It's a page flipping into now, and then into the next now, your mom's grass grows on it—.' Shafiqq tucked his hair into his dastār. *'It's everybody's hopes and dreams that get us to now.'*

'That's 'cause you haven't felt hard rubber tread on a throat.' One more gulp of fresh air before in the unit and suffocation time. Right off the lake the cold, earthy air dug into the ears. The throat opened wide and got the wind in far, far as far back as muscle allows.

Lights blinked across the water. Rochester, New York. Heaven, man. Bet cops over there don't have to drive around in piss. They probably have rights. Torontonians need to learn that Peace, Order and Good Government comes from fresh air at the heel of a jackboot.

Sessy

Sessy cleared the living room carpet to the front door. But, as she flew, the vertical lines between her and the front door rose up to capture her. A cage. A corral. A prison of elevens. She froze. Up and down lines pressed into her from every direction. The two doorjamb mouldings, the three struts of the coat closet, the four machetes of wall joints, the walls needling the doorway to the kitchen—she dropped to the bottom stair and pressed her face into the railings. Prison bars, as tens of elevens, crowded in from everywhere. Oh, dear God. Somebody break her free.

The doorbell rang again.

A growing tenor of trumpets came inside of her. She knew that melody. Jeff!

When she opened the door, her stinking flesh fell to the tinkling of ivories. One loafer tapped its toe. Fred MacMurray. Star of stage, screen, and TV. Or was it?

Hello, Sweetheart.

This fellow was no ordinary Fred MacMurray. This Fred MacMurray tapped on the door moulding as "Steve Douglas," the dad, from the 1960s American TV sitcom *My Three Sons*. He's a widower with 'three' sons—get it?

Chip, Ernie and the older cute one. But this Steve Douglas-Fred MacMurray tipped a devilish fedora at her and licked his lips. "Steve Douglas" never wore a hat like that. Oh, she knew. She knew exactly who this was. This is a "Walter Neff" Fred MacMurray, the fall-for-a-dame insurance salesman from *Double Indemnity* (Wilder, Billy. Feature film. Warner Bros. 1939). This Steve Douglas-Walter Neff-Fred MacMurray popped the pizza box lid. But, no, wait. Since when did a Fred MacMurray of any kind have curled mullet strands? Jeff?

The tinkling fell away. This Steve Douglas-Walter Neff-Fred MacMurray could be Jeff in disguise. She drew back against the wall. Oh, please, please, please. Don't blow it. She'd have to play coy. He must be seducing her. A role play. Oh, baby. *Mr. Mac*—.

Call me Walter, baby.

Just 'Walter'!?

'Save the rest for later, Toots.'

'Toots!'

He leaned in close. *You're playing it real good, sweetheart. Real close to the bone. You gonna let me in?* He drew his finger along the length of her forearm.

A Steve Douglas-Walter Neff-Jeff could mean trouble. But not necessarily. "Steve Douglas" never hurt anybody. Who doesn't love "Steve Douglas"? The overture from the *My Three Sons* theme-song spilled out from the baseboard heating units.

Sing me the tune, baby.

'Da-da-da-da, da-da-da-da, doo-doo-doo-doo, doo-doo-doo-doo doo—.'

A rainbow of the dancing prison bars encircled them. In the show's opening, multi-coloured bars bounced up and down and then apart to open upon the episode's first scene.

It occurred to Sessy that she might be dead. This could be her heaven. With Steve's show being off the air so long, Walter Neff-Jeff delivered her to the pearly gates —her own front door. Steadying herself on the wall, she stepped back to see if her body still lay on the shag. Nope. She patted her tummy. Right here. All accounted for. *Yes, Walter or Walter Neff-Jeff. You don't mind if I simplify your name, do you? Please, come in.*

He stepped inside. *It feels good to be back, baby.*

She put a finger to his lips to shush him. *I vaguely remember you from another life.* This 'Walter' seemed more 'Jeff' than the other Freds—or the one Jeff, for that matter. She could kind of sort of make out her husband's jaw line underneath the stage make-up.

Walter Neff-Jeff pulled her close. He talked low and through his teeth and perfectly balanced the pizza. *Oh, that is my name, baby. You just remember, 'Walter,' baby. Forget about thems that pushed you aside. Forget about all those busters. Walter's my name. Don't you forget it.*

She yanked her arm away. He's testing her. This Walter Neff-Jeff is testing her loyalty to see if it's safe to come back home.

Your pizza, Mrs. Dietrichson. He flipped open the box with one finger.

Two could play this game. *Pepperoni?*

Just like you ordered. Eleven dollars.

Eleven! She got into his neck real close. Jeff's Old Spice. He could break her free. Who cares about names? What's in a name, anyway? *What is with the 'eleven'?*

Eleven, sister. One and one. Side by side. You and me, baby. It's a storm out there, Mrs. Dietrichson.

She lunged to him and pulled the arms that didn't seem like Jeff's at all around her. *There's a storm in here.* She moved his warm palm to her breast. *Call me Phyllis. I might explode. Don't make me explode. Don't—.*

He shoved her away, now vicious, now cruel. *Well that'll be fine, Mrs. Dietrichson, that'll be fine.* Now he stepped in close again, teasing her, toying with her heart. *Listen, baby. Pull yourself together. We're all going to go very carefully tonight. You, me, Uncle Charlie, the boys—.*

What are we going to do? Her knees wobbled. Oh, why must torture hurt so bad bad? Her fingers pawed at his unshaven chin. She smelled them. Life! She tip-toed along a very tall precipice. Family. Family, she repeated to herself. Daddy-Mommy-Me. Jeff-Milk-Nobody. Steve. Walter. She knew now. She could never be enough for any man. All she had is herself.

He pressed her into the shadows and into the door-jamb. *We'll get her too, see?*

Her, too? Who? What?

Her. That Lola.

Oh, she knew this game. He means 'Patricia.' *Her.*

We'll formaldehyde and truss 'em up in the trunk. Bound and gagged.

He certainly has come to his senses. She tore the curtain away and looked to his car. Uncle Charlie, gruff, waved at her. Sessy did not approve of violence. But exceptions prove the rule.

He gave a little sinister laugh. *Then it's us, baby. Just us. Justice.*

Her head swirled.

Don't sweat the small stuff, sweetheart. You'd be surprised how good old Uncle Charlie is with details.

Uncle Charlie sure keeps his cards close to his vest.

Chip and Ernie are good for their piece, too. I'll tell you, it's Robbie I'm worried about. Robbie—you may have to do a little work on him. He thinks he's a grown man, he thinks he's big stuff, he's a little slow, so you might have to warm the kid up. Can you do that, baby?

She couldn't take it. *Yes, yes, oh yes, my darling Steve Douglas-Walter Neff-Jeff.* But no violence.

Get your things. Let's go.

Milk

Maybe what Tad did to Mr. P. is like those assholes at Columbine or that prick at *Polytechnique*. Maybe Tom is no different. Or you. That carport went up in flames. Maybe it ignited the building. Maybe that boy in the window is charred dead. Maybe Jeff. Maybe your mom. Maybe you two are Ern Trues. Ask Smith. Ask Suong. Ask Mr. P.

Fucked-up Ern True dug trenches from the wall of his basement to the ravine under the Bloor Viaduct. A neo-Nazi with a hard-on for calculus, he ordered SS daggers from the Dark Web that had *Alles fur Deutschland* engraved in the handle. A *CZ Waffen 78* (snub nose) tucked into his belt. He had the Visa card and he got the gear. His parents capped his credit card monthly auto-payments at two grand. But you can get more than you bargain for with 2K and no questions asked. The True house stood behind Castle Frank TTC and the Discovery Walk at the Vale of Avoca ravine. Ern's parents mined the Canadian Shield for their driveway, walkway and fence mount re-dos. This required the leasing of a horizontal precision drilling machine with some vertical capacities and a work crew. Being a smart cookie,

Ern got the crew to teach him how to use the equipment. Two days after his folks ducked out to Europe, Ern told the crew the family'd been struck with rubella. The crew took the week off and Ern began drilling an escape tunnel from his basement to the Discovery Walk. A straight shot and he's in the ravine. This all came out in the trial.

Out on the school lawn that day, the fresh-mown grass mellowed in from the parking lot. Outside the classroom window, the seagulls were flinging old mac and cheese noodles at you, caked and pasty, into the air before dive-bombing and gulping them whole. They tore at each other and the noodles, going at each other's throats and when they got stuck amongst each other's wings, they flapped, pushed and kicked furious all the way to the edge 'til they had to lift off and fly up, thrashing their wings and cawing.

After third period, Ern True backed William Thibidault up against a locker with the snub nose at the centre of his forehead. William peed himself. Ern popped William, who dropped. "Nothing personal."

Somebody had just peeled open some of that new tropical fruit gleam gum, the gum wrapper crinkled, the pineapple scent hit you. Crack. Crack. Crack-crack-crack. Everybody froze. CRACK. CRACK. Everybody lunged. Desks jerked, kids ducked. Duck, drop, roll, run. You know the drill.

The air stung bitter sulphur. Get the classroom door. You dragged the new kid to the floor. Get the door. You scramble. Low-slung, back pressed into the wall. Sweat trickles from behind Jessica Needham's ear. The chemical pine lemon of Fogle's cleaner swirls with the stink of

gunpowder. That first round died off. Down the hallway, Ern is growling and heaving.

Mr. Smith tip-toed to an overturned chair to ease
Prank Tilter and Jessica to the ground. Once Jessica hit
the linoleum, she shot a scream almost drowning out
that next snap of gunshots.

Plaster dust floated in from the hallway.

Smith seized kids, yanking and dragging them by
the collar towards the windows. Wrong move. The windows were on the far side of the room, opposite the door.
In the direct line of fire. Phuong vaulted, jerking those
same kids, heaving them to the wall on either side of the
classroom door out of firing range. *Go, go, go.* Mr. Smith
windmilled his arms. *Go.*

Ern cracked a shot in the hall.

Smith whipped so fast to Phuong, his glasses flew off
and skated all the way to the windows. Suong, Phuong's
sister, hurried to catch them. Smith tore through the
door and faced Ern head-on. With no glasses, he didn't
stand a chance. *Put it down, Ern.*

Suong straightened up. Massaging the arms of
Smith's glasses.

In the hall, Smith talked low to Ern.

You black pig.

A crack and Smith came flying backwards back into
the room. He twisted onto his side. And then, writhing,
his huge weightlifting muscles pulsing in his back and
that yellow golf shirt flowering in a scarlet bloom, he
crawled, pawing at the concrete floor and gathering his
intestines now spilling away. With nowhere to go, he
straightened one leg and then the other.

Ern clomped into the room. His fresh-shined black jackboots flopped too big. He teetered under the weight of the gun. Ern wavered, but you did too. Your path opened.

"Do me, Ern," you wanted to say. "Kill me." This is it. You were born for this moment. To feel that metal in you. "Please, Ern," you'd say if you could make your mouth move. But you could not speak. Your legs stuck.

Tad leapt a desk and body-blocked Ern out of the room. He threw himself back at the classroom door and, somehow, yanked it shut. *Lock it, lock it, lock it.* Like the geese that day watching football practice with Mr. P., everyone lifted, fell, scattered and squawked. *Get down, Get up, Stand back, Move up, Move down, Take him, Do it, Don't.* Tad got the door locked and then dragged Smith, eyes peeled to the kids and clutching his gut, out of the line of fire. Ern landed at the door then, jerking and kicking it. He shattered the door window with the butt of his gun. He backed away. Quiet. Then he kicked the door. It held.

Jessica shook and spit. Phuong pissed a pool now inching towards Mr. Smith fading fast and heaved himself into the corner. Suong watched her brother's pee inch towards Smith. Being a pianist in training, she played imaginary notes up and down her arm and then dropped Smith's glasses.

Outside, seagulls alighted back on the dumpster and dabbed at lunch napkins.

In the hallway, Ern got fed up. He stomped and hollered, his boot laces snapping at the linoleum. And then, he returned. The rifle nose poked through the door glass, easing in and out same as a pool cue. He cracked a round.

Suong spun. The back of her head shattered spraying blood and skull across the windows. Her body landed on Smith's glasses. Her blood spilled onto the linoleum in a widening blossom. Phuong froze.

Ern rifle-butted the rest of the glass out of the door's window and got his face through. Shards of glass slit his temples and cheeks. *Yoo-hoo, I'm here, chicken fucks. Meet your maker.* He got the nuzzle through and sprayed the far wall with rounds. The hiker in the *Dreams Come True* poster took the brunt. Everybody flattened themselves against the wall on opposite sides of the door.

Sirens howled from way, way off. The gulls long gone.

Ern yanked at the door, shook it and kicked it more, good and hard. *Let me in*, he yelled. *Chinny-chin-chin.* He let loose and unloaded into the door.

Hey. Tad hissed and jabbed at the windows. He darted over to the far end of the room.

Ern worked his face back into the window, the glass bloodied from his cuts.

Tom got the window open, jumped up on the sill and stomped its steel pane down and flat.

Ern got his arm came through cracking shots with his Luger. Pieces of ceiling tile, chips off the desktops and dings when the desk legs got hit. But Phoung, out of nowhere, lunged at Ern's hand holding the gun tearing at it with his teeth.

Goddamn it, Ern screamed. And dropped the gun. Phuong kicked it away.

Come on! Tad motioned you and Julie Gietbaum, who'd been holding onto your thighs though you didn't even notice, to the window. *Get over here!* Nobody could move. *Move!* He scurried, whispering and incanting, *move, move, move.* Ern had pulled back out into the hallway.

The rifle came through the window again.

Tad lunged off the sill, pulled you close and heaved you at the window. *Go, go, go.*

You threw yourself out. Your shoulder bit the dirt and you rolled down into *The Pit* where the burnouts hang.

Melanie Hernandez and Julie hurtled through after and then Scott Heitz and Jessica. Phuong hurled through, his mouth bloodied and then spitting.

A whole slew of crack-a-crack-cracks followed. You dug your faces into the upslope. *Stay down, Don't look, Who's hit; Dude, Smith; Fuck, Suong; Ern True; Whack Job; Don't.* Julie spazzed, shaking, and elbowing your gut. You crawled on top of her.

Tad stuck his head out of the window above. *They got him!* His fist in the air. Julie threw you off and hurried back up towards the window. *Is he dead, did they kill 'im, did the cops come* and so on.

A SWAT team rushed at you, guns drawn. *Get down, get down, get down. Flat, flat, flat.*

You hit the dirt. Tad dropped out of the window and strolled towards the cops. *I think he's down, Sirs.* He shook out that golden brown 'fro of his.

On the ground. Now. One of them shoved Tad with a black leather glove landing him into the worn grass gulley where the rain had washed it out. He pinned Tad with his boot heel. *What do you want to get your head blown off, Curley?*

Tonight, Time itself came on. Rushing at you like a clear-cutting weed-wacker hellbent on taking out a forest. Getting on to eleven-fifteen by the time you got the limo out from the cemetery, atoms had shifted.

'K, we can't sit here all night. It's his body.

He curled a strand of 'fro around his finger. Dude, you got a hat in here?

You dug at the denim weave on your thighs.

Milk. We go now.

Your arm wouldn't come up off your thigh. The distance between your arm and the ignition key stretched for miles. Turn the key.

A wind carried dirt and moss, stink and mould through the cracked window.

Okay, Tad took the reins. Now. Keys. He lunged to turn the ignition. Give it gas. Now. Shift.

The foot wouldn't move to the pedal either. What a trip.

Now. Drive. Milk. Go.

You are disappearing.

Don't go whack.

I'm not even here right now. You dug the frozen leatherene steering wheel cover into your forehead.

I didn't like kill kill him, Milk.

The ceiling pressed. The doors squeezed. The floor mats rose.

You don't know, man. You do not know. Like——. I'm in there, Milk. Doing my thing. I'm jamming and singing "O Come, All Ye Faithful." I am in there jamming and——. And then, there's Mr. P. standing there. Right outside the ATM booth glass. Watching me. Like he's my reflection but the booth's window-glass reflection is laid over him like a Photoshop filter; the cash dispenser machine with its green light, the 2% interest signs. He comes around. Opens the door. He comes in. Tom stopped. He looked at you. And then at, like, the sidewalk or tombstones past the fence. But I gave him the idea.

Tom popped open the door. He hopped out onto the curb. You got out, too.

Tom walked to a telephone pole and then turned around and came back. He went to the trunk. He pressed against the lid and dropped to his knees in the snow and slush. I taught him. It's me, Milk. Maybe I did kind of kill him. Maybe it is me.

But you said—

The squeegee has a lead strip, right? You and me we welded lead to it.

The teeth of some turning gear clunked into place in your gut.

The streetlight glare cast the street into a blinking gold-orange filmstrip.

If you hadn't held that squeegee while Tom moulded the lead to it; if you hadn't held it while he melted the metal with the torch; if you hadn't scraped the lead into place before it dripped off—Mr. P. would be alive. He'd be right there with his wife.

Cemetery rot seeped through the fence.

Tom burrowed his face into his forearms. He just takes my squeegee—like he was surprised it's so heavy.

You took a step back.

The sound, Milk. How am I ever going to get that sound out of my head? Why did he do this to me? What did I do to him? I don't understand. Tom's mouth hung open. Who is going to like believe me, Milk? Who? I made the squeegee. No fucking cop is going to believe that. It just, like, stuck there. I froze, Milk. That instant—.

If you changed your orientation, Tom and you could spin into some other reality.

The snow shunted in then, pounding you into the car.

We just got to go. Go. Tom brushed at the gunk on his knees.

But where to. I want to see him, Tom. I have to see Mr. P.

Go look, if you got to. We might as well just sit here until they come find us. We might as well just call the police.

So. Let's call the police.

And what? Tell them I literally built the murder weapon. I did like what he wanted. Like, he kind of worked the squeegee, the rubber-leaded part out—that I put there, okay—. Tom whapped the window glass with the back of his hand. Jesus. We were in that closed-up little glass ATM booth and I kept the lights on. I shut my eyes. I know. I can't even believe like someone didn't come in. Boom, boom, boom. Then, like on auto-pilot. I dragged him out of there, I locked the booth and hit the lights. I put him out around the back, I got the limo and pulled him in the trunk. I don't even know how. And then I went back. There's a hose in the cleaning closet. Sprayed down the entire inside of the booth and then, me too, like my coat but outside. No one came, Milk. I put the limo on the street. You pulled up, man.

You shifted the car into "Drive." I don't need to look.

The body had to go somewhere. Eleven o'clock chimed in. You took the D.V.P. south past the check-points going north. Then Eastern as far east as Cherry and then South. Maybe The Beaches, maybe the Spit.

The Spit.

You shifted into gear and pulled away from the curb. Parliament heading south. Snowbanks whizz past. The tires crunch the ice and slush. A distillation begins. A tide lifts you from shore.

Sessy

Right out in the driveway the lights were spinning. Red. Blue. White. Police. Blink. Blink. Blink. No measure, no help. Sitting there in the back of a '70 Impala, she could just about make them out. Chip, Ernie, Robbie and old, grumpy Uncle Charlie. She didn't care if they saw. Know her. Hear her. Uncle Charlie tooted the horn. Couldn't she just have one little love-minute more with her man?

She flicked up Steve-Walter-Jeff's tie pointing down. *Oh, you. You.* That arrow shot her to new lows. Her gaze soared to the height of that torso, that chest, those shoulders—she could never taste enough. *Follow me, You.* Men are so so weak.

You're a real queen, baby.

She tucked him close and planted a good smacker in. *Spider, darling. I'm your Black Widow.* Don't tip him off. *You standing there all night with that pie or are you gonna show a lady how to eat it?* She dragged him to the kitchen by his tie. *Oh Steve-Walter-Jeff-Neff—whoever you are. You don't know and I can't bear to—.* She threw herself across the kitchen counter. *I can't take it anymore.*

Walter perched on the stool Milk sat on that morning and gently rubbed her back. *I'm here now, baby.*

Whyn't you have some pizza? Pizza'll do you good. You got to conserve your strength, Doll.

She couldn't stand it: it's too much, too long, too never-ending. *Oh Walter, Walter, Walter. You, too. I know it. You're just like all the rest of them. One long chug of heartbreak sucking the life out of me. Pedro in junior high. Craig in high school. Fifth period. What could I do, Walter? Love. I need love. Does that make me so bad, so cruel, so evil, so used? Tell me I am not used up, darling. Tell me, tell me, tell. Tell me that you are not like——.* She could barely speak his name. *Jeff.*

Oh, darling, darling, darling. Walter had slid a long thick slice from the box. It oozed roasted red peppers, aged Reggiano and extra-extra virgin, pure olive oil. He caught her hair and steered her face into the pizza. *Eat this, baby.*

That yeasty crust split her open so that she gulped every drop of oozing mozzarella. Her tongue found it first, darting out catching the littlest taste of sweetness spice nectar, that special Grecian sauce of crushed and sun-dried organic Cretan tomatoes stewed with old country parmesan and Mediterranean hillside basil.

That basil blooms once a year, and on steep rocky hillsides, baby.

But this annum it erupted in her mouth. *Oh, Walter, Walter, Walter. I want it all, give it all to me——.*

Easy does it, baby, easy does it. Don't take it so fast, darling, there is enough to last for now, for then, for eternity and as far as the horizon of your heart——.

Can't you just smell it, Walter? She did. The dough filled every fibre of her being. It descended into her, her throat rose to swallow——

The doorbell rang.

Sessy gripped the shreds of the pizza box. The doorbell rang, again.

She steadied herself on the sink. Walter no longer sat on the stool. She looked under the table and opened the broom closet. Gone. Where had Walter gotten off to? He's pulling something.

She lurched from Jeff's La-Z-Boy to the front door.

A gentle knock thundered.

She cooled her cheek on the steel above the doorknob. She turned the handle and opened it just a slit.

A police officer.

She recoiled. She looked to the top of the stairs. Peeked towards the back. Over the officer's shoulder. Uncle Charlie vanished. Chip and Ernie, too. *Robbie, oh, Robbie!*

The officer appeared to be working a seed through his lips. He spit and tipped his hat. 'Evening, Ma'am.'

Sessy curtsied.

'Is your son an "Evan," Ma'am?'

Oh, God. Oh, God. Oh, Jesus. This is why she should check to see first before opening the door. This is why she didn't want him to sign up. This is why. Oh, god. Just like in the movies. The ones where the War Department telegram delivery comes: *We are sorry for your loss.* Oh. Milk didn't even have a chance to get wounded over there. He was born to be wounded. Let him live. Wounded first, killed second. Oh, but no now he'd never take a bullet. He'd never live.

'Ma'am. There's been an incident.'

Oh, God. Oh, God. Oh, God.

Authorities did this to her mom and Uncle Louise once with her older brother Adam. It practically killed

Adele. A soldier with beautiful lips mistakenly delivered a telegram from President Nixon that honoured his work, dedication and ultimate sacrifice. The family got scribbled in there somewhere. Her brother, Adam, it said, got killed in action at Penong Yang. Oh, why does everyone have to go to war? What did the United States want with everybody else's business anyway? She couldn't remember it all. It had got so cloudy, so murky, so immersed in words she could not understand. The President had signed it, she remembered the signature. A short checkmark with a long tail. Like Kohoutek Comet but with a line through it. Like the legs of those goliath brown spiders on the Queens Quay.

Uncle Louise had clutched his wife's shoulder, held his stomach with one hand and waved the paper in the air with the other. Grandma Jean Sloan backed away from the soldier and bowed her head. Adele only nodded as if she were expecting it all along. But fortune favours fools; the telegram had come in error. As far as Sessy knew, Adam had lived past sixty scratching out poetry to his late beloved on a mountain in woods near Big Bear, California.

'Nothing major, Ma'am.'

Oh, how could this copper say such a thing? If it were his child, if it were the human being who had peeled the curtains of his labia aside to push his way through, if he had pushed night and day, month after month, year in and year out just to make sure he reached an age to fulfill his potential, if he had striven to buy organic day in and day out, to go forth and change the world—if that were so, this gentleman, this soldier cop, would not be so cavalier.

'A small fire.'

Oh. Now she understood. Patricia called the police. 'Officer,' she leaned in close so as to not be over-heard. She caught a whiff of Grey Flannel.

The officer looked over his own shoulders to the right and then the left.

'Just who called this in?'

'Oh, I am not at—.'

'You can tell me, Off—.'

'Actually, I can't. I am not at liberty to say that information. Ma'am, we want to know—.'

'If I know where he is, and I am not saying I do, but—.' Think, think, think, she thought to herself. Did this cop honestly think that she would betray her son so that that that Patricia could continue to infect her family?

'Ma'am. We've had a report that some folks saw a limousine near the incident. You know anyone with a black limousine?'

Milk comes first. No matter what. 'Thomas Meuley. You find him.' He knew his future. His dad could buy him out of trouble. Milk had only her. They couldn't count on Jeff. Not after he choked her boy last night. Not after the carport. He had nothing. 'Thomas Meuley. Find him.'

The officer kept his cards close to his chest. 'Continue.'

'Well, he certainly is an acquaintance of my son's. But distant. A *distant* acquaintance.'

The officer scribbled notes.

'M-e-u-l—.'

'Got it.'

'E-Y.'

'E-Y.' The officer confirmed.

"E-Y." Oh, God. Milk's life hung in the balance. She said too much. 'They hardly know each other. Not *really* really.'

'Is your son at home, Ma'am?'

'Home?' Sessy zipped her lips. 'No. Nada. Nope. Never.'

'"Never"?'

She folded her arms and leaned in close. 'You do not have teenage boys for kids, I can tell. Do you have children?' She had to demonstrate her maternal wisdom and experience.

'When do you expect him, Ma'am?'

'They do not stay home. Teenage boys gallivant.'

The officer tapped his pencil lead into his pad of paper.

'He is——.' Think fast. 'Swimming at the lake.'

'At the lake?'

'With his grandmother. Up north.'

'Up north?'

'Down south.' Goddammit. 'In Chile. A lake in Chile. It's summer down there. His grandma has a cottage in Chile——.' Oh, if she could just remember a city in Chile. 'Near Bogota.'

'Bogota is in Colombia, Ma'am.'

'Right. Well, you know——.' She tucked her arms in even closer. This demonstrated her precision and thoughtfulness. 'All those cities and people down there, they just sound and look alike sometimes, don't they?'

The officer half-shrugged.

'Well. Yes. My mother has a summer home there.'

'Nice.'

'Yes. Yes, it is, isn't it?' The officer bought it hook, line and sinker.

He handed her a card. 'Call me if you hear from your son, Ma'am. We got a few questions we'd like to ask him about this "Thomas Meuley".'

She gripped the card and showed him so. 'Got it.. Yes, Officer. Will do. Tom Meuley is a nice boy and it probably maybe wasn't but it could possibly be him that started your tiny small fire.'

The officer retreated down the sidewalk.

'Tom has a future,' she said.

The officer paused—and half-turned.

'You smell awfully nice this evening, Officer.' Heavens to Betsy, she had almost got the door shut. 'Goodnight.'

He skittled back to her. 'You know him? Tom Meuley? About his future plans?'

Oh! How come her gums had to flap that way? 'No.' She dismissed the thought. 'No, no, no. I was—.' Think fast, sister. 'See. I was. Well … I went to see, see? At the Main Office at school. One day, the way you know how you *know* know?'

The officer tipped his hat back.

'The truth is that I went in there after the shooting, right? I mean wrong. Ern True? I'm sure you recall that. Those poor kids. Well, I am at the school, you know, just checking in, see? After something like that, you just want to make sure that the school is doing the bare minimum, that security measures of some kind are in place. Implemented, right? Since when are children running around with guns and ammo? Since when do almost grown-up kids shoot up the place? It makes no sense how that could happen.' It made perfect sense to Sessy. People can only take so much. They get pushed beyond the fence posts of *right* and *wrong*. At that point, they will do anything to survive. She knew the feeling. Herself, she could do without. But not her boy. Milk would fulfill his destiny come hell or high water.

She had to throw Officer Friendly off the scent. 'There were a lot of us parents, concerned parents—You just don't think it'll ever happen. Not in Canada. Not in Toronto. But then, you know that psycho on that Greyhound—.' Her eyes welled up. 'He cut that man's head right off.' She clutched the delicate base of her neck. 'Some of us parents just had to see the bullet holes with our own eyes. Nobody gets a chance to see real bullet holes except on TV. Probably exactly why it continues.' Her eyes welled up. 'To see the jagged, cragged rips in the wall.' She put her hand on the officer's forearm. 'To poke your own finger into where bullets ripped, teared, and shattered your own son's school walls—.' She fingered her scar.

'I understand.' The officer pulled his arm back. 'Are you alright, Ma'am?'

'I am just for real, Officer. I, for one, am a very real person. I am not a fakey fake. I am not a copy of a mother. You cannot imagine, Officer, how healing it is to stick your finger in a bullet hole.'

'And your son, Ma'am. Does he have a future planned out?'

Oh, God, she'd never shut up. 'You know teenage boys.'

'What's he going to do?'

'Astronaut-Fireman.'

'Ah.'

'Yes. Yes.' She crunched her lower lip so that he'd know she meant business. 'He's going to put out fires in that last great frontier—.'

'Outer space.'

'Outer space.' She half-shrugged then, too. 'Defying gravity. Putting his life at stake for planet Earth.'

'Admirable.'

'Like you, Officer.' She clasped her hands together in sincerity. 'There's no one braver than a police officer.'

He nodded and tucked his pencil into his shirt pocket. 'That's all I need for right now, Ma'am. If you hear anything—.'

He tipped his hat.

Once he left, she closed the door and pressed her back into it. She pressed harder until it crunched just this side of a dent. Her stomach sunk. She had to find those boys. Maybe an Ern True's on the loose.

She got on the horn. She had to warn the boys. If they were going to be on the lam, she would help them. What did she have to lose? She could tip them off. Don't be scared, she'd tell them. I've got your back. Panicking wouldn't help. Panicking wouldn't help at all. The telephone handset wasn't in the cradle. That's okay, she'd use her cell. Oh, but her cell got left in her purse which she left … in the car. She'd use the landline. Now, the last time that she'd used the phone was was was (think fast) when she called the school to tell them Milk would be late. Right. But, that was a hundred years ago, this morning, before the lemons, before Patricia, before Walter even. Walter, Walter? Walter-Neff-Jeff? Gone. Vamoosed. Ditched.

The kitchen counter, sticky with dried lemon juice and strewn with bits of Reggiano, lay otherwise bare. No phone. The floor, too. She looked into all the corners and underneath the chairs. Somebody stashed it in the freezer once. Back by the kitchen door, she hit the phone locator button. It chirped again, like it did before, but this time from upstairs. Sluggish, with her mind racing, she climbed. At the door to she and Jeff's room, she listened. Nope. Not the loo, neither. Milk's room. She found it in his duvet covers.

On her back on his bed, she tapped out Milk's number. It rang. And, rang. And rang. Maybe she didn't have the number right. Again. It rang. And, rang. The cops know something she does not.

She thought it through. Somewhere kids hang out. If she were Ern True, where would she hunt them? Cherry Beach. Sunnyside Pavilion. High Park, maybe. She knew her boy. The Spit.

In the Tercel, she figured her best route to the lake, tonight anyway, had to be the D.V.P. At the Don's bridge on Bloor, the traffic had backed up so she took Parliament south, instead. 1:27 a.m. Come hell or high water, she'd find those boys.

Ton'

Behind the wheel, Shafiqq rapped on the squad car window. 'Hurry it up, Ton'.'

Ton' jumped in. A stew of stink-piss funk.

'Grow up, dude.'

'You grow up.'

'We're going to go back up Church Street and we're going to see your Julio—. The Mac-10s.'

'I don't have a Julio. You got something on the Mac-10s?'

'Better stick to business with Julio.'

Don't tell Ton' he don't stick to business.

'Ton', I got you.' Shafiqq tapped his temple with his index finger. 'You don't wipe your mother-in-law's hiney and not have a heart. You care.'

Ma's neck jack-hammered and Little Fuck, Ton's tiny brother, floating face-down in a halo of sauerkraut wrenched vice-like at his chest.

'If I say Heidegger, what do you say?'

'You always got an angle.'

'If I say Care, capital "C"—what do you say?'

Care coming with a capital C means the steel toe of a jackboot. Or a stiff prick.

'What you pay attention to is what you care about.'

Care is lifting a pale, dead brother from the sea of kiddie pool and slipping amongst steel cages of juvenile detention in Upstate New York. Ton' could tell Shafiqq all about Care, with a capital 'C'. It starts with an 'S'.

Sometimes people see things about you you don't see yourself. A guard, Solomon, at the Northwest New York State District Regional Juvenile Detention, Rehabilitation and Education Center (DREC) working laundry detail ragged on him about getting exercise, helping Ton' and connecting him to an immigration judge relative. But Ton' picked his battles. In the exercise yard, he kept his mouth shut. In places like DREC kids disappear body, mind, and soul. That's the point. 70,000 kids in these places. City, state, feds. A playhouse for predators. Every single one.

In the yard, Ton' did push-ups. The fresh-cut grass smelled like freedom. Green.

This guard, Solomon, fingered his weapon, clocking him.

Just come and get it, dude. Ton' did the deed. Dropped trou to feed Brenda working nights or Vazquez that everybody else's scared of. Give the people a little nutrition.

Ton' got busted in Buffalo. A sitting duck. Under a poplar tree at Rainbow Bridge park, Tweek told him to sit still, don't talk to anyone. I'll be back. Two grand, man.

But Tweek got jacked. Ton' dug his heel into the dirt and goddamned, sure as the sun spit through those pear-shaped leaves, two cops blocked the sun. They got him around the neck and pressed his throat into the fresh-cut lawn. Like to remember what 'outside' smells like. They found the extra stash, tied him to Tweek and got all 'don't-they-call-you-Curley?'

The judge tossed the key. Three strikes. The States went apeshit with contracting prisons out back then. It might as well have been Alabama 1954. Chain gangs, free labour. Two judges sit on the board of DREC and remand to keep the state contract intact. The more kids they can keep locked up for longer periods the more money they collect from the public purse. Good for politics, good for business. Legal, tight and proofed against fluctuations in the economy. The kids were lost causes. They'd never amount to anything. Ton' saw the writing on the wall.

Solomon saw him through the cage fence and hung there. Eyeing him.

Incarceration is like being inside of a washing machine that's lost its balance. You can't wait for the lid to open. One dude yells, another hollers back. One dude scrapes his bars, another one's stomping up and down. Steel doors slam, buzzers buzz, alarms squeal. Walkie-talkies and intercoms buzzing. Chains rattle, pipes groan. Ton' scored wads of cotton and melted rubber seals off the cheap-ass sneakers for earplugs.

Solomon stared at him.

Just take it, man.

'You fold a good one.'

Keep walkin', dude.

'What're you 16, 17 years-old?'

Check the file, man.

'Can't stay away from the U.S.A., can you?'

Ton' rolled his canvas bin to the others roping down the hall.

Solomon tightened his belt.

Yeah, daddy. Whatevs.

'*Don't the laundry bins look like a line of mules? Or storm clouds rolling in?*'

A line of hostages is what they looked like.

'*I don't know Mr. Gonzalez, maybe you're going about things in the wrong way. You seem like a nice kid.*'

At DREC, 'nice' means lube.

'*I got you your more rec time in the Yard.*'

Ton' pulled out another batch of sheets and piled them on the table.

A thousand dead flies clouded up the fluorescent light overhead.

The guard came closer.

The body don't hurt like the mind.

The guard's fingers, thick and copper-coloured, pulled at the bleached sheet corners. Then, at his goatee. '*Maybe I can help.*'

This dude. What about the three feet rule?

He passed Ton' a power bar and a pack of Camel Lights. '*Health food.*'

He pocketed the bar and smokes.

'*I got a brother who's an immigration judge. Two in one. Get your dope case though him and an immigration application. You could be an American.*'

Nobody wants to be an American.

'*Why not?*' asked the guard. '*We're freer.*'

Fuckin' Americans.

'*I just think we could do with more kids like you over here.*'

Say it, dude. Don't work so hard.

'*Think about the police academy.*'

Americans do not give up. Yankee Doodle Dandy.

'I see you. You can take it.'

He could take it. Got that right.

'You might dig it.'

Groovy, man.

'You won't make twenty-five.'

He don't know nothing. Twenty-five. That's seven years. He'd be back in Mama's rye fields by then. Sell enough dope to get Ma a house back at home. *Hasta luego, El Norte.*

'You're one of those kids. Mom came on a temporary work visa. As a housekeeper or a nanny. You start dreaming about back home and start selling.'

Fool-ass motherfucker.

'Anthony. Make something of yourself. It isn't that bad. It can be home. You're North American now.'

──── Solomon got his case set up. Back in T.O., he turned eighteen, did the online application for police training. Twelve weeks in Aylmer and he had his badge. A couple weeks after that he's with Pat-Pat selling bricks to ghosts under Sherbourne Street.

According to Shafiqq, DREC is a classic means to transfer public dollars to private hands. 'It's all about Care. Transfer wealth to the top 2%. They aren't playing. It's getting to be the same in Canada. Follow the money.'

'You know,' Ton' pressed his palms into his thighs, settling into his stew of curry and piss. 'You're the best partner I ever had.'

Milk

The limo rolled to a stop. Lakeshore Boulevard cuts the city off at the ankles. A border crossing. Lake Ontario's shoreline is a hodge-podge of untamed land. The Spit, a man-made peninsula built upon the hollowed-out remains of two centuries of downtown Toronto, pokes into the lake just past the traffic light at Leslie and Lakeshore. A conservation area teeming with weeds and wildflowers, broken concrete and steel coils—the dumping ground of City development. Migratory birds crouch amidst its wrecked and dented sinks and in the crevasses between ancient bathroom tiles. Insects scurry from coyotes hunting the feral cats and dogs seeking shelter there. At Leslie, the lake mounts the wreckage of the city and presses into a fortress of condo buildings.

Run. Dude, you got to stop this car and get away from this dirt bag.

But it's me, Milk. I had to help him. I wanted to.

Captive and caged in a cragged and rocky cave, Odysseus blinds the cock-eyed Cyclopian prince, Polyphemus. Holding his face, the monster moans who could do such a thing? Odysseus answers: *Nobody*. The wounded one-eyed prince declares his attacker's name:

Nobody. Tom is the prince, you are Odysseus—Nobody. Untethered and free, you will find a way out of the giant's grip; out of the cave. William Thibidault could have turned down another hallway. Maybe he could have ducked. He could have stayed home with a cold. He would be done with his college applications. He'd be finding out who's having a New Year's party. Ern could have blown off steam shooting up lockers.

Run. Run. Back to Lakeshore. Back to Carlaw. Take the bus. Get to Broadview. Disappear into the glare of the Canadian Tire floodlights. Be a rat. Run into the LCD beam of the Loblaws Garden Centre. The automatic doors peel wide and swallow you whole. There is no running for your life. As want withdraws, your life remains. A snowdrift keens towards the water, Lakeshore goads you to myth and memory.

⬤ Once upon a time, you row into the weeds. Uncle Louise draws his bow to his knees. The trout gulp below. He extends his forearm, you fasten the arm guard to the muscle there. He lifts the bow, you hand him an arrow. He seats it the string and fixes his eyes to yours. In a T, its shadow pokes at the water cresting, lapping and troughing over the worms, algae and fermentation. The two of you lean over the edge of the rowboat. In that pure lagoon, the pesticide run-off, the bird and fish droppings, the McDonald's sacs and dead animal fur now steam a blurring stink of organic combustion and chemical ferment. A blade of yellowed grass floats by, dry so late in summer. Deer flies lumber to chew at the meat of Louise's chicken leg, his back, and to swarm at that breast. That left tit, the lone survivor, glum and holding down the fort; its nipple worn to burnished plum scar. He cut it off at the age you are now. This murder is yours, too.

About the time he finished high school, Louise met a clan of Radical Ladies who trained as archers and warriors against the patriarchy. To cement their loyalties, they cut off their right breasts and unmoored from "woman." Life lands many blows and that is good and well enough but it is deploying the blade of Self that allows the smoothest drawing of the bow's string. Armed just so, one withstands the whim, wind and chance of fathers. Out here, Louise could take his shirt off.

You may be blown, Milk, onto strange shores, as the Amazons themselves were, although fine and noble seamen too, you may be forced even to mate with a Scythian but your customs are your own.

The Radical Ladies laid him in the Fontenelle grass beneath the harriers and osprey howling and circling as that tallest and fairest one got held Louise's head with their free hand gesturing to the others to tighten the noose: *no, more; yes, more; yes, more; yes, keep pulling there. There, that's it,* she whispers. Louise's throat choked, the blood vessels bulging, the Lady began to speak; the warmth of her breath softened the thin skin of the ear dusted with the tiniest pearl hairs standing tall as the Spit marsh fields swaying in their bend west from Iowa. His eyes now drowsy flit open.

Remember, the Lady whispered in Louise's ear; the blade bites bone to cleave fat from skin: *the Lilliputian Family Circus snatched from the platforms at Auschwitz, all seven of them a family of little ones plucked from the planks by that great winged and paradoxical demon Dr.*

Mengele to study and inspect their blood, their frenula, their vaginas and every little thing that makes them tick. Why 'paradoxical,' you say. Well, if the good doctor had not rushed from his cozy bed tripping over his own feet to catch this fortunate family hand-delivered in the middle of the night just for him, they would have been gassed with the rest.

They cut Louise of his own cloth. The blade threading the skin with what became himself, dabbing the absinthe to his lips like the others have done with every fibre and sinew sliced clean, so that from then on no one would mistake him for her.

Remember then, those little ones, whose blood withdrew into great jars day in and day out in order that the grand doctor could gather the material for twenty years work. For this, Mengele thanked a God that had cast him out long ago. And so every day the blood of one poor dwarf-child; or a parent, sister, or brother; a mayor, the owner of the Lilliputian General store, the druggist, or the postman—one is emptied, and then another, while the others sit shivering on wooden benches dolled up in January the same as when they arrived to camp in the windswept hours of a May night.

The Ladies inched their forearms between the dirt and Louise's lower back to arch his body as the breast, still clinging to its body by muscle, is lifted to face its sky above.

The wee darlings perch there as in their circus days, lips scarlet, skin clown white, ringleted hair; the men with a good neat part in order that Herr Doktor could map the boundaries of vascular onslaught. They clutch each other's hands on those splintered spruce boards—some frozen in fear, others still weeping, others plotting a futile escape. For, in a world of shadow, where shall they find light? The spirit of Lilliput, as it were; I tell you they were plucked by the Angel of Death, their faces scarred with a lipstick brewed from the muscles of their neighbours, the fat of their tiny village mayor creaming its viscosity—who, in his day, bellowed and crowed that their town should never worry over darkening skies. He, now spread on their lips they knew for he had a distinctive scent, a spiced lemon gas emitted from him which, if truth be told, earned him his office—it must have been what was Romania at that time. You mustn't ever forget. Remember Louise, no matter how they dress you up, no matter the paint they find in the rivers of your blood, you are who you are, and what you are is what you are. A man through and through.

Uncle Louise left his breast on the floor of the Fontenelle Forest for the coyotes, bobcats and field rats. Though it had no milk, the meat would feed spinning into vitamin, mineral and enzyme. And from that ordeal there on the forest floor, like that family of little folks, Uncle Louise was to step away, shorn of one breast to be sure, but what he lost in a sack of gristled tissue, susceptible to cancers and tumours and pockets of putrescence, he gained in self and surety and the clarity that men need to put one foot in from of the other. Now, he would draw his bow firm and true unencumbered by biology and meaning. Your Uncle Adam wrote you a lyric once: *a warrior's aim true / as yet unchecked by circumstance.*

Louise with bow and arrow raised. He draws the tendon string. He wiggles his fingers. The arrow shoots. You, and then Louise, leap up. The boat lurches. He jerks himself, and then you, for balance. He lifts his lone breast to the sky. Grateful. The fish freezes to roll its own pearl breast skyward. It gums for air and is everything you've ever wanted. To witness agony. Struggle. The fight to stay on the planet. A gut-clench of viciousness and hate. You're both in on this. Mr. P.'s murder is on you, too.

The blinking red light at Lakeshore Boulevard flashes on your reflection in the rear-view mirror. Your pig eyes and lop-sided ears. Lakeshore is the borderline. Your own leaded squeegee. To tear at the soft meat of the gulping mouth, to beat at the throbbing skull, to frustrate the very pulse of the heart—to fight back against the avalanche upon you. Not Tom. Not Jeff. You. To matter now is to revolt. Against never being enough. Against not counting. You would have done it, too.

Tom fiddled with Marine Joe.

Hey, hand me him. You got your finger in through the snaps of his shirt. You felt the indents of his chest and the hoop made by his six-pack. That plastic warms to your touch. Nobody. *Nobody* born to escape the Monster; to fill the Joes, nothing more than ABS plastic, with meaning. Joes are the Tupperware of Terror. The killing of Mr. P. will be poured into the plastic cast of your life. There is room enough amidst the striations of Jeff's letdown, Louise's grief and Saddam's oil fires. Room enough for Nobody. For you.

Tom poked you. Green light, Spaz.

Right.

Through the chain maybe. You shifted and rolled forward.

Ton'

They made Queen St. from Lakeshore coming up on Moss Park—where Ton' used to deal. Nobody in the park deals Mac-10s, but they got their ears to the ground. 'We go ask 'em.'

'Dude—.'

'Do not "dude" me. Mac-10s, okay. That's our job.' Shafiqq's a mobile boot camp obstacle course.

"K. But your wife buzzed in.'

She did not.

Shafiqq pulled to the curb. Wind shook the car.

'I tapped the glass to tell you, Ton'. When you pee, you don't listen.'

Goddamn, this dude. 'Schelle's knows better than to bother him on duty.

'She says her dad's not back home.'

And?

'He ought to be by now. He went out to get cash.'

Cookie crumbs clogged the gear box. Snickers wrappers stuck to his boot heel. Between the dashboard and the trash, their squad car might as well be a trashed washroom. Ton' peeled crinkling cellophane from the sole of his shoes.

'It's all Patricia's, maybe.' Shafiqq tapped the steering wheel.

'Then, we circle back to Moss Park after seeing her moms.'

Or they could just hop in and out.

▬◄ Back in the day, Ton' could not get better than selling in Moss Park. Bound by Shuter St. to the north, Queen St. on the south. Sherbourne St.'s got the east, Jarvis St. on the west. Ton'd jimmy the fence behind the playground and tuck out of the wind against that wall there. Come August, the smell. People taking dumps close to his spot. Pissing right on the wall. The bugs down there'd get under his skin. He'd scratch the scab bumps on his ankles and pecs raw. Droplets of juice oozed out onto his neck. The lower leg, too, above the heel and behind the knee.

Mama'd cream plantain onto his shoulders. *'You lay down with dogs, you get up with fleas.'*

She'd choose the oozing oar-like leaves from behind the St. Lawrence Market and boil them; pulp them and mix in spoonfuls of raw cocoa butter. But it wasn't dogs, fleas, flies, or August pee stink causing those bumps. They were the hives of anxiety. Of getting seen and heard and found out; of people watching him everywhere. The blisters of Child Welfare workers: one eye on him and one eye on their quarterly progress reports; detectives slowing down and then speeding off wagging their pink, sausage fingers. He needed bank. Like, otherwise they'd be on the street. Like, Mama's cheque would ever pay rent. Fuck the government. Months before the cops nailed him in Buffalo, the Richmond Walk-in Clinic diagnosed him with an ulcer. *Milk*, Ma said. She'd seen it before. *'Su papa, su abuelito. Los nuestros.'* Ton's dad had disappeared the year before Little Fuck, his gut chewed by how-come and what-if. *'Este su sangre, mijo,'* Ma told him. She knew. She's the one pulling her boys from the deep.

Way back, Ma blistered the sausages on the grill. His brother, Little Fuck, stole the sauerkraut and tripped into their kiddie pool. Ton' stared at his brother floating belly down. Slivers of kraut floated out from his head. Dude can't put food in the pool. Dumb ass. He wasn't moving. Start kicking, man. Play-acting. Throw the meat. The kraut collected around his head and neck. Holding his breath. Stop play-acting. Ma, Ton' yelled. He's playing. What must've been one, two or five minutes, and even with Ma throwing her massive body at that tiny plastic pool her plate smashing into a hundred arrows. She slapped at the side of the pool, putting her whole weight to bend it to empty the water out. She scooped like crazy and even before she stopped she lifted Little Fuck to the sky with both hands, shaking him, pounding his back, dragging him to the concrete, opening his mouth, doing her best to give him breath. Fuck lay face up, his skin pale grey. Minnows of sauerkraut streamed along the sidewalk. Ton' hadn't moved. His stomach burned.

Parked on the edge of Moss Park, wind spiked down into the bare baseball diamond, spinning up snow.

Shafiqq phffed him. 'Think there's anyone out there?'

'There's always somebody out there, man.'

The Eden comms lit up again. 'Schelle.

Ton' put her on speaker.

'Dad doesn't go out at this time of night. He should be back by now. He's just getting cash for the guys tomorrow to get rid of the bats.'

God, everyone's so wound up. 'Don't think the worst. He's making a clean start getting rid of those things.'

'Ton', go check on them.'

'I just did.'

'Five hours ago. Ton'. A lot happens in five hours.'

'You go, 'Schelle.'

'They think your stuff might stick this time. I got to stay still.'

'Schelle's in-vitro's holding on for dear life.

'Mom and Dad aren't answering, Ton'. That's weird.'

'We got time, Dude.' Shafiqq had to stick is nose in. 'We go over.' Shafiqq whispered, waddling his head. 'We check, we go. No prob.'

'Man—.'

'I'm still on here, Ton'. Listening.'

'Sit tight.' He poked the disconnect.

Shafiqq steered them away.

— Ton' let himself into his Albert and Ale's mostly dark house. The dragonfly lamp glowed in his in-laws' living room. An orange night light cast a glow over Ale's bedspread, carpet and up the baby blue walls. Ton' sat on the bed.

Ale's green eyes opened. She got his forearm. 'You're cold.' She looked to the window. 'It's night.'

'Early morning. Storming off and on.'

Ale nodded slug-like. She pulled at some imagined jacket hood and tightened its strings. 'I was going off a cliff. In a car.'

'You're dreaming, maybe. Where's Albert?'

Her gaze, pulled by some invisible wagon, landed on a coffee-stained volume of Carol Shields. 'Bank. Machine.'

'A while ago? Where we were. You and me, maybe. Getting gas—or.'

Albert ought to have a cell phone. It's, like, the 21st century.

The wind had kicked up. The branches beyond the window glass whipped like crazy. Sometimes, he and 'Schelle'd lean against the trees past the playground fence at Lyons Primary School to see what their kids would be like. They wanted to know what they were getting into. *That one's like you,'* he'd tell her following a cartwheeling girl flipping over head to foot, end to end. *'Can't wait.'* 'Schelle just knew their kids would dig cartwheeling. She'd teach them all of her secrets. *'Watch.'* Right there on the curb, between the tree and the street light, 'Schelle'd do a cartwheel. He'd clap. *'That's nothing,'* she'd say. *'I used to be able to cartwheel from one end of this playground to the other. My mom said it make my wrists weak but dad said it'd make them strong.'* Behind the fence, closer to the school building, the kids jacked themselves up and down, bouncing and jerking and twerking.

Street light flickered into the room. Shadows washed over Ale's face.

'K.' He brought her hand to his lips and kissed it. 'If you were my lady, I'd never leave you.'

'You butter me up.' She dug her fingertips into her forehead. 'I dream and dream.'

Shafiqq tapped on the bedroom door. 'T.'

Ale's eyes darted to the door, to Shafiqq's golden dastār, to Shafiqq and then to her bedspread. 'What'm I hosting a party?'

'Excuse me, Ma'am.'

Ton' pulled Shafiqq into the living room. 'You made me come out here. Give me two seconds.'

'J. says we got to go. Like now. It's a 10-18 on a maybe 10-87.'

'You told J. I'm visiting my mother-in-law?'

'Chill. I explained. But, like this, he says, is urgent; maybe drug stuff.'

Ton' righted a tilted lampshade and then tucked in a flap of linoleum with his toe. 'Albert, man.' What about hitting Moss Park?

'Residents on the Islands called it in. A limo's out there, that's what a guy with binoculars said. They're afraid of raves.'

'What is it with the limos tonight? Raves, man? Raves?'

'Nah, man. Let them get Ray Hong or Pete.'

'They're on the D.V.P.'

Ton' strategized. He and Shafiqq would hit the Spit, check out the 10-87, then back to Moss Park. Like they're supposed to make progress on Mac-10 gun traffic chasing teenagers doing X. 'The D.V.P. gets to search trunks and under seats; apply breathalyzers—we get fifteen-year-olds blowing dope.'

'It's just the call, Ton'.'

Nobody raves anymore. Ton' whispered sweet dreams into Ale's ear.

They closed the door quietly behind them. The trees in the front of Albert and Ale's house shook. Pterodactyls caught in sandstorm. He had to remember to

show Shafiqq the bats. Nobody'd believe it if they didn't
see it.

Out on the Gardiner, the traffic crawled. The D.V.P.
checkpoint backed up traffic even this far. All the way
out by Islington and the Black Creek turn-off.

'Put the overheads on.' Ton' flicked the switch. He
put on the siren for good measure. They tore up what
there is of the shoulder over the Cherry Hump to Leslie.
To chase a limousine. Probably the mayor smoking out.
Or his brother.

'I am talking to J. about this matter. I am a good cop.
You are a good cop. He's got us out here chasing high
school jerk-offs. I mean, like, what's our priorities? Bet
it's not like—remember Central Tech.'

Shafiqq flitzed his lip. 'Ern True.'

'What makes a kid do that?' Ton' remembered pressing that kid with the 'fro's head down. They said he'd
gotten all of them out of the window. That one kid
by himself.

On the south side of Lakeshore Boulevard, at the bottom of Leslie, the Spit disappeared behind a curtain of
ink-like night. The entrance chain lay busted at the gate.

'They drove right through it.'

Ton' opened the door and pulled himself up to look
into the distance. He swung himself onto the hood. The
trees wouldn't quite give him a clear view as far as the
road break.

'We got to go out there.' Shafiqq meant to do his
duty. They ought to be on the D.V.P. doing some good.
Ton' jumped and skidded into the snow. He brushed
himself off. 'Nothing there.'

'You're like a monkey, man.' Shafiqq worked earmuffs down over his daster.

'Man, you got to go racist and dark.'

'No, Ton'.' Shafiqq pulled on his gloves and packed his fingers into them one at a time. 'I mean, a monkey. Just a monkey. You're a monkey-frog man.'

Shafiqq ought to just speak straight. It'd save everybody a lot of trouble.

'We got to go check it out, Ton'.'

'I climbed up, I scouted, I looked, nada. Re-con done, report filed.'

'Ton', maybe they turned their lights off.'

'Don't go old lady.'

"If we left and kids're out there and get hurt, there goes detective constable, man.'

'We didn't see anything.'

'You stay here, then. I'm going.' Shafiqq rushed for the car.

Ton' leapt to cut him off but Shafiqq body-blocked him and got behind the wheel.

'Get in the car, Ton'.'

'We get stuck out here. You are digging us out.'

'We get stuck out here, we radio for a tow truck.'

'And J. will take the cost out of our cheques.'

'Such an old lady.'

Past the chain, a set of tire tracks stretched ahead of them. They rolled the car past the boulders that surfaced out of the snow marking the dirt trail along the lake edge. For some reason the arm stood up by the guard booth. In the summer, the inland harbour tottered full with bobbing sailboats and mini-yachts. Beyond, downtown Toronto glittered wrapping the sit-and-spin CN Tower in light. On the left, beyond the boulders and all the stories Shafiqq says were in there, the lake trembled. Across the water, Rochester's lights blinked.

'They're lucky the snow wasn't so deep out here.'
'They're lucky? We're lucky.'
They got as far as the three massive snow-cloaked boulders blocking cars from going any further. The headlights illuminated where the snow swept into low hills as boots and cargo passed. Scattered footprints coalesced into a smudged line tracking up a bluff.

Sessy

She headed for the Spit. The Tercel didn't slide at all since they kept the south-bound lanes salted good. At the bottom of Parliament, Sessy hung a left on Lakeshore, and then a right on Cherry, one of Toronto's oldest but long forgotten streets. Her headlights cast over the Don River trickling through in spite of most of its tributaries being buried in concrete under the city. She tapped out Milk's number on her phone. *This number is out of signal range.* She dialed it again. *This nu—.* 'Out of signal range.' His antennae had broken from hers. Out of signal range. Steady, Girl. She'd find them old school.

If the Don River is the esophagus, then Cherry Street is the gut leaking into Lake Ontario. Back in the day, the whole city pitched their dead horses, rotted lumber and overflowing cisterns into the marsh and wetlands below Cherry. Ignorant of cholera, the locals dipped their ladles to drink the water before heaving their guts and retching to their gruesome deaths. Finally, in an effort to keep a few people alive and fund the next year's budget, the Portlands Water Treatment plant sprung up there alongside an oil-drilling concern. The Toronto city government never could see beyond the end of its nose. It had, and has, the vision of a bat in full daylight. It grants private corporations the right to tear up pristine natural habitats to turn a short term tax bump—Sessy saw it now in the big box Canadian Wheel, Food Basement's, and Buyer's Drug Mart all capped with a Moonbucks coffee shop that'd wiped out generations of muskrat, beaver, otter, and water fowl habitats to make way for asphalt car parking, shopping carts and sliding glass doors. Nature, which always has a trick up its sleeve, plopped a stand of bamboo down there to purify the water over a few centuries. Purifying other things, the gay boys found those tall grasses. Out of contagion, came belonging and pleasure. There's a reason it's called Toronto the Good. She had to face the facts. The boys could be hiding in that bamboo. They wouldn't be the first.

Take the queers. Take poor Adam. He made the mistake of protesting the Bathhouse Raids. Cops clipped him from College and Church St., packed him into a cruiser and took him on the "Cherry Beach Express." 52 Division officers dragged him kicking and screaming, landed him more than a few kicks and punches to teach him about gay rights. *Disease-ridden faggot* is what they called him. Being a good sport and taking a fist for permission, Adam became a tiny local celebrity doing his inimitable rendition of Pukka Orchestra's "Cherry Beach Express" at high school dances, open mics and, since AIDS never ended, in on-going resistance marches: *That's why I'm riding on / the Cherry Beach Express / my ribs are broken / and my face is in a mess / and I made all my statements / under duress.* The road went all pot-hole since the businesses left and the queers stayed on. In the summer, they are always popping into the sunlight from the stands of bamboo down here.

Thunder cracked. She did a three-point and took bumpy Unwin west. She hung on a bone of ice and rolled down to Leslie. At the entrance to the Spit, a drift half the size of her car blocked the way. A snagged chain clung to collapsed poles along with a shredded, neon orange flag flapping in the breeze. She could dig tracks around and make her way out onto the Spit. She probably shouldn't do that at all. If she got stuck, there's no getting out. Jeff probably gave her auto club card to his cardamom chickee. She tapped the accelerator. It jammed. The car lunged; she slammed on the brakes. A second try went smoother. She popped her window.

Waves crashed in as the lake rustled and roiled out there in the dark. Cottonwood striplings shuddered in the halo of her headlights like naked boys shivering from a cold plunge. The purple-fingered dogwoods pricked through the drifts.

She had to pee. She clenched her thighs. She squinted through the windshield. And then out the passenger and driver's side window. Not a loo in sight. She pressed tighter. It had to be pushing two in the morning.

But then came a cop cruiser plowing right to the edge of that buffalo drift and blinding her head-on. The Toronto Police Services. If she played her cards right, they might have beans to spill on the boys. Hands on the wheel, she checked her eyeliner. She beamed, nodded and twiddled her digits. My god, she had to pee. Bastards ought to dim their headlights. She punched her beams to dim. They did the same. But not their blasting flashers. Christ. Police are drama queens. She's not a criminal. Not yet. She bared her good teeth and grinned for their dashcam.

The officers clomped out of their car. One, a tall drink of water. Nice, thick moustache. Hesitating. He packed the goods under that snow coat, she could tell. He tugged his earflaps. The other one, coming closer on her side had a turban on his head capped by earmuffs. They blinked sideways at the snow shooting into their faces and zipped up their navy blue parkas. The moustache one leaned on the patrol car moaning, a cow lowing in quicksand. She held her hands up. Like a thief in the night. No sudden moves. No funny business. Take it slow, Copper.

Turban got his free hand closer to his waist. His holster tucked tight under that flap of jacket. He could blow her head off so fast she wouldn't know Monday from Tuesday. Moustache would finish her off. She'd be like Faye Dunaway in *Bonnie and Clyde* riddled in a ballet of bullets as her blonde blonde hair spun over her frozen eyes seeing the last thing ever to see—that foolish and trusting Clyde. Turban came to her side of the car.

The other one, Moustache, had come as far as the front of her hood. That one's face rested tight and focused. No doubt chewing something over. She could see it the way he kept looking off to the left and behind him. She could tell.

Turban knocked on the glass.

She stared straight ahead. She didn't want to look. What if he had a gun on her already? She gritted her teeth. This is how it would end. Just beginning. Jesus

Christ. Give her one last look at Milk. One last glance.
She peeked.

Turban bared his fangs.

No gun. Not yet. Don't move her hands.

Turban wagged a finger.

She'd know this from TV. She lowered her window.
'Officer?'

'Ma'am?'

'Can I help you, Officer?'

'That's for me to ask. Anything I can do for you?'

'No. No, no, no.' I'm just looking for my son that's
just blown up G.I. Joes under his father's Saturn. If that
wasn't a sluice of Saussurean signifiers, she didn't know
what was.

'The park is closed. Tommy Thompson Park is closed
—9 p.m. weekdays. Besides, the road is a mess out there.'

The other officer backed up to the squad car.

'I'd get stuck.'

'Most likely.' He studied her back seat.

Stay one step ahead.

'Did you need something out there, Ma'am?'

'Oh.' Think fast. 'Yes. Yes.'

'What's that, Ma'am?'

Hmmm. Haw. 'I thought …'

The officer looked back at Moustache who clung to
their squad car.

'I meant …'

'Yes?'

'I am a writer. A novelist, actually.'

'Oh.'

'Yes. Yes, I am. And—.'

'You're doing research.'

'I am.'

'On what?'

'The Spit.' Think fast. 'In winter.'

Turban nodded.

Oh, he bought it hook, line and sinker. 'Yes. Yes.' Think, Sessy. Think. 'Just what happens, for instance, to all of the rabbits in the winter. Where do the otters go?'

'Right.'

'Yes. Yes. In summer, this place is crawling with otters.' She never heard of an otter being out here. 'They think, well, this is the accepted explanation, you know I know because I've been researching, that a family of otters had migrated over from the States and—.'

'Everyone wants to come to Canada.'

Sessy guffawed. Too much. 'Well. They used to.'

'Ma'am, we have to move you out. It's an emergency.'

She bit the inside of her cheek.

'Come back and do your research when the park is open. I have to ask you to turn around and leave.'

Oh, Officer, that just isn't an option.

'It's an order.'

An 'order'? Something bad happened. Okay. Okay. She could do this. Pull down the access road and go in on foot.

'Please turn around.'

Oh, he's so smart. 'Um.' She had to convince him she's for real. 'Can I just ask you then? Where do the rabbits—?'

'Underground, Ma'am.' The officer cleared his throat. 'Contact the Toronto Conservation Authority they'd be happy to—.'

Moustache covered his mouth with his hands.

'He doesn't look so good.'

Just past the end of her bumper, the Moustache one blew a stream of orange-chunked vomit. He almost splattered Sessy's bumper.

'Jesus.'

'Just a second, Ma'am.'

That police officer gripped the side of his car now. Holy cow. The pressure cops endure. People got to treat police officers better. She shifted into reverse.

Turban leaned back over to her. 'Ma'am?'

'Got it. You take him to a hospital.'

Something's cooking out here. Please don't let it be Milk.

'Officer—?'

'Yes?'

She leaned from her window. 'Have you seen a limo out here?'

Turban stepped back.

She shouldn't have asked that.

'What about a limo?'

'Oh. I only just—.' Think. 'A butler in this fanciful, untrue and not real novel I'm writing, he has it so hard but he, this butler, has a limo and visits the Spit—.'

'No.'

'So, I'm just wondering if you—.'

'Ma'am. Please. It's an emergency—.'

Now, Moustache bent to hold his knees.

Turban seemed torn. 'Please.'

"Night, Officer.' Sessy rolled the Tercel back out and did a three-point at the corner of Unwin and Leslie. Those cops knew something or her name wasn't S-E-S-S-Y.

They could lead her straight to Milk. She did a U-ee a little further down into the bamboo off Cherry St. and backed out of sight. Milk had gotten himself into something. She could read the signs—the tell-tale suffering on Moustache's face.

Milk

Leslie St. spat you out at Tommy Thompson Park (a.k.a. The Spit). Mr. P.'s body in the trunk had thrown you onto open seas. A heavy-duty chain cut straight across the entry to the park. Breathe.

You're panting.

A chill had creeped in like down the back of your neck.

Hold your breath.

You did.

Tad got his boat boots up under the dash. Hang on, Milk. It's gonna get worse before it gets better.

Like Nobody.

Tad scoped out Leslie Street back all the way to Lakeshore.

We're the one-eyed monster.

It's me. All me. I'm not a beetle caught by a magnifying glass. I lifted that squeegee, and I stepped off the shore. Me. Totally me. But a me that never had, like, potential to exist before. Not even the me that's sitting here. Not the me that sat in calc this morning.

You dug into the grain of the leatherene ceiling. You know this story. A neutrino can be one thing unknown and unseen but then passes through the lead wall of experience and becomes a thing known and seen. From μ (*mau*) to t (*tau*). All potentials collapse into what is but then, just as fast, spin into something else. We tell the cops what went down. We go home.

Right. I'm the guy that killed the teacher he loved. I love him. I wouldn't've killed him if I didn't love him.

You didn't choose it, Tad. It's a potential.

That came into being, Milk.

One of many. A *mau* ion and a *tau* ion are not the same. And the *tau* ion is invisible. So whatever you became holding that squeegee spun into something that no longer exists. It is not you. We only know it's real because there's a body in the trunk.

Tom snaked his fingers into your hair.

Which means that you had just as much potential to kill Mr. P. as Tom did. Care matters. Attention matters. Makes things real. It's quantum.

He massaged your scalp as you talked. He shook his head. Where I fucked up is I would've helped him. Like with Mrs. P. or like anything.

Wrong place and right time don't equal guilt.

Tom inched closer.

It could have been me.

Oh, the guy knew I'd be there. He pulled at a thread on the inside-out seam of your jeans. It's who's ever going to believe Mr. P. did that to himself. *How could we with our bare hands—*

—leave—

—heave—.

But why would Mr. P. do this to Tom? What is the differential equation that puts a seventeen-year-old kid in this position?

He knew I would do it. He couldn't do it alone. You or me would help him. He knew that. But not if he asked. He had to compel us through circumstance.

But why you, then. Why not me?

Simple. Think about it, Milk. First, I'm pinned down to a single place. I'm at the bank machine. Enclosed space. Isolated. He hunted me.

But why *you*?

Love. Dude knows you of all people, Milk. He watches what Jeff does to you. He's not going to destroy you. You don't have the room in you, man. You got no room for random. What kind of monster would he be if he took what little wiggle room you got inside of yourself and, like, damned you to make it all about him? Like, for the rest of your life. No, dude. I'm all potential. I got privilege. I got a room. I got all the random. He pressed his face into his hands. It's not like I can be something I'm not. Like, I can't be myself. I can't be in some other life.

At Charlevoix, Grandma used to take you to the American Legion cottage she and Uncle Louise rented in July and some years, August. A string of Canada Days lit up with sparklers, burnt marshmallows and mosquito welts. Late mornings, you two'd waltz down the grass tracks, stopping now and again to trace deer whose hoofprints vanished in the stultifying heat. With each walk, a fresh coyote dropping might appear. A worn beaver dam or a used tampon led you two off the beaten path.

The two of you ducked birch boughs weighted with midge into clouds of gnarled and buzzing wings. She'd hook her paw in yours and then climb onto a shag of pine needles. *Listen,* she said. Wind whinnies through the red pine, lifting her sweat-yellow hair from her patch-quilt vest. A mosquito brandishes her proboscis high above your snouts before plunging it deep, un-relenting and unforgiving into the thin sheath of skin at the bend in the elbow where the bone is hard and the blood is good.

She inhales in a short sharp start, her arms lift. On her funny bone, the insect gorges herself; the bands binding her abdomen swell with the tide and trough of drink; she tippy-toes to the brink of a compulsive and unnatural moulting. Stuporous now, her thorax throbs with Grandma's pulse. Grandma sinks to her knees to paw at the pine needles saying, *See yourself in these gentle birds, Milk. As their tiny bodies fill to make room for Life, so does room for you.* Her Tussy anti-deodorant crème draws a brazen second, and then a third, insect to feed.

➤ Tom dug in the seat for more smoke, then in the back and then his pockets. He and Mr. P. were not so different than your Grandma swinging you round and round before missiling you into waves so that you might become something.

➤ *Get to Ithaca, Milk,* she said. *And you shall be reborn.* You and she standing on tippy-toe at the edge of the exposed cement porch. All Kristi Yamaguchi and jump-ing off, repositioning, up on one leg, singing out *la.* Then, after beating her bare, manly chest to the wicked wind, she'd hang on the flag pole and sing *Life is like / Getting home / Ithaca home, Ithaca home.* A song she made up. *My baby's bones at Ithaca home, Ithaca home.* She'd clap her hands together, lunge and get you good, gathering you to her tummy, holding you tight in the storm, hammer-dancing, pulling your pants down, slapping your bottom, yelling *beat cha* and tearing off to the water, her feet big as flippers so she'd get there first and catch you if and when you were brave enough to leap off the dock or the beach even and holding tight to her forearm she'd drop you to fly like a butterfly into the water. And then, closing your eyes, and giving over to lie on the surface of the waves as she led you past the drop-off. Out there, she planes you in circles, your eyes closed the whole time, the rush of water on your forehead when you lifted. Oh, god, then she'd lift you up incanting: *Not they—they upset—*.

And if you got it right, you giggle-shout: *Our palace day and night / they butcher our cattle—*

—our sheep, our fat goats/ feasting themselves on our glorious wine as if—

—there's no tomorrow. There's no tomorrow. With each plunge, you became somebody new.

Knowing no sissies, she would double-cross you and skid you on the surface, laughing hard enough to not catch your breath or make the words and then then then she would rocket you into the water, sluicing down down down 'til two-hundred gallons rested on your fragile shoulders and then she'd pull you up into the burning air, a horse fly lumbers by, and out out, she'd throw you up and let you go, releasing, and the water bore into your sinuses erasing your entire being. Down there you'd stay. Holding, holding, holding. Wait until the lungs would burst. Wait until the lake expels you, dizzy and deconstructed. Dunes of her Tussy underarm deodorant cream your vision before cracking the surface.

As you break through, you are not who you were. That
horse fly hovers. And you offer your arm to sup.

—*back that slab he set to block his cavern's gaping*—
—*maw.*

When you got home you couldn't wait to tell Tom
Meuley the little pieces of the text that you'd learned:
our palace night and day—. You couldn't wait to tell him
that you are now what you foresaw.

Tonight you were disappearing into the cave shed-
ding your skin to become Nobody. You got out of the
car and held held held your breath and rattled the chain
link. The headlights blinded.

With the driver's door wide open, Tad shifted the
gears. The limo zipped by, the door slam-bamming, the
car clipping the chain, the pole, and an orange warning
flag. You leapt, caught up, and cracked your head getting
back inside. Jesus, fuck. Ouch. You put on the brakes.

Steer.

Eff, Tom.

The lake spun black discs of shadow through the fog
rolling into the cottonwood jiggling like the dancers at
Jilly's; leaves and branches bushing out against the sky.
Birch and silver maple had taken their posts, their feeble
leaves tittering, their trunks scarred by land and lake.
Excoriatingly drastic is what this is. Snow devils sprung
through the trees now. The wind tricked out fractals in
the downtown glow.

Tad twisted to face you. It's all action to feed the
function.

The night slipped into a differential equation.

He went at your neck. His lips and breath hot and
stale. He pressed himself back where the seat belt starts

and wrote in the air. 'F' is function, Milk. A result. Everything is a function of things that've come before. He made air brackets with his fingers and thumbs. You bracket whatever you want to analyze—like say how tonight happened—and that everything is a function of a set of variables. Tonight is a consequence of variables colluding to produce change. Tonight, like, we've got the mythic: the storm, your grandma. Desire: me squeegee-ing for bank, Mr. P. to cut loose.

Tom's lips filled and tiny hairs glimmered gold on the curve of his chin. He scooted closer.

Tonight, like, every variable in the equation is maxed out in value and upsetting the apple cart: myth, your grandma, me, Mr. P. We're weighted, Milk. His eyes rut into yours, the lashes longer than your own. He flipped on the overhead light. Blood bloomed to his cheeks and ear lobes. He turned it off, putting his arm on your shoulder. The meat of his fingers pressed in.

Your whole self shook. You bit down hard. Fold into him. Collapse. Withdraw. Disappear. Your teeth clenched; your jaw tight.

His mouth came and coaxed. You ate into each other. He: your neck. You: the crown of his nipple, the tuft of his pit. He lifts himself onto you; the heel of your hand tracks the line of his spine. Pop buttons. His pants kick into a squirm of Safeguard, his hands pawing at the ceiling.

You take him whole and no way is it ever enough.

He came at you, coaxing you to his cushion lips. You ate into each other carried to his chest, your neck, the crown of his nipple and the cap of spit. Him onto you so that the heel of your hand tracks his spine to unhook buttons, then seconds, then thirds forcing his pants down as he lifts in a steam of Safeguard. You take him whole, your throat opening and it is never enough. As if he were going to speak, his air comes shallow, fast and sharp. He has your head in his hands. His spine twisting, fingers grabbed to get him up, his boots off, the jeans gone, then he's fingering himself and then spreads, you gut into him entering too hard, too first-time. You dig and shift. Drive the spike, cinch your grip.

He gets your chest and unspools a condom onto your cock. Like he knows how. Like easy, Tad lifts himself up and off, up and off. Then down. Up and off. Down. Up and off. His skinny spider thighs, hold him up as he lowers. He chews your neck and tongues your ears. He hooks his arms through the steering wheel bracing his elbows on the dashboard, lifting and lowering, lifting and lowering. His throat was lit by the glow of the bluish lake reflecting the city. His Adam's apple erect, for an instant, this seemed anything but new. Like you knew how all along. Like you'd felt his working the condom down. He lowered himself taking you in and surrendering to some pull. His fingers dug into the sides and back of your neck, then your shoulders, as he loosened you into the stream of particle exchange from who you were to who you are. Every clutch at the seat or paw at the ceiling, released you from Jeff's fist eviscerating you from what you had been. Jeff's punches, the fear in his eyes when he looks at you—these have flung you far. Every push into Tom pulled you home, and propelled you into something new, to the fragility and groundlessness of name and self. This is your feeble bridge from sea to shore, the several weakened bricks upon which you could, if you choose it, walk. The outcast snatches his chance and lurches to the beach, to mattering. Like when you snatched at the grass scrambling to get out of the line of fire from Ern True in tenth grade.

All feeling shot to your groin. A muscular thrust pulled. Hollowing out, you buckled. You could not bite down. He pulled you deeper into him, holding. If you looked, this would be over. Never again. Not this night, not with Tad, not like this. Now, you got seen. Now, you felt. You lifted him from the abyss and back into your mouth.

After a moment, he pulled away and collapsed on the seat. Goose pimples came up on his thighs. It's cold. He got his pants around and held his head in his hands —the smell of your bodies scenting the air. He rubbed his scalp hard like figuring out the slope of a tangent in differentials. Damn. He studied you like you'd filched something from him. Bathed in the blue light, he popped the lock.

The snow devils spun off into the dense fog, splintering out into what must be black water.

Maybe you should've had a smoke, turned on the radio; apologized. Maybe maybe.

He shot a tentative glance your way. This is fucked.

The car submerged into dense tufts of cloud.

We got to get him out.

A boner came up again in your pants.

Tent pole.

Fucked up, Tad.

He leaned forward and laid his cheek on the dashboard. He still had his eyes on you. I am, I got to—. Mr. P. did this to you, too. You're a function of this.

You plugged me into the equation, Tad. No deed or meaning of my own, I'm plastic. A G.I. Joe. I'm Tupperware. I'm a neutrino. Even Ern True is somebody.

Tom rested his chin on the dash and pulled at those little hairs. Can't see a damned thing.

You could. Out past the headlights, the drifts had twisted into peaks alive and seeking.

After the
Midnight of:

Ton'

'**There could be** a meth lab out here.' Out past those three boulders, he and Shafiqq balanced on the oil drum bridge.

Shafiqq had to show off. He'd already reached the end of the rickety so-called 'bridge.'

'That's what you're thinkin'. That's what you're hoping for.' Ton' got hold of the stinging copper railing, wanting to shake it with everything he'd got, wanting to rail at the clouds fomenting a grey quilt. The lake circled him in a cobra coil of black ice. The moon tore into the night sky past the tippy top of the Fairmont Hotel's spire. What a joke tonight is. His life was anchored to rusted drums. Fuckin' geez-fuck. Water. Licking its chops. He ground his hip into the bars to balance but then dropped to his knees, clinging.

Shafiqq sprung to the far side. 'Cool your jets, dude.'

Whatever those teenagers dragged for their rave party, they brought it up here.

'Gonzalez', man. Now, who you callin' "sissy"?'

Ton' pulled himself to standing. He got his footing in the rusted steel treads. 'I, for one, love the water. Love the lake. I could jump right in,' he said. His stomach wobbled. Holy fucking Jesus Christ. 'Jump with me,

Puss-ass So-sick Sissy Shafiqq Sinha.' Ton' threw a leg over the chain railing. 'See? You don't scare me.' His palms sweat. Fuckin' man fuck-fuck. He pumped his weight into the deck. 'Come on, Puss-Ass Mo-Fo, Shafiqq. You first.' On that flimsy strip of steel, his life wobbled. Jesus. Skeins of light nipped at his legs and flickered across his gaze. Jesus fuck-me God. 'Okay, I'll do it.' Keeping just one toe on the bridge (holy fucking christ), he dangled himself further out over the water (oh man oh man oh man). 'Motherfucker, Shafiqq. Puss-Ass Pussy Puss. SISSY!' They'd trawl his torso, all worm and snail eaten. They'd lift his head and limbs chewed by eel and boat motors. Retrieve his remains by cord and pulley. 'Man is first a sea creature, Shafiqq. We are not so far from ocean birds.'

Shafiqq hopped up, touched his knees to his hands and landed on the slushed shore.

Ton' dropped to the bridge floor, again. 'Don't think I won't, Shafiqq. Don't think I can't.'

'Ton', take a pill.'

Ton's breath wouldn't come. He saw red. Coloured balls exploded in his eyes. He gripped the railing. One step. Two step. Please, please, please.

'My grandma's got the balls of two of you, Ton'.'

He teetered at the edge of the bridge and land; earth and sky; life and death. Maybe he should stay put. Stay on the bridge. Hold the railing. Don't move a muscle. Choose Life! Moulding moss ground into his nose. 'Something died out here.' Please dear God Jesus let it not be him. Not tonight. Not when 'Schelle's flat on her back and his little ones have staked everything on a swim against the current. The steel lip could slip. He'd sink into the lake; into the gunk black of night. He lunged clearing the bridge and landing on all fours. He clawed at slippery grasses sheathed in sleet. Bracing himself, he pushed himself up the upslope.

Shafiqq got ahold of his collar and pulled him up.

'It's dick-stupid to tromp around out here.'

'Walk, Ton'. Just get up and walk. We bust a meth joint, we make D.C.' Shafiqq clapped his gloves together. 'Eyes on the prize.'

The wind cut into Ton's boots.

'Bust a lab, man, make Detective Constable.'

Ton' jerked his shoulder out of Shafiqq's grip. 'Just walk. Man.'

'You.'

At the top, his thighs cramped. He dug his thumbs in. 'I am.'

They don't call it 'The Spit' for nothing. Fish. Stink. Humber innards. Decay gunked up the air. Leaves, fish, rats, mice, dogs and cats all sweeten the breeze. All the chopped-off arms, legs, and feet they find out here. Mob jobs. Boyfriends gone berserk. Rogue cops on the D.L. The lake shore and its environs came littered with Torontonians making bad choices. That head caught in the Peace Bridge and decomposing in a Glad bag. Those legs bound to that sunken fender. Montreal ain't the only war zone death trap. Out past the cottonwoods, the downtown Core twists a golden necklace of blinking lights. In the marina, a wire cable dinged a steel mast.

The tracks faded into the ice pack of blacktop tunnelling into trees closer to the water.

'That way.' Shafiqq lit off.

A siren peeled from Lakeshore and Leslie. The Spit lighthouse shot a beam brushing through the leaves higher up.

Snow gummed up Ton's boots.

'Come on, Ton'.' Slowpoke.' Shafiqq took off.

'It's cold out here.'

Shafiqq cleared the upslope beyond the bridge. Freaking jackrabbit hopping up off-road over milkweed and sweetgrass. The tracks merged into a path burrowing into a dogwood stand. The snow slowed.

Scotiabank Plaza's reflection rippled on the waves. This area turned gull territory come summer. The tracks led further into other stands of poplar, elm and birch. They pressed further through tangles of cottonwood. On a chain-link barrier, a yellow CAUTION sign flipped in the wind.

One jump and Shafiqq hopped over. Fucker.

'Do it, Ton'. You can.'

'I got boots on.'

'You don't see me in ballet slippers and a tutu.'

Man. 'Break my neck back there, break my neck out here.'

'Just jump.'

The wind stung his neck. Ton', for one, didn't need to be a show-off. He got a boot and a hand on the pole to steady himself. Just as he lifted, his legs slicked out.

'I'm just saying.'

'Help me.'

Shafiqq heaved Ton' up. 'Climb over.'

Man.

Everyone knew about that jut of elm trees shooting up from past the bush and around that curve down there. April to September, it's one long squawk of birds.

Shafiqq pushed at him, 'Easy, eh?' He raced down. Show-off.

Hanging onto each other's elbows, they pursued the tracks sinking, splitting and disappearing into the trees. Two distinct and parallel lines.

Just like when 'Schelle squirts toothpaste in two lines directly onto the bathroom mirror. *That's your life,* she pointed to the left line. *This is mine*, she pointed to the right. *And this,* she smushed dabs into the space between them. *This is called "the focus space." I may work at a construction joint but I have a degree in cognitive linguistics and I am telling you that in the focus space between is where "wobble" lives.* She wiped her finger with his shirttail. *Mind your wobble, Ton'. You wobble with or without me.*

'What were they hauling is the question.'

Way high up, the branches whipped in the wind.

'Come July—those trees are dripping with cormorants.'

'I ate cormorants before.'

'No, Ton'. You did not eat those.'

Prick. Ton' got his footing.

They cleared the dogwood and hit a clearing. The air cleared. The ground sketched out in an arc, charcoaled between where they stood and the water. The path wound into a knot of trees. The T.O. skyline spilled east like a dump bucket of Legos or G.I. Joe accessories: tanks, vision helmets, ammo satchels. Nobody appreciates G.I.

Joe anymore. Like when *The Baroness* explodes to save *Destro*. Yellow. Red. Black.

'Cormorants are those black birds, Ton'. Like Canadian geese, but black. You don't eat 'em. They're polluted.'

'I do.' Ton' never ate a cormorant in his life.

'You know what you're standing in.'

Ton' lifted his foot.

'Guano.'

A gun-metal glacial sheet spread to the water and into the trees.

'Bird shit.'

A brush of snow swept over Ton's boots. He jumped up and down.

'Two feet of it out here. Avian permafrost.' Shafiqq jumped up and down. 'You can't break through. A jack-hammer maybe. There's guano islands in South America.'

'You can break it.' Ton' leapt up and landed. Again. Harder. Again. He squatted to check. The stuff didn't crack. 'Mine cracked.'

'You dig into this stuff,' Shafiqq dug with his heels, 'you find everything we are ingesting.'

Man, Shafiqq never heard him out.

'In the air, Ton'. Every time you breathe. Everything. Birds are the ultimate environmental historical record.'

'Of what?'

Here, the wind pressed the ends of branches to the waters' edge.

'Bird shit, dude. Check it out. They eat—.'

Oh, boy, Professor Sinha stepped up to the podium.

'Pesticides, man. Contamination. They eat beetles, ants, worms, blue gill; boom, guano. Mosquitos. A fossil record of global warming.'

'We're all going to die anyway so who cares?'

'Ton'. Hello. You want to be a detective. There is a lot of information in guano. Get curious.'

Ton'd like to know how many cases got cracked from bird poo.

'That's not the point, Ton'. You're such a frog in a well. Clues right under your nose. Traces of what went down are everywhere. Everything leaves a clue. A mark, a scar, a difference. Like this drag path.'

Like they're going to find out what went down out here from bird shit.

'Be a detective. Open your eyes.' Shafiqq took off to the stand of trees farther off.

Kids partied. Got jacked. Went home. End of story.

Mr. Ballerina had gotten ahead into a tangle of elm and poplar. He pushed into a poplar trunk. He squatted. He stood. He backed up. He shook the trunk. A Sufi thing probably.

'What do you got?', Ton' asked. Humber stink sailed in. 'Man, it is perfume out here.'

Shafiqq spoke, but Ton' couldn't hear. His eyes stung and teared up in the iced wind. If he had a jar, he'd collect them for Ale.

The trees scratched at the sky like they wanted out.

Shafiqq poked with his foot.

'Find something?' Shafiqq is such a fucking pussy. He's never going to get Detective Constable.

'No. Nothing.' Shafiqq gripped a sapling yanking his boot loose. 'My boot caught.'

'Your meth lab? A campfire?' Not being Canadian, Shafiqq wouldn't know how to smother flames in snow. 'That's all they were doing. Partyin'. Making a fire.' Ton'd have to show him how. 'Stomp it, dude.'

'My boot. Is all.'

Ton' stepped closer. 'You don't want the whole place to go up in flames.'

Shafiqq put a hand on Ton's chest. Ton' jerked away. Shafiqq shoved him.

Ton' fell back holding on to a sapling. He got himself back up. But, his knees flooded with air. His stomach sank. 'What?'

Shafiqq planted himself in front of whatever he was kicking. 'Back off, Ton'.' Shafiqq shoved him.

Ton's cheeks stung. Shafiqq and the trees blurred. He wiped his watering eyes. Jesus. Weird. Little Fuck floating in the sauerkraut surfaced, his tiny legs rotating slowly with the body. But then, too, Ton' peeking through their bedroom doorjamb with 'Schelle holding the jar under Ale's eyelids. The doc saying 'leukemia' kept them in that room for what seemed hours. Ton' made a whole meat loaf, baked two potatoes, and sat with his arms folded on the couch that afternoon. Ale's news came the freaking day after their first IVF. Not making a peep, he squinted through the crack. They pressed their foreheads together just the way he used to press his into Ma. Ton' blinked. The trees folded back into focus.

'My boot, Ton'. It is just my boot.'

'Don't fuckin' hit me.' Ton' took a step forward.

'Don't.'

'Don't "don't" me. A detective would look. I got to look. What, it's more of your guana guana?'

Ton' stepped closer.

Shafiqq put his hand up. 'Ton'?' His voice warbled.

'Stop "Ton'-ing" me.'

'Ton'.'

He stepped. A pile of logs. So what.

'Jesus.'

Ton' saw. A stick. A little thick stick. Poking up out of the snow. That's all there is there. Kindling. He stepped into Shafiqq's boot tracks. He steadied himself on that sapling. He squatted. He had to keep his ass out of the wet.

Shafiqq hopped out of the thicket. 'Ton'.'

'Pussy, Shafiqq.' That old song he and Ma used to jiggy to cut clear through the stink and waves from a party boat farther out on Lake Ontario. *I love you, baby. / And if it's quite alright / I need you, baby. / Through all the lonely nights——*. Ton's eyes adjusted to the shadows cast amongst the branches.

The snow and ice sparkled refractions of city lights.

He leaned forward, supporting himself on a small branch digging his toes in. Oh. Wait a sec'. That bark is a knuckle. He got himself sideways some. That's a finger. A fat finger pushing up through the snow. Okay, so what's a dead body to professional detective cops? Cops get hardened by nights like this. You seen one dead body, you seen 'em all. Actually, Ton' had never seen a dead person before. Save for Little Fuck. Shafiqq the weak definitely could not handle a dead body. Ton', though, had the guts to handle a little death. He reached for a twig. He got a grip at the crook of a branch to break it.

And froze. That finger. But, he knows that finger. The fat of that knuckle. That finger is Albert's. That is the crook of Albert's finger. Ton' dropped into the snow next to the body. He pawed and scooped at the snow at the neck, on the chest, the other side of the body, in between the arms; he swiped at the legs. He took Albert's cheeks, grey in the loam, in both hands. He lowered himself to feel the breath on his own cheek.

'Albert!' He slapped at the cheeks. 'Dad!' He shouted. He got his arms around the shoulders to lift him up but the body did not bend.

Shafiqq had tip-toed closer. 'Ton'. Come on. We'll call it in.'

Shafiiqq called from a parallel universe. Two light years and five feet away.

Ton' could just stay here. He'd just stay here with his father-in-law and everything would be okay. Everything would get back to normal. He would stay here and figure it out.

He snapped the twig and steadied himself. He didn't know. That's a fact. He did not know for sure. Sometimes his mind played tricks on him. There's no guarantee. There's no official ruling. Who says it's Albert? Nobody said that. That had not been stated. He only thought it. It's not real. Every finger's got knuckles. Every finger's got those lines. All fingers crook crooked.

He brushed aside a bit more snow. One unbroken crease on the index finger, with a cross bow wrinkle shot through. That is the finger that had gripped dripping pizza meltdown to his mouth. Albert's. Ton' got a good hold of a birch sapling and pulled himself up in. 'Yeah. Okay. Right? Can we call? We just got to just call.' Ton' bolted. He jumped back. Cleared the trees. Landed two feet far away.

Shafiqq circled him. As if facing a wild animal.

Two minutes ago this hadn't happened. Two minutes ago, Albert sat next to Ale at home. 'Schelle bugged him to go check things out. He did. He did. Ton' did what he was told to do. He fulfilled his duty. How did Albert get way out here? How did this happen? Ton' did what he was supposed to do.

Shafiqq had his hand on his shoulder radio.

Ton' plunged back into the trees. He had to see. Maybe he was wrong. He could be wrong. A thin stream of pure, sweet breeze rushed his face. He leaned, he squatted. He got closer and scooped even more of the snow from around the face. He touched the skin. Taut, hard and clay. The half-moon of Albert's eyeball rose from beneath the lens of his wire framed glasses. He had had something in his sights. Ton' stomped and jammed and cracked twigs, branches and discarded steel to clear room. The eyes were open and steady. He got down to eye level with Albert's gaze. It wasn't his killer the old man caught with his eye. His crow's feet were relaxed. He expected the blows. People squint in a panic when their killer's in sight. Figure it out, Ton'. His heart thundered. What went down. Ton' cleared two feet around to make way. He'd give him in a halo.

'Ton'. Just come on.'

Albert's hands were not clenched, he did not fight back. His knees were bent. Probably from the initial fall to the ground and then rigor mortised in transport. People tend to twine themselves in the death pangs, fighting back as if caught in a net. The skin mottles: reddens, yellows, and mattes. His limbs bent in the bush but the body seemed tidy. Like it'd been placed here. He didn't die here. His coat had fallen or blown open. City light caught the purple tie 'Schelle had gifted him, now flipped over off his shoulder. His lips had thinned as the blood had drained. The whole right side of his skull mis-shapen, the side of his face smeared. His white shirt dis-coloured with oxygenated blood, gunked and black. Before Ton' knew his plan, he kicked the body. It may be a movie dummy. The kick landed like into Ma's sacks of basmati rice.

"Kay.' The saplings dug into Ton's palms. "Kay.' He braced into the wind; the trees, now smooth steel rail-ings overlooking waves crushing under the bow of the ship he pounded from, into a sky cloudless yet clinging to the earth absented by what-was-left of the city's re-flection velociting shooting ricocheting ping-ponging to Shafiqq now taking his shoulder even while Ton's mind returned a strange fruit so particular, so peeled clean that he leaned into the touch, that impression, that undeni-able kindness landing a sucker punch. Now.

Shafiqq clipped his arm.

"Kay, kay. So. Okay. We have to call.'

'Ton'—.'

Ton' stopped. No. He had to see again. For himself. Just to know. It could be a joke. It could be some kind of sick fuck joke. He watched his step. Took it slow. If that thing were real, it would be there when he made it back.

'Ton'!' Shafiqq tapped his shoulder mic. 'Ton'. Don't look more. Let's go.'

He got up close. Angled to get Ton's eyes wild as they took in the trees, the blue-grey sheen of the snow fields, the trees inking skeletons against the city, the low-slung clouds gorging on the coming storm. 'We'll call, Ton'.'

Now Ton' rode the breeze angling over the lip of his collar to a choke hold. He flew. He jettisoned back to that oil drum bridge from what the crook of that finger meant.

'I do. I am. I saw it.' He stopped dead in his tracks.

Ma came out of the trees. Snapping first a stripling, then a firmer intact one, lurching right, then left but easy, not rushing, she came stepping over triangles, squares and ladders laid there seeming like by Nature as the deck of the ship she steered through obstacles but also as markers, measurers, as geometrics of navigation is what they'd say in Ton's Investigators' textbook, the architecture of crime they say, in a blink she squatted next to Albert's body, poking his skin to cry out to her but so focused and intent balancing herself on a branch behind her and Albert's gut in front, the blood coagulating at her feet as maybe just after he'd fallen the flood filling his throat his esophagus, his epiglottis, a lone red-sheened bubble of oxygen pressing forward back into the life now speeding from sight, away from all those he would leave behind, look there how Ma gets herself lower still so that she is able to fold herself in amongst the birch branches fetally close to Albert perhaps to comfort and soothe him. Ton' noticed then, that she had him, her son, in the purview of one eye.

She watched Ton' in his gob-smacked silence. She began, then, to unbutton Albert's shirt, un-peeling the fabric back to reveal his chest chalky in the glow of the city and its snow. One eye on her boy, one eye on Albert. Rooting at the skin of his chest, just below the stem of his sternum, his skin now glistening though he couldn't be sweating, she didn't dig hard but with a ferocity in her finger's press tearing the skin, allowing one finger first, and two to enter that cavity. Once she had two fingers in, she made it three and then four and before Ton' took a single breath, her whole hand up to her wrist but now her elbow disappeared inside; and slowly, slowly slowly as if she were detaching this piece or that, she withdrew her arm in pulls so minute one could miss them unless watching filmstrip like, and out came Albert's entrails: his intestines, his liver, two kidneys and that pale lima bean stomach one would have thought to be bigger. At last, now, she got up on her free elbow, finishing the disembowelment and held there, resting perhaps, and miraculously it seemed to Ton' given all the things she could have tripped over with all of her balance problems, but with still that one eye locked on her son, Ma stepped back over the branches, over the triangles, squares and ladders to spin off further towards the lake. But once Ma cleared those struts and beams, the woodsmoke of a cook fire came—hadn't they come to look for ravers, for partiers, weren't they a part of all of this, wasn't there a limo they were after.

Ton' stepped himself now around Albert, back past the gutted body out towards where Ma had gone, over the triangles, the squares and the geometrics of navigation and when he got far enough, Ma crouched stirring the entrails in a skillet sprinkling tiny tidbits taken from her pockets, one eye still cocked on Ton' and, with her cooking complete, she waved him to come closer, his chair reserved on the rock next to Ma's fire, having his plate now filled full without asking but because they shared molecules and incidents, bloodlines, and terrors.

He stepped towards Ma. But something caught her eye the same as she had caught Ton's a minute ago creeping forth out of the trees. Ma's eye whirled around just as the clouds cleared and the full moon shone forth washing first the lake, then the beach, third, the smooth side of the fallen trees to, fourth, the rocks of concrete debris circling around her fire. He followed her finger, now lifted and tracing a path from these woods to her skillet and for a brief moment just past the tip of Ma's finger, he descended into a lunar canyon and when he surfaced his skin had hardened even more than a moment ago but clean clean clean as if he'd been washed not by water and not by experience no way but by the fine dust of a lacuna opening only at the pit of unexpected circumstance that one knows, in spite of his best intentions, to be warping the wires that make him up.

'Ton'—.'

On his knees, Ton' pressed his cheek against the marble of Albert's.

Milk

Tad laid his hand on your thigh. Driving west on Queen, the Spit faded behind. Sirens peeled. A long ways off, east of Leslie. *Jamaican Jerk Chicken* broke past. And then *Jilly's Strip Joint, Dangerous Dan's Death by Burger* and the *Dog-U-Wash*. Past *Coffee Planet, Sushi Marché* and the *East Side Community Care*. Past *Magic Oven, Ya Bikes* and *Kim's Convenience. The Beer Store, Stephen's Place*, and *Acadia Books* bloomed in streetlights. Way back at Carlaw, sirens cut through the night. Curtains of snow swept into the sidewalk.

Tom shook his 'fro and curled his lips under. Tonight's the physics. That back there, what we did—do not lose your cookies. It's physics. Quantum, right? What else would explain it?

Mr. P. buried in birch is the lead membrane through which you spin. Into presence. Into absence.

Maybe it's like "see our future," Tom said. See me. I'm at U of T, right. I'm there. You help people. The *bacha bazi*.

Asaan. Whatever plans you were thinking about helping Asaan couldn't be separated from Mr. P.'s forehead and those branches; from the bark, the birds, and the sculpted angels; from your mom's photos, the stink of Jeff's ass and lighter fluid on fire; from silver shorty-shorts and cops riding your bumper. From the scruff of Tom's jaw and his muscles pulling you in. Just now, you had signed the dotted line of Tom Meuley's insides, you had cast your signature upon his skin. A line drawn in some sand. You were not going back. There's no getting Asaan or his brother out if convicted for murder. Lose him now. Cut him free. The die is cast. Your lot divined.

Let's rent an apartment.

Back there in the trees, purple blotches of burst blood vessels mottled the lines in Mr. P.'s forehead. Gouges from the squeegee left shards of dried meat and pearl-white skull. By now, snow would have collected in the nostrils but the cold would slow the bloating. Come March, the coyotes and microbes would eat their fill.

It's what that old lady at the gas station said, Milk.

Like the one at your bedroom window.

Ferrying the dead, that's what we do, she said. Doing her windshield, climbing up her door, getting around—you should've seen her, Evan. Hair yellow. Long. Stringy. Floating thread fairy hair, all-electric in Petro Canada light. She pulls herself up. But, she's not strong enough so I did it. I let my pump click and ran to her. She could fall, right. Her hair lifting up like your grandma in the hospital, it's all in my face, you know, and I get her around the waist, and—swear to God she expected it. She doesn't straighten up. She falls into me. I hold her, she cleans her freaking windshield. The entire station wagon of hers is full of lawn frogs, broom handles, Barthes' *Image Music Text*—books. Clothes piled up like in your mom's basement. A polka dot photo album even. She starts to squirm to get in her car. And—.

Tom shook his head. I couldn't believe it. You won't believe it. Guess what she hands me.

The Odyssey.

Exactly. Read that, she says. The cover's fake marble and her mouth's gushing steam. You read that part, she says, where he carves that gulley so his dead mother can speak. So, all the people he's killed can speak. He's not trying to get home. It's to paddle. To cut the waves open for story. Cut the trench so story can flow. We paddle, we cut, so that the dead can story. The dead story the living. Every fibre of their being, every cell, every blood cell, are the ships in which we travel. Their histories, their lives; their loves are the blades cutting Life loose. The stories we tell are the vessels in which we sail. The passion, the hungers, the sufferings—the rivers on which we set sail. We must have the dead! Or we might never find our way home; to ourselves; to now. And so, we *are* home. Now. Row, Young Man! She hollered, shaking her fist. Row! You'll never reach those balmed and blistered shores, but you must cut your trench! Row! As if your whole life depends upon it! For it surely does! Watch the dead roam, she says, at Queen and Markham, at Bellwoods and Strachan, at Parliament and King. At the Don River and her buried sisters: Taylor Creek, Mud Creek, Taddle Creek. She got her dried twig of a finger in my face. God or your Mighty Zeus never made a land of the future, did He? Flashers blistered off Caroline St. and disappeared north.

Tom pressed his forehead into the dusty dashboard.

You could feel her ribs poking through her coat. Black ribbons streaming from her hood were all Earth smell. Soil-like. She had them in her teeth, chewing.

The closer you got to Parliament, signal lights shook frantic in the wind.

Your thighs pulsed the imprint of Tom's mount and gallop there.

At Broadview, a hurtling squad car clipped the corner, took the curb and spun straight for you. It squawked. You jammed on the brakes and braced. Tad shot his arms out. The unit swerved past. The red and blue flashers blinked and faded.

No way they could have found him yet.

The sirens thinned.

Maybe I got to go home, Tad. Maybe that squaring off inside of you is wrong. It could be Jeff like playing with you as a kid one minute and choking you the next. Nobody can figure this out. You didn't lift that squeegee. You weren't in that ATM booth.

Go.

I might still get out of this.

You two crossed back over the Don and made your way to Sherbourne.

You anchor at Moss Park. Straight ahead, a streetlight lit a baseball diamond and a pile of Zamboni scrapings by the back door of the community centre. The Canadian Air Force tank gun at the armory aimed straight at the Queen's Mental Health Centre. Crackheads huddled against a wall on the basketball court; Scotia Plaza and the BMO tower loomed.

Let me go. There's still time I might make it.

Cops are not going to be on us already. Not all of the evidence gets online right away. They build their case. They sweat you out. Don't spaz.

But, I'm a trench, Tom. I'm Tupperware. I'm G.I. Joe.

Let's go to my room, then. Sleep, he said.

Ahead, kliegs lit the baseball diamond.

They'll never find me in Kabul.

Use my credit card.

Sweet. Find Asaan. Then, Sakar. Get him. Then, what? Come with me.

He pulls that old photo of you treading water in Lake Charlevoix from the glove box. Grandma put it there on a trip to Metro. Like the story of your life.

In a stand of trees, a lighter flashed.

Queen Street had become a wind-blown snowscape pock-marked with periodic manholes and rock salt that didn't stand a chance.

Behind the baseball diamond, dealers ducked along the hi-fly fencing and disappeared into the tree line.

A current had you now. You could feel it taking you around the legs, the water rising to your hips. A pull from shore.

Nobody knows it's us, Milk.

Ton'

Albert's teeth bulged. The face screwed up from the birch. Ton' had seen that look before. The ravine. With Pat-Pat. That dude stopping smack in his tracks when he came to Ton'. No way. The brain mixes input under stress. Training taught him that.

But the light falling through the trees; the lips baring teeth like corn kernels. The same. Tonight, the lips had fought to do their work. Ton' forced them open; the gums too dark for the living. A funeral home would use the splits and fault lines tracking there to thread the mouth like Ma's in her casket. Ton' traced Albert's mouth with his fingertip. He knew its lines. He knew that finger.

'Schelle called it a "habit of mind." They had all gone to Giorgio's Pizza. Albert'd start some story, choose a piece of parmesano porcini, and suck the sauce from his fat index finger. He'd hold the slice in mid-air, between the pan and his mouth on the verge of starting a story.

'Eat your pizza, Albert.' Ale laid slivers of anchovy onto her pizza slice. *'Or I'll put some of these on it.'*

'Blech.'

Ton' knew 'Schelle's dad from somewhere. He couldn't place it.

'*Dad. Eat your pizza. Don't lick your finger.*' 'Schelle held out her own pizza slice to her mother.

Ale speared thin grey-brown slivers of fish and laid them onto 'Schelle's slice.

'*Ton'?*' Ale dangled an anchovy. '*Want some?*'

Fish on a pizza. Jesus. '*Sure.*'

Ale pulled the saucer of fish away. '*You're just saying that.*'

'*No, I really do.*' Christ.

'*Ton', you don't have to.*' 'Schelle forked a couple more slivers for her own slice and exhaled into his face. '*Get used to it.*'

Gross.

Albert nodded to Ton'.

He had to please these people. He didn't know why. He never wanted to please nobody else. Except Ma.

'*We love you fish or no fish.*'

But Ton' recognized Albert from somewhere. It was the way Albert held his pizza slice in mid-air about to take a bite. It was his short, tight nod to Ton'. He'd seen that exact look somewhere. That exact face.

'*Dad does this.*' 'Schelle lifted her Diet Coke glass and held it in the air. '*Like he's struck by lightning. That's what he tells me about the bats. You don't know the bats, but—.*'

'"*Schelle.*' Ale held her hand up. '*We're eating.*'

'Schelle cupped a hand over Ton's ear and whispered. '*He staples dead bats to our garage whenever he's struck by a thought that won't let him move on. It's disgusting.*' She took a bite of pizza and then returned to his ear. '*Or like for my nightmares or something.*'

Ton' snapped his fingers. *I know.* His face flushed red. *I think. That day at the school. The Ern True kid. The shooting. I saw you there. Maybe.*

Ale put her fork down. *You were at the school that day?*

Were you outside on the lawn? Ton' thought of all of the locations at the school where he might've seen Albert. Funny what the brain remembers. *A bunch of kids on the side after coming through the windows.*

Albert shook his head. *I don't think so.*

'Schelle piped up. *Dad's too modest. He pulled a bunch of kids into the janitor's closet. Right, Dad?*

Ale placed both hands on the table. *If you went to that school that day, Ton'. Just thank you.*

It's the teachers. Some of those kids.

Albert shook dried hot peppers onto his slice.

Dad, too. I'm just saying. He stayed in there protecting them.

Albert shook even more peppers onto his pizza.

Dad. That's going to be hot.

Ton' couldn't quite nail it. Maybe he didn't know Albert from that 10-71.

Albert had been in the middle of explaining economic troubles in the States. *What do you think, Ton'?*

Ton' shrugged. *Sure. Totally.*

'Schelle kneed him under the table.

He's scared of you, Albert. Ale pointed her knife at her future son-in-law. *Call him "Albert."*

If I had time I would tell you about this friend of mine that lived in the Vietnamese jungle. As a child—.

Albert. Please. We're eating.

'Dad.'

He brought the slice towards his mouth. But, then stopped. His mouth frozen.

Out here on the Spit, a dried leaf had caught at the crook of Albert's arm slanted behind the left thigh, the face relaxed. Boot tracks roped the body.

Shafiqq tracked the line of footprints.

Beyond, saplings sagged truncated and broken. Storm fencing strung out from where Shafiqq stood to the path where they'd climbed the caution sign, to the up-slope down to the chain-link bridge, to the boot-tracked path towards that barrier they climbed, and then on out to the three blocks of granite, and then to the road ending at Leslie. T.O.'s haranguing din had faded, that song had ended.

Ahead of Ton', waves lurched loud into the rocks out past that hard pack of bird shit. He maneuvered sticks from under the head and over the torso.

Leaves keened and crickled above.

'He used to get ready to tell something and then just—.' Ton' forced himself to study the steel cable of that road barrier. Those stones and these trees had seen what had happened here. That barrier and those trees knew. Mama knew.

'We got to call this in, Ton'.'

'No. No. We do not. We leave it.'

'Ton'—.'

'No. We take care of it.'

'They are going to know that we left a body out here.'

That reek curry crap smell flung itself onto Ton'.

'Sorry. Not "a body." Him.' Agitated, Shafiqq's held tight to the sides of his head and his dasti. He paced. 'Here. They told us to come here.'

'Don't be nervous, Shafiqq. I got these fuckers.' Ton' stepped away from the body. 'Say I'm in shock. Say I couldn't take it. Say I melted like a little baby.' He had this.

Shafiqq tightened his turban.

'No. Better. I got it, Shafiqq. We leave it. Okay. We leave him. We. We find it out. We take care of it.'

'"We."'

'We. You. Me. We.' Ton' got around the body into the sticks, got a good grip under the shoulders, and lifted him.

'Sorry, Ton'. Not me. Crime scene, man.'

Ton' lifted Albert so Shafiqq could see. The head flopped over, the eyes soaking up the city in their not-seeing. 'Call it in then, Shafiqq. Call it. You think if it's your dad or your father-in-law. You get a picture in your head of your own dad, Shafiqq.' Ton' hoisted the dead weight to his chest. Albert's head now slumped forward. He studied the piles of snow, the tracks; the tiny twigs they broke bringing him here.

The waves still smashed into the rocks beyond the trees. Must be one of those cargo ships docking at the Redpath plant had broken the shoreline pressing out to deep water, carving their way now up to Lake Superior.

'Got the picture?' He laid the body down. And smoothed its hair. 'I'll get 'em, Albert.' A cold sweat broke on his brow and neck. Hold it together, Ton'. His stomach turned upside down. Go find who did this.

They crawled back to the main gate at Leslie Street. A Tercel blocked the way out. Some lady wanting to go in. Lost. As soon as Ton' got out of the car, air plunged into his guts and bones. He blew. Puked. Too much oxygen. He'd surfaced too fast. Shafiqq dealt with the lady. They had to find those fucks. He wiped his face with handfuls of snow. He turned from the woman, scooped more into his mouth to get rid of the taste. He walked to the trunk and spit it out.

Once they made Leslie and Lakeshore, Shafiqq took a left, hyper-slow. 'You could fishtail out here good.'

'I'm right, Shafiqq. I have to. You get that picture.'

'So, what. We wait?'

'We find those fuckers.'

'In the limo?'

'Yes, of course, that limo. That must have been them. 'Bet they're the ones that we were supposed to bust. That got called in.'

'That lady was looking for a limo.'

'What lady?'

'The one in the little—.'

'That lady back there? The Tercel or whatever?'

'I told you. She told you. Not like she hid it. She asked if we saw a limo.'

Ton' jacked in his seat. 'You let her go?'

'What am I to—.'

'Hold her for? Murder, motherfucker.'

'Easy.' Shafiqq crawled through the right on Cherry.

'She's got to know something. Did you get the plates?'

'No. She got mixed up. A writer or something.'

God puts the cunt smack down in front of him and this jack-off hands her a get-out-of-jail-free card and sends her on her way.

A Diet Coke can got lifted by the wind—and hurtled at their windshield. They ducked.

'Damn.' They ought to clean this road better. 'How come they don't salt out here? Don't they know this town is on a downslope? Don't they know a tin can gets thrown out at the top of Parliament and rolls to the lake?'

Ton' could do tonight. He could. He would.

The can blew back towards where they'd come from. 'Ton'—.'

'You don't see how things run together, Shafiqq. Who is the frog in the well, man? That limo. Put two and two. A Coke can comes flying. But where from? Ask that question.' He slapped the dashboard. 'Story, man. Story.'

'That lady doesn't know—.'

'Oh, yeah. Lots of bitches out here looking for limos. At the Spit. Tonight. Wake up. Right where—.'

'You're right, you're right. Stupid. You were puking—.'

'Okay. Okay.' Ton' sat on his hands. Think. 'Here's what we do.'

They passed a billboard for the Lower Donlands development. The lanes to the D.V.P. were jam-packed.

'We call in an A.P.B. that Tercel. And the limo. We triangulate.'

'The limo has one.'

'Put another.'

'J. will want to know why.'

'Fuck J.'

The way Albert's mouth buckled under the shivering cormorants.

'Get up further.'

Shafiqq put on the overheads. They had to make the up ramp.

'You got to—.'

'Get over, man.' The whole right side of Albert's head, the whole front portion caved in, almost as far back as his ear.

Shafiqq had his eye on the traffic behind him, then to the right and then to the left.

'He wasn't even bleeding out there.'

'They did it elsewhere. They brought him out there.' Shafiqq cleared his throat.

What they must have done is get him out of the trunk by the three boulder barriers and half-dragged, half-carried him into the trees. 'Were there drags over that bridge?' Ton' gripped the seat edge.

Shafiqq tugged at his dastār.

'Like I'm supposed to tell 'Schelle?'

'Let me.'

'No, me.' Fuck this traffic. 'Take the shoulder.'

'Ton'—.'

'You are real good to them, Ton'.'

Not good enough. Maybe Ale didn't have to know.

'Take the shoulder, Shafiqq.'

Shafiqq took a deep breath, whoop-whooped the siren, hit the horn.

There she sat. That woman in the compact. A Tercel. In the right lane exactly where they were crossing. Ton' slammed his hand into the dashboard. 'There she is. Man. It's her.'

Shafiqq glanced to the left, to the right, in the rear view.

The woman brought her hands to her face. You can't hide now, lady.

'There. There, there.' He pointed to where she dipped now behind them. They were on the shoulder. Ton' yanked at the seat belt, and then rolled down his window. 'Stop. Stop. I'm getting out.'

'You aren't getting hit.'

Ton' leaned out waving for that bitch to pull over.

She zipped through an opening into the opposite lane. Cunt.

'That bitch knows. She knows.' He pushed back into his seat, keeping an eye on her. 'Go back.'

'Ton' we can't—she can't get off the D.V.P. without us getting her.'

The Eden's screen lit up.

'They've got the limo up there. It's two boys.'

In some parallel stream of events, what would be had already unspooled. Flashes of 'Schelle this morning and of Ale slapping his face surfaced and disappeared. He wiped sweat and hair wax on his pants.

➤ What came at him equalled when he and Ma had blown that tire on the 427 coming in south past Black Creek. The right rear tire blew, the whole car massively swung, the rear pulling around and now leading, Ma slammed on the brakes and then the accelerator. Centrifugal force heaved and twisted, the rear spun ahead of the front. The car surged forward barreling into that trench. When they hit the upslope on the opposite bank they cut a trench open full-on, popped up in the air, flipped and landed upside down. The windows blew out. As they skidded, Ton' hung there, suspended by the safety belt, as an eighteen-wheeler plowed straight at them not 25 feet away—so this is how it ends is what he thought at that moment. He hoped Ma was okay. Up-side down, they skidded all the way to the far shoulder and came to a rest facing north. His body hung there, but he was long gone. He'd flown somewhere deep inside of what had been himself, crouching and hidden, as if in a deep dirt hole, waiting for it to be over.

━━ 'Just get us to the checkpoint, okay? I bet they got 'em.'

'Ton'.'

'I am not going to do anything bad, Shafiqq.' The hell he wasn't. 'I'm not. I got it.'

'Think of 'Schelle.'

'Schelle, who? She is back there on planet earth. Sitting at home. Her legs up to keep his cum inside.

'Ton'.'

'I got it.'

Untie their ropes and let the lake take them. The blows sink, the shore recedes.

Sessy

Close enough to see but far enough to hide, Sessy backed the Tercel into the reeds. She'd tail the coppers'd back towards the city. The limo, the limo, the limo. Sure as Mother Teresa, she should not have asked about Tom Meuley's limo. They probably had an APB out for the boys. You-know-who (Jeff) said *what do you need a police scanner for, what a waste of cash* and *how come she didn't understand the value of money*? Listening to that *gets you paranoid*, he said. Foresight is nine-tenths of the law. He's got some nerve calling her paranoid. Just who is catting with a kitty and who is not?

She dug deep under the car seat. Something rotted down there. A Little Debbie caught between the gear shift and the seat lever. She creamed her finger in and then sucked it clean. She opened the door and wiped her hands in the snow. She gripped the steering wheel and lifted herself to standing. From over the Tercel's roof and the reeds, she could spy on those officers.

By the Leslie St. entrance, the cop with the doo-wrap on his head got back out of the car, hanging on to the hood and getting around back to where the metal posts bent in crooked 'Ls' now. Probably trying to hook that barrier chain back up. Good luck. The joker that mowed that down wasn't fooling.

Vapour steamed from her lungs—the bowels of the earth.

Towel-head got back in his squad car and they backed out of the Spit. Those cops were on their way and would lead her to the boys.

Sessy took three long breaths to bide her time. Give 'em a head start. Stay back. Don't raise their suspicions. She traced her scar again. Those coppers had something on their minds. The boys.

There must have been a crush of warm air pushing over from Michigan. The snow up Leslie to Lakeshore glistened packed and crunching. The mess pounded down, thunking. The snow fields shot off the shoulder sailing out away from the road, surging into the tornado fences lining the sidewalk. The drifts out there, with their new weight, could have been the gently swooping surface of a tub of Cool Whip.

Maybe Milk and Tom are down in one of the ravines. Maybe the coppers will rappel down the slippery slope, flashlights beaming, radios squawking. They'll fire a rope gun into a rock and capture the boys in a giant net. Or worse. The boys could have parked just south off of Yonge on Merton. Or worse. They could've ditched the limo back down along the beltway, hopped the fence, cut across Mount Pleasant Cemetery and boogered down deep. Maybe that bat-hooded lady, the ghost of ye ol' Edith Nordheimer, would lead them through Taddle Creek to action, adventure, and her Castle Frank woods.

Back in the day, Edith would go in there to escape Samuel, to wrench at her hair, hike her skirts, and skin those beavers. It's the one job the old girl insisted on doing for herself. At what is now the drainage ditch south of Davisville she'd tuck her hems into her belt and squat slitting the throats of the little guys one by one. Those woods down there are made for secrets kept and tongues bitten.

Edith caught the little buggers in a cage wedged into the shore. After slitting their throats, she'd fling the bodies to dry land. Them others screamed and clawed and scratched at the steel drain screens waiting for their kingdom come. Their sweet goddess drained them of life's sweet goodness. They rotted; caught in twigs, leaves, logs, and fashion.

If the boys hid in the ravine, they'd have a few hours before the daylight gave way to search parties.

Maple leaves tingled in the quiet. Cardinals, nuthatch, and beady-eyed finches squawked.

She pulled out of her hiding spot and pulled closer to keep them in view. That cop car took a yellow light onto Lakeshore. West. Maybe that Patricia had called the police on the boys for attempted murder. Jeff wouldn't back up his own kid. He'd throw him to the wolves, selling him down the river. Sessy dug into the family size peanut M&M's and got a handful. She dug the candied shell off a blue M&M with her teeth. The boys must be in the Core or up the D.V.P. Dang. Christ. Goddamn. The light went red. So, what. She gunned it. But, she blew too fast and fishtailed. She spun the wheel right into the turn, straightened out, and shot down

Lakeshore. Her summer as a barrel-driver served her well. Nobody's leaving her in the weeds.

She caught up to them at Cherry. One right and they headed past the Distillery. If they took a right at Eastern, then they were headed up the D.V.P. That would mean the boys were stuck in that D.U.I. boogeroo checkpoint she'd seen heading south. Nobody ever takes Cherry. It's a snow drift. Cars were half-buried next to the fence at the Donlands condo development.

At the stop sign, they took a right. Heading east on Eastern they went under the D.V.P. and hung a right to get to the entrance ramp.

Some yahoo came speeding up behind her. She gunned the accelerator. It jammed. Then released. She slammed the brakes and skidded whipping into tight circles. She covered her face. The Tercel flicked out of its spin. And stopped. No one honked. She had spun to the shoulder and stopped cock-eyed to the road. That yahoo had disappeared. Probably in the ditch. Straight through the barriers and crashed face down into the left lane of Eastern Avenue. She tippy-tapped the accelerator after shifting into reverse. Her calves were soaked. Maybe piddle. She couldn't tell. She backed up far enough to get her wheels turned. Headlight beams blew into the Tercel as another car entered the ramp. They slowed, she got her shoulders right, did a three-point turn, and gunned the gas. And, made it. At the top of the ramp, she blinked her headlights, waved a friendly little hello to some blond joker in a Hummer. 'Thank you,' she mouthed. Once merged, she couldn't see a damned thing up ahead. Packed in like sardines, the traffic crawled.

Anybody drunk would be sober by the time they made to the Checkpoint Charlie ahead. She inched. And inched.

The slopes off the Don had been carved out by glaciers in the Pleistocene retreat. From that height she might be able to see Milk. From that height, she might have known better.

The traffic on the Don Valley Parkway, a.k.a. the D.V.P, wasn't moving at all. Probably a D.U.I. checkpoint. That's the Toronto Police Services for you. A checkpoint in the middle of a blizzard.

But the glaciers pushed forward tonight.

She pulled at the seat seam. Okay. Okay. Focus, focus, focus. She might as well be an Edith Nordheimer stuck there on the D.V.P. fleeing her high-falutin beaver balls flinging off the stinking, fresh-killed fox stole she had draped over her Imperial beaded lace gown, snatching her own 'Samuel Nordheimer' to hurry past the townsfolk lined up at the sidewalk waving flaming torches and chanting that they wanted a piece of her pie. Sessy tipped what was left in a Pringles canister into her mouth.

Like Edith, her tummy sank and then leapt. She put the car in park, got the door open and puked. She spat the Pringles coating her throat.

Milk

Up there, ahead on the D.V.P., traffic poked. Red. Blue. White. Lights. Police. Spin. Blink. Blink.

Tad dug into the glove box. Roadblock.

Black woods ran along the Don Valley Parkway.

What's down there?

The river.

The ravine runs from Rosedale out here; past Ern True's and Castle Frank. We shoot down, stay under the overpass.

Like that wouldn't draw attention.

It's one night, Milk.

The limo, Tad. It'll be sitting here empty.

There's a drainage tunnel, it's just sticks and debris. It's got a metal screen. Get in out of the wind. Tuck in. Wait. There's water running through there. Dogs can't smell us. Remember *The Fugitive?* He's in the drainage pipe. Tommy Lee Jones can't find him—. That's us maybe. He strained to see over the edge. The veins in his forearms bulged. We do it. One night. Then, up to Taylor Creek, then Mud Creek to Mount Pleasant Cemetery.

Carved out by glaciers, the Don Valley and its river had been ripped from Mississauga peoples.

People freeze to death out there. That's where all those old people wander off to.

Those molars are out here somewhere.

After pumping chemicals into the Don for decades, a plastics company built solar-powered and elevated wet lands in the shape of giant molar teeth to draw the polluted water out, filter it, and then feed it back to the river.

We can get water straight from the molars.

Sheets of sleet plugged the view.

We get out. We walk.

Licence plates, Tad. Provincial databases.

He still had the glove box open, digging. We take them off. Got a screwdriver in here. The heater kicked in again, whack-a-whacking.

You cracked the window and the wind ripped at your forehead.

You could slip into the ravines until you come up by the buried lake at Rosehill Reservoir.

Behind you, a line of cars streamed back to Eastern Ave. Snow slashed bright across the headlights.

It's like a funeral procession. Isn't it like what that old lady getting gas said? Dragging the dead along with us.

The limo pressed in on you: the mahogany dashboard, the quilted ceiling.

Like the wagons ferrying the dead across Paris. Tonight is one of those trips across the city. We're the Charon ferrymen rowing the dead to Hades. Your mom, too. Her keeping photos ferries the dead to the present. Taking eighty-seven steps into the catacombs, that's it too. We're how the dead find their way home. We're the light on the porch; the candle in the window.

You and Tom were ferrymen. When you tell a story, like Orillia and bakery. Like Grandma and getting the nitro-oxygen exchanges just right. Like putting a foot on the floor in the middle of the night; like just looking out the window. The outcome doesn't matter; it's the act. The living are pressed into action by the dead. It's us that pull their wagons. If you're the ferryman, play your part. Get it right. The lives of the dead ride on your back. You could actually say what went down with Mr. P. The story of what he did. This is an inkling of the part to play tonight.

Tom's face scrunched up. You got your panties in a knot.

At the very edges of the sky, dawn with her rosy-fingers reached out.

Out there on the D.V.P., maybe you could be James Dean; or Walter to Tom's Phyllis. You could be like that Anne Perry who helped her friend off her mom. You could be the organizing principle Smith talked about in class before Ern got him. Like the ropes and lines of muscle showing through his tight polo shirts; like at home, too, when the basement flooded and those waves lassoed the washing machine, the dryer, your mom's *Looks* and *Life*'s and *Reader's Digest* editions; all her Marilyn Monroe's and *National Geographic*'s; the dirty clothes, the detergents, the washer and dryer lifting them off the ground and swirling them towards the drain amongst centipedes paddling to save their lives.

Sheets of snow torpedoed west now.

Tom chewed his fingernails.

Tell them the truth. He made you do it.

Kind of.

Doing what he made you do isn't a 'kind of.'

No. Tom splayed his hands. I mean, like, before to-night. He kind of, kind of.

A few cars ahead, OPP dragged people out of cars. Their haloed forms moved in and out of headlight beams.

'Kind of kind of' what?

'Kind of kind of' you know. He half-shrugged. Like he did it to everybody, right? He's a lech if I think about it.

He studied the back window. Like tonight even me doing it—I wasn't actually doing it. It was like kind of happening from him through me.

You knew exactly what he was saying. The part of that Rose story in the book closet you keep secret is Mr. P. holding you close. That's just Mr. P. But you not telling anybody is the thing.

Always like my story's there for him to put his name on. Tad opened his door. How'm I going to tell them that? He slipped out.

Shit.

The freeze bit your neck raw where he was chewing.

A tripwire of red brake lights shivered up ahead. Snow ripped down in jagged lines out beyond the passenger side window. Maybe he slid down the embankment. Whose story is tonight anyway?

A rap on your window. Light. White. Beam. Officer. A mountainside rumbled and loosened somewhere. You kept your eyes locked on that string of brake lights.

The officer knocked again. Open up.

The ground shook, the trees shivered.

You nodded.

Hands where I can see them. The officer flattened against the door. Out.

Maybe Tad had flown tracking under the overpass and out to Pottery Road. He wouldn't be as far as Taylor Creek, but he could be at that parking lot where they all cruise. You popped the door.

Out. The officer got you belly first on the car. You got everybody pissed, kid. *Action Soldier, Action Marine, Action Pilot*—you even burnt up *Action Nurse*. Brutal. You messed with the wrong crowd. Cops are G.I. Joe freaks, he said.

They didn't know about Mr. P. maybe.

Arson's serious, son. Give me your name.

Shouldn't I see a lawyer?

You get a lawyer if we book you. We don't book you 'til we know your name.

He thought you were born yesterday.

You know my name.

Thomas Walter Meuley.

Thomas Walter Meuley? Is that your dad? Who owns the car? What's with your coat? How come you got the seams wrong-side out? He squinted at your leg. Even your pants. He patted you down, shaking his head at your inside-out pants and having to dig in there to get your wallet. No driver's licence. What is this like a teen thing? Like a club? From the radio?

I forgot my—.

Too bad. Tonight's not going your way.

But then, there Tad stood. Hands flat on the roof.

It's me. I'm Thomas Walter Meuley, he said.

If the light were falling in some other way, you could read the crease at the side of his mouth.

Hands on the roof. You stay here.

You could: drop between the cars; bore yourself through the embankment piled high; bypass the overpass straight to High Park; tunnel out at Summerhill and—. Sure.

Going north, a wall of brake lights blinking. South, a rope of fairy lights—. Shit.

Your mom. Pounding the steering wheel in her cranberry Tercel hollering.

Ton'

Up ahead, the boys were in the back of a unit. According to Pat-Pat on the radio, they got their clothes inside out. Do to them what they did to Albert. Just up ahead. A hop, skip, and a jump. Thirty feet maybe.

Honking set in from behind them.

Shafiqq sunk the emergency brake. 'Play this cool, Ton'.'

'Oh, I am cool. I am very cool.' Ton' stepped into the unflinching onslaught.

The air cut shards out here, the down blasts and side gusts stung foreheads and necks. Curtains parted to let History pass through. The Great Peacemaker, Dekanawida —He whose name one does not speak—perched here on the bluffs overlooking the longhouses tucked into the meadows. His fields fed by buried rivers running purple still from the days of chemical dyes draining into the Don below.

The boys. Eight, nine feet ahead. Boys had done this. Kids.

Pat-Pat stomped his boots free of gunk and wheezed.

A kid does this. A child. 'You know Dekanawida, Pat-Pat?' Six, seven feet.

'Deka-who?'

'Dude.' One step at a time. 'The Iroquois Confederacy.' Pray the Lord, their veins to leak. 'Know the ground on which you stand, man.'

That limo's rear end dangled over the embankment. The wind whipped, the crust crunched.

The ropes anchoring Ton' to tonight frayed. Five feet, now. Four.

Pat-Pat spit.

The wind bit. The molecules of Ton's breath cling to each other first hovering and then spinning into the few feet between he and Pat-Pat. Three, two. Kids out playing.

Pat-Pat shot a glob of snot from one nostril.

Maybe Albert got himself in over his head.

'Check out them turning their clothes inside-out. Check out the pants.' Pat-Pat pawed at his 'stache shuffling to the limo's trunk. 'A real battleship, eh?' Pat-Pat pushed off the limo and punched Ton's shoulder.

The boys were greyed-out blobs in the back seat of the cruiser. 'I am glad we got 'em. Stoker's holding them on a 433.'

Ton' played dumb. 'That carport fire thing? G.I. Joes?' He wanted into that trunk. Blood spatter, hair follicles, epithelial transfers. He had to get the boys to himself first. 'They could be ours. We had a thing on the Spit.'

'I say more like they're the carport 433.'

'You don't know that.'

'Don't I? Black limo, two teenage bullshitters. On a night like this?' Pat-Pat's a dog with a bone. 'There's a *Marine Joe* in the back seat, friend.'

Exactly.

'These boys're my inventory. J. wants numbers, J. gets 'em.'

The night's still young, Pat-Pat.

'But that ain't all of it, Ton'.'

'No?'

Pat-Pat dangled a Hot Wheels-size plastic bag of powder in Ton's face. 'D-U-I. Bingo. Ka-ching.'

Ton' snatched the bag. Sniffed. Good stuff. Sour. 'You don't need the numbers probably, so we'll do you the favour. You're too old to be up all night typing paper-work on a 433. Go home to Carley.'

'You are not taking them.' Pat-Pat went still. He stomped a foot. 'No freaking way.'

Ton' put a finger to Pat's lips. 'I am.'

Pat-Pat yanked away. 'Ton'. Don't.'

'Don't "don't" me.'

Pat-Pat pulled his officer's cap back. And hacked.

'What do I got to do?'

'What do you got to do?' Pat-Pat wouldn't let go.

'What do I got to do?' Ton' squared off his stance.

'I found the stuff. I did.' Poor Pat-Pat whined his case now. 'Everyone's looking for booze, and I scored this stuff.' Pat-Pat tucked his chin into his coat.

No way he found that bag in the limo. No way. He planted it.

'You can't tell nobody.' Snot gunked into Pat-Pat's 'stache. He spit, and leaned in closer. He whispered. 'I'm the Mac-10, Ton'.'

Pat-Pat's been playing it all along. And fucking him-self royally. Ton' knew it. You can't save people from themselves.

'Don't say nothin'. J's got me on probation. My pen-sion, man. Ton'. Car—.'

His daughter, Carley, had Down Syndrome.

'I mess this up, no Beaverbrook, Ton'. She practises to say it: Beaverbrook.' Pat-Pat flapped his elbows. 'Ton'. My age, what'm I gonna do? Sell cars? Nobody buys cars anymore.'

Cars honked, idled, and revved their engines all the way down to Eastern.

'J.'s going to generate a stack of lawsuits 'cause of people stuck in traffic to catch drunk drivers."

'The Civ panel. That's bad news for you, huh, Pat-Pat?'

Pat-Pat cocked his chin. Defensive.

Eyes on the prize, Ton' defused. 'One—.' He worked up a wad.

Pat-Pat got up his own, 'Two—.'

They horked side-by-side loogies. Every cop bound to the other. To serve and protect.

'J. brings the heat, the Civ Panel's got me. Proliferating weapons and other matters. They think that, Ton'.'

Duh.

'They just got to say it to the *Star*, to *NOW Magazine*, to the *Sun*. They'll sack me to prove they're onto corruption. Just wreckin' lives—.'

Ton' wondered what else that panel had on cops.

'It's just me so far, J. says. Blood is in the water.'

Got that right.

'I just got to demonstrate. D.U.I. Numbers.'

For the first time since he and Shafiqq had turned off Leslie onto Lakeshore, Ton' landed back in his body. He dug a fingernail into a vein on the back of his hand to feel it.

Pat-Pat's breath reeked.

Psych the dude. 'Take 'em, Pat. Do the D.U.I. Or we split it. You get possession, we get the carport 433.'

'Stoker's got the 433.'

'Fuck Stoker. We got seniority.'

'Okay. "Fuck" Stoker, sweet. You take the carport 433 and the kids.'

'Plus, you get the D.U.I., Pat-Pat.'

Pat-Pat clapped his hands. 'That's me four for the night. Lieutenant says we got to bust six on the minimum. Two more.' He clomped off, and then turned back. 'But, I got that, right?'

'Like that.' Ton' snapped his fingers. 'Go jack 'em. Think: Carley.'

'And don't forget what I said about you-know-what.' Pat-Pat pistol-shot his thumbs, put a gloved finger to his lips. 'Bang, bang.' He tromped off into a vapour of idling vehicles.

People get in over their heads. Take that queer kid doing nothing but coming home from his sister's birthday party got bashed and run over smashed by a bunch of boys in an SUV at Church and Richmond. They never found those kids because they didn't ask whose SUV went into the city that night; who saw those young men piling into an SUV in the entertainment district heading east towards Church. Which drivers saw them? Who they swerved around? Church St. wasn't empty. It never is. Who read the paper the next morning or watched the CP-24 News or Global or the CBC and thought *man, I was out there. That's right. I saw a vehicle like that.* That boy got caught in the random nature of violence this world whips around its head like a link chain in a street fight. Maybe that's the way it is with Albert. Maybe with those boys sitting there in that cruiser. But it'll eat them from the inside. It'll drive them to do things they wouldn't do otherwise. Maybe Albert forced the boys into something they didn't want to do. Maybe it's not random. Maybe it's payback.

Shafiqq caught up with them. 'The unit's on the shoulder.'

Ton' put it to Shafiqq. 'Doesn't make sense, right?'

Shafiqq pffed.

'You had something like that before. You used to work Cherry Beach, right?'

Shafiqq seemed to study the CN Tower poking through a bank of storm.

'You think he brought it on himself.'

Shafiqq pulled at his chin. 'Ton'—. You know. But, man.'

'"Man," what?'

'Nothing.' Shafiqq put his hand on his heart. 'I just don't see—.'

'Spill it.' Dude knew something.

'Just that Cherry Beach shouldn't be a thing. Like kids don't have meals. People get shot. There's more important things.'

Ton' stomped off.

But Shafiqq blocked him. 'All I'm saying is who cares, right? Dudes having it off in the sub-zero temperatures more power to 'em. It's on us, man. It's just sex.'

The spinning cruiser lights—blue, red, yellow—lashed out blinding. Damn.

'You paint things black and white, Ton'. Just saying that can leave you in the dark.'

Sessy

A cascade of cars poked south back down to Eastern. Her throat stung. What she'd give for a sip of water. Maybe she'd cup her hands at the trickle being spat by the solar-powered molars purifying just past Taylor Creek. A good wind could flip her into the Don River. The grey bouldered clouds lumbering at her on the Don Valley Parkway had to be cousins of those that'd storm over the trees towards the rowboat she and Uncle Louise used to go bass fishing. Planted on the shoulder, fists of wind shook her car out here but it sure wasn't her first time riding a bronco storm in a tin can claptrap. A sunny day had gotten up to a devil of guck under clouds tumbling in, falling over themselves in a roil that tipped their colours from autumn burnt orange and golden crust to ice-bound permafrost sucking pretty from their texture. Soon, squalls cut into the undertow and thunder rattled the resting oars. The bait slugs tipped over, worming over each other to burrow their heads into a spill of dirt. The lake went choppy. Then, choppier still. The hull jerked up, then down. The boat lurched, the waves tipped in. On the right and then the left. First, starboard and then port. Right, left; to, fro. To the stern, back to the aft. Given her sweaty palms, Sessy couldn't get a grip. The oars were long gone.

We're not going to worry about that, Louise said. The nipple on his breast hardened and he did up a button on his flannel shirt. *The current's got us.*

Louise.

Don't you worry. The storm is called Life.

Sessy had frozen. Sediment surfaced from far below the waves in blossoming, muddy mushroom clouds.

Tonight, on the D.V.P., she rowed in a backed-up sea of Vipers, Aspires, Taurus', Yaris' and Echoes; the pulse of petrol. A constellation of floodlights lit out from a police checkpoint across the lanes of traffic up ahead. She slapped herself good. Wake up.

She dug behind the seat. A Twizzler. Her eyes played tricks in this glare. With the snow coming down, and rectangles of car roofs stretched out like quilt sheets of Glossy II photo paper, one of them could be Tom Meuley's limo. Maybe she had imagined this whole night. Maybe she's lying in her bed right now; maybe Jeff's fingering her; maybe Milk's counting sparrows.

Clouds of exhaust leaked in through the air vents twisting her thoughts. Brake lights pulsed in cyclic dances. Engines heaved their steel bodies inch by inch. Cops darted in and out of headlight beams as bats do in the leavening of night.

Sessy shut her eyes. And then reopened them. Colour blurred. These intermittent flares of exploding reds and yellows muddied the licence plate ahead of her, to the right, and to the left. Three cars boxed her in behind, two on the right, and three to the left. No where to go. She pressed her forehead into the steering wheel. Just make it to the checkpoint, Girl. In this sick asteroid tinge, she knew what was what. If Milk were safe, he would call her. If he were near his phone, he would see her text.

A cold sweat wet her torso and a narrow gap opened to Sessy's left.

That Hummer next to her dawdled. The blonde lady driving danced in her cab wearing headphones the size of disc satellites.

Sessy nudged in. She waved, honked her horn, and then beat her chest to get the woman's attention. She shook her steering wheel huffing in and out. Calm down. Calm down. She pressed her forehead into the steering wheel. Somebody, please. Open more. Her eyes watered. No. No crying. There is more than one way to get into the next lane. Her phone showed one signal bar.

She put the car in 'Park,' got the door open, and climbed up on the driver seat to wave at the Hummer lady. She hollered and pounded her car. With one leg swung onto her windshield, she caterwauled into the void. Pulling herself onto the roof of the Tercel on her belly, she pointed, she waved, she gesticulated. A string of pearls strung all the way from where she stood to Eastern around to Cherry St. and beyond that even. The boys could be lost in that thread.

The pounding in her chest drove her up to her tippy-toes now. History itself had blown in tonight driving her to wit's end. To the west and behind her, all those office tower windows were shaking free of their steel, concrete and glass structures in some collective condensation of hope; a rock and fire of desire and despair detonated and freed them, and her, from the rules of architecture. She could be something. She could matter. More than scar, more than meat for Jeff to peel, more than some gutted and puking beast. She punched out another text to Milk. The phone responded: *Try again?* It's one bar long gone. She thrust it flush to the sky. And then tapped out a text: *Call me.* But then: *Try again?*

To get any signal at all, she needed higher ground. With one foot on the rearview mirror, she pushed herself onto the roof of the Tercel. Flat on her belly, she cleared snow to make room. Out here in this cold, airless vacuum, anything could blow open. Signals might reach her. Maybe even Jeff.

The yoo-hoos behind her laid on their horns. She got to her knees and held the phone higher still. She slid to one end of the roof and then the other. She studied the blinking lights ahead and back behind her. She just bet that Tom Meuley's limo had been caught like her in the coils of this snarl. If only she could make out its long, sleek body in the stinging onslaught. She brought the phone down and seeing no bars held it high. To the right and to the left.

"What are you doing you crazy bitch!"

Spits of snow tore into her cheeks, her neck and down the back of her shirt. The cold bit straight through the cloth at her thighs and flayed, absolutely peeled, the exposed skin of her calves. No hollering could stop her. Winded and weaker, Sessy got to her feet. She waved the phone; her arms now lead, her knees cement.

Hummer lady caught sight of Sessy. She did a double-take. Her jaw dropped.

Sessy leapt off the top of the Tercel and became herself again. Free. Free! A Nadia Comaneci doing three somersaults in mid-air and landing just ahead of the

Hummer on the back trunk of an old Nova before bouncing back to the hood of her Tercel.

That Hummer lady brought her hands to her mouth.

Sessy got behind the wheel and eased the Tercel right in and all the way into the lane. If only——.

There. The limo. Milk. Right there. Belly against the car. Hands on the roof. A police officer pressed her boy's head into the roof of the car.

"Milk!"

The officer yanked him back.

"Hon'!"

And now he had a hand on his back shoving him to move away.

"Son!"

To walk farther on, to twist between——. Tom Meuley!

"Milk!"

That little tribe, Milk, Tom and the officer pushed off farther.

"Hon'! Son!" Sessy put the car in 'Park,' got the door open, and tore towards the guys on foot. Around the Tercel, she slipped catching the hood of a BMW. "Milk!"

Stunned onlookers looked up from their texting, finding a radio station, watching a DVD, painting their nails, finding the right page, brushing crumbs, flossing teeth, digging down for a pen, hunting for the USB port, holding their phones up for bars, drawing a map, taking down directions, pleading a case, loosing a goose, asking for forgiveness, bleeding a heart, cooking a liver, kicking the bucket, baking bread, breaking bread, remembering a punchline, counting their chickens before they're hatched, regretting the past, threading a needle, rewriting history, taking one step forward and three back, telling the truth as we know it, knowing better than the last time, learning from past mistakes, waiting for the other shoe to drop, being left at the altar, not having enough for everyone, filling to the last drop, leaving the stinking bastards behind, asking too much for too little, always thinking of themselves, having faith in spite of everything, recalling their first kiss, doing their online banking, remembering that their lives had become unmanageable, taking their words back, fighting injustice in Ottawa and Washington, donating money to Haiti and the tsunami, editing their Kickstarter videos, tagging friends on Facebook, never saying goodbye, dropping a bomb, cooking a hit, ticking a spliff and digging for the last fries in their McDonald's bag. They shook their heads, honked their horns and tried to run her over. She charged on, hardly keeping a toehold.

But, over the roofs of cars, their three heads dropped from view. The boys were being put into a police car. She hopped up on a bumper—oh, if only she could see. If she could just reach them, she could explain. Milk sought to protect her. Blame her. Imprison her. Incinerate her. Wouldn't they do the same? She squeezed through two sedans practically melded together and bracing herself, lifted herself high enough to catch the squad car fading into the shards of blackening night. On the roof of that cruiser, "54."

Milk

The two cops that'd taken you from the limo, handed you over to a doe-eyed brown cop wearing a cornmeal doo-rap. A Dastār. Maybe Asaan wears one of those. A ripped, Latino officer elbowed in to take Tom's elbow.

Don't think you're all about something, kid. AAOOO! He howled at the stars scratching in. HA! You, he jabbed a finger into Tom's chest. Are a pig. He yanked Tom's cuffs up behind his back and pressed him into the cop car.

The dastied one ground your cheek into the stinging iced limo roof. He jacked your legs apart; his breath pushing into spruce branches. Stache got hyper-close to Tom's ear, whispering.

In their squad car, Dastie asked if you were comfortable. He turned south on Bayview. Must be from 54 Division. If they hit the Gardiner, they're from a division out there by Jeff's carport.

The terrain sunk low out here. Clumps of elm beaten by D.V.P. exhaust and maples stripped bare.

At Evergreen Brick Works, they turned into a vacant lot overlooking Roxborough. And stopped. Dastie caressed the steering wheel, the engine ticked. We don't want to get stuck in here (something).

You nudged Tom with your foot.

Tom cleared the window fog with his 'fro.

Pornstache popped open the driver's side door and, stepping outside, zipped up his coat.

Kicked in by the wind, the snow drove straight in between the seats.

Dastie zapped the lock on Tom's door and shouted at Pornstache. On' or Bon', he said. His name, maybe. The cops stomped farther off.

You leaned against Tom. He tucked in closer. You can't put this on you. It's Mr. P. He did it. Him standing watching you the window. Him coming in. Him getting the squeegee.

Yeah, but I could've ran.

Those cops had stomped off even farther, huddling.

I didn't have to.

He took the squeegee, Tad.

The seams in the car seats reeked of piss.

Blood filled his mouth. He couldn't get words. Help me, help me. It was me, like, watching me.

Grandma begged you to saw her in half. On her walkabout to drain fluid in St. Mike's Queen's Wing every step killed her. Every tile. Every linoleum square. Her jaw clenched. Two days before she died she dug her forehead into the doorjamb. *It's the way through, Evan.*

Through the door glass, at the twenty-first floor stairwell landing. She had her eye on the railing. Patients pissed in that stairwell. The stink seeped into Grandma's room.

You are—the words hissed from her lips same as the breathing machine in her room.

Her lips darkened with her oxygen levels decreasing. She smiled, *The bends.*

You weren't sure if you should touch her, help her or what.

Get me to the railing.

Grandma, no.

Get me. There.

The stairs spiraled down.

Grandma.

Love me.

You did think. This is what separates you from Tom Meuley. You thought. The nurse in the lemon jumper came. She got her free elbow. *Adele. Come 'ere.*

Grandma yanked her arm back. A yank that shoved her into giving up. She fell into the doorjamb, her lips purpling even more. You and the nurse caught her. On the far wall blinkered the Urgent Response button. *Hit it.* In one fell swoop, you shifted your share of Grandma's weight to the nurse and kicked the switch with your foot. Her broken body collapsed into itself, withdrawing.

Oh, Adele. The nurse wiped Grandma's mouth.

The cops clicked open Tom's door. Flurries rushed in, settling in the creases of the gearshift, flitting to the soles of your boots. Pornstache dragged Tom out of the car.

Dastie maneuvered you out. But, you fell. Dastie lifted you gently, though, and held you to the car.

We got to talk to you face to face. Up close.

Across the roof of the squad car, Tom blew you a kiss. Hey, he asked the coppers, what's going to happen to—? Pornstache pushed his head down.

Dastie tightened his grip on you.

Pornstache ground Tad's head into the limo roof. No questions.

Tom wrenched. The officer kneed him in the back. Fight me, kid. Fight me. Come on. He shoved Tom into the roof again. Tad wrenched his neck from the roof to keep ahold of your eye.

Pornstache whispered something in his ear, pulled Tom up close and held him eye to eye. He chewed the strands of his moustache in his teeth. Big mistake tonight, boys.

Tom pressed his forehead into the metal.

A team effort? Two to tango?

Ton'. Dastie named 'Stache.

Don't "Ton'" me.

Ton'.

Do not.

Tension could work for you and Tad.

Dastie huffed. Shit.

What do you know about G.I. Joes?

Your knees ballooned with oxygen.

Tom pffed.

The gas can in the trunk. It reeks back there, okay.

If he's talking about the gas can, then Mr. P. had not been found. Blood came back to your legs. He's only talking G.I. Joes.

We kind of know what you did.

Dastie's the cool-headed one.

Not 'kind of.' We know. 'Stache didn't give an inch.

But we don't *know* know, Ton'.

The Ton' one stepped back, but then came in real close to Tom's ear. You ever hear of a jar of tears?

Ton'.

Right. I get it. But I'm just saying, Officer Sinha.

He caught you looking at him.

Like what you see, bitch.

You went cold.

My wife—that's right, even people like me are married. My wife, her mom, her grandma, they all pass down this jar. And you know what the jar has in it? Tears.

Dude is playing you.

How much you know about American history? Canadians don't know nothing about American history.

You knew American history. Grandma and Uncle Louise told you. How they had to leave the United States. How they ran from Nebraska. The haters. Grandma Jean Sloan had to leave too to get decent work in Michigan. First at Olds, then at Pontiac Motors.

My wife's mother is from Arkansas. You know Arkansas, right? Pig-farmers, Bill Clinton?

The temperature plunged again.

You know how come Arkansas?

Ton'.

Officer. I told you with the "Ton'-ing" me. How come Arkansas is because my wife's great-grandma was marched there. On foot. He finagled his arm under Tom's nose. But, look at that. Brown. Pigment. Stain. Taint. My wife don't look like that on the outside but she and them that come after are scarred on the inside.

Dastie stomped his feet in tight, precise circles. It's freakin' cold out here, Ton'.

How come it is that people count. Okay. Black people. First Nations people. Women. They matter, man. You don't get to put the lights out on people. My wife's

great-great-whatever grandmama escaped the Trail of
Tears. Some people get away. Some don't.

The CN Tower stabbed at the sky over the downtown core.

The dog tails of his moustache flicked up. He saw
past the numbed look on your face.

My wife's grandmama took off from the that death
march and lived on roots. Raw roots, man.

Her whole family had their heads bashed in—.
Right, Officer Sinha? Bashed?

Sinha stopped circling now. He stood off some, his
lips moving very fast, quiet and low.

Yeah, Officer. Pray.

Tom squinted at you. The Ton' must be stoned on
something.

Guess where that jar is. On my dresser. That same jar
that great-great grandmother found discarded, a piece of
trash, unburned, un-bashed, in the hills over Jonesboro,
Arkansas. She cried it half-full up in those mountains. If
she made it out alive, no more boo-hooing.

Dastie had moved right behind you.

Maybe getting ready for some kind of confession.
They would have said by now if the carport hurt
anybody.

The speaker squawked in the unit.

Ton'.

The officers popped the doors and squeezed you in.
As he pulled out of Evergreen, Dastie rolled down his
window and pulled at his stuck wiper.

The headlights boned into the trees lining the parking lot. Once on the southbound D.V.P., Dastie flashed
his lights taking the traffic in weaves. 54's the only station

south. He clicked off at the Richmond exit, landing at Parliament and King in the parking lot of 54 Division.

Fluorescent kliegs flooded the back entrance of the 19th century brick pile.

A pin-point red eye read the key card. The steel door ka-chunked and crawled open. You stepped through. It clunked shut. Its bolts locked. Two cameras hovered at the hallway ceiling. A stink of chemical clean had soaked into the cinder block.

Ton' turned his face away.

The hallway, a gold-flecked sluice of yellowed linoleum stretched ahead. In sci-fi movies, some guy, disoriented and sweating, walks walks walks runs runs runs finally the door at the end of the hallway comes into view but it is so so far away getting first closer then farther, the harder and faster he runs, the farther door pushes from him. He finds hope in the sliver of light under the door. The hallway is an endless plank now, stretching and unfolding in bewildering ways. The harder he runs, the harder it gets; the more he breathes, the less oxygen he gets. Sluggish now, he falls farther behind, but forces himself to jog and jog. He can make out the thump and scratch of the boot. Then, there's another set that joins the first. The scrape of footsteps following, clack in a cacophonous din. Over his shoulder, no one is there, but the chew of their boots is deafening. He cannot escape, but he must. He cannot outrun this river. The current has him, the footfalls thunder, their rumbling kicks collide now with waves to thrash, slosh and pound his legs, his torso, his heaving breast. At first, just one set of footsteps follow but by the time he is hoping to mount the surf, it is hundreds, maybe thousands in hot pursuit, hunting him and getting closer. He can hardly stand it, what has he done, what is he guilty of? He can't see these ghostly hunters, of course; these villagers stay hidden and buried, their pitchforks seeping into the cells of the cinder blocks mixing with the corrosive chemical cleaners feeding on it like the dead do when Odysseus' mother says cut the trench well, like vampire ladies feeding on Jonathan Harker before Dracula hauls them back. He speeds now best as he can slapping and pushing the waves behind, pulling his pace as best he can. He cannot be faulted, look how fast he is going; he's giving it his all, look at the progress he's making, look at how far he's fallen behind, look how off course he truly is; and still, he will not give up and quickens his step even now; he gives it everything he's got. The door recedes. He stumbles, trips and falls flat smack into the surface of the waves. He thrashes for hold, he gulps for air. The waves close over him. He is gone. It is as it was; the din dies.

In the lobby, Ton' slammed Tad into a chair. The grass-plastic moulded chair screeched with his weight. Dastie stood you next to Tom. Air gushed in from vents up high. No air vent could stop you. Unscrew it. Ahead of you, a wall of black and white portraits of officers long gone. One lady cop had her hair piled up like your mom does when she plays *I Love Lucy* at Halloween.

At Halloween, she would plant herself at the front door to rifle your pail. *Hold it right there, Mister.* She snatched the Tootsies and Kit-Kats for herself and freeze your bite-size Snickers. *That's the fattening stuff,* she'd say, caramel and wafer out of her teeth, wadding up the wrappers and sticking them in her pocket.

F-A-T, Milk. You do not want that. Trust me, you don't. It sucks the life out of you.

After eating five or six or twelve Kit Kats, a handful of Kandy Korn or two and eight to fifteen caramel squares she'd go toss her cookies. The more you ate, the more you disappeared—like her. The two of you shared a yearning to disappear in plain sight; to not be seen; to not be counted; to be missing but accounted for. She'd come out of the bathroom, wiping her mouth. Just think of poor Princess Di. The doorbell'd ring, she'd goose her Lucy hair up and open the door wailing, *Waaa, Ricky!*

The kids cringed at the porch railing. Give them *SpongeBob, The New Scooby Doo, Lady Gaga, Witches,* "Bella" from *Twilight* or *Harry Potter.* But "Lucy Ricardo"?

It's Lucy! I'm Lucy, get it? Waa, Ricky!

On the sidewalk, parents slapped their thighs. What a gas!

See? Your mom would point. *Your folks get it.*

The kids'd hold up their bags: *Just the Kandy Korn, Lady.*

Lucy is *TV, kiddies.* She'd aim and shoot lime suckers from Dollar Depot into their bags and whisper, *Not like this malarkey they got on these days.* Then she'd call out to the parents, *Teach 'em Lucy!*

Freaked out, the kids'd tear to the Eisele's for Fruit Rollups or even better.

Waaa, Ricky! She'd call after them closing the door. *It's not like when I was a kid.*

➤ Ton' popped the hand-cuff bands. Sit.

As soon as Dastie got his bands off, Tad landed in the chair next to you.

Ton' hit the front desk.

Let me look, Ton'. The officer on a rolling chair blocked him.

You know what I want, Horst.

Wow. The desk officer sat on his hands, clamped his lips, and shot a glance your way.

Ton' got into the officer's face. The muscles in under the fabric of his shirt, snaking and sweating. Just below his holster, his thighs pushed back against the material. Big dude. Big. 6' 3", 6' 4".

Tad dug into the cracks between the floor tiles with his heel.

Dastie ducked into a hallway farther down.

The officer at reception, 'Horst,' shot to his feet, pacing and pulling at his ginger sideburns. A bank of monitors blinked and washed his face out, alternately. Grey, to chalk. To grey. To chalk. Ton' squeezed around Horst to rifle through something on the desk.

If they did a blood test on you right then, they would've found the nitrogen globuling enough to sink you to the bottom of Higgins Lake.

Ton' caught you. Keep smiling, kid.

You wiped the smile off your face.

You'll see how funny funny is.

You seep into the wall now.

He pivoted, disappearing down the hall you'd just come from.

Except for Horst at the desk, you two were alone.

Look for the camera. Tom whispered, but wouldn't look up. His lips moved. The camera. Your skin hummed. The red light's blinking.

Tom turned his mouth from the camera. You could've went to Kabul or Khakon.

No. You're right where you're supposed to be. Not saving Asaan or Sakar from Americans or the Taliban. You belonged here. To shake off Jeff's punches so that you can surface. So that you might matter. You call the shots now.

Dawn's rose-fingers began to push the day into view. The golden halls lengthened. The walls fell back.

Behind the monitors, Horst kept an eye on you, but made no moves.

Go home, Tom mouthed. Tell 'em. Me. I did it. Go.

You slipped into that hall that Dastie had disappeared into.

Milk, Tad hissed. Come back.

You are long gone.

Wow! Horst tore out from behind the monitors.

But you made the corner.

The Wee Hours of:

Sessy

Those cop car taillights skit a pink glow over the drifts lining Pottery Road. The cruiser slipped through the blow, sliding over a mound, fishtailing a crest. And then sank out of sight as if Milk were being ripped from her breast.

Her grip slipped. How could she be herself at a time like this? Who's to say what or who herself was at all— or wasn't? Where's Walter? Where's Uncle Charlie? Where are the compatriots, fellow soldiers, Radical Ladies and the Lady Pyrates of the Caribbean? Where's Phyllis? Where did Edith Nordheimer get off to? Where were the ones who made sense of things? What's to become of us if, and when, our ghosts run for their lives? This must be, as Uncle Louise said, like Grandma Sloan said, like her mom would have said (if she had opened her heart past her penis) a night that poetry enters the world. The prayer of TV heebie-jeebie (*MedicalCenter-LostinSpace-MyThreeSons-IDreamofJeannie-Bewitched-BionicWoman-DoubleIndemnity*) brings the gods clamoring. Poetry will not be denied. It's in your throat; it's scratching at the window. There's no tomorrow like today.

Car keys. Her fingers tightened. Gone. Dang. The light grew dim. Oh, Christ, no. Nada. She patted her waistband. Nothing. She cracked her clamshell purse roping her neck. Zero. Oh, Christ. She dug into its front slot, the side flap, and the zip pack. Zilch. Oh, Christ Jesus. Crap. God owed her one and tonight she called in her chits.

She made her back to the Tercel. Took the long way around an old-time Cutlass, leaned on the hood of a Jeep Cherokee and pulled herself along using the buck-eyed antennae of a Beck's taxi. That antenna took her weight and kept her balance. Oh, and then a swoosh, an evil onslaught of cold, biting wind took her chin and spun it Linda Blair. She blinked and fought forward. Oh, the snow blew in now into her as a hurtling buckets of sofas. She covered her face. Ammo plowed into her forehead, cheeks, and the backs of her hands. A maple leaf bumper sticker bleated that *Tomorrow Should Be Ours.* "Tomorrow"? Damned Canadians can't never appreciate what they have and the moment they have it. If only they were her.

Drivers gawked at her—a wild lady.

They flashed their headlights and honked their horns. Some joker in a van threw open a rear door yelling, 'Get in here, get in here.' He lurched splattering his rice noodles and broccoli onto the ice. He slammed the door back shut.

Sessy tore through the steam cloud of salty rich soy. She made it back to the Tercel.

Holy Toledo. Its front tires spinning, the front end dangled over the edge. Damn. Crap. Darn. The front left wheel lifted into the air. One little dink and it's in the Don River. She could push it back.

She strategized. Play your cards right, girl. *Don't get ahead of yourself. Think before you act. Don't be absent-minded. Keep your wits. Careful. Too big for your britches now, huh? Fancy-pants. Cow. Counting your chickens before they're hatched; biting off more than you can chew; two in the hand's worth three in the bush. Who do you think you are?* Easy. She did a Discovery Channel rock climber. Tread lightly. Maybe this bumper, maybe that one. The dash lights were out. She laid her fingertip on the hood. No engine hum. At the rear, she took a step and—

Holy tomoley. There sat that same old lady again chewing on her hood string. Right behind the steering wheel. Miss Cut-Your-Trench-Well. Sessy crept closer. She got up close to the window. That ghost pressed into the ceiling with both hands. Her coat splayed wide open. The woman hammered her legs into the accelerator revving the engine. On her breast, were two live beavers clawing and feeding and swatting their leathered tails at the steering wheel like that painting she saw where the Mother of Christ, or the Commonwealth, or Nature stared at the roaring Don. Sessy had to be seeing things.

The car reared forward with each acceleration. The emergency brake held. The car hung. Teetering.

She eased her fingers under the door handle. One. Two. Three. She flung the door open. A raft of urine blasted Sessy. 'Get over, get over—.'

The woman jerked; her hands flew to her face. She ripped the beavers from her bleeding breasts by their necks and flung them, screeching, to the ground at Sessy's feet.

They skittered off.

The car tilted.

She shoved the lady with her right elbow and then kicked at her.

The old bat gripped the seat. She didn't budge.

'Get over, get over——.' Sess' shoved with both hands and her kicks now. No room for error. If she goes over this cliff, Milk is stuck. They got him. They've captured him. No one will free him. Sessy walloped the lady with a right hook. 'Take that!'

The crack of bone to bone popped in the Tercel's interior.

Sessy pushed at her. 'Go go go.'

The car lurched forward to rest at an odd angle. The back end groaned.

The lady scrambled into the passenger seat.

Sessy pulled herself in and the back end threw itself up with her weight. She got the gear to reverse and gunned the gas. It was no use. The front end pitched cockeyed. And shot forward. They sailed off the shoulder above, a rocket launched, careening towards the river, taking with them piles of snow, and then saplings, only to clip the glacial boulders strewn there.

Sessy clutched the wheel. Time stood still.

Bam! The grass came at her in a piney moss colour and Christ who'd've known they stayed so green in winter underneath all of this snow burrowing into, all of these feet of snow, who knew it got so deep out here, it smelled different deep in it like this too, that is fresh, that is the smell of fresh, but rot too, that is rot isn't it, what is rotting here, well that would be leaves and grass and maybe, isn't that rot too this far down and in, this is the kind of thing not seen from back up there on the D.V.P., they'd never ever see this, and speaking of that no one would see her digging in so fast, smash, her fingers clawing at the leatherene and vinyl ceiling, no one would fight to cover their eyes plowing into snow piles bursting over and burying her no doubt, crash, exploding now with the impact of the rock they just hit, slamming jolts of pain into her tailbone and lower spine; they would have to be very very very close to the water now, rush, maybe they were already in it but there no way she could yet open her eyes, oh, she felt it back and down there, she could tell that when they hit, the Tercel popped up some, landed with Sessy's window exploding, she could tell, and thank god she's letting terror run free there's no way she could yet open her eyes with the glass and snow shooting into her left cheek, her forehead, her earlobe. Then, as if that weren't enough, the car rocked and tipped over, now spinning with a centrifugal force that seemed to never let go before tipping to a rest parallel to the river. Upside down.

Don't move. The wheels whizzed, spinning at the night in frenzy. *Stse, stse, stse.* Car innards dropped. Broken glass fell to rest. The car's steel body groaned. She took inventory. Neck? Check. Shoulder? Ouch. Her chin dug into her knees. Her left cheek flattened into the upside down leatherene driver's seat. Light seeped through her eyelids. Her neck bent cockeyed. Biting air blew onto her forehead. Cold chewed at her neck from behind. The steering wheel pinned her into its cave between its underbelly and the feet of the driver's seat.

The car's metal grunted in its settling.

She moved. The engine revved.

Above her, the wheels spun in futile wheezing screams. *Stse, stse, stse.*

She moved again. The engine roared. Her foot wedged into the accelerator. *Stse. Stse.*

The Don's rot rooted in.

The woman.

Sessy held her breath. And listened.

The river rushed. the wheels whizzed. *Stse, stse.* The car's body groaned.

Maybe that lady got thrown out, maybe she's dead. Maybe she ditched Sess', high-tailing back up the hill.

Sessy flit her eyes open enough to let a little light in. Her right arm didn't want to come. Ache shoved into her ribs pounding at her tailbone. She inched her foot free of the gas pedal. And pushed up a bit.

The driver's door and window had twisted open into a grotesque maw of chewed-up steel, grass, and splattering funk mud. Its glass broken free. If she could just get her left arm loose, she could pull herself up and out. Blood rushed to her brain.

Glass chips, shards and shreds showered her from the backseat. *Stse. Stse.*

She got one finger, and another, hooked on the steering wheel. And pulled herself up even more. Her arms free, she leapt to throw an arm around the back of the driver's seat. She dangled; her shins found ground in the steering wheel.

Outside, the river churned as it crushed past.

She dabbed her forehead with a knuckle; blood. Her skull throbbed. Oh, Jesus. Please, Jesus. Cut me free. Get me out of this and you'll never see me again. I'll ride those wheels out there and spin into nothingness just like Milk says. God, please. Make me a neutrino, too. You want me to find Evan. I know you do. He's yours, too.

Hollering came at her from far away. Her skull rattled. Dings dinged. Bells donged. She had to keep it together. Life pumps in her still. She could make 54 Division. That'd be a starting place. It's the closest. She had to.

People ought to be coming maybe. Don't people just have to drop what they're doing and help? Like when Princess Di died? Isn't that Canadian law?

She licked her lips. Blood.

The hollering got louder. Maybe right now they'd hopped the guardrails up above and were sliding towards her down the embankment.

She willed herself to lurch forward. She timed it: one, two, three. Oh, Jesus Lord God Christ.

Dogs barked now. But, aways off. Maybe dogs, maybe people. The panic-pitch squawks of female voices and the grunt harrumphs of men reigning them in. The soundings gathered themselves into words. The slings and arrows of her outrageous fortune came at her in a pounding of footfalls, bodies slipping and sliding; the crack of claps and yelling; her consciousness ebbing. She seemed to have been down here forever, but she couldn't have been. It all flooded back: Milk, Pringles, those officers; Jeff. *Her.*

With one arm hugging the head rest, and the other braced on the steering wheel, she angled her legs to get one foot, and then the other, farther out of what was left of the door. Lowering herself bit by bit, she ground a foot into the mud for traction and in one fell swoop heaved herself out of the car to standing.

And, they nailed her. A pack of hyenas. Do-gooder rescuers pulled at her from the right and the left. They hugged her, kissed her, and collared her arms 'You're all right, Ma'am.'

Some balding wanna-be superhero brushed her off. He snorted in and out of lips fatter than a hungry she-bass in mid-winter. 'You're going to live.'

The D.V.P. surged from back up by the guardrail like a monument.

She shook the man off and made a beeline to the base of the hill. A saucy potato with golden hair bounded right alongside of her. She snatched at Sessy's sleeve. 'Let me.'

Sessy whacked her off too.

'You're bleeding!'

'Easy, Fella.'

Another joker tackled her and some jerk got her arms. Sessy could play this. She went limp. She relaxed. They got the coat in their grips. But Sessy slipped through its arms—and beelined up the hill. The only way to break free is disappear.

Milk

Taking the corner, you spin into the room. A toddler fiddles on the floor. You jump over her.

At the far end of the room—a crash bar looms under an EXIT sign. Reach that door, speed past.

The little bugger digs at the shiny, gold flecks littering the linoleum. S-ow-ku, she says, twitting her fingers.

Phones ring. Drawers open and then slide shut. The crack of a voice. A soda can dings into a garbage can. A toilet flushes.

Fairy dust, you whisper. And wiggle your fingers like snowflakes falling.

S-ow-ku. She pulls at her purple leggings. S-ow-ku. She wears one pink croc.

You could swipe her up and stream into that choked night.

S-ow-ku.

Sparkle.

The Ton' one is right around the corner. You could smell it.

A printer took up paper further down the hall; a faucet ran.

The crash bar twinkles. No lock. No bolt. A current rushes through ceiling pipes. Listen.

The girl squeals.

You bolt. The air rushes into your skin, lifting your bound wings. Steve McQueen on a motorbike; sail up over longboats and the longhouses, clearing the Spit lighthouse to where buried rivers burrow.

Turban steps out from the room on the right.

You for Tom.

Don't. He pulls at his peach fuzz goatee. Don't run. It won't go well. He ushers you into the room he'd stepped out of.

The blood sludges now. Drop to the floor. Fold up. Die.

A cubicle-like printer room, steel-cage walls lined with shelves: books floor to ceiling, left to right, bottom to top. Dust-ridden HPs; a dot matrix. Magazines, reports and file folders jammed into each other. Wads of paper overflowing from a trash can.

I know, you know?

You don't know nothing.

Me, too. This place reminds me of a teacher you and me had. His storeroom.

Your stomach bottoms out.

I'll know whether you tell me or not. I've been there, Evan.

'Been there,' too. Right.

Fill me in.

You tell me.

I'm you, Evan. You're me. Before.

It's easy to block interrogators. Put your attention elsewhere: the green in this room is the green paint of Uncle Louise's oar.

My sociology teacher. He treated me like I'm human. Looking like I do, wearing a dastār—what he did mattered to me. He saw me. I'm a cop 'cause of him.

He studied you. Crinkles appeared at the corner of his eyes. Tufts of black hair dangled to his neck. He presses his back into the doorjamb, fiddles with his boot. Something happened.

Ask the car. Ask the carport. Ask Jeff.

I don't see it in you. Maybe. What do I know? Tell me. Right.

Help me, help you.

You didn't ask for help.

Officer Gonzalez. Man. We just got to get on-sides. Or else. He pushed the trash can with the paper wads. I'm back here typing the report. A record. There's got to be a record, Milk. Officer Gonzales does not want a record. Do you understand?

The 'Stache guy can't just pretend he didn't detain you.

Yup. He can. He will. Officer Gonzalez is persuasive. We just don't see certain things.

Sinha had the brown eyes of Jeff's wildlife TV gazelles. The animal stops. Dips its head. A twig cracks. A rifle blows. Turban cocked his chin to the side, towards the top bookshelves.

The guy I'm watching with my daughter out there— not sure it matches the story Gonzalez is cooking up. Let's just say, I saw you.

A cockroach darted under the bookshelf.

What am I going to write on that paper, Milk? What's the story going to be?

I got to see Tom Meuley.

Turban stepped aside. Go.

You could have stepped out and spun through the emergency exit. But, you are a neutrino now. You always have been. Take the blame. This thought cements you. It coheres. It matters you. You for Tom.

Just past Pashi puttering—Ton'.

Ton'

Ton' held his badge up to the laser door release mechanism. The green light blinked. And went out. He whapped the thing. Automatic apparatus, my ass.

'Ton',' warned Shafiqq.

'Don't Ton' me.' This time, his chest straight onto the glass. The green light blinked. And went out.

'Let me try.' Shafiqq hopped in front of the reader. The green light blinked, and the lock clicked. The door eased open.

'I'm nice to it.' Shafiqq sailed right through.

Ton' pushed the boys into the long hallway toward booking. Focus. Albert. He could hear it already: too young, not responsible. Ton' knew better. The youth defence is for white kids. If Solomon's judge didn't throw him a bone, he'd still be locked up.

'Take a breath before blowing a gasket, Ton'.'

Shafiqq's always got something to say.

'We don't know 'til we know.'

Ton' knows. Every face in the world is a story carved into the eyes, the mouths, the way they lean against a wall. Look at these two. Their gaze. Once he got them into the Reid Technique Personal Zone (< 18"), the bug-eyed kid wouldn't sustain eye contact with him. No eye contact indicates culpability. Watch the lips thin, the jaws tighten. The clearing of the throat. That means pulling for a pre-conceived narrative.

➤ Ma had no more story. All she could do is look him in the eye. After Little Fuck died, a horseshoe crease opened from her chin to her throat. That crease, and then the accident, choked whatever tales might've come. That right rear tire blew, spinning them ass-end first until they slammed, head-on into the upslope, popping them upside down, still spinning but in the opposite lanes pirouetting with semi-trucks headed straight at them. The windows exploded. Ton' blinked, sure enough knowing oh that this was how it would end, maybe he was dead already, he couldn't really tell—this could be what death was. But then they stopped. Truck and car horns screamed. Glass tinkled.

He couldn't hear Mama. When he finally did get turned around, Ma stared stunned, her eyes pinned open like seeing Little Fuck floating; her neck jammed into her spine, her spine slammed into her brain. She didn't move. And stayed that way, immobile, her skin taut over her teeth, eaten alive and gumming for words. 'No No No. We go to Him. We go to Him.' The walls of her story collapsed.

➤ Doing his best to control his narrative, the Tom Meuley one had his feet up on the bench. Ton' got him. 'Pick your feet up, prick.' He knew the side of that face. The cut jaw, muscle-cock nose; the whack-down 'fro. They had met before.

The kid went limp.

'Pick yourself up.' Ton' yanked the kid into the Personal Zone, pulling his chin around to get a good look. 'Watch these eyes.' He shoved him past Horst fiddling on Facebook. 'Heading to Holding.' He booted the prick into the wall.

'Wow, you take it easy, Ton'.'

Go ahead. Stick your nose in Horst. Do it.

Fucking Shafiqq's nowhere, dicking around with the other one fudging the report.

Meuley stumbled and sank.

'Ton'.' Horst shot over to the scuffle.

Ton' lunged, the kid cringed. 'I am your future.'

Ton' waved Horst off.

The kid jumped but one foot caught the other. He fell.

Ton' blocked the cameras pulling the kid up and so tight to his chest he could feel the pant of his breath; the pound of his heart. Ton' came down with his fist. 'I'm your future.'

The kid whimpered.

'Cry.'

The kid shook his head.

Ton' remembered. He took a handful of that curly orange mop and flipped the head side to side. He knew him from somewhere.

The kid covered his head.

'Ton'. Man. Wow. You got to—.'

Ton' let go of the kid but shoved Horst. He straightened his uniform. He folded his arms. 'What, Horst. What do I got to do?' He poked Horst's chest. 'You tell me.'

'Ton'.' Horst nudged with his chin up towards the ceiling camera unit.

Ton' turned from its view. "Shut it down.'

'Ton.'

'Off.'

'I can't.'

He'd do it himself. 'Watch the kid.' Ton' made a beeline back to the front desk.

The kid made a run for it, speeding to the front lobby. Ton' leapt the desk and nailed him.

'Please, please.' The kid begged Horst standing there wincing. 'Mister. Officer. Help me. He'll hurt me.'

Ton' yanked him.

The kid flinched good.

Ton' dragged him up.

His rubber boot soles streaked the floor black. 'Please, Officer. Please.'

He could smell the kid's pot rot breath. 'Officer Horst can't help you. Tell him, Officer.'

Horst knew better than to stick his nose in. He made his way back to the desk. 'You don't have to be saying our names all out like that, wow, Ton'.'

'Officer Sutton Jameson Horst, watch him for a sec'.' He pushed the dick towards Horst. 'I'm getting Shafiqq. And the other one.' He pointed at the camera. 'That goes off.'

Somebody ran up that far hallway, up from the printer room; heading right to the corner into the hallway. Oh, yeah. The other one. Sweet. Don't fuck with a sprinter. Come on, boy. Into his arms.

Sessy

She set her sights on the soaked ground. The Tercel's belly lay exposed to the sky. Its wheels wheezed, teetering as inebriated harpies. Above, the cliff from which they'd torpedoed loomed with a growing crowd of lookie-loos. Mud pulled at her sneakers. She lifted her arm against the pummeling blizzard. Back down the slope her rescuers hooted and hollered like a jug band escaping from a disco dance fire sticking their heads in through the shattered rear windshield and yanking at the doors wedged tight. She knew Canadians. If they caught her, they'd lock her into a care facility. Thing is, sane people know when they're crazy.

At the hill's base, she hit the first crunch of crust driven from the west. She leapt onto the upslope, landing on all fours. Up to her forearms in gunk and snow, she snatched at weeds, vines and rock—anything to take her weight and act as a foothold.

'Ma'am! Ma'am!' The rescuers had her in their sights. 'Ma'am! You'll hurt yourself!'

No hill, no rescuer, would get her now. She went to her knees, the ice sand-papering her knees.

'Ma'am! Aren't you cold? The blood!'

Cold-schmould. Her boy will be free. All four of her limbs power-drilled into that ice sheet, hammering, and carrying her up up up. Beams of flashlights hit her from above and below; from the right and from the left. Onlookers pointed from the steel railings above. She hit the dirt. She squished herself flat into the snow. She went ghost, phantom, winter sprite. If only she wasn't her. Disappear.

Her rescuers tired out and lost sight of her. They shuffled back down the hill to the wreck. A bevy of them toppled down the hill. Up above at the guardrail, gawkers pointed; one had binoculars. She'd have to move fast. Like the wind, she made the crest.

'There she is!'

Never underestimate a mother. She swung her legs up and sideways. With a scissor kick, she flew to the guardrail. She darted along the embankment. Keeping low, staying stealth. She'd get to 54 Division. Before they hurt Milk.

A field of honking cars, blinking headlights and bouquets of exhaust stretched from up where that cop car had disappeared and all the way back down to Eastern probably. She propelled herself through Acuras, Toyotas, and Buicks. Astros, Nissans, and Chevettes; VWs, a Lamborghini, and two GTIs gunning their engines; a Dart, a Hyundai and the owner of a Suzuki pounding on its hood. She hugged the shoulder first before slipping back in amongst the steel cattle. Deep gulps of gaseous exhaust gave her the strength to carry on. Before she knew it, she had practically landed in that cluck of cops.

At first she stood straight up and strolled along getting closer to the flash red, blue and yellow lights igniting the chiseled chins, the chick cops and the shadow side of the bills of their hats. She trailed a finger along the rubber seal of this car. And then the next one. She played the part: just a girl on a stroll.

Squeals pierced the steady hum of engines. That horde of Mongolian banshee rescuers pole-vaulted over the hill she'd just climbed, clocked her, and headed for her. She dropped.

'There she is!'

That Hummer she had climbed over twenty minutes or a lifetime ago lurched ahead. How many hours ago had that been? How long had she been out here? Oh, when when when would she see her boy? Clawing at its massive iced hood, she climbed over a Viper to bang on the Hummer's passenger door. That blonde woman punched at the door lock button. Sessy moved faster. Yanking the door open, she launched over the woman to land behind the steering wheel. She blocked the badger with her forearm.

'Don't kill me don't kill me don't kill me,' the lady squealed.

'Sssh.' Sessy peeked in the rearview mirror. Those fire ants were swarming two cars back, looking in car windows and under their wheels. Their voices garbled, then clearer.

'She's a bleeder!'

'She's got a red coat!'

'Check her head wound!'

'Hey—!'

'Over here!'

The Hummer lady shook her fists like in a TV movie. 'Murder! Murder! Murder!'

Sessy clamped the joker's mouth shut. 'Sshh.' She held the back of the woman's neck with one hand. And hid her face in the lady's lap.

The lady stiffened. Flashlight beams pressed into the cab and the roofs and trees surrounding them. Sessy stayed low. When they passed, she popped up. 'Look, you, my son is in desperate straits—.' She checked the rear view, in the centre, the right, and the left. 'I don't expect you to know—. I don't expect you to understand. I am not going to kill you. Give me the wheel.' She grabbed the steering wheel with one hand and got her foot to the gas.

The woman shook her head and then her finger. 'I I I I I—.'

'Right.' Sessy jammed the thing into 'Drive.' The last clutch of flashlight-bearing hooligans streamed past squawking and hollering.

Sessy pulled the wheel to the left. She'd go straight over the hoods of the cars surrounding them. A Hummer does that. Take a clean shot to the shoulder. Circle around the coppers. Checking the rearview mirror one last time —she didn't want to kill anybody—she gave the thing some gas and pressed forward to the left, pushed back to the shoulder. She nudged a Rio to give her room. She shoved a Cavalier. An Elantra pulled ahead at the last minute. The driver jumped from his car, screaming, and beating the sides of the Hummer. Sessy plowed the tin can into the ditch. She had to. Her shocked but thrilled passenger beat Sess' with her stocking cap. Sessy held her off.

Oh, but now trouble bore down. Behind her, oh oh oh she could see them—those police officers were snaking up on her like a string of beetles taking out roadkill. By God, that is not the way tonight is going to go. Tonight she would cradle Milk in her arms, tonight she'd smooth his dampened brow with the back of her silk hand. Tonight—.

'Out of the car.' A bull horn blasted. The Hummer shook.

Goddammit. She had to pee, again. She clenched.

'I know how to get rid of you.' The woman undid the top button of her jeans.

'It ain't that kind of party.'

Then, the second button.

'Out of the car. Now.' The bull horn sounded again but from the roof above.

'Out.'

This chick had her pants at her ankles. A real professional. She tightened her teeth and clenched her fists. She pressed the soles of her feet into the dash. She lifted herself some.

'Don't even think about it.' She couldn't be thinking what Sessy was thinking.

'I will. I will. You're. Going to. Make me.' The woman focused and pushed. Hard.

A fist slammed the roof. 'We're counting to five. Five—.'

A stinker cut loose.

'Oh, for crying out loud.'

'Four—.'

'I'll do it.' The lady squeezed even harder. 'Swear to. God.'

'Three.'

Sessy got her hand on the door handle. She'd ditch this shindig.

'Two—.'

'Oh, you are not.' Sessy stared. Paralyzed. Conquered. WTF?!

She leapt out of the cab and, as soon as she hit the ground, bounced back up onto the hood of the Elantra, and did what news reports later said was a back flip landing her off the beaten path at Pottery Road. She hurtled herself down the embankment towards the river. Crothers' Woods Trail down there would drop her on King St. and from there hop, skip, and jump to 54 Division.

Catching her breath, she gulped for air on the trunk of a beech. And listened.

The tick hum of the city and the irritated groan of the maple and oak in the wind put her back on the planet. The unadorned cacophony of Nature drowned out the fuss back there. Focus. For Milk's sake. The Don surged below.

A wisp of wind, she'd slip through to her boy if it killed her.

Ton'

Ton' blocked the kid with his arm. 'Ding, ding.' Railroad crossing.

The kid froze, caught his breath, and folded his arms. His golf-ball eyes landed on Ton's, first, but then clocked the Zelitzer's red light.

That's right. Lick your lips. Relax your jaw.

The kid peeked back over his shoulder.

Tight neck, folded arms: a textbook Reid withholding. The Reid Technique gave Ton' precise steps to read a suspect's behaviour. First, track the physiological: the eyes, breath—its rhythm and extension. He had maybe an hour before the shift turnover to nail these fuckers. This kid is a Chapter 5 "Intermediate Progressive Situational Pregnant Pause" situation. That calls for the Interrogator to do eighty percent of the talking; the interrogated does twenty. Then, if he plays his cards right, it flips: 20/80. Silence is the crowbar of truth.

Ton's got what other cops don't. Shafiqq, Horst, Pat-Pat, or Lt. J.—they don't see what he does. Some folks face a cop and shake in their boots; others drop to their knees. Set the baseline of physiological reactions.

Perspiration dotted the kid's upper lip. (check)

'You're pretty warm for there being a blizzard.'

A glance. (check) Blue bugaboo eyes.

Think twice before you speak, kid. It's Canada. What you say will be used against you.

'You got to be a sprinter. To run like that.'

This fuck sprints like William Lyon MacKenzie. He had handlebars the size of grapefruits hooping over his belt. Get him off-guard and off-topic. Eighty percent. (check)

'I look at you—you. Not your friend. You. I see an out-of-the-box thinker.'

The kid shut his eyes. (check).

Ton' lowered his arm. 'I got you.'

He knows he's caught.

Pregnant pause. Ton' checked first to make sure the Zelitzer camera couldn't catch him at this angle.

The heat of his breath bloomed on the boy's neck. A test would tell. He pressed his cock to the kid's thigh.

A press back. Instinctive. (check) A pull away: fear. (check)

Ton' had him.

The throat swallowed. The body don't lie.

'I work my way through a chain of Reid Technique clues. I ladder your responses.'

Back down where he left the 'fro kid, somebody scraped chairs on the linoleum.

Ton' got behind the kid, purring. 'My dead mother came to me at the Spit tonight. We poked around a true crime scene.'

The kid turned away.

'Don't get jigged. The Dead are always coming around. You open your eyes, you take them in. Like air or water. The door's cracked, in they come. Boom. It's the spin of forces greater than ourselves. They got to hang tight to this world. Their claws in this world are where our scratch marks come from: the hurt feelings, heart ache, being pissed off, the suffering. Their hanging on is what care is.'

The tongue wets the lips.

'Thirsty?'

Then, they tighten.

'You two got it into your heads to blow up a carport in Black Creek tonight. Tonight. Of all nights. Maybe it's —we were parked right behind your limo in the Village? No accident.'

The eyes study the shoes.

A cool customer. The lips narrow. The wheels turn.

'What's your name? Evan, right? Go down over there with your friend. No running.'

The data points percolated into alignment.

'Call me "Milk," Officer.'

Okay. Okay. Eighty, twenty. 'Milk. Huh. Like that's what they call you?'

One arm stretches. The cuffs were wearing. Reid him.

'"Curley"'s what they used to call me. I don't scare you. I can tell.' The kid don't even know he's tapping his thigh. Baseline. 'Everybody knows I'm a sweetheart.'

The eyebrows jack. Milk had something to say.

'You don't look like a bad kid, Evan-Milk.'

Down at the print room, Shafiqq ground the cage lock and slammed the door. And headed their way. Ton' could probably get Shafiqq to work this Milk to spill; he'd get at the Meuley one.

Time to up his game. 'Start talking anytime.'

The arms tuck in.

'Milk.' He worked it in his mouth. 'Funny.'

"Milk" shifts his weight. First to one leg and then to the other.

He snapped his fingers at Shafiqq. 'Speed it up, Officer Sinha.'

'Ton', man.'

The kid looked like some corn doll statue planted alone there in the hall.

Ton' spilled his own beans. 'You know, by the way. Your ma, in her Tercel. We saw her out on the D.V.P. Right, Officer Sinha?' The kid sucked at the inside of his lip.

'Ton'.' Shafiqq pansies out.

'Don't "Ton" me.'

The boy stood stock still. A good soldier.

'Your ma is a very bad girl.'

Farther down the hallway, by the front lobby, afro-head Meuley sat still as stone on the chair down there. Head in his arms. Horst had come around from behind the desk and planted himself down there to keep watch.

'Officer Sinha, let's do a bench warrant on Milk's mom. We got her Tercel. She's implicated. We know what we know.'

Milk made the biggest move he'd made in five minutes. He looked at Shafiqq now behind him.

'I, for one, do not believe her story about researching.' He got a handful of Milk's shirt and pulled him down the hall towards the lobby, Horst, and the Meuley kid. 'Yeah, we talked to your mother. Pick up your feet.' Ton' yanked him straight. And then shoved.

Shafiqq dawdled along behind.

Horst scrolled through one of his hook-up apps.

The Meuley kid leaned back in his chair as Ton' dragged Milk past. 'Get Meuley up, too, Officer Horst. Heave the keys.'

Meuley stood up ready.

Horst threw the keys. Shafiqq caught them.

'Ton', wow, do not ask me to help you.' Horst headed back to the front desk.

'Just buzz us in.'

Milk

Taking that corner, the Ton' one jacks his arm up and blocks your way. He's grinning. Black hairs sprout from his chin. Purple veins pulse at his wrist. The ventilation system kicks on through his snow-white teeth. A lemon stink seeps in. Cleaning fluid. You fall onto the beach of his forearm. Here, multiverses birth and burst; die and expand.

Fluorescent light fixtures buzz and blink detonating electric current and gas. Nearer the ceiling, dawn chipped away at the ceiling pipes. Night withdraws into its black hole, sucking grief and memory from the linoleum.

Doors groaned open and then crawled shut out of sight. Turban hurried to Tom.

You are a neutrino. An anvil presses upon your throat, your lungs, your liver, your heart. You are spun into walls, moralities, identities—any solid thing—leaving no track no trace. No longer there, you become. μ to τ way faster than this Ton' can think. He pulls you to your feet.

If you were a "You" caught in the lens of that security camera, you are, too, a snapshot you here but there too in the basement digging through dirty undies with your mom. You here but there too as "Marilyn Monroe: 10

Years Later" in *Life* magazine; you here but there too as a centipede oggling; and you here but there too in her throat singing *what about Love/you might need it someday*. Your striving catches the ties that bind and the architecture of this hallway—these walls, that moulding, this floor tile, that smell, and this electric hum. It glues the hallway tiles here at 54 Division to Mr. P.'s storeroom to his tacking of bats to the garage; to Jeff's hand on your throat to his humping his mistress; to you in the kitchen this morning to the sweat on your mother's neck cutting her lemons; to you, here, weak in the knees.

This Ton' is the cave from which you crawl; the scaffolding of your atomic ribs; the weight of your photon brain. He is the white hole of an undetected universe. He is the antimatter into which you have been spat. Ton' is the *Passage Brady, de Choiseul, Joffrey*, or *La Gallerie Vivienne* through which you and Tom collapse into particle or wave. You are the one-eyed monster feeling his way in the dark.

Tom sits in shadow at the other end of the hallway.

Outside the storm booms thunder again but now, too, out over the lake gathering for an assault on Rochester. Dawn now, too, fingers the corridor igniting crooks and crannies, waste cans and shards of Kleenex dropped. A rumble, maybe a streetcar, rises and falls.

That old woman slides into the hallway between you and where Tom sits. It must be her. The one scratching at the window last night. Wild hair electrified and that frail body fading in and out of materiality. She takes a step or two. She stares at Tom who does not seem to see her.

The Ton' one didn't see her either.

You're fucking losing it. Must be.

The lady hesitates and looks over her shoulder. Oh, the distance she's come. Her shoulders lift with a ballast shoving onto rougher swells. She oars now, each step cracking the walls.

Chips fall from the ceiling. Smoke erupts. Concrete dust collects in your nostrils.

She takes the length of one linoleum tile now. And then another, and another. She will not drop anchor, she will not harbour. The air thickens. You cover your mouth to preserve your breath.

The cop pulls you into his chest now. There, an eddy of spray starch and sweat oozes from his polyester threads and cushioning your knees. Oh, to be sewn into his shirt. Your upper lip carves the border of a perspiring and undiscovered country. The handcuffs cut your wrists; the wounds sting with sweat. You are not going home.

That woman shuffles closer still.

Don't look.

Ton' tightens the cuffs saying that the two of you were out-of-the-box thinkers or some shit. That you two were Sanford Fleming or William Lyons Mackenzie. That you two were more the same than not, that you better think twice before you say one word. That this wasn't the fucking United States of America. That this is Canada, what you say will be used against you. That the writing's on the wall, he can keep you as long as he wants. That they saw your mom at the Spit and what a piece of work she is. No shit.

You dug your fingernails into the meat of your finger. Cut in, draw blood.

His hot breath soothes your ear, the meat of him on your thigh. When he gave his name, the 'o' had the scrape of 'home.' Each press of him throws a ship's rope and scores the knot. His chocolate eyes anchor, his voice pricks. The die is cast, the bond is set. He moors you. And you are free. No mother can solve tonight.

In mid-air, Ton' outlined his words with the fat of his hand: how the night had gone, how his mom had come, how the dead point the way, and how people like you know that. 'People like you and me are different.'

The hallway brightened. Probabilities hummed amongst the specks in the floor and in the soil of his uniform. A snowplow's shovel landed on the asphalt out and beyond that crash bar. Its engine revved as it began taking the skin off of King St. Or maybe Parliament.

Mr. P. had been left in debris from the old City of York. Kitchen walls, basement foundations and exploded chimneys; cheating dudes, frantic wives, and a thousand kids jerking off under sheets. Each scrape of dirt and design slingshot from what mattered to them to your quivering belly now, from this cop's voice here and the computer's ding down by Tom.

The observable universe is *seulement des portes* (Tom would say), doorways, bridges, and organic highways to some other equally viable option. If you could spin faster than the speed of light, if you could actualize your neutrino self, you could loosen the ties that bind: Jeff's grunt and disgust, that squeegee coming down, Sakar's flight out of Khakon, and the fat of this cop's hand on your bum.

Behind you, and to your left, the hallway you'd come from stretched. A stillness only disturbed by Tom's occasional fidget.

And that woman comes. On her knees. At the wall, she lays tools. A hammer, maybe a railroad spike, some printed document; a chain. Getting a good grip on the spike in one hand and the hammer in the other, she sets the spike in grout. As if chiseling fine china, she taps taps taps. The concrete trembles. Cracks open threading the brick as varicose veins.

Ton' one had an arm around your neck, holding you close. He didn't see what you saw. He went on about his dead mom.

She clings to the walls now riding the waves of crumbling cinder block. The pee-yellow linoleum fractures. The gold flecks spin galaxies tipping you and Ton' into an abyss opening in the hallway. She dangles now from ceiling pipes bellowing to *Come, Come* wheeling her free arm as if an oar paddling towards a portal of stumbling peoples, crumbling monuments—even City Hall collapses on itself right past the ladies' washroom; the CN Tower shoots in headfirst with the pleadings of thousands of old timey people, First Nations families; squealing critters skinned within an inch of their lives; soldiers staking their bayonets and pulling themselves towards the hole she has opened.

She falls to the floor, looks at you, and sets her spike once more. She lifts the hammer and wallops with every bit of muscle left. She gives it her all, lifting a little off the floor. Three-quarters sunk, she posts the printed document there. Hoisting ho, she steels herself gasping for air clipping a coiled length of chain to the spike, she holds it high and with her last breath, it seems, holds it higher still and heaves it to you.

In a rush of air and shoe squeak, Turban appeared.

The Dawn of:

Sessy

At 54 Division, she pressed her back against an exterior wall. She clocked the perimeter: new sidewalks, smooth blacktop, chrome pillars, steel perp doors; lighting by *Battlestar Galactica*. The boys had to be inside. If not here, then 52 Division over on Dundas. But if 54 brings them in, then 54 gets the credit. She did a visual recon of the immediate area. No voltage signs; no trap doors. No customers approaching; no streetcars passing. Not a peep, inside or out. Don't think she didn't see that beady redeye camera watching her. Don't think she couldn't see its iris shrinking. No army of nincompoops would take her down.

Clouds scurried from east to west. Telephone wires whip-snapped in the wind. The glass jaw doors peeled open.

Moist warm air blasted her. She vanished into the wall. If Milk were breathing, she would know it. His pulse pumped in the hum of the heating vents and the doors whizzing to a close her. He's here.

The lobby bent left to an L shape. All along the wall on the Parliament St. side, old time police uniforms, newspaper reports on tacky posterboard and a phalanx of photographs carpeted the exposed brick. They planted a camera there, too. She knew their ways. The rat-a-tat-tat of someone typing bounced from deeper within.

This wasn't her first time at the rodeo. Who broke Jeff out of that D.U.I.? Who bailed him out on account of hot-rodding his e-bike? Who thumb-screwed his lawyer to wrangle a warning over a ticket? Who never allowed one Swanson's dinner to pass her boy's lips? The cop on desk duty had no idea of the tornado that just spun into his lobby.

She tip-toed to the corner.

'We got you on the Zelitzer cam, Ma'am.'

Drop. The urine-gold linoleum heated to her touch. She burrowed into her coat. A cave. She dug her fingertips into the floor tile grout.

'Can I help you?'

She showed herself.

A copper with some shred of humanity leaned over his desk.

She folded her hands. She brought her legs close. She scanned the floor tiles. And gave him stink eye. To get to Milk, she'd have to work it.

'Yes, Ma'am?'

Only one way to play this. She played bashful, shy; not at all sure of herself. 'You know who I am.'

'I don't, wow.'

'Don't be coy, Officer.'

The officer leaned back in his chair, licking his chompers. 'I don't.'

'You do.'

He put his chin on his hands. 'I don't. But suppose—.'

'I tell you?'

'Please. Tell me.'

She did a Princess Grace hop forward. 'I bet you will.'

'I will what?'

'Know me. I'm here to see someone you might be holding.'

'Name?'

Maybe he didn't know about her car crash. 'Not so fast, Officer—.'

'Horst.'

My god. 'Horst?'

'Horst.'

'That's a song.'

'Wow, it's not a song. It's my name.'

'Horst-Wessel is the marching song of the National Socialist's Nazi hooligans' SS.' She knew her history. Grandma Jean Sloan would sing her the Horst-Wessel song when they went to Germantown for cabbage and kraut in Detroit. 'My grandma sung it.'

'I never heard it. You want to see—?'

'You google Horst-Wessel, Mister—.'

'Officer.'

He's playing hard to get.

'Two boys were brought here. I am one of their mothers.'

Officer Horst didn't blink. 'We're not holding anyone.'

'You are, too. I saw you handcuff them.'

'Not here. Not 54. 52, maybe.' Almost imperceptibly, the officer leaned forward to look down a long hallway.

If she'd have blinked, she'd have missed it. 'The police car had a big "54" on its roof. I want to see my son.'

'I'm sorry but no one's been brought in.' His computer dinged. 'Tell me your name.'

'Then, your people are holding them somewhere else.' She headed down that hallway he'd glanced to.

He punched a button. 'Where you going?' He hopped out from behind his desk and blocked her way. 'Authorized personnel only.' The phone on his desk rang.

'Somebody wants you.' There's more than one way to skin a cat. She slid onto his desk to smoke an imaginary cigarette in a very long holder.

His shoulder-mic buzzed. A tall drink of water. Blond, blue-eyed, and oozing out of his polyester uniform pants. 'You go out in public like that?'

Horst turned red. His phone rang again. 'I'll call you a cab.'

'All packed in like a wiener schnitzel?' You got to twist male circuits.

He smoothed a lock of golden sunshine back from his forehead. 'Have a seat over there.' He pointed to green plastic chairs. 'I'll see if 52 has them.' Officer Horst answered the phone and held up a finger. He leaned into his screen for a closer look and then up at her. He leaned back. 'Got it.' And hung up. 'As far as they know, nobody's at 52 either. I'll call you a cab.'

'You said that.' He's lying. With a blizzard bearing down, they brought them here to "Cherry-Beach Express" them, maybe. To disappear them. She knew exactly what to do. 'That wind out there goes right through you. But, you'd know that. Wouldn't you? In those pants?'

The phone rang, again.

'Popular fellow you are.' She caught the hallways in her peripheral vision. The boys were either being held to her left or down that long hallway where an odd green line thrust down mid-way past the ladies' room. She scootched off the desk and into a plastic chair. A row of them lined up next to a stake driven into the cinder block. Some kind of paper tacked there flit in the air conditioning blower. She knew just what to do. Officer. I'd like to see the blotter.'

The officer faked it like he didn't know. 'You mean, like a—.'

She gestured to the document staked to the wall.

'I don't think so.'

'If you don't have a blotter then why do you have one tacked to the wall?' She pointed to the wall. Right below the stake, cement dust fanned out on the floor.

'Have you been drinking?'

'Do you have a powder room?'

His brow crinkled.

'The ladies' is down the hall. I'll take you.' He stepped around the desk.

Sessy flipped her hand up. 'I am old enough to fizz by myself. Thank you very much.'

Before he could say boo, his phone rang, his mic buzzed, the computer dinged. Horst held his finger up. 'Jus' a sec'.'

He studied her. 'Tell me your name again?'

She Betty-Boop pressed her knees together. 'I really really super-duper have to go, Officer.' She squeezed. 'Stress incontinence.' And curtsied.

He glanced away.

She shot down the hall disappearing into the ladies' room. 'Be right back,' she called. 'Oh, God,' she yelped for authenticity. 'Oh oh oh!'

He yakked on the phone.

Slipping into the loo, she cracked the door to listen.

'Didn't get her name,' he said into the phone.

'Patricia.' She called through the slit. 'Just call me, Patricia.'

That officer would probably wait outside to nab her. She ran the tap, got on her knees and listened through the door vent. Bingo. Horst ground his teeth right outside the door. A frosted-glass window blinked at her from over the stall. Snow caked it. She knew what to do.

A Parliament streetcar rumbled by outside.

She'd slip through like a beetle and drop to the sidewalk by the entrance. Horst would still be hmmming and hawing in the hallway. She'd zip back through the front door.

Horst knocked, but by then Sessy had one foot wedged to the wall and the other to the top of the stall. Shoot.

'Miss?'

Police always underestimate the power of ladies. She leapt down and slipped the bolt on the washroom door. In two leaps, she landed back at the window and took aim with her elbow. She undid the latch, tilting the steel frame open. One good grip and three yanks-up broke the hinge.

'Ma'am!' Ol' Horst's sweating now. He banged on the door. 'Miss!'

She held her breath, made herself super-small and only heard Horst that second time. The shock of landing on the front sidewalk altered her being. No cabbage-eating cop packing a sausage to the size of Mr. Owser's knackwurst could block her. She sprinted back in the front door, through the lobby and hung a right down the hallway with funny green paint knowing that Horst wouldn't've never have sent her to the left if the boys weren't to the right. Oh, oh, oh—

Peanut shells. Right at the leg of the green chair where she sat: a clue. Milk.

She zipped into the hallway to the left. She flew down the hall jerking and twisting door knobs and slamming at handles. She tried one door and then another. Every one locked. She pulled, kicked, and spit to lubricate. The glass windows shook with her beating.

'Don't be scared, Ma'am.' Horst balanced on tiptoe towards her. 'We're not going to hurt you.'

She froze. She smoothed her hair and wiped her mouth. She did Judy Garland in *Judgment at Nuremburg*. 'Vhere ee-z my son?' She clenched her eyes shut.

'You're Sessy Mae.'

'You don't know who I am,' she murmured. 'Don't get me for who I am.'

'Ma'am—.'

'Nobody knows me.' She grew weak in the knees.

'It's okay, Ma'am.' He nabbed her elbow. 'Wow.'

She pounced on him with all fours the same as she took that upslope escaping from all those banshees out to tan her hide. 'You take me to him or I'll, I'll, I'll—.'

Horst pulled at her. She punched with every fibre in her being.

'I will, Ma'am. I will.'

Oh, a Jacob's Ladder unfolded from the cruel and unflattering fluorescents above. 'You will?'

Ton'

Near the hallway ceiling, hail and snow machine-gunned into the glass. The wooden panes shook. They dragged the fuckers step by step on the piss-sticky vinyl flooring.

Shafiqq punched the code and Horst buzzed them from the front desk. 'Get in here, boys.'

Ton' zapped to Horst on his shoulder mic. 'Kill the Zelitzer.'

'Nothin' stupid, Ton'.' Shafiqq led Meuley into the concrete holding area.

Stupid is all you're gonna see, dude. Very stupid. 'Take the wall.' Ton' got the Milk one's collar.

'Think Detective, Ton'.'

Fuck 'Detective,' Ton' had thirty-five, forty minutes 'til the shift change. Pat-Pat, the crew. Maybe J. All stomping in from the D.V.P. He'd take his sweet time.

The air conditioning cranked ice air into his neck. Shafiqq ought to unglue his head from his ass. 'Let's Reid 'em, Officer Sinha.'

'Ton'.'

'I got the baselines.'

Ton' shoved the Milk one further into the room.

'Not Reid, Ton'.'

Meuley shivered against the wall.

'You got to pee?'

Meuley nodded.

'So do I. So what.' He could wet himself for all Ton' cared.

'Ton'. No Reid-ing. 'Schelle doesn't even know yet.'

Ton' had the pattern of eye movements; the changes in respiration.

That Zelitzer's red cam light blinked.

Ton' hit the button on his shoulder mic. 'Horst.'

The Zelitzer blinked again. All four studied the bulb.

'Kill the Zelitzer.'

Horst would feed the tape to the Special Investigations Unit.

'Turn it off.'

Ton's mic buzzed.

Meuley studied the dot. He squinted. His teeth clenched. His lips thinned. Pray, fucker.

Two blinks. The cam died.

Shafiqq's not into The Reid Interrogation Technique. *'Eyes moving, respiration rates—it's all interpretation.'*

Exactly. First, get the physiological baselines. Then, the next-level baselines via non-threatening questions. Chit-chat snaps attention from amygdala to the frontal lobe; reptile to confession.

Ton' locked the door. And sucker-punched Meuley. 'We go easy on them, Officer Sinha.'

The kid fell, scuffing the tile. 'Don't mark the floor, Thomas Walter Meuley.'

Tom shrunk back into the dark corner.

'See,' Ton' scratched at the scuff. He knelt to sniff it. 'Right. Officer Sinha. ABS plastic resin. Burnt. You know what that means.'

Shafiqq buzzed on his shoulder mic.

The Milk one stepped towards his friend.

'Don't, kid.'

He stepped back.

'Ton'.'

The Meuley one's the money shot. 'Milk can take it. He's going to tell us about where that ABS plastic resin got on his friend's shoes.'

Milk seemed to be counting the dots in the ceiling tiles.

The bulbs up there buzzed and crackled.

'What went down tonight.' Ton' leaned an armpit right over Meuley's head. He tickled his chin. 'Say something. I'm on your side.' He tapped the kid with the palm of his hand. First on one cheek, then the other. 'You. Me. Let's talk.'

The kid didn't give an inch. He stared straight ahead.

'You're scared, eh? Ern True doesn't scare you but this does.' He brushed Meuley's cheek with the flat of his hand. 'I recognize you. You're him. The G.I. Joe from the Central Tech shoot-up.' He forced Tom onto his belly on the floor. He dug one foot on his back. 'Remember?'

Ton' slid his boot to the kid's neck. 'You're scared now. *Dime.*' He let go.

The kid scuttled back to his corner. Beetle.

Albert's mouth came up in Ton's mind's eye. That fork about ready for bite. 'Someone very important to me—.'

Shafiqq fiddled with his keys. 'G.I. Joes, Ton'.'

'Right. G.I. Joe.' Fuck that. A mob of vision rushed in: Albert shielding his head; 'Schelle's tear sliding into her jar; Ale peeking from under the blanket.

The Milk one stuck out his chin, while Meuley fondled the wall next to him.

'Tell me what went down. You meet up, you go to Black Creek, you go to the Spit—.'

Their breathing modulated: now precise, measured, deliberate.

Shafiqq clapped his hand together. 'Tell us and you're out of here.'

In a flash, Ton' had the Meuley one's leg up, dragging him out of his corner wrenching his boot free. With both hands, he whacked the floor scuffing a dark black scar. He spelled it out: 'On that side of the line'— he pointed to the door—'is before right now. On this side'—he pointed to himself and Shafiqq—'is now.'

'You,' he squatted and got his finger in the murderer's face. Meuley. 'You are coming with me.'

 But the Milk one appeared next to him. 'I did it.'

'Like, what'd you do?'

Clock mouth muscle contraction; eye contact: maintain in Q & As, avoid during denials; keep it conversational; even if you know the answer, ask like you don't; if you don't know, ask like you do. Three keys: did you do it; should I believe you; why should I believe you? 'Making a statement of guilt, Milk?'

'I am.'

'Ton'.'

'Officer Sinha. I warned you.'

Tiny creases appeared around Milk's mouth and then relaxed.

Meuley's lips thinned; his emerald eyes remained stuck on Milk.

'Guilty of what?'

Milk held Ton's gaze. The cheeks paled, the throat quivered. Liar.

'You set them on fire.'

Fucking Shafiqq.

Milk nodded, but broke eye contact—to the right.

If one is recalling actual events mentioned, the eyes move to the left. If lying, to the right. This kid's remembering the hammer slamming into Albert's head. 'We need to get you in on tape.'

No eye contact from the Meuley one means Milk takes the rap. Whether he did it or not. He could start with Milk and take his time with Meuley. '46's avail, Officer Sinha? Let's get this monkey on tape.'

'It's prepped.'

'Good.' Ton' made his way over to Meuley on his haunches at the wall.

Ton' squatted close and personal to him. 'Letting your friend take the hit for what you did?'

'Rocky, Skip, Ace, African American Adventure' From over by the door, Milk shot his blanks. *'Mike Powers Atomic Man—.'* Eyes lit; cognition activated.

Don't fuck with a fucker. Ton' had this: *'Bullet Man, Eagle Eye, Roadblock—.'*

Shafiqq moved to the hallway door.

'Chameleon, Valor, Venom, Matt Trakker, Snake Eyes, Viper: Gyro, Alley, Laser, Night, H.E.A.T., Sludge, Flak, Sand, S.A.W., Techo, Tele, Pit, Terra, Toxo, Trace—.' Shoot 'em up partner. Ton' kept a bead on Meuley. Deceptive people may display heroic complex.

Milk loaded his rounds: '*Range, Motor, Neo, Night, Nitro, Shock, Rock, Vypra, Cyber Ninja, Dark Ninja, Lady Jaye, Kim Arkashikage, Blind Master, Crimson Guard, Marine Joe, Cobra, Gallows.*'

Ton' leaned in even closer to Meuley. The tiny blond nostril hairs flit in the force of a panicked wind. He laid his palm on the kid's head.

Meuley pressed into Ton's push.

'Arson,' Ton' said.

The kid looked up at him. Direct eye contact.

'Criminal Code of Canada, Part Eleven, Section 433-436.1 and maybe 437 and 445.1. Arson. Damage to property, damage to own property, fraudulent purpose, by negligence, possession of incendiary material and maybe Section 437: Other Interference with Property and Section 445.1: Cruelty to Animals—if there were any pets in the immediate vicinity. Disregard for human life. Every person who intentionally or recklessly causes damage by fire or explosion to property, whether or not that person owns the property, is guilty of an indictable offence and liable to imprisonment for life where (a) the person knows that or is reckless with respect to whether the property is inhabited or occupied; or (b) the fire or explosion causes bodily harm to another person. R.S., 1985, c. C-46, s. 433;1990, c. 15, s. 1. Arson.' He had him.

Meuley's mouth hung not five centimetres from Ton's. He could eat him. 'This is what's going to happen. One at a time, first Milk, then Meuley are coming with me to 46. To tape. Maybe your dad, Milk, did something that honestly deserved that life-threatening retaliation. Maybe not. Tell us your side of the story.'

Shafiqq's shoulder mic buzzed.

'Let's go.'

'Ton. Horst has it happening at Patricia's carport.'

'Our Patricia?' Last time he saw her, she was show-ing off her new dentures. Her ex knocked her lights out.

Milk

The camera's red dome light blinked. Like Ern True's bullet in William Thibidault's forehead. You stared. Tad's arms floated up from his sides, lips parted. The Ton's one's jaw pulsed. Sinha licked his lips. The light went dead.

Ton' shoved you into the room with Sinha buzzing behind, 'Ton', don't.'

Think fast. He pops you upside the head pushing you to the floor. The tile sinks cold into your cheek. Focus.

Melting snow had puddled around Tad's boots. Ton' stomped at Tad's ankle taking him down too.

Think fast.

He's got Tom's hood now. Heaves him up; tickles his chin. He's on your side, he says. Whacks Tad with the back of his hand. One cheek, first. Then, the other. He drops.

You lunge towards them, but Sinha blocks you. Don't.

Yeah. Yeah. No one's going to—. You little fuck. He knows you from Ern True. He plants a foot on Tom's neck grinding into him. Picture the skull caved in, man. *Dee-meh*, he says.

Tom gets a breath.

You kneel. Let me.

Let you.

Your brain is dinging. Let me.

Ton'—.

Don't fucking, Ton' me. Get the Zelitzer.

You all keep Ton'-Ton'-ing me.

You just—.

I am taking this suspect to 46. Okay? That's it. Got it? Okay?

Sinha is no match for this guy.

You're going to stay here with the other one. He cuts to the chase. You two meet up, right. Black Creek, first. Make a bonfire, blow up daddy's chick's house. Then, hit the Spit.

Sinha cuts in. Ton', it's—. But—.

He rips Tom's boot off and carves a coal black line in the tile.

Sinha launches at his partner, shoving him against the wall. His hands at his throat. The Ton' one spit and snarls. Sinha holds him nose to nose. Behave yourself, Ton'. Think 'Schelle. Think Detective Constable. Think your—.

Ton' shoved; Sinha pinned him to the wall.

You can't beat me, Ton'.

Ton' put his hands up. Sinha released him. And stepped back. Ton' kneed him in the balls. Hard. Sinha buckled to the floor. Ton' pressed his boot onto Sinha's neck.

I got you, Shafiqq. I told you: don't Ton' me.

Shafiqq hissed. *Albert.*

A weight came down on your chest. Albert. Albert. Albert. Mr. P.

Now you were on your feet. Ready.

Not so fast. Now your turn. Ton' slams you to the wall, digs into your sternum with his fist.

You fucked with the wrong old man, man.

He reaches down, wrenches Sinha's shoulder mic free, stomps on it. Black plastic shards scatter. Takes a step back, high-kicks the Emergency Call button. Shatters.

Tom covered his mouth.

Above, the fluorescent lamps crackled. Sinha gulped air deep. Your chest caved. Ton's throat pulsed. They found Mr. P.

Tom chewed his cheeks.

Officer Sinha, you're going to watch that one. He pointed at you. But then, cupped Tom's face pulling him to his neck. You, with me.

I did it, Officer. It's me, man. Just me. You had to say it. Tom couldn't take it. If there's one thing you're good at, it's taking it. It's what Mr. P. used to say. Some people have some things in them, but they don't have others.

He yanked you down to your knees.

You sure? You know what you did?

I got born.

Tom knelt next to Sinha.

For real, Officer. It's me. The way to convince someone is just to put the facts on the table. Don't press it. Leave space for their imagination to write the story. Don't hurt, Tad.

Ton' smirked. You set them on, like, "fire"? He did half-hearted air quotes.

Oh. Maybe you heard wrong. Maybe they didn't find Mr. P.

His face revealed nothing. He licked a lip. The turban one played it cool. Tom's eyes darted from one, to the other, and then to you.

Tape, Sinha. Room forty-six.

Holding himself, Sinha had his hand on Tom's back. Room's a go.

Tom's gaze tracked the linoleum lily pads, the gap between two tiles.

Ton' hunched in front of you. Lips pumped full, almond eyes almonds. Black stubble reached out for him from the caramel skin.

Rocky, Skip, Ace, African American Adventure, Mike Powers Atomic Man—. Win this. The musculature of superhero strength blasts through any tunnel, any doorway, any escape hatch. You are a neutrino. Lock and load: *Bullet Man Eagle Eye Roadblock Chameleon Sludge Trace Motor Night. Arkashikage.*

He spits out arson code at you; a finger under your chin. He stands, you follow. His scent. Safeguard. Like Tom. The fat of his hand at the back of your neck.

Sinha's mic buzzed.

You, fuck. Hands clasped together, he draws his finger along your jaw. I got you.

Your blood pulses. You want him. Take me.

Tom lurched up. Ready to pounce. But paralyzed.

The Ton' hit the door buzzer; it swung open. He yanked you to your feet and pulled you into the hallway. Left.

You wrenched yourself free of this Ton'. Do not hurt him. Whatever you want. Do it to me. Let him go. You straightened up. Faced him. Just like Jeff. He can't hurt you. Not really.

The hallway reeks of pine cleaner and archaic piss. An old skool lead plate sign on the door reads, 46. He shoved you towards the door.

Don't shove me, Officer.

He pffed, wiggling the knob. He kicked it. The hinges exhaled as the door opened. A black hole room. A pit. An abyss. A plank of hallway light flopped to a drainpipe on the far wall.

You step in. Dark pools at your ankles and rises to your knees.

Go on in. Ton' checks the hallway to see if the coast is clear. Go on.

Shadows tangle now catching at your neck; what's still visible of your face.

Go on. You're safe.

Hinges wheeze. The door swings shut.

You're underwater now.

Ton'

The steel door groaned to closing. The kid took a step into the darkening room reeking a sink of black, grey and silver. And piss. That pipe ran the length of the far wall.

The kid clocked Ton's position.

'I got you.'

He stepped into the centre of the room.

'I got your back.'

He took another step.

'Move.'

A hammer of fluorescent poked at the peach fuzz on the kid's neck. Ton' stepped in.

The door lock bolted into place, the cave went black.

Ton' rounded the walls. A blind gargantuan now, his vision widened to fracture. The pipes burst, the panels above fractured, the black sea of tile cracked. The ceiling withdrew as he rounded the cave. The eye in his forehead blinked, the one in his back stung. The antennae at his nostrils got the Pine-Sol and the kid's citrus sweat. The tickle in his gut tacked his exact location in regards to the emergency exit. His shoulders grew great; his arms, biceps and thighs followed. What he considered himself disappeared. Now mountain, he propped up the night. Now peak and abyss, the kid would be truthful. Milk would spill.

The kid inhaled. Held it. Let go.

Ton' had him. Reid. Set the stage. 'I'm obligated to inform you that everything you say is being recorded.' There is no recording. Everything the kid says can and would be used against him.

'Part of interviewing is where we sit at a table. I ask you questions. Lights on. I like starting in the dark. It gets us to the light. It's fairer. The Interviewer and the Interviewed got no visual cues. No distractions. We can play it straight.'

The kid was masking his gulps for air with non-committal grunts.

'Sinha mentioned Officer Patricia Khahali. Patricia. Tell me your connection to her. Why do you want to blow her up?'

The kid shifted. 'Like you don't know.'

Ton' leaned, letting the wall take his weight. 'Like maybe I don't. Tell me.'

'Get to something you don't already know.'

'I have a stake—a personal stake—in what you tell me.' Not a peep.

Reid: approach common themes. '*Sigma 6: Bat, Baroness, Buzzer, Destro, Duke, Destroyer—*.'

'Not *Destroyer.*'

He's playing. 'Right. You know Joes, I know Joes. *Firefly, Hawk, Heavy Duty—*.'

'*Hi-Tech, Jinx, Kamakura.*'

'Right.' Feeling along the wall, he circled the kid now in the centre. Once Ton' got to the other light switch, he'd pinpoint his location.

'The one thing I can tell about you is that you know the difference between right and wrong.'

The kid pop-popped and then *stse-stse*'d his lips.

'Not that I, myself, am some Sir Sanford Fleming or William Lyon Mackenzie.'

'It's all me.' The kid hunkered low. 'Tom Meuley doesn't know about the Joes. Or anything else.'

Or anything else. 'Right. See what I'm trying to understand is the mental mechanics behind what you say you did. Versus what exactly you did. Versus what exactly we know to have gone down.'

'Tell us why we're here. Exactly.'

A bus lumbered by out on Parliament.

'You don't cop to nothing, huh?'

He stirred. 'My dad's fucked is the mental mechanics.'

'You know why you're here. Exactly. Officer Khalali never hurt anybody.'

'She's boning my dad.'

Ton' thought of 'Schelle and that little bitty thing clinging to her insides. This kid could be his own son someday talking 'Schelle about Julio and the others. Get to Albert. 'Direct question.' He had a sixth sense about the dark. If Ton' were an animal, he would be a bat. The dark gave him a sixth sense. He chewed his lip, he got his crotch in both hands. The sensations shot up his spine, across his shoulders, and down the outside of his forearm. He dug at that scar 'Schelle cut. 'What makes someone hurt someone that didn't do nothing to them?'

'Getting' all Degrassi, man.'

A car horn bleeped from somewhere.

He wishes. 'What did Officer Khalali ever do to you that you'd want to blow up her apartment building is

what I'm curious about; because I am hoping that tonight you and your friend will help me to just get what is
the switch that goes off, that particular switch, that says
someone else should be exploited, taken advantage of, or
taken down even for your own gain. That someone's life
should be, how do you want to put it, taken, yeah, erased
even for another person's gain. Walk me through that.'

'Dude. Like. My dad hates me. Hate, man. My existence. I'm just a kid. He fucks around. You should see my
mom's face. He's killing her. She doesn't deserve it. Just
takes it.'

The kid's playacting. Ton' felt for the light switch.
He let it dig into his shoulder.

The ventilator shafts ticked. The flagpole cable
whacked outside.

His shoulder mic fizzed. He clicked it off. Ton'
crossed his legs. He held his crotch. He had all night.
Fifty minutes. 'Shoot. Go ahead. Tell me. You speak
Spanish? *Dime.*' He had to piss. These pants were tighter.
He leaned away from the wall to pull his junk to the
other side.

'I didn't mean to hurt anybody.'

Whoops.

'I didn't. Burning G.I. Joes is stupid, I just wanted to,
you know, lodge a protest. Fight back. I'll never amount
to anything so who cares.'

Ton' popped his tongue. 20/80.

'My dad—I just got pissed at it happening. I didn't
mean for it to go that way.'

'You and your Thomas Walter Meuley are in together
tight. In and out.'

'We were just hanging; the storm was coming.'

'How you found your dad at that house is what's impressive.'

Ton' trailed his fingertips along the wall to the right.

'I stalked him.'

'So, you kind of thought about it first.'

'He's always killing me over too many G.I. Joes.'

The kid dragged himself towards the left a little.

'Like grow up, grow up, grow up. The future, the future, the future. School, school, school. Money, money, money. How, how, how.'

'Pisses you off.'

'It'd piss you off—right?'

Ton' could smell it. The kid didn't know if their conversation was about arson or Albert.

'You had a right to get pissed.'

'He won't shut up.'

'Take off, then. Go to L.A. Go to N.Y.C.'

'Can we turn the lights on?'

He's going to clam up. The kid's soles squeaked. On the move.

'We're doing pretty good in the dark.' Ton' moved back in the direction of the door. 'It's to your advantage. They analyze the interrogation tapes for additional evidence of truth telling or lying.'

'I'm not lying.'

Maybe. Maybe not. Time would tell. 'The way you describe it, you have a sense of justice. Fairness. What the right thing is. If there's anything wicked done to you—you can tell me. That hurt you.'

No air brushed Ton's cheek. Slippery fuck.

'I didn't mean for it to go down that way.'

Now he had him. 'What way is that?'

'After, we see him and we leave him and we were maybe going to go back home or—.'

'But he's messing with you. Assaulting you.'

'Not tonight.'

The kid loosened.

'You don't know what it's like in my house. Nobody does.'

'Right. But I'm not talking about your dad.'

The kid froze. Got him.

'Let's cut to the chase. Any assault to you in any way?'

'No.'

'Just bashed his skull in.'

The kid hadn't moved one inch. 'Yup.'

He could ask how he did it, but it didn't matter. He could ask what the tool was, but nobody cares what he used. He could ask where it was done but, bank or Spit, it don't matter.

'It just came over me, I just did it. Tom Meuley had nothing to do with it.'

'Right. You keep saying that.' Ton's forehead got wet.

'You think I'm lying.'

'Tom wanted me to like call you guys. Like "Call 'em, call 'em." It's on me, man. Totally.'

Ton' had an idea. 'What's the exam on you going to tell us?'

The kid had gone silent again.

'The kind of exam I'm talking about on you, on Tom Meuley, what's the story going to be coming outta that?'

The kid inched to the back of the room.

'Keep crawling.' Insect. 'The room is sealed.' Horst better have bolted that fire exit.

The kid stopped. 'Don't worry. You'll get your quota.'

'No quotas at work here. What's the story between you two and Mr. P. is what you got to tell me.' Maybe they did shit for cash. It's not like teenage boys never murdered nobody. 'We do examinations. We will find out.'

The kid had pursed his lips to get more oxygen. Ton' could tell. People purse their lips in imminent danger.

'Like stick a finger in my asshole?'

'At the least.' Ton' took a play from the oldest interrogation technique in the world. He asserted uncertainty. 'It's hard to tell why one kid—you're smart, obviously—why you'd take the rap for your friend.'

The boys could've been defending themselves. Albert wouldn't be the first teacher to pluck cherries from sixth period.

'He wanted it. Just walked up to me. Just handed me Tom Meuley's leaded squeegee. Saying do it.'

Albert would do that. 'Describe to me exactly what happened.' As the kid explained, Ton' moved closer.

'I was waiting for Tom to finish—.'

Ton' took a long step.

'His windows. And all of a sudden Mr. P. was just like standing there and he had one of Tom's squeegees in his hand and he—.'

Ton' held his breath and took another long step. He'd gone to that restaurant up on Church once, where all the waiters are blind and they lead sighted people in to eat by the shoulder. Once they shut the door, the black swallowed the light. Ton' made no sound. His heart thumped, he held his breath. Moved when the kid was talking. Right next to him now. Right out from the thermometer.

'He he he had me get Tom to like go out to the limo. I totally totally like didn't know what was up. But I did. I told Tom, like get me a squeegee from the limo and I'll help you so then we can get all of this done and get out of there. I wanted to party and and the storm was on its way. I mean like come on. Tom's brilliant and Mr. P.'s our teacher. Why would we just like kill him?'

The kid huddled at his ankles now. What Ton' ought to do is lift the little guy up and rap his head into the concrete and smash that fucker like he was a pup or a rabbit or a chicken. Like what Ma told him about what they used to do back home. He could whack him in the head first with his stick. He'd knock him silly and dash his brains upon the tiles and scoop them up and devour them with a glass of that raw milk Ale gets delivered from her cow-share near Buffalo. His forehead was soaked, and now the back of his neck. Ton' stomped hard.

The kid yelped and dropped to the floor.

Exactly.

The kid cowered now. The breath: short, sharp, shocked. In the centre of the room. On wide open seas. He curled himself into a ball. Curly bug. Squirm. Fetal. 'Mr. P. says just kill me.'

Milk

The cop slammed the wall. The door shut to black.

You dropped. Grit floor. Crawl.

The wall pipe fizzed. The officer seethed.

A phone rang somewhere. A door buzzed and then squeaked open. And then closed.

You are Uncle Louise leaving his breast on the Fontenelle floor. You are an insect digging at the earth. You are the granite Shield dragged to Ern Tru's driveway. You are the goat unpegged and fleeing the blade. Your flock ninnies from beyond the beast's lair.

Outside, the blizzard sea surges.

You hold your breath. Ton' wasn't making himself at home. He wasn't taking off his coat. He was jazzed up, over and around. Ahead of you. He was yapping superfast about the interviewing process, the dark and everything you said can and would be used against you. He crossed the room to right up behind you asking about who is Patricia, who do you think you are, and didn't you know she was a cop and your dad's fuck buddy; and if you know what's good for you give him the rundown on everything you and Tom did tonight.

Sigma 6: Bat, Baronness, Buzzer, Destro—.

Not *Destroyer.* Keep your mouth shut. He moves around you now rattling off Joes. He follows the wall to the right. The linoleum chews into your knees.

The low-slung radiator spews heat and rattle.

Oh, how come you guys didn't slide out and down that hill on the D.V.P. How come Sir Sanford Fleming again.

The windows shake in their panes.

Don't think you're going to take the clip on this, Milk. I got that fuck and you're going to assent to what he did before you leave this room.

What he did? What kind of mischief was this? What trick being played? You turned your back so he couldn't hear your breath. This was like in bed with Jeff. He'd pull you in so close you couldn't breathe, and if you did, he'd press down harder so you couldn't breathe more, and you had to make yourself as small, as insignificant as possible to exist at all. There wasn't a single movie or TV show or book or nothing that this was like. Maybe it was like that kid hiding in the shit in *Schindler's List.* But that kid put himself there, didn't he? Maybe it was Steve McQueen in *Papillon*, stuck in that cell. He got his coconut raft and jumped off leaving Dustin Hoffman picking his nose. Maybe it was like Odysseus pinned down and held prisoner by Cyclops or Calypso.

It's me. I told you. Tom didn't do nothing with what went down.

What went down?

That siren pins the great warrior keeping him supped with wine, goat and perfumed cheese. The stink of her captures him to make herself into something other than a lost and liquid spirit gunning for wayfaring sailors.

My dad's fucked.

He was spinning it around now pleading with you to come clean. To escape with the cheese for yourself. Don't let the siren snare you, weigh anchor and set sail. But, she has been gutted stem to stern and vomits nothing but straight A's since there is no connection, no basement, no no more. There, on the far shore, lifts the maple fleet surging to Kabul. You feel Tom, his muscles holding and pulling. Unleash your ropes, empty the ballast. Leave the milk tipping with whey. Come away, come away. Come. When was he bringing up Mr. P. was what you wanted to know. You scratched at the floor letting the suction cup feeders on your hairy and spindly legs crouched beneath your scaled and sectioned shell claw for every mineral, every nutrient sprinkled there. You had eaten your fill tonight but left none for the gods. And you knew better.

When Uncle Louise took his breast he left it in the woods at Fontenelle Forest for the coyotes, bobcats and field rats. Though it had no milk, the meat would feed spinning into vitamin, mineral and enzyme. He had gone to the Radical Ladies who laid him in the grass there beneath the harriers and osprey howling and circling high high high and when he turned his head a pill bug unfurled and skittled away as one Lady whispered. That tallest and fairest Lady had gotten down on her knees and held the back of Louise's head with one hand while gesturing to the others to tighten the noose no no no more yes more yes more yes keep pulling there there that's it. As they cut just below the collarbone he had closed his eyes while they pulled the noose they'd roped him with to 86 his air, cutting him of his own cloth and threading him through with his own presence and his own originality married to his own attention enough with absinthe to his lips like they did in Civil War days when the Ladies first came up as gaggles of runaway Union wives eager to soldier for the blue and the gold dodging the fists of their husbands, with every fibre and sinew cinched for the slice that wouldn't feel like nothing, and knowing that from then no one would mistake him for her. One mustn't forget who he is. Before she began speaking, the warmth of her breath softened the thin skin of his ear dusted with the tiniest pearl hairs standing tall as the Spit marsh fields swaying bending down from the north.

Louise, no matter what they find in the annals and canyons of your blood you are who you are and what you are is what you are—. You are that poet, that bug; that breast rotting on the forest floor; Uncle Louise unfurling himself.

A zipper opened.

Talk to me about tonight. What was going down?

Hang out. Dump the Joes. Like, he had me by the throat last night.

How'd you find him?

He thinks I don't see what he does.

To your mom?

It's just a car. He's got insurance.

But you want to get him good. You want to make him suffer. Make him squirm.

A buckle dinged the wall.

You slipped left. Yeah, man. He pissed me off. I don't want to like *hurt* him hurt him. Just freak him out. You can't just be recording me without me seeing you.

His jacket scrunched off. It's to your advantage.

You're so mistaken if you think I'm lying. My middle name is Truth.

Milk Truth.

I got nothing to hide. You are a neutrino. Spin to μ. What if the men were to serve the monster, to wash his feet, to comb his wooly hair, to feed his comrades, to milk his flock. But you are the living and so not yet story. You are a neutrino. This is spinning. You knew that you had to get yourself spinning so fast that you would disappear and become a τ. Get to τ.

If this were a movie it would all make sense. A ways off down the hallway a song spun up: *I need you baby / and if it's quite alright / I love you, baby / all through the lonely nights—*.

The cop froze.

Then, it came together. You are a bacha bazi running the snow plains of Khakon. Pull yourself by branch and stone. Push, as rock faces tear. The White Teeth posse, the cacophony of hounds yelping and snarling pound into the gulley below. You got to rescue yourself.

A sink runs. A toilet flushes. Water rushed through the pipe above.

That kid whose family got slaughtered in Vietnam, that family where the mom threw him a fruit and all the kids sunk back into the jungle, the ones that hid down in that hole until morning when, climbing out, they saw their aunts, their uncles, their whole village flayed and played over tree branches, strips of meat baking in the sun. Blinking in the sun, streaming through and not believing their eyes. That was this. How smart you are doesn't count. You are in a shit hole, stuck on an empty dry rock snow plain, taking your mom's breast down from a tree.

You shut your eyes to hear better. He will kick you and you will feel again. A punch, a kick, a loving embrace. You fizz your breath once. And then again. Bacon. He smelled of bacon.

You lean onto your knees; pull forward. Hold. Drag farther.

You're not going anywhere.

Wait 'til he is in front of you. Get out of his path. Wait 'til he is in front of you. Stand up, shove and run for your life. Two minutes ago or two hours, whatever it was, you had given up. But this spinning in you made things different. The centrifugal force gathers the momentum of the water in you generating more energy and force the more you spin, the more you move. You made your ankle muscles—and then your calves, your quads and glutes—push you to standing. You are dangling at the end of a string. Stand. Run for your life.

A pinpoint green laser sensor fidgets on the far wall.

He crosses the light and circles your way. I got you.

You ducked back. Doubled-up tight. So small you could spin from sight. Arms up to protect your head.

He scuffs to the far wall, struts left. He marches the half-perimeter in a tease, coming to the corner behind your left shoulder, breaks the emerald thread beam, and lands behind your right shoulder.

The dude don't stop. Now he skitters along the far wall muttering fuck fuck. He lands again. Behind. He slips closer.

A zipper rizzes.

His jacket, or something, is coming off. That bacon smell presses in. He comes closer still.

Hand me your shirt. Take it off.

You tangle in the sleeves until he yanks it off. He finds your hair. He fills into your nostril and lips. You fist-punch his thighs.

He guides your head closer. Smell that?

He pulses through the polyester.

Ton'

Oh, man, you got this fucker. 'Don't play-act with me.' Ton' stepped left.

'Officer, Mr. P. stood there. I stood there. Tom hung, I think, back at the car.'

'You think.' Keep the kid on his feet. Ton' stroked the glass of the blacked out viewing window. 'But you don't know.'

The kid hunkered into that dark field. 'You don't want to believe me.'

'Just tell me.'

'You know.'

'No. I don't.' Ton' got himself in a bit towards the centre, closer to the kid.

At least they reno-ed this room tight. Just that spaceship green sensor light breaking the black.

'Mr. P. was messed up over his wife.'

Ton' held. 'What makes you say that?'

The kid was low. 'You want me to make up something. Tom and me helped him with a hospital bed.'

A pushing came from the backside of his neck. In turn, he squared off and got air in sharp intakes. 'She's sick, huh?' He crept right up to over the kid. The kid's heat blossomed.

'It was—you aren't going to believe me anyway. Shouldn't you be farther away?' The kid reached his hands out into the dark.

'What happened?'

The kid was crawling away now. Just try.

He landed a few feet over. Crouching. 'He said Milk I got something I need you to do. It's the most important thing you'll ever do in your life. It was the way he said it, I guess. Like all Rings cycle.' He crawled even further.

'I don't do hobbits.' Ton' caught up to the kid.

'Wagner Ring cycle.'

Ton' didn't know what that is. Maybe a washing machine. The black swarmed thick. He'd be on his bum now, arms pulled tight to his knees.

'He held the squeegee up. They glide on the glass with the lead we put in. No streaks. No marks. Like he wasn't ever there.'

The kid's compass sucked. He moved near Ton's leg.

'Mr. P. says he's going to start it but I would have to finish if it wasn't if it wasn't—.'

Ton' held his breath and stepped further off.

'And so then he did it. He didn't wait for me. No yes or no.'

He could just see it. He could see Albert's jaw stiff while lifting those heavy planters for Ale; he could just see Albert's jaw slack while battening bats with a staple gun; he could just see that foul mouth fixed forever with not a shred of doubt now out at the Spit. Ton's own mouth now was wide and silent in the interrogation room. His legs had become tree trunks; his feet burrowing down to root deep into the linoleum clawing east, back west to the Don, to Taylor Creek, and to Castle Frank; finally his tentacles could surface to where Albert lay to cocoon and to digest, to be subsumed by wolf, worm, and bacteria. It was as if that squeegee had come down into his own skull, by his own hand; and oh how could a person do that to himself; and why bring this poor kid into it; why after what he himself had been through; the times and throats into which he'd emptied as one self-loathing ingests that of another. It was exactly what 'Schelle had spit at him. That when he gets angry, when he goes over the top, that that is when anger and indignity—she used the word inhumanity—was transferred from one person to another.

He had never considered that he and Albert and all dirty-rotten faggots were alike in this way, that each of them were driven to one extent or another by a desire, a want, a hunger to connect their kick-sad shame to other human beings and to do that by shoving themselves down throats as if a squeegee; the spunk wets the blade to cut the humanity from some other; not only of their lives, which depend so little on the heart, the kidneys, the brain but on some other organ; he could see now some river from which humans drink that transcends this room, interrogation techniques, and professional status yet was the one and only thing seeding the weather; that storm that moved all things forward always yet it is that same engine powering a ferocity that propels kindness and forgiveness and forgetting.

'Don't make me tell it. Did you see him?'

Snow had collected in the cold crux of the corner of his eyes by the time Ton' knelt to Albert. 'Vicious.'

'I wanted him dead.'

Albert didn't do that to himself and drop to the floor. 'Did he die just like straight out?'

'He knew I'd do it. I love Mr. P.'

'He had blood stains on his knees the same that one gets crawling in the grass. You didn't help him.'

'No way. He begged me not to.'

'Tom Meuley could have—.'

'I shoved Tad back. He wanted me to stop the bleeding, to call—all of that—.'

'When Tom was saying let's call somebody to him, I said fuck no.'

'You did.'

'I did. I picked up the squeegee. I drove it, dug it in more.'

The kid's not speaking from direct experience.

'We get trained in these things, Milk. You didn't do it. Tom Meuley did. Talk to me.'

'Officer Gonzalez, oh it was so awful. He lifted the squeegee and brought it right down into, like, above his forehead. It stuck in his head. It didn't even—. He was rolling around. Do it, Milk, do it. Do it do it do it.'

The kid's breath heaved.

'You alright, Milk?'

The kid's arm found his boot now. He pulled himself closer to Ton'. He hung there, at his feet.

Ton' nudged him off.

But the kid pulled himself back. He held tighter wrapping his arms around Ton's calves. He laid his cheek on Ton's thigh. His fingertips found the tendons there.

'Know what?' A roiling rose, then, ripping and searing. It came from far off in the boy's pulse pressing itself into Ton's skin. The skin peeled back from every hook-up, every alley and bumper fuck, every tear he had made 'Schelle cry into that jar.

Ton' pushed back harder, but the kid held tight. He wouldn't let go, god he had to piss, he balled up his fist and landed a blow to what must have been his shoulder or ribcage.

The kid clawed at his trousers, his zipper, his belt.

Ton' backed away kicking and pushing the kid off but he was a strong mother fucker who now had his belt pulled and oh—not not not—with Albert and 'Schelle and Ale but then he slammed into the wall and slapped around for the light switch they must be on the far wall he couldn't tell in the dark and the kid had his zipper open now—he pushed at the kid—oh god he had to piss and then the kid had him had him whole and took him down and—it came up out of his legs where the blood and tonight had pooled and burned into the kid's throat before relaxing like the long arcs he drew on the Spit fell to a stream and and and with each contraction of the kid's throat he was removed he thinned and dissipated and was not there. When he was done, the kid did still not let go but lingered resting with Ton' thick in him, his cheek on his hip.

A heat came from the boy's pulse pressing itself into Ton's skin. The skin peeled back from every hook-up, every alley and bumper bang, every tear drop he had made 'Schelle cry into that jar.

Milk

And for a split second, a picture in your mind of what's going down. The flow stings your cheek and *Paris, Je t'aime* runs for cover. Surface and spin into something. Find the stream and take what you can. Your life is summed in the cough to swallow and the gulp of gush. Drink. Live. Be. This must be surfacing and spinning into something. Nothing could change the hot stink sting. Tad would go free and you would exist. And come to matter.

He lifts you to standing. Wipes your mouth, chin, and neck with the fat plain of his palm; the brazen scratch of his forearm hair lingered.

Your T-shirt: a cooling, wet wad at your feet. Your teeth chattering. The spill of his soak chilled.

Watch your eyes. He flips the light switch on.

You squawk and cover your eyes. And flutter them open.

He's unbuttoned his own T-shirt and gets you into it. One arm, and then the other.

Put that on.

He tipped his hat and leads you through the steel door. The interrogation room had been pitch black, but this hallway, one square tile of yellow-speck linoleum after another is bathed in fluorescent light and its glare in the floor wax. Your eyes sting and water. Put one foot in front of the other. Bring this to a close. End this night.

Ton' punched a door lock button and buzzed his mic. Prepped.

You stood in front of the last door on the left. Its lock released; the door popped ajar.

He nudged you into the room. Hang tight.

You shielded your eyes. The light here blasted like floodlights. Another interrogation technique.

It won't be long, he said. The door closed behind him. The small square window in the door just above head height revealed no shadow out in the hallway. No movement. You press your ear to the door.

A printer feed takes up paper somewhere. A door lock buzzes. No footfalls. Maybe Officer Ton' crouches on the other side of the door. Maybe he's pressing his ear to yours through the steel. His drink coats your insides, soaks into your gums and the surface of your tongue. Your esophagus, painted with him, tingles. His trickle leaks enzymes and proteins; his dirt hormones and the silt of his rut seeps in. From nothing, absence, and non-existence into something, presence, and nourishment. To story.

Your eyes adjust to the hyper-bright fluorescents. Four cinder block walls. Ceiling swinging low. A pipe there cut the room in two. Your shoes stick to the floor and you clench your toes to keep them on. Far off, chair legs scrape the floor; a door squeaks to a close. A spaghetti of graffiti plasters the far wall. Stepping across that gummed-up floor, arms outstretched, you balance yourself. Eyes to the floor, the bright lights blot out the ceiling glistening slick with drip and moisture. From the corners, a putrid gunk of festering pong: piss, mould, sweat. Ton's taste remains.

The lights flickered and went normal. You blinked your eyes to get your bearings.

A centipede scuttered to the corner and froze.

You gripped the floor with your suction cups. In the far corner you were heading towards, a weak bulb flickered. You got this game. The floodlights will come back on. Then, go out.

You lean on the damp walls to read the hieroglyphics there. You follow a scratch which, at its top, loops to the right. The wall stretched with carvings. *pUta, africa RISING, I Am Innocent, j'ai faim, ayuda me, Demon + Julissa, Brittany, Money, Circo, Sleepy, La Chica + Consacres, Raul +*. Hieroglyphics, lightning bolts, A's as steeples. Maybe William Thibidault carved his name somewhere tucked around a corner locker. Maybe William knew on some level that Ern True had him in his sights. Maybe Suong scratched her name into a desk top or wrote it in a book to identify its owner. Maybe names hang inscribed ready for random, unconscious couplings in unforeseen terrains: press reports, court documents, and the skins of those involved.

You have a choice. You can matter.

That one pipe ran out from the fluorescent to just over where 'Raul + '. A camera pointed at the centre of the cell.

A chair. You kicked at the metal door.

The sound shot against the walls and then fell away.

You kicked again. One hard time. A second one. You pounded with your fist. Hey! You listened. Hey, cocksucker! You kicked again. You got one of your boots off and stood on one leg. You beat the door with the heel. Hey! You listened.

After a minute or so, a clomping grew louder. You pulled yourself up to the window in the door to peek at the scuffed-up linoleum tiles. You dropped back down.

When the Officer got to your cell, she opened the door tucking her hair up. Her shoulder mic squawked. She folded her arms.

Please. Ma'am. I need a chair, Ma'am.

You got the floor.

The floor, Ma'am, please. It's disgusting. My shoes stick. You got to give me something to sit on.

I don't got to give you nothing. She snorted.

It's in the Geneva Convention.

She rocked forward. You having a chair is in the Geneva Convention?

It is.

This ain't Geneva. She stepped up to the window. It's Toronto. And walked away. The door swung to close.

You spit at her. It landed. Right where she stepped.

She stopped. Clicked her mic. Whispered. Turned around.

Please, I really, really, please, Ma'am. Please, a chair. Just, please. You held the door open. You chattered your teeth. And again. I'm cold on the floor, Ma'am. I have a weakened immune system.

She inhaled deeply and then mumbled low. You get yourself kicked to next Tuesday for a move like that. She walked out of view.

The door closed. The centipede made it halfway up the wall but then fell. You followed the hieroglyphic cracks in the poured cement floor. A sluice of fluid roiled through the pipe straight through the far wall. After a moment or two, it returned.

She popped the buzzer and the door swung ajar. A chair clacked into the room by the door. Is there anything else you'd like Mr. Your Royal Highness?

Yes, Ma'am. The door inched to close. You jammed your foot in.

Take that foot away.

I want a pen.

No pen. Boy.

Ma'am. I've never been in jail. It's freaking me out. I write and so like I could write on the wall. Like them. You pointed to the graffiti.

Who? You and your friend.

I'd really appreciate it, Ma'am.

No. Get your foot out of the door.

You did.

She stuck her foot in the door and leaned back in. Self-harm. Not on my watch.

Once she was long gone, you moved the chair under the pipe in the middle of the room. Hopped up and ducked for the ceiling. You got a good grip on the pipe. It took your weight, sort of. Slowly, very slowly, you bent at the knees and eased your weight from the chair by lifting your ankles. For a few seconds, you didn't let go. You should have done push-ups like Jeff told you to. The pipe groaned. It held. You let go and hung full. Sweet. But then you saw the pen.

Back by the door. She must've dropped it. Self-harm with a pen's going to be the least of her worries. Back on the floor, you tested the pen's ink on your hand. You broke the clip off and dug it into the plaster.

The plaster gives way easy. Just below *Raul* + you scratch *Milk* + You step back to look. If you are a point on one of those grid sheets from Geometry, z-axis, you could draw lines out to your mom, your grandma, Uncle Louise, Mr. P., and Asaan. Sakar. Jeff. G.I. Joe. Mr. P.'s wife even. That cop. Tad. You do mean something. When people think of you, they can follow those lines out to those people. Maybe that's what that old lady did looking in your window last night; maybe those twigs of frost scratch a map shows her once but never again; maybe it is from those lines that you are drawn from those sketches you find form; you are made visible. A kid like you could see your name there. Maybe that's all a name is, after all. A roadmap. A schema. A chimera covering the what's what. You scratch 'Tom Meuley' next to the plus sign. A mark, a scar, a difference.

Back up on the chair, goose bumps erupt in the chill. You twirl the Officer's shirt roping and spinning it. You wipe your hands on your pants. Tying a good slip knot in the right arm sleeve, it fits over your big noodlehead. Tie the left sleeve. A couple of loops and a square knot. Left over right, right over left. Grip the pipe on either side of your head and figure you'd do a few pull-ups after the chair falls away. Clench your fists, swing a leg out—the chair knocks back. Its legs and plywood slam into the concrete floor. That lady'd be back in here.

Hold and lower. Do a chin-up. And then, another. Last time you did chin-ups, you got five. You're way stronger now. You do a leg-lift straight out in front. You pull yourself back up to the pipe. It doesn't give at all. Galvanized. Lower back down. Pull back up. Maybe that lady would come, maybe she wouldn't. Don't be a wuss. Hanging in the air. One black cormorant among many.

You never spoke. From when you were born. You didn't cry, you didn't wail. Maybe you were on the spectrum. Maybe you were a bean head. You watched, you waited, you smelled, you touched. December stings your skin tearing after Jeff down the sled hill at Broadview Park or in August, same hill, when all the Chinese ladies pick bush fruit; it's Jeff plunging down the up-slope, you'll never scrape enough skin for him to gather you close; the suckling lip of his coffee breath and the flat of his hand pressing your head in deeper to the dead maple leaves and calling your name: Evan. You climbed as far as his ankles, but he kicked at you. You held on for dear life. Swing back. *Because even you don't give up.* Even. Evan.

And leapt—. Milk.

Sessy

Knotted neatly to the pipe, the line of that blue sleeve tricked her to the top of his head. Not Milk's shirt. Graffiti curtained the cement walls: plus signs, lightning bolts, and Z's reaching to God or something greater. Oh, god, the long feathers of his hair spilled there catching the fluorescents and radiating the glory and transcendence of that little boy.

Her hand came to her mouth. Milk hanging there. Spinning first this way, and then that. Away from, and then towards, what must be Parliament. The tops of his feet were just this close to brushing the floor. It had not been long. Spittle caught the light at the side of his mouth. His stare a frozen and barren beam amongst the scattered boulders of pipe, cave markings, and cracks in the floor. First this way, and then that.

Oh, the force of oceans crushed into the tendons of her neck. She keeled forward as the waves crashed. Her breath would no longer come. That old ghost lady had left her to herself. Maybe she, herself, Sessy, no longer felt her feet on the concrete. No longer her, herself, forcing the buzz from the fluorescents rocking into her skull. Her boy Milk Milk Milk there oh you goose you berry you chunk of fruit. She fell to her knees.

She crawled to him. Hunkering low, and using her back, she positioned herself under his feet to stop the awful creaking of their spin. She pushed just the littlest littlest teeniest pressure up so that he would have a piece of earth to stand on. Oh, walk on me, Milk. Walk, walk, oh, Milk step here, lay your burden here. Break my back to take one step. Break it, Milk. On all fours, she pressed up taking as much weight as she could.

Just there, next to her right hand, his pee had puddled. Keeping him on her back, she inched to plant her palms deep into his cooled waters. Oh, smell him. His insides and, oh, his sweet-sweetened soles digging into her back laying some sacrifice onto her skin—he let his mama lift him.

She dipped her second to the last finger, the make-up finger, in the pool. It applies the least pressure, mama said mama said. You smooth foundation out with that one.

She held that finger to her third eye. And let the liquid drip its tiny river. She dipped again, this time getting enough so that Milk's juice would dribble down from her forehead, and again to feed the current, and again so that it would curl around her nostril, and one more dot to reach her lips. Her tongue met the stream it sought. She got herself around and got a hold of his legs. The tips of his fingers were flush with the blood that had drained there. She made herself reach out to them. The very tip of her index finger touched a joint in his thumb. Warm. She pulled him closer and held him. She reached the chair on which he had stood, now kicked over, with her leg and dragged it to her. Setting it upright, she moved Milk's body and got her arm behind his knees. If she climbed up on the chair, it would take some of the pressure off of his neck probably. She lifted him into her arms.

A police officer stared her down from the door. She knew him. That moustache one.

'Ma'am, climb on down.' He held out his hand to help her down.

She pulled her boy closer. Milk's head flopped to her breast.

The officer stepped closer, 'Ma'am.'

'Don't "Ma'am" me.'

He got a hand on the chair, the other up stretched to her. 'I'll help you.' He wasn't looking at Milk.

'Back off.'

'Ma'am.'

The Horst-Wessel cop eased into the room. 'Wow.' A lady officer stepped in alongside him. Her hand to her mouth.

'Let him go. I'll climb up and cut him down. He is mine. I got him.'

'Ma'am.'

But then, but then, but then. Tom Meuley. He pushed his forehead into the doorjamb there. And she broke. 'Tom. Tad. Help me.'

The boy pushed past the coppers to her.

The Turban one from the Spit had appeared behind him and lunged after him, and oh it's the one that'd puked in the headlights that now swung to get him but Tom Meuley dodged his reach, and jumped up on the chair with Sess'.

They both tipped, close to falling but, instinctively, used their body to steady themselves.

The poor sick officer lunged, but Turban blocked him.

'Don't you.' Turban wielded a pocket knife.

'Tom, we know it wasn't you.' Turban handed the knife to Tom. 'Cut it.'

Tom Meuley reached up, his breath overtaking him, his mouth falling into a jagged gasp; with one cut Milk dropped free.

The weight surprised them, they tipped.

Puke and Turban caught and steadied them.

'Lay him here,' the lady cop motioned past Milk's puddle.

Sess' and Tom and Ton' and Shafiqq laid the body on the concrete floor.

Milk's eyes were seeing something.

Sitting there on the floor, Sessy had a fullness she had not known before. Appetite departed. She had no need of Pringles, Twizzlers, or cake. No food could fill her. The void behind her boy's eyes dove into nothingness. At first droplets of dew, and then sprinkles of rain and snow began to accumulate on the prow of the vast desert she oared with him at her side. The storm of Milk's last breath pushed a flood onto the plains in her chest and the dry gullies of her gut. Her boy had reversed the natural course of things. Him flying from her at birth, now returning and filling her with a mattering of his own pregnant design. She smoothed his pretty hair. Tom Meuley kissed his forehead. He smoothed his brow. Sessy pointed. On the wall, an etching in her boy's hand: a mark, a scar, a difference.

Acknowledgements

With Gratitude
Vajdon Sohaili who never wavers in his
care for me or what I imagine.
Lisa Vernon Pender who knows of what
I speak and still holds me dear.
With me from the start:
Adèle Robbins, Béatrice Pettovich, Mary Michael
Hanbury, Lisa Boone, Donna Howland, Lueann Hart,
Dawn "Sissy" Komljenovic, and Karen Quick
For the *gite* and camaraderie over the years in Johnson,
New York, Paris and Marseilles: Reineke Hollander
and Daniel Turbow
The Toronto Arts Council
The Ontario Arts Council
Canada Council for the Arts

To the Kern-Pages: Valerie, John, Erin, Terra, Grady,
and Jasper. Thank you.
Barbara Radecki and Ken Murray for their
commitment to this manuscript.
Alison Smiley, Richard Elliot, and Rob Champagne
for their unwavering support.

About the Author

thom vernon is a multi-media artist, teacher, and scholar. His first novel, *The Drifts* (Coach House 2010) was called "a significant contribution to CanLit" (*Globe & Mail*). A professional actor (*The Fugitive, Seinfeld, General Hospital, Grace Under Fire, Saving Hope*, and others), he also holds a B.A. in Philosophy (*summa cum laude*), an M.F.A. in Creative Writing, a terminal Masters in Gender Studies, and a Ph.D. in English Literature—Creative Writing. HIV positive for most of his adult life, thom is a Vanier Doctoral Scholar, a Social Sciences and Humanities Research Council (SSHRC) award recipient, a Dr. William S. Lewis Doctoral Fellow, and a Magee Doctoral Fellow. See thomvernon.com for more.

MIX
Paper
FSC® C100212

Printed by Imprimerie Gauvin
Gatineau, Québec